About the author

Nathan Dylan Goodwin is a writer, genealogist born and raised in Hastings, East Sussex. then completed a Bachelor of Arts degree in Radio, Film and Television Studies, followed by a Master of Arts degree in Creative Writing at Canterbury Christ Church University. A member of the Society of Authors, he has completed a number of local history books about Hastings, as well as several works of fiction, including the acclaimed Forensic Genealogist series. His other interests include theatre, reading, photography, running, skiing, travelling and, of course, genealogy. He is a qualified teacher, member of the Guild of One-Name Studies and the Society of Genealogists, as well as being a member of the Sussex Family History Group, the Norfolk Family History Society and the Kent Family History Society. He lives in Kent with his husband, son, dog and chickens.

By the same author

nonfiction:
Hastings at War 1939-1945
Hastings Wartime Memories and Photographs
Hastings & St Leonards Through Time
Around Battle Through Time

fiction:
(The Forensic Genealogist series)
The Asylum - A Morton Farrier short story
Hiding the Past
The Lost Ancestor
The Orange Lilies – A Morton Farrier novella
The America Ground
The Spyglass File
The Missing Man – A Morton Farrier novella
The Suffragette's Secret – A Morton Farrier short story
The Wicked Trade
The Sterling Affair

(The Mrs McDougall Investigation series)
Ghost Swifts, Blue Poppies and the Red Star

(Venator Cold Case series)
The Chester Creek Murders

A Venator Cold Case
The Chester Creek Murders
An Investigative Genetic Genealogy Mystery

by Nathan Dylan Goodwin

Copyright © Nathan Dylan Goodwin 2021

Nathan Dylan Goodwin has asserted his right under the Copyright, Designs and Patents Act 1988 to be identified as the author of this work.

This story is a work of fiction. Names and characters are the product of the author's imagination and any resemblance to actual persons, living or dead, is entirely coincidental. Where the names of real people have been used, they appear only as the author imagined them to be.

All rights reserved. No part of this publication may be reproduced, stored in a retrieval system, or transmitted by any means, without the prior permission in writing of the author. This story is sold subject to the condition that it shall not, by way of trade or otherwise, be lent, resold, hired out, or otherwise circulated without the author's prior consent in any form of binding, cover or other format, including this condition being imposed on the subsequent purchaser.

Cover design: Patrick Dengate
www.patrickdengate.com

For Faye & Lucy

Author's Note

On the 28th September 2020 (or September 28, 2020), I ran a Twitter poll asking my followers whether a book that is set exclusively in America with American characters, but which is written by a British author, should use British English or American English spellings. Ninety people cast their votes, giving me a damned-if-you-do-and-damned-if-you-don't result of 52-48 in favo(u)r of American English spellings. The comments attached to the poll were equally equivocal and divisive. Having considered the matter carefully, I decided to settle for American English spellings, thinking that only those who know that I am British would find it odd for me to write in this way. So, if you already knew my nationality, pretend you didn't and if you had no previous idea, pretend that you haven't just read this paragraph.

Chapter One

Sunday, March 1, 2020, Downtown Salt Lake City, Utah

Madison Scott-Barnhart sighed as she gazed out of her office window on the fifth floor of the downtown Kearns Building on Main Street, Salt Lake City. It was snowing again. Heavily now. Great. The ride home on the I-15 would be a crawl at best. And she had wanted to go for a run tonight. *Needed* to go for a run. But there was just no way that she would be able to in these conditions—not for a good few days after the snow had stopped at the earliest. Maybe she would head out to Park City or Alta on the weekend and ski instead. It was no coincidence that the only two sports that Maddie actively enjoyed taking part in—those being running and skiing—were solitary ones. Although at times she did both with other people, it was generally those isolated moments that she most savored. Being alone and outdoors, combined with the speed of movement, helped to clear her head, giving her the space in which to think—usually about the myriad of complex cold cases on which she was working in any one given period.

Maddie watched the thick snowflakes falling unremittingly onto the muddle of life in the city center. Three lunatic teenage boys on the city's rentable scooters were dodging and weaving through a gaggle of pedestrians who were scurrying towards an incoming tram.

Mesmerized by the snow falling, Maddie resolved to take her two kids out to Park City with her on Saturday. It had been a few weeks since they had last all skied together; it would do them good as a family. The fifth anniversary of her husband's disappearance was looming, like an offshore hurricane that nobody spoke about but that everyone knew was coming. A general oversensitivity in her two kids, which had coalesced unhappily with the usual teenage apathy for life, had been murmuring below the surface at home for the past few days; an unsettling glimpse into the next few years ahead, Maddie feared.

She turned from the window and sat back at her desk. Her unattended laptop had switched to displaying a buoyant kaleidoscope of dancing color as the screensaver. She could wiggle the mouse and resume her work, or she could fold down the lid and head home. She rarely came to the office on the weekend but her kids' being out with friends all day meant that she had been able to clear her backlog of admin in preparation for a new cold case that was due to start tomorrow.

She gazed around her small office. She had a desk that was cluttered with note paper, stationery, two mugs containing the tell-tale residue of today's drinks and framed photographs of Michael and the kids. All around her were bookshelves sagging below the weight of copious amounts of files, paperwork, books and folders that the job routinely generated.

Cozy—and probably very unrealistic—thoughts of heading home and making something nice for dinner, followed by a device-less evening together with the kids, compelled Maddie to shut her laptop.

She switched off the light, closed her office door and wandered out into the main working space of the company—Venator—which she had set up here two years ago. At the center of the open office was the nucleus of their operations: a six-foot-wide, high-definition, digital whiteboard screen sandwiched between a glass writing board of similar dimensions and, on the other side, and with equal proportions, a regular whiteboard. Each of the three, central in bringing together the cold cases on which the team worked, were revealingly blank. Angled towards these were three desks, the state of each offering an insight into the personalities of the members of her team who operated from them.

At the back of the office were rows of bookshelves laden with files, each labeled with the name of a particular case. Those on the shelves closest to the window had the pleasing addition of a SOLVED sticker appended to their spines. *The Broadview Strangler. The Candee-Lee Gaddy Murder. The Fall Point Killer. The White Lake Ripper.* And the case that had propelled Venator into the media spotlight last year, *The Winterset Butcher.* It had been Iowa's largest unsolved serial-murder case, in which nine young women had been brutally hacked to death between 1979 and 1984. Maddie had been given nothing more than the killer's DNA to work with. Three months later, using investigative genetic genealogy, Maddie and her small team had solved the case that had confounded more than two hundred police officers for over thirty years. Venator's identification of the suspect had resulted in the successful conviction and life imprisonment of Dexter Beynon, a sixty-three-year-old former police detective. The knock-on effect of Beynon's conviction was a dramatic increase in the number of law enforcement enquires coming in from around the United States.

Maddie studied each of the open and active files in turn, bringing the specifics of some of the cases to mind. Some, such as the *Cleveland Cannibal* or the *Mount Vernon Serial Killer*, were currently dormant, awaiting new DNA matches to appear in the databases. Others, like the *Boys under the Bridge*, a pro-bono case for the National Center for Missing and Exploited Children, happened as and when time permitted.

She sighed, wishing—as she always did—that she could wave a magic wand and bring justice and peace to the families involved. With her husband Michael missing, Maddie knew better than most the exhausting desperation that they felt for answers.

The personal anguish, she knew, had taken its toll on her. With her quirky dress style, naturally blonde hair worn in shoulder-length curls and a general appearance which she was told was attractive, she looked good for her forty-five years. But the damage was there, manifest in her permanently furrowed brow and in the dark circles below her eyes, optimistically hidden beneath her make-up.

Maddie turned from the folders and walked to the cloakroom area of the kitchen on the other side of the office. She pulled on her vintage shearling jacket, placed her trilby hat on her head, switched off the office lights and headed past the reception desk for the door.

Tomorrow, a major new case for the team would begin: *The Chester Creek Murders*. Now, though, it was time to head out into the snow and get home to her family.

Two months earlier

Chapter Two

Park Police Department, Media, Delaware County, Pennsylvania

Detective Clayton Tyler was working late. His official shift had finished more than two hours ago, but he had come down to the cold-case vaults in the depths of the police building basement. The permanently arctic temperatures and deficient lighting rendered this storage facility an eternally unappealing place to visit. He didn't have much choice in the matter, though; he had to take a look at his share of some of the department's one hundred and forty-six cold-case homicides that currently lined four floor-to-ceiling metal shelves, spanning the entire length of the basement.

Clayton stood in front of the shelving and yawned, trying to dismiss thoughts of being back at home with a few cold beers at hand and his feet up in front of the television. He was forty-two years old and freshly released from a marriage that had been killed by the infinite hours that the job had demanded of him.

He walked slowly through the vault, inwardly cursing his difficulty in viewing the spines of the files that he was passing due to the number of blown lightbulbs above him. It wasn't even as though he was short of work—he currently had thirty-two open investigations sitting on his desk, vying for what little time and resources he could put their way—but the department, like every other one in the country was being besieged by constant demands from media outlets for information on all cold cases with the designation of 'open-inactive'. The applications came under the cursed entitlement of Public Disclosure Requests with which the department were legally obliged to comply. Not only did the PDRs dramatically increase his workload but they also massively jeopardized the possibility that the case might one day be solved, its having been plastered all over a newspaper, blog or been the subject of some amateur sleuth's podcast or a gratuitous Netflix documentary. Consequently, all of this department's cold-case homicides, of the one hundred and twenty thousand across the whole of the U.S., had been divvied out to each detective in the department, thus rendering them 'open-active' and no longer within the legal remit of the PDRs. The laudable but unrealistic idea was to triage each case, ranking their solvability as high, medium or low. Those deemed to be medium or low were sent back to the vaults until the next round of reviews. Those with a higher chance of solvability might just get to join the bottom of the pile of cases on his desk. Part of the problem was the demoralizing statistic that just one percent of cold cases in the US ever got solved.

He paused every few feet to squint at the case titles that he was passing. Every unsolved murder for the county, dating back to the early 1900s, was held in thick binders down here in this windowless gloom. Some of the cases, particularly the earlier ones, were contained in just a single volume. Other generally more recent ones were held in up to a dozen ledgers.

The scale of the task was daunting; a proper, systematic review of every homicide was all but impossible.

Clayton stopped and pulled a file from the shelves: *Jane Does 476*. Opening the folder at the summary page, he quickly recalled the case. Two unidentified females, late twenties, raped, murdered and dumped at the side of the I-476 on July 4, 2000. He thumbed past grisly crime-scene photos to the case notes at the beginning of the ledger. No DNA evidence. No witnesses. No persons of interest.

Snapping the file shut, Clayton placed it back on the shelf and continued beside the run of shelving.

He stopped again, ran his fingers through his short dark hair and sighed, as he squinted at one of the less familiar cases beside which he was standing: *Chester Creek Murders*. Six huge binders, stuffed with notes, photographs, witness statements and evidence.

For a time, he simply stared at the folders, trying to bring to mind the specifics of the case. Although Clayton had spent pretty-well his entire life in Delaware County, he had been just a kid when the murders had happened and, thankfully, his parents had spared him the contemporary reporting of the crimes. His first real knowledge of the case had come during high school, when tales of the Chester Creek murderer had been filtered through repeated childish and fantastical exaggeration. Grave warnings had been passed from the older students to the younger ones about not visiting certain parts of the school grounds alone, for that was where the Chester Creek murderer had captured his victims. As Clayton had gone through high school, the tale had reached mythical proportions with the implausibly elderly janitor's being framed by successions of whispering students as the unvanquished killer who would chop up his victims and tip the pieces into Chester Creek so that the final tally of his crimes could never be known.

By the time Clayton had graduated from college, the Chester Creek murderer had reached the apocryphal status of a fictional killer from the movies, someone akin to Freddie Kruger or Jason Voorhees.

He grinned at the memory, as he hauled down the first of the six files pertaining to the case. He angled the ledger towards the closest overhead light to try to lift the words of the cases' opening summary out of the darkness of the vault.

The Chester Creek Murders (1982-1983)
Three Caucasian females aged 17-19. All raped and strangled. Bodies dumped in the Chester Creek, Delaware Co., PA. Witness statements taken. DNA evidence procured from each victim. No persons of interest to date. Open-inactive (Reviewed: 1995, 2003)

His childhood knowledge of the case, which had grown into a grotesque nonsense, far removed from the truth, clashed starkly with the words in front of him. Real victims and a real serial murderer who had evaded capture for some thirty-eight years.

He could still be out there now; alive and dangerous.

Chapter Three

November 3, 1982, Glen Riddle, Delaware County, Pennsylvania

Mary-Jane Phelps knew that she was being followed. Unfortunately for her, on this stretch of the Glen Riddle Road there were no sidewalks and no street lights. For the level of isolation in her current surroundings, she might as well have been hiking on a disused maintenance track in the middle of a state park.

She now wished that she had listened to her father's simple instructions. He had warned her not to walk home from the party but to call him to come get her or to catch a ride with one of her friends; just not to walk home alone along the Glen Riddle Road because of the tendency for it to be used as an after-dark racetrack by some of the town's younger drivers.

She continued her striding walk, fleetingly more anxious about what her father would say when she got home as she was about the intentions of the driver in the car that had been following her for the past few minutes.

Mary-Jane looked down the road behind her and saw it again. The car—cowardly concealed behind the glare from its headlights—appeared around the corner at a crawling pace.

It stopped.

She looked down at the light muscular tremble in her legs and realized then that she was standing within the illuminated fringes of the car's headlights.

She was definitely being watched.

From somewhere up ahead came the low grumble of an approaching vehicle. The idea that she might flag it down disappeared as quickly as it had arrived, when the speeding truck, hogging most of the road and seemingly unaware of her, compelled her to jump sideways onto the narrow grass shoulder.

Mary-Jane inwardly cursed as she watched the truck fading fast into the distance.

The car continued to creep towards her.

A nervousness rose inside of her. It couldn't be Daniel or Jack trying to spook her as she had first suspected. By now they would have driven past with the windows down, laughing and making some dumbass remarks. Even they, with their warped sense of humor, wouldn't inflict this terror on her. No way.

She exhaled as she stepped back onto the road and continued towards the turning for her home on Martin's Lane, increasing her pace as she went.

It was just a few more feet.

Mary-Jane felt her blood run cold, as the car slowly—very slowly—began to close the gap between them.

Looking around her in panic, all she could see was the distant glow from the exclusive homes dotted sporadically along the road's length, nestled away in their private grounds behind high fences and electronic gates.

She turned again. The car was just thirty feet away, still crawling towards her.

An involuntary shudder ran down her spine when she caught her first glimpse of the car: a red Dodge Coronet—*not* a type she knew any of her friends or family to drive.

She uttered a pitiful yelp as she broke into a run, her bag falling from her shoulder as she went.

The car was now just behind her.

Tears filled her eyes and began to diminish her view as the car drew up beside her. She pushed on, using all of her energy to get to Martin's Lane.

Just a few more feet.

She chanced a quick glance to her side, trying to see into the car. Nothing. Just darkness.

There was now no question in her mind that the person in that car driving alongside her meant to do her harm.

But suddenly, it lurched ahead with great speed, leaving Mary-Jane running through its belch of exhaust fumes.

She slowed down, unsure of what was happening, then stopped, panting and gasping for breath.

Then she began to sob.

The car had stopped ahead of her and a male figure, silhouetted red by the taillights behind him, began walking towards her. He was carrying a long, thin object in his hand.

Mary-Jane Phelps screamed as loudly as her tired lungs could manage and twisted around to run back in the direction from which she had just come.

Tears were coursing down her cheeks. Another scream lodged in her throat.

He was running behind her, his breathing a series of loud determined grunts.

Getting closer.

Closer.

She glanced around her in desperation. Not one house within sight. No cars. No people.

Anger suddenly curdled her terror and she spun herself around, facing her assailant head-on and, wasting no time, booted her right foot towards his groin. But he was too fast, as he grabbed her leg, twisting it over painfully and sending her crashing headfirst onto the road.

She gasped from the pain in her head.

Then…blackness.

Chapter Four

January 3, 2020, Park Police Department, Media, Delaware County, Pennsylvania

Clayton Tyler was sitting with his chin propped in his left hand, elbow on the desk, reading the case notes of the first homicide in the Chester Creek murders.

He had cleared his desk in the usual manner, by sweeping everything in front him—computer keyboard and empty mugs included—as close to the edge of his desk as he possibly could manage without it all cascading domino-style off the side. With a small space free in front of him, he had switched on his lamp and began to read through the first file, making notes on a legal pad as he read.

His desk was beside a window in the open-plan office that he shared with the other ten officers in the department. Only Detective Clint MacRory—mid-sixties, overweight, forever single and a social hermit—was still working, which depressed Clayton all the more. His colleagues had already drawn mocking comparisons between the two men, with suggestions that Clayton was on an evolutionary journey where he ended up becoming the department's Clint MacRory in ten years' time. He didn't want to become that guy. He wanted a wife, kids and a decent home.

'You want some?' MacRory asked him, raising a slice of pepperoni pizza from the take-out box in front of him.

Clayton realized that he had been staring in his direction. 'No,' he said, a little too harshly, before adding, 'No, *thanks*. Daydreaming.'

'That a cold case?' MacRory asked, wiping the back of his hand across his mouth.

Clayton nodded. 'The Chester Creek murders.'

MacRory snorted, then laughed. 'Good luck with that one. I was part of the original investigation…*and* the review—in what, 2002 or 2003—when we found nothing new. The guy's probably dead now, anyways.'

'Maybe.' But that was beside the point. The three victims would still have family who had never had full closure. And this damned file would forever be consigned to the cold-case vaults, hauled out every few years and given the cursory once-over, all in order to avoid its being handed over because of some small-time journalist filing a PDR.

Clayton rubbed the stubble on his chin and looked back at the notes that he had just made. Mary-Jane Phelps had spent the evening of November 3, 1982 at a friend's birthday party. When it had ended, around 11pm, she had taken the ill-advised decision to walk home alone. The journey should have taken her around twenty minutes, but she had never made it home. Police and search parties, comprising concerned friends and relatives, had spent the following days searching for her. But it had been an elderly couple, out walking their dog, who had happened upon her in the end. Her naked body had been discovered lying face-down in shallow water on November 6 with visible signs of strangulation and a severe wound to the side of her head. The pathologist believed that she had lain in the river for two or three days prior to being discovered.

'So around two days Mary-Jane Phelps was unaccounted for between the night of the party and when she was found?' Clayton checked with MacRory.

'Yeah. Same for one of the others. We kinda came to the conclusion that he picked the girls up, knocked 'em out and took them somewhere to...well, you know. One of 'em—the second one, I think—the pathologist thought she'd been raped several times and not necessarily all *before* she died.'

'Christ,' Clayton muttered. The idea that this monster might still be out there some place sickened him.

Just one witness—a local truck driver—had seen her walking in the direction of her house. According to his testimony, he had a vague recollection of passing a red Dodge Coronet and a white Toyota Pickup around the time that he had seen her.

'The red Dodge and the white Toyota Pickup...?' Clayton called across the room, already anticipating that the answer would have something to do with the prevalence of these vehicles at the time.

MacRory waved his pizza crust in the air and spoke with his mouth full. 'Hundreds of 'em.'

Clayton nodded. 'And it says here that the truck driver was interviewed again during the review of 1995 but not the review in 2003.'

'Dead,' MacRory said.

Great. The only witness to have seen Mary-Jane Phelps after she had left the party was now dead and the only vehicles of interest were a dime a dozen.

The pathology reports had confirmed the obvious: that Mary-Jane had been strangled to death, having likely been rendered unconscious by a blunt trauma to the side of her head. A small lock of her hair was noted as having been cut out, believed to have been taken by the killer. Also confirmed in the autopsy was the fact that she had been raped peri-mortem.

'DNA?' Clayton asked.

MacRory nodded. 'Pretty good.'

'And presumably it was run through CODIS?'

Another nod from MacRory.

CODIS—Combined DNA Index System—was used to cross-check DNA samples taken from a crime scene with the Convicted Offender and Arrestee Indices. That the semen specimens taken from the three girls matched each other but had not matched with a suspect in the database implied that the killer did not have a criminal record. Except that it wasn't anywhere near as simple as that. Tens of thousands of convicted felons in the state of Pennsylvania alone had not been asked to provide DNA samples even though their convictions had demanded that it be taken. It was the same picture nationwide: the DNA of hundreds of thousands of convicted criminals had not yet been entered into CODIS when it should have been.

Clayton turned to read the case file on the next victim, Terri Locke. On the second page were the crime-scene photos.

'Jesus,' he said, turning away. 'I need a break.'

'Terri?' MacRory intuited.

Clayton nodded, rising from his desk. 'Want some coffee?'

'Sure. Or, we could wrap up here and maybe go grab a beer?'

'I'm going to be here a while,' Clayton answered. It was the truth, but it also provided a solid excuse not to be seen drinking beer with Clint MacRory outside of office hours. He could only imagine the whispered jokes around the office about the two sad loners' quietly getting drunk together.

'Black with two, then,' MacRory said.

Clayton flinched as he headed out of the office to the break room on the next floor. In this job, he'd seen pretty much everything, the results of every kind of human depravity; yet, still, when he came face-to-face with photos like those he had just seen—or worse still, the actual crime scene—it always shocked him anew.

At the vending machine, he punched in his coffee selection and watched as a thin plastic cup whirred its way into view on a robotic arm. After a guttural grunt from the machine, a steady stream of a terrible murky solution, masquerading as coffee, poured into the cup.

As Clayton watched the liquid slowly flowing, his brain mulled over the case so far. Apart from the DNA evidence, he struggled to think of any viable leads worth pursuing. Maybe a fresh media appeal? he thought, removing the cup before selecting MacRory's coffee of choice.

He carried the two drinks back down to the office and placed one on MacRory's desk.

'Thanks,' he muttered, not looking up from an NBA match that he was watching on his cellphone.

Back at his own desk, Clayton took a sip of the coffee and winced at both the temperature and the flavor. If nothing else, the caffeine would see him through the next couple of hours of reading and reviewing.

Reluctantly, Clayton opened the file and began to examine the crime-scene and autopsy photographs of Terri Locke.

Chapter Five

January 1, 1983, Granite Run, Delaware County, Pennsylvania

'Happy New Year!' Terri shouted across the street to the couple heading away from her arm-in-arm. She didn't wait for an answer but continued dancing along the sidewalk. Twirling. Twisting. She laughed, then stood still and squinted down the street at the intersection, watching the pavement below the traffic signals become washed in red light. Pretty.

Her white dress—bought new yesterday for the party—was sliding off her shoulders, making her shiver. She pulled the straps back up and gazed down the street. Where was she? No idea! She giggled, then felt a bilious gurgle inside her stomach. Water, that was what she needed…or maybe a McDonald's. Yes! A big fat juicy burger and a milkshake. And fries! Definitely fries.

'Do you want that large, Terri?' she asked herself.

'Hell, yes. Thank you, Terri,' she answered herself, flicking her long brown hair backwards.

She turned around. Now, which direction was McDonald's, anyways? It was around here someplace. She knew *that* much.

A car was heading towards her, hooting its horn as it passed.

'Happy New Year!' she shouted at the guys dangling their tongues out of the rear windows. 'Wait! Take me to McDonald's! Come BACK!'

The guys didn't come back. They ran a red and were gone. Damn them.

'Thanks, boys,' she whined. 'I just wanted a burger and fries.'

She stood still for a moment, flicking her head to and fro, now not even sure from which direction she had just come. She turned around and stared into the blurred distance. She was pretty certain that she'd just walked from *that* direction. She twisted around. No. Maybe the party had been *that* way. The party! She should go back to the party and get one of her friends to drive her to McDonald's. Yes!

But…which way?

Terri laughed as she tip-toed to the edge of the sidewalk. She thrust her arm out and raised her thumb high into the air. 'I need a ride!' she shouted. 'Please can someone please take me to the McDonald's party…PLEASE?'

A gray pick-up, just starting off from the lights, was headed in her direction. Terri jumped up and down on the spot. 'Stop! I need a ride!'

The pick-up was slowing down! Yes! It stopped beside her, and a black man wound down the window.

'What's up, Miss?' he asked.

Terri pretended to cry. 'I REALLY need a McDonald's,' she said.

The pick-up drove away.

'Jeez. What *is up* with these people?' she mumbled, calling after him, 'Happy New Year to you, too!'

Concentrate, Terri, she told herself. She studied the intersection for a while and decided that she had *not* crossed it to get to where she was now. 'Which means, the party is *that* way,' she said, spinning around.

The signals turned to green and, again, a car headed towards her.

Terri pulled off her heels and then waved frantically, jumping up and down, singing the chorus from Maneater.

The car was stopping!

Terri giggled, watching as it drew up beside her.

'Need a ride?' the driver asked through the open window.

Terri pointed at the man, scowled at him and sang that she was going to chew up him.

The driver pushed open the door to the red Dodge Coronet and Terri climbed inside.

Chapter Six

January 3, 2020, Park Police Department, Media, Delaware County, Pennsylvania

The dismal coffee was untouched and stone cold by the time Clayton Tyler had finished reading the reports into the second of the Chester Creek murders. He rubbed his tired eyes, then looked at the copious quantities of notes on his legal pad.

Terri Locke, 19, white, attended a New Year's Eve party at the apartment of two of her college friends. Left the party at some point shortly after midnight. Witnesses saw her displaying drunken behavior beside Lenni Road just before 1am. No witnesses or sightings of Terri alive thereafter. Roommate phoned police later that day. Her naked body was found in the same location on the Chester Creek, just below New Road. M.O. similar, though not identical, to that of Mary-Jane Phelps. Mary-Jane suffered a single blow to the head; Terri had endured multiple strikes to the skull). Raped. Death by strangulation. Good DNA sample. Small lock of hair cut from her head. Trophy?

'Did he take hair from all three?' Clayton asked.

'Uh-huh,' MacRory confirmed. 'Souvenirs.'

Clayton didn't want to read on into more detail. He blew air out from his cheeks and stretched. What time was it? He looked at his wristwatch. Almost 10pm. 'Are you going home any time soon?' he asked MacRory, needing some encouraging solidarity to help him pack up and leave.

'What for?' MacRory replied.

Christ. That would have been *his* answer. What was he going home to do that was more important than *this*? He glanced to the stack of files and paperwork perched precariously on the edge of his desk: the rest of his workload for which he and only he was responsible.

Push on, he told himself.

He forced himself to look back down at his notes, at the circle he had drawn around the single word which gave him some glimmer of hope that the case might be solvable: *DNA*. Given what the killer had done to Terri, strong DNA had been extracted, confirming what the detectives already knew; that the same person who had killed her had also murdered Mary-Jane Phelps.

Clayton drummed his fingers on the desk, wondering what could be done with the DNA evidence, given that the perpetrator had not shown up in CODIS. Then he remembered reading something online or watching some news story about *The Winterset Butcher* finally being brought to justice through a specialist DNA company. What *was* that?

Pulling his computer keyboard back in front of him, Clayton ran a Google search for the infamous murderer, finding a short news item about his capture among the first results.

Winterset Butcher suspect traced using genealogy websites
Iowa prosecutors say genealogy websites played a key role in tracking down a man accused of being one of the state's most notorious serial killers. Dexter Beynon, 63, is suspected of being the so-called Winterset Butcher and has been accused of a string of murders between 1979 and 1984. DNA had linked the crimes, but police had failed to identify the attacker until Venator, a Utah-based genealogy company, stepped in to assist. Dexter Beynon, who was arrested on Wednesday, has been charged with nine counts of murder.

Clayton stared into the middle distance, allowing his brain to do the thinking. Then he turned to face MacRory. 'What do you know about these companies that track down serial killers by using genealogy?'

MacRory shrugged. 'Nothing.'

Helpful, Clayton thought. 'Is the Chief in tomorrow?'

'First thing,' MacRory confirmed.

An idea was forming in Clayton's mind. He ran a Google search for Venator. They were based in Salt Lake City, headed up by a professional-looking businesswoman named Madison Scott-Barnhart. Their website listed several cold-case homicides that they had solved using something they described as *investigative genetic genealogy*. Clayton was impressed. He didn't really get the specifics but, from what he could understand, all the company needed was a decent DNA sample to run through their systems or databases or whatever it was that they used. If the Chief and the DDA agreed to it, then this cold case could be given the status of high solvability.

Clayton left the Venator website onscreen, as he turned back to read about the final victim of the Chester Creek murderer.

Chapter Seven

October 28, 1983, Granite Run, Delaware County, Pennsylvania

'Where do you want to go now?' Jason asked, tapping the steering wheel of his dad's Plymouth Road Runner as they cruised down Howarth Road.

'Home,' Nicole answered from the back seat, promptly yawning to underline the point. 'I'm done.'

'Come on,' Jason pleaded, meeting her gaze in the rear-view mirror. 'It's like just after nine. Aww... Do you need Mommy to tuck you up in bed, Nicole?'

From beside him, in the passenger seat came a fawning giggle from Jason's new girlfriend, Kristina.

Sadie Mayer, sitting in the back beside Nicole, rolled her eyes. It was pathetic the way that Jason had suddenly become an alpha-male douchebag as soon as he had started dating that giggling gink. Sadie shot a look to Nicole, receiving further confirmation of their general disapproval of Kristina and the seismic personality shift that she had brought upon their high school friend, Jason.

'I have class first thing and want to get a good night's sleep,' Nicole said. 'It's really not such a big deal. We were going out to the movies together and that's what we just did. Now, I'd like to go home, please.'

Sadie watched as Kristina placed a hand on Jason's thigh and said, 'Hey, it's okay if *she* wants to go home.' She leaned in closer, moving her hand over his groin, and murmured. '*I* don't want to go home yet.'

Jason turned to her and kissed her on the lips.

'Looks like I'll be going home, too, then, if it's all the same,' Sadie muttered to Nicole. 'Three's company and all that.'

'Okay, okay,' Jason said, pulling off onto Mount Alverno Road. 'If that's the way you want it.'

'The end of the road's just fine,' Nicole said. 'I'd really rather my dad didn't see me getting out of your car; I told him I was studying at your house, Sadie.'

'What? Walk home alone?' Sadie said. 'No way. There's some serial-killer guy on the loose out there. You are *not* going on your own.'

'It's fine,' Nicole said, trying to reassure her. 'I can see my house from the end of the road. I'll run.'

'Anyway... Is he even actually a *serial* killer?' Kristina asked, turning to face the back of the car. 'I mean, does two count as serial? He's hardly Ted Bundy.'

'That's not important and wasn't really the point I was trying to make either,' Sadie countered. 'Two girls of our age have been horrifically raped and murdered not far from here in the past year. We need to be vigilant.'

'Nothing's happened for months now. For God's sake, it's totally fine,' Kristina scorned.

'Yeah, right. He's probably retired,' Sadie said, unable to hide the incredulity from her voice. 'Two gruesome murders… That was probably enough for him.'

Jason turned into Nicole's road, pulling over just a short distance from her house. 'A compromise,' he said. 'We can still watch and make sure you get in from here, but your dad won't see.'

'Thanks,' Nicole said, unbuckling her seat belt. 'See you guys tomorrow.' Nicole patted Sadie on the leg and whispered, 'Good luck.' Then she climbed out of the car.

'Bye,' Sadie said, twisting around so that she could keep her eyes on Nicole for the short distance to her house. She watched as she strode along the sidewalk, past Nicole's mom's Datsun and an unfamiliar red Dodge Coronet, and finally up the short flight of steps to her house. The porch light pinged on automatically, as she approached, and Sadie was able to see Nicole opening the front door and disappear inside.

She visibly relaxed now that her friend was safely home and turned to face the front of the car to say that it was okay to leave. The sudden nauseating sight of Kristina sucking the life out of Jason's face made her exclaim, 'Jeez,' a little too loudly.

'Problem?' Kristina said, un-suctioning herself from his lips and scowling at her.

Sadie theatrically placed a hand on her chest. 'Me? Sorry, I didn't realize you knew I was still here.'

'Why *are* you still here?' Kristina asked. 'I mean, you know he's never going to date you, right?'

'Kris,' Jason protested weakly.

Kristina shrugged and stared at Sadie. 'What?' She faced Jason. 'You said it yourself that you think she's got the hots for you.' She frowned at Sadie. 'It's. Never. Going. To. Happ-en.'

'You're right,' Sadie said, unfastening her seatbelt and climbing from the car.

'Wait!' Jason said. 'You don't have to get out like that. At least let me give you a ride home.'

'I'll get Nicole's dad to take me,' she said, slamming the door and marching towards Nicole's house. She stormed along the road with her arms folded across her chest, as she heard Jason's car powering noisily away.

Jerk. He wouldn't have behaved like that two months ago. She guessed their friendship was over, now. Maybe it was always destined to happen, anyway, since they were all headed off to different colleges next year.

Any idea that she might once—*maybe*—have ever liked Jason Laird had now been well and truly obliterated. She sighed as she reached the bottom of the steps that led up to Nicole's house. In the front room she could see Nicole talking to her dad. She thought for a moment as she watched their interaction. What could she possibly say as to where she'd suddenly sprung from? After all, Nicole had told her father that she had been studying with her all evening and now here she was showing up on their doorstep. He'd see straight through it all.

A plausible story began to form in her mind but was quickly cut short by a strange sensation on the nape of her neck, as though someone were breathing on her. A split-second of confusion gave way to the appalling realization that someone *was* actually standing directly behind her.

The certain gravity of her situation dawned on Sadie Mayer the moment that a hand curled around her face, determinedly clamping down over her mouth. Another hand encircled her midriff, thrusting the air from her lungs as she was dragged backwards off the sidewalk.

Chapter Eight

Monday, March 2, 2020, Downtown Salt Lake City, Utah

Maddie was sitting at her desk in her office, catching up with an abundance of emails that had rolled in overnight, when she heard Ross, her receptionist, welcoming someone to the office. She stopped typing to listen. It was a man's voice, very likely belonging to the detective whom she had been expecting fifteen minutes ago.

A knock came at her door and Ross poked his head around. 'Maddie, Detective Tyler is here.'

Maddie nodded. 'Offer him a drink and I'll be right out.'

Given that he had kept her waiting, he could now wait a couple of minutes while she finished the email that she was composing to her insurance company about her mother's condition. After Michael had disappeared five years ago, her mother had moved in with her to help out with the kids but just over a year ago she had been diagnosed with early-stage Alzheimer's. Truth be told, her mother was now more of a concern to her than her two teenage kids. Right now, she needed some idea of what future assistance or support she might receive when her mother's condition undoubtedly started to worsen.

She clicked *send* on the email and stood up to check herself in the small mirror on one of the bookshelves. 'Urgh,' she commented. She'd had no time to apply any make-up or do much with her hair this morning. Not exactly the best impression for a new client, but then he wasn't here to see her.

Maddie picked up a legal pad and pen and walked confidently from her room out into the general, open-plan office. She poured herself a fresh coffee as she looked across at her team. Kenyatta was engrossed in something at her desk. She was a middle-aged, third-generation African American who was Maddie's deputy in all but name. She was a member of the City Presbyterian Church, worked with the city's homeless and had an unshakable sense of the need to bring justice to the cases on which she worked.

Becky, a young woman just a few years out of university, was sitting behind Kenyatta. She was hard-working and, like Maddie, also into running and skiing, as well as a wide range of other extreme sports. She was attractive with shoulder-length mousey hair and sporting a pair of thick-rimmed glasses. At this moment she was frowning as she scribbled something onto a pad.

Finally, there was Hudson. Only twenty-five years old but, despite his age, his knowledge of investigative genetic genealogy was second to none; he could always be relied upon to provide the science behind their work. Hudson was standing, talking to the detective, pointing at the solved cold-case files on the shelves. Maddie smiled inwardly, pleased with the pride her team held for their job. As it was with her, it was more than a job for them all: the cold-case victims took on an elevated role in their lives, as though they were members of their own family. Solving the murders had become their burning passion. It wasn't uncommon for Maddie to get a text message in the middle of the night from one of her team, who had made some discovery or other in one of the cases upon which they had been working in their own time.

The detective looked impressed at whatever it was that Hudson was telling him. Maddie was inexplicably pleased to find that he was around her own age and wearing jeans and a sweater, as though he didn't take himself too seriously. Some of the cops she had worked with had been walking clichés—exactly the hapless idiots often depicted in the movies. This one seemed different somehow. Normal.

'Ah, here's the lady herself,' Hudson said to the detective. 'Maddie, this is Detective Clayton Tyler.'

Maddie smiled, extending her hand as she walked towards him.

The detective switched the coffee cup to his left hand and took her hand in his.

Good handshake, she thought, recalling the numerous occasions when other male detectives had found it necessary to exert the full force of their finger-crushing masculinity in an attempt to compete with her authority in the room.

'Clayton.'

'Nice to meet you,' Maddie said. 'Good handshake, by the way.'

'Oh, thanks,' he said with a nervous laugh. 'Not sure it's something I've ever been complimented on before.'

Maddie shrugged and took him in fully. He was slightly taller than her and well-built, although there were signs of previous tone having softened with age or inactivity. Handsome face in a rugged kind of way. Nice green eyes, like hers. 'So,' she said finally, 'have you got a presentation for us and the access details for the DNA kit?'

Clayton nodded and fumbled in his jeans pocket, producing a flash drive and a folded piece of paper which he duly handed over to

Maddie.

'Thank you,' she said. 'Hudson, could you do the honors, please?'

'Sure.' Hudson took the USB stick and inserted it into his computer.

'Two minutes, team,' Maddie said loudly, before facing Clayton. 'Ready?'

Clayton looked a little tentative as he responded, 'I guess so...'

She offered a sympathetic smile and touched his right forearm which was pulled across his chest. 'Don't worry, Detective. We don't bite…hard,' she said, taking a seat beside Kenyatta.

Clayton moved so that he was standing at the front of the room between the three different writing boards; he turned to see the first slide of his presentation projected onto the six-foot digital whiteboard behind him. 'Wow. Impressive,' he said.

Hudson handed him a remote clicker and quickly explained its operation.

'Okay, Detective, it's over to you,' Maddie said, taking a cursory glance at the rest of the team; each of them was ready with a pen poised over a notepad.

'So, um, the Chester Creek murders,' Clayton began, somewhat nervously. 'Er, anyone here heard of them?'

Silence.

Maddie shook her head, having only taken down brief details when the Chief of Police had called up to discuss Venator's taking on the case.

'Okay,' Clayton said, advancing the remote clicker too many times, flashing through a series of images, maps and text, all of which abruptly terminated on an horrific autopsy photograph that instantly folded Maddie's stomach over. The police really didn't need to show them this stuff, but Maddie knew that it was their way of pressing home the arrant awfulness of the crimes. 'Sorry,' Clayton said, skipping back to the start. 'Right.'

'No problems, Detective,' Maddie reassured.

He nodded and clicked the slides back to the beginning. 'So, the Chester Creek murders.' His presentation moved on one slide, showing a high-school photograph of a teenage girl. 'This is the first victim, Mary-Jane Phelps, seventeen years old. She walked home from a friend's party on the night of November 3, 1982 and was found dead in shallow water in Chester Creek on November 6. She'd been sexually assaulted, had a blunt force to the skull and was strangled to death.' He shot a glance at Maddie. 'Is this the kind of detail you need? Too much? Too little?'

She nodded as she made notes. 'Perfect. Keep going.'

The detective went on to explain exactly where Mary-Jane had gone missing and where her body had been located.

'How was the body positioned when it was found?' Kenyatta asked.

'Face-down in the water. One arm up above her head. The other tucked under her stomach. One leg out straight. The other bent at the knee.'

'So, *dumped* rather than *placed*?' Kenyatta pushed, bouncing the end of her pen on her chin.

He nodded.

'And good-quality DNA was taken from this victim?' Hudson asked.

Another nod from the detective.

'Any clue about the perp from witnesses?' Maddie asked.

Clayton shook his head. 'No. A red Dodge Coronet and a white Toyota Pickup were seen nearby, but no firm link was ever established between the three murders and either of these vehicles.' Clayton glanced at the team, then moved the presentation forward to show what appeared to be a family snapshot taken at a beach. Dominating the foreground was a young lady with long dark hair, seemingly photographed unawares. To Maddie's mind, the only resemblance to the previous victim was that both would be considered pretty, young women.

'This is Terri Locke, nineteen years of age. She'd been at a party on December 31, 1982 and, in the early hours of the following morning, was walking home; alone, again, but this time along a busy street. She was intoxicated and witnesses saw her trying to hitch a ride. The likelihood is that she took a ride with the killer. She suffered a worse fate than Mary-Jane did, probably because she put up more of a fight. She was sexually assaulted, and her body was found on January 3 in the same part of Chester Creek…under the New Road bridge.' Clayton faced Kenyatta and preempted her question, 'Terri's body was also dumped. It appears that he stopped his car on a short bridge over the water and then just tipped them over the side—no attempt was made to conceal her or any of the victims.' He moved the slides on to show images of Terri's body in situ, followed by the images of her body on the autopsy table.

Maddie flinched and had to look away. She'd seen enough of these now for them to be commonplace, but, still, each time her mind managed to superimpose faces from her own family onto each deceased victim. She now had the very clear image in her mind of her daughter, Jenna, lying on the coroner's slab with her skull smashed in.

'So,' he said, pushing the slides on to a photo of the third victim. 'This is Sadie Mayer. She was a week away from her eighteenth birthday when she was taken from somewhere on or close to Mount Alverno Road on the night of October 28, 1983. She'd been dropped off outside the home of her best friend and was reported missing later that night.'

'Ten months after Terri Locke's murder,' Maddie commented—as much to herself as to anyone around her—as she studied the photograph. Appearance-wise, young and good-looking was again all that she seemed to have had in common with the other two girls.

'That's right,' Clayton confirmed, moving the presentation on to show the crime scene. 'Same M.O.: Sadie was sexually assaulted, strangled and her body left at the same location in Chester Creek. One difference here, though: she wasn't dumped until six days after her abduction.'

'Any reason for that?' Maddie asked.

'Not that we've been able to work out, no.'

'Was anything ever made of the fact that he left the women in the creek?' Becky asked. 'Like, any significance of the river to the crimes?'

Clayton shook his head. 'At the initial enquiry and the two subsequent reviews, it was felt that the location chosen was a convenient disposal point, maybe on his way from one place to another.'

Maddie glanced at Becky and could see on her face that, with her background in geo-profiling and criminal psychology, she questioned this assessment.

Clayton clicked the remote in his hand, bringing up the image of Sadie lying on the pathologist's table with a green sheet pulled up to her neck. 'All three girls suffered fractures in the laryngeal cartilages, had petechiae hemorrhages in the eyes and face, and bruising around the larynx: they were strangled to death, in other words. And he took souvenirs from each victim: a small lock of hair.' He clicked again, sensing the mood of the room, and on the screen beside him appeared a police composite suspect sketch that made Maddie shudder. He had a long, thin face, was unshaven and with military-short hair. But it was his eyes that drew her. Horrible, haunting eyes with dark circles beneath them. What those eyes had taken such heinous pleasure in witnessing, Maddie thought, before Clayton spoke again. 'This is a person of interest. Sadie Mayer's best friend, Nicole, recalled seeing a man she had never seen before, sitting in a car parked outside her house. It was dark, she couldn't recall anything about the car but did remember that he had had a long face, short hair and—how did she put it?—'scary' eyes. He's never been identified, so remains a person of interest, although he may have nothing at all to do with the murders.'

'Do we have an approximate age?' Hudson asked.

Clayton sighed. 'She really couldn't be more specific than twenties to fifties.'

'That's quite wide,' Hudson commented, making notes on his pad.

'What about ethnicity?' Becky asked.

'Again, she couldn't be sure. It was very dark. She didn't think that he was black but also couldn't be certain that he was white.'

A small silence settled on the room, before the detective moved the slides on to a page with small lettering that read END OF PRESENTATION at the top of the screen.

'Um, and that's the Chester Creek murders in a nutshell,' he said. 'Are there any more questions? I've put everything you need to know about the names, dates, locations, etcetera on the thumb drive, as requested.'

Becky raised her hand, appearing perplexed. When Clayton nodded in her direction, she tucked a loose ribbon of hair behind her ear and said, 'I was kind of expecting more…'

Clayton flushed red in the cheeks. 'Oh, sorry. I…um…what do you—'

Becky laughed and interrupted, 'I didn't mean more from *you*. I meant that I was expecting more *bodies*. This seems to me like it should be more the mid-point for this kind of a serial killer. Three murders in… What, eleven months? And then nothing. It's unlikely. It's also highly improbable that Mary-Jane Phelps was his first sexual assault. Was there really nothing more in CODIS?'

'Just these three,' Clayton answered. 'But, yeah, you're right. It is unlikely that these are the only three. The review from 2003 proposed the most probable scenario was that the perpetrator had died soon after Sadie's murder.'

'And is that what you think, Detective?' Maddie asked.

He gestured to Becky with his open hand and said, 'I would tend to agree with your colleague that there *should* be more bodies, which leaves three explanations as far as I can see. One, he's deceased. Two, he's no longer in the immediate vicinity of Delaware County. Three, he's being much more careful about what he leaves at the crime scene…if you know what I mean. Back in the early 80s, this guy just needed to worry about not being seen or leaving fingerprints behind. Then DNA came along and—wham—it's a whole different ball game.'

Maddie nodded, liking his open assessment of the case. The number of detectives she had dealt with, who had had rigid, unshakeable ideas about a particular homicide, was startling.

'Does that make a difference to your searches?' Clayton asked. 'If he's dead or alive, I mean?'

'No, it has no bearing,' Maddie replied. 'Personally, I'd like him to still be alive to face justice, but maybe if he died soon after Sadie's murder, then *that's* the best-case scenario.'

'So, what happens now?' Clayton asked.

Maddie stood from her chair. 'Now… I access the DNA kit online and assess how solvable the case is, then triage how we're going to proceed.'

'Oh,' Clayton said, taken aback. 'I thought it was pretty much guaranteed that you'd be able to solve it.'

Maddie smiled. 'Unlike some companies in this field, we take on any case, no matter how hard it is. *But*… if the matches just aren't there in the database right now, then we'll have no choice but to wait it out.'

'So, effectively it becomes 'open-active' again,' he said, blowing air from his cheeks, 'but now on your shelves as well as mine.'

Maddie observed the detective who was clearly disappointed that she was offering him no guarantee of success. 'Let's take a look-see, shall we?' she said, trying to sound reassuring as she pulled Kenyatta's keyboard towards her. She opened up an internet browser and went to the FamilyTreeDNA website. Taking out the piece of paper given to her by the detective, Maddie typed in the kit number and password, and signed in. The page, appearing in full on the digital whiteboard at the front of the room, displayed several tabs and option boxes. The one that she clicked, and which was central to the entire solvability of the case, was headed *Family Finder*.

Maddie briefly cast her eyes over the familiar eight gray rectangular buttons. *Matches. Matrix. Chromosome Browser. Advanced matches. myOrigins. Data Download. ancientOrigins. Learn More.*

She clicked on *Matches*, then, as the page loaded, glanced to the rest of her team, noticing the shared apprehension as they waited. Only the detective, blissfully unaware of the decisive weight of this initial step, was watching the screen impassively—his arms strapped across his chest, his hands tucked into his armpits—as though he were waiting for a movie to begin.

'Yes!' Kenyatta cheered.

'Great,' Becky echoed.

The screen in front of them was now populated with a long list of people's names. One thousand nine hundred and seventy-one people's names to be precise, all of them having one thing in common: the misfortunate distinction of sharing varying amounts of DNA with the Chester Creek killer.

Maddie noted the cause of Kenyatta's and Becky's evidently delighted outburst: the results were ranked in order of closeness of matching DNA quantities, and at the top of this list was one Kathryn Simmons who shared sixty-nine centiMorgans of DNA with the killer, thereby receiving the approximate relationship range of second-to-fourth cousin. She scrolled down the page, seeing several further family members with ever-lessening amounts of DNA, but who also fell into this relationship bracket. 'It's *good*, Detective,' Maddie said, smiling at him. 'It's not amazing, but it's good.'

Clayton grinned. 'Well, I'm sure glad *you* know what you're looking at here because, except for the people's names, the rest is like a totally alien language to me, I can tell you.'

Maddie laughed.

'So, it's promising, right?' the detective pushed.

Maddie nodded. 'Yeah.' She stood up to address the team, facing them in turn as she issued her instructions. 'Okay. So, we're probably looking at around two to three hundred hours' work, here. Hudson, pass me the thumb drive, then I want you to get cracking on the Y-line and EVCs. Kenyatta, start clustering. Becky... admixture and geo-profiling. Ross, print me out all the victims' details: names, dates of abduction and discovery, photos and witness details. I'll upload the kit to GEDmatch, then move all the case details to the shared drive.' She looked at her watch. 2:46pm. 'We'll have our first briefing at 4:30pm. Everyone okay with that?'

Nods and murmurs of agreement came from the team as Maddie cast her eyes around the office. She noticed the look of bemusement on the detective's face.

'Why line? EVCs? Clustering? Add mixes?' he said with a laugh. 'What the hell do you people do here?'

'Witchcraft and sorcery, Detective,' Maddie replied, dragging her chair over to Becky's workstation.

'But I mean what are you doing here that CODIS can't do?' he asked.

'Okay,' Maddie said, staring at him as she thought for a moment. 'So, CODIS will only produce a DNA hit for a direct match or their parent, child or full sibling. It *won't* give you the perps' uncles, half-siblings, grandparents or cousins because it's only comparing up to twenty DNA markers, right?'

'Right,' he confirmed.

'We're testing over *four million* markers, which means we can pull in relatives as distant as sixth or seventh cousins. If we can work out how those cousins relate to the DNA sample, we've got your serial killer.'

'Wow,' he said, clearly impressed. 'It sounds so easy.'

Maddie laughed. 'It really isn't easy, but we're getting good results. Where CODIS runs at less than fifteen percent chance of producing a positive ID for a perpetrator, in this office, we're running at around eighty-five percent.'

'Incredible. Can I stick around and watch?' Clayton asked, as Hudson leaned over and passed Maddie the thumb drive.

'Thanks,' she said to Hudson, then screwed up her face and replied to Clayton. 'I'm not sure there's too much point, to be honest; you're not going to get any answers for a good few days yet. Maybe even longer.'

Clayton nodded. 'Okay, well… I'm staying at the Hyatt House Hotel until I leave in two days. It's just a couple of blocks from here. In case you have any questions, I mean.'

'Thank you, Detective,' Maddie said, sitting down beside Becky who slid the keyboard across in front of her. 'I'll be in touch.'

'So… I think he was hitting on you,' Becky whispered, nudging her elbow towards Maddie.

'What?' Maddie said, pulling up the GEDmatch website and then pausing to face Becky. 'What?'

Becky tilted her head towards the door. 'Clayton. I think he likes you.'

Maddie turned to see the detective strolling out through the main office door. Flicking his head sideways, their eyes briefly locked before he was gone. 'Don't be absurd. *I* am married and God knows what *he* is.' She returned her focus to one of the two computer screens on Becky's desk, logging in on the GEDmatch website. From a long menu of options, Maddie clicked *Upload your DNA files* and was then taken to a new page to register the kit. In the *Name of Donor* box, Maddie entered 'Chester Creek' and 'LZ031' as the killer's alias. Next, from a raft of upload options about the DNA's source of origin, she chose *DNA obtained and authorized by law enforcement to identify a perpetrator of a violent crime against another individual, where 'violent crime' is defined as murder, non-negligent manslaughter, aggravated rape, robbery, or aggravated assault*. She selected the DNA data file from the thumb drive and then clicked to upload.

'Let's see what we got here,' Maddie muttered as she returned to the front page of the website, where all of Venator's previous cases were listed. At the bottom was the Chester Creek kit, noted as *processing*. While DNA-cousin matches would take up to twenty-four hours to populate against the kit, certain functionality was instant. 'Over to you,' Maddie said, sliding the keyboard back in front of Becky.

'Thanks,' she said with a grin.

Maddie stood up just as the receptionist, Ross, approached her, offering a small pile of papers. 'Here you go.'

Maddie thanked him and carried the paperwork over to the large blank whiteboard, ready to write up the known concrete facts of the Chester Creek murders. Almost all of the process of investigative genetic genealogy was about hunches, blind alleys, rabbit holes, wild goose chases and a whole bunch of maybes, likelys and possiblys and very little in the way of absolutes until the end of the case drew close and a list of suspects had been identified. She picked up the red marker pen, prized in the office for being reserved for indisputable facts, and began to write up the case notes. THE CHESTER CREEK MURDERS, she wrote at the top of the whiteboard. Then, she carefully stuck up the color photographs of each of the three victims. For a moment, she simply stared at the young women, meeting each of their silent stares in turn, respectfully acknowledging their role in this work and willing them to speak out. The ends of their lives had been unimaginably horrific and violent, and for almost forty years their families and friends had been trapped in a perpetual state of grief and uncertainty. 'We'll find him,' she whispered to them.

Taking a long inward breath, Maddie steeled herself and wrote the names of each of the three women below their photograph and the details of their abduction. Then she sifted through the paperwork that Ross had just printed out for her, settling on the police suspect sketch of the killer, shuddering again at how the artist had managed to depict such evilness in his eyes. She stuck the photo to the whiteboard and, taking a blue marker, which signified unverified information, wrote up the description given of this person of interest. Beside it, Maddie added the details of the possible two vehicles seen around the time of Mary-Jane Phelps's abduction: the red Dodge Coronet and the white Toyota Pickup.

She stood back and looked at the whiteboard. For the moment, the vast majority of it was completely blank, but with hers and her team's best efforts, she was confident that would all soon change.

Chapter Nine

Becky Larkin watched from her desk as Maddie finished adding the case notes for the Chester Creek murders to the whiteboard. As happened every time, the case had reached into Becky's heart and she had formed an instant, palpable affinity with the three victims. One in particular, Terri Locke, resonated deeply. Becky stared at her photo. Athletic and with an exuberance for life was exactly how Becky herself had been at that age. She still was, truth be told. Terri would likely have been the same today, had she not unwittingly fallen into the path of a serial killer. She shuddered to think that the same might just as easily have happened to her.

Turning back to her desk, Becky pushed her black-rimmed glasses onto the bridge of her nose and began to work on the breakdown of the killer's admixture—the technical term for ethnicity. It was still an evolving science and one based upon *very* loose approximations. In some of their past cases, it had provided important clues in the DNA of a victim who had had very evident Jewish Diaspora heritage and another with high Native American ethnicity.

Selecting *Admixture* from the GEDmatch website menu, Becky chose the MDLP Project which was a global calculator that attempted to break down ethnicity into different regions of the world. Having entered the killer's DNA kit number into the search box, a colorful pie chart and accompanying table of information loaded onscreen.

South and West European: 47.84%
North and East European: 39.40%
Caucaus Parsia: 6.65%
Middle East: 2.63%
Indian: 2.07%
Melanesian: 0.63%
Mesoamerican: 0.56%
Paleo African: 0.20%

The killer was of overwhelmingly European heritage. What the chart did not tell her, however, was for how many generations he or his ancestors had lived in the US.

Becky clicked to print out the results, then logged in to the FamilyTreeDNA website. Where Maddie had previously clicked to view the killer's genetic cousins, Becky selected *myOrigins* from the options in the Family Finder menu. Choosing *All Ethnic Makeup Percentage*, she was presented with a table displaying the 24 global regions that provided reference populations against which the killer's DNA had been compared.

British Isles: 72%
West and Central Europe: 23%
New World: 3%
Scandinavia: <1%

Significantly, the percentage ethnicity from Asia, Africa and the Middle East was zero. Therefore, taken alongside the admixture estimates from GEDmatch, it was probable—but by no means conclusive—that the killer was white. The most valuable aspect, however, of knowing even the approximate ethnic heritage was that it could help the team know where to look when they began the onerous task of rebuilding the killer's family tree.

Becky sent the results to the large copier-printer underneath the windows. She walked across the room, collected the papers and gazed out at the relentlessly falling snow. Darkness was pulling in early today as the heavy gray clouds continued to hunker over the city.

'Is it still bad out?' Kenyatta asked.

'Pretty much, yeah,' Becky replied, heading back to her desk.

'Oh dear,' Kenyatta muttered.

Now it was time to begin the second phase of her work. She glanced at the clock at the top of her monitor: 3:23pm. Just over one hour until the briefing, which Maddie liked to have at the end of most days in order to bring everyone up to speed with each other's work.

Pulling up the case information from the shared drive, Becky found the abduction location of Mary-Jane Phelps and typed that address into Google Maps. The satellite view of the area presented the roads as gray snaking lines superimposed over an otherwise densely green, rural landscape. Becky estimated that the Glen Riddle Road ran for around one mile in a north-east, south-west direction. She zoomed in closer and, as she did so, the names of minor subsidiary roads began to pop up on the map.

The road upon which Mary-Jane Phelps resided, Martin's Lane, came into view, spurring off Glen Riddle Road and running south for approximately one hundred yards before terminating at a cul-de-sac.

Part way down that road was the house that she had never reached.

Switching to map mode, the winding blue line denoting Chester Creek appeared, running parallel to Martin's Lane before turning sharply under Pennell Road. The other two victims had been abducted fairly close by.

Becky sat back in her chair and studied the map closely. The murders appeared to have had little planning and, based on the evidence of their abductions, it seemed as though the women had been selected at random. The killer, she believed, likely knew the area intimately and, when the impulse took him, he would drive around until the threshold of his requirements had been met. In Becky's opinion those requirements were fairly rudimentary: a lone, young, nice-looking woman coinciding with the availability of the amount of time that it would take to overpower her and get her into his vehicle unseen.

Returning to the case notes, she wrote down the location where the bodies had been found. On each occasion, he had dumped them in the same place in the creek, making no effort at all to conceal them. He had either been in a hurry to dispose of them, panicked, or simply arrogant enough to believe that he could get away with it. She had studied several serial killers who had wanted their crimes to be discovered quickly, gaining as much pleasure from the hype around the investigation as from the murders themselves. If the first condition had been true, then Becky would have expected the killer to have dumped the body almost immediately post-mortem, and yet, in each case it took more than two days for him to dispose of them; six days in the case of the third victim, Sadie Mayer.

Using FBI descriptors, Becky found the killer to have been disorganized in his selection of the victims but organized in the disposal of their bodies; this dangerous combination pointed to his being an arrogant, spontaneous serial killer.

She pulled up the images of the crime scenes, taken under the bridge of New Road, trying to observe them dispassionately as her studies had taught her. She had a bachelor's and master's degree in Criminology from Simon Fraser University in Canada, specializing in geographic profiling, yet still she found such imagery hard to look at as intensely as the role required of her.

As the detective had said, no attempt had been made to hide the bodies, they had been thrown the twenty or thirty feet down into the shallow waters of Chester Creek like garbage. Their bodies were forever immortalized in the photographs as adopting hideous, unnatural positions, with joints and limbs forced into impossible configurations.

Becky took a deep breath in, slowly zooming in to the first picture of Mary-Jane Phelps's body. She wanted to analyze the detail of the surrounding landscape, trying to figure out why the killer had chosen this particular location. With nothing obvious coming to her from the image, Becky went back to Google Maps, where she clicked on the miniature orange man in the bottom right corner, dragging him across the map and plopping him down onto New Road.

The little orange man landed the Street View in the middle of the road, directly in front of a small triangle of grass at an intersection with Mount Road. Situated in the center of the green was a Second World War memorial, from which protruded a flagpole hanging the stars and stripes.

Just as it had appeared in satellite mode, the area was surrounded by full, mature trees and long stretches of neatly trimmed lawns. Becky looked at the date on which the stitched photographs had been taken: July 2019. In the top-left corner of the screen, she slid the date-selection bar down through the three available dates to the earliest images which had been captured in August 2007. It was still twenty-five years after the murders but, from the switch between 2019 and 2007, it appeared as though very little had changed in the area over time.

Becky slowly turned the view three hundred and sixty degrees, noting a small children's playpark and two detached houses that, significantly, did not have a direct view of the bridge over Chester Creek. Also of interest to Becky was that in all three sets of Street View images, taken five years apart, not a single car had been photographed on the road. A perfect quiet spot to pull up in a vehicle and launch a body over the side of the bridge, the walls of which she noticed were barely knee-high and would have demanded little effort from the killer to get the victims over the edge.

She looked at the coroner's report into Mary-Jane's death to help understand the killer's movements, hoping to see an approximate time of day when her body had been thrown into the creek, but he had only been able to offer a broad period of one to two days.

Becky took a selection of screenshots from the Street View of the bridge area, then sent them to the printer and saved them to the shared drive.

Now, she needed to examine the crime scene photos for the other two victims to try and identify any potential patterns or similarities. But time was running out; the briefing was in just thirty minutes' time.

Chapter Ten

Hudson Édouard was waiting impatiently for the coffee machine. He looked across the office at how diligently the rest of the team were working. Kenyatta was flapping a piece of paper around in her left hand, while she directed Maddie's attention to something on her computer screen. Becky, with her back to him, was nibbling on her thumb nail, as she scrutinized some hellish crime scene photograph. As far as possible, Hudson steered well clear of the gory sides of the cases, much preferring to concentrate on the genetic genealogy aspects, those being his absolute passion in life. Being an eclectic mixture of heritage himself, he'd held a fascination with his ancestors and their exploits since the age of twelve. He was a good-looking, twenty-five-year-old, third-generation American. His paternal grandparents having been born in French Guiana, Hudson had inherited their olive skin, deep-brown eyes and jet-black hair. From his maternal Canadian side came less of his physical appearance but more of their dogged work-ethic, compassion and resilience; a good mixture, in his humble opinion.

The machine finally finished. 'Anyone want anything from over here?' he called across the room.

There was a unanimous but polite rejection. Hudson smiled, knowing that they were all up against it, wanting to have something decent to relay at the briefing in just twenty minutes' time. He could relax…a little. As was to be expected at this early stage of an investigation, he hadn't yet made any major breakthroughs, although he would still be able to contribute something to the briefing.

Back at his workstation, Hudson set down his coffee and returned to his previous focus. Halfway down the page on the FamilyTreeDNA website was information pertaining to the killer's Y-DNA, something that passes relatively unchanged from fathers to sons across generations. Hudson clicked on the Y-DNA *Matches* option and was presented with a list of nineteen men who all shared a common paternal ancestor with the Chester Creek murderer. In theory, since it is the tradition in most Western cultures to pass surnames down from father to son unchanged, all the men presented as matching the killer should all have the same surname. In practice, he had found the reality rarely to be so. There were seven different surnames in front of Hudson and none of them was necessarily shared by the killer himself; generations-old illegitimacy tending to be the largest contributing factor to this misalignment. The killer's closest match on his paternal Y-line was one John James Smith. Nice and unusual surname, Hudson thought sardonically.

According to the Time Predictor tool on the website, there was only a 24% chance that the killer and John James Smith shared an ancestor within four generations. To achieve a 91% chance of finding a shared common ancestor, from whom they both descended, it would be necessary to trace John James Smith's paternal line backwards sixteen generations; an all-but-impossible task.

His final job before this afternoon's briefing was to work on the killer's phenotype, the evolving science of predicting EVCs—externally visible characteristics—from DNA. Like so much of the work in this office, it was based on a great deal of maybes, probablys and likelys, running at around a 70% rate of accuracy.

Accessing the Hirisplex website, created by the Department of Genetic Identification of Erasmus MC as a tool for forensic and anthropological usage, Hudson opened up the killer's DNA profile. It was a plain text document, filled with 677,864 lines of DNA coding. He was pretty well the only person in the office who understood the science behind the data. The others would usually glaze over when he would extol the biological aspects of their investigations. Of those 677,864 pieces of code, just forty-one helped point towards an idea of the killer's eye, hair and skin color. Maybe. Possibly. Hopefully.

Hudson pulled out the corresponding forty-one lines of information. After ten minutes of careful extraction, he clicked *Display Predicted Phenotype*. A short moment later, the results were in front of him. He studied them carefully, noting them down on his pad.

'Two minutes, please, people. Two minutes.' Maddie called across the office.

Hudson picked up his coffee and took a sip. As he did so, he glanced at the photograph on his desk. It was of him and his wife, Abigail, on their honeymoon in Hawaii. Three years ago, he thought with a smile as he picked up the picture. It was a selfie taken on the beach and all around them was brilliant-white sand, reaching out to the perfect clear sea in the distance. The happiness on their faces had been real, if naïve. It was after their return to normal life that their problems had started. The move to Salt Lake City eighteen months ago was supposed to have been a fresh start for them.

He returned the picture to his desk, just as Maddie strode across the office to the enclave of the digital whiteboard, the glass writing board and the whiteboard upon which she had already added the known facts about the killer.

'Okay, guys,' Maddie said, reaching for the red and the blue marker pens. 'Let's have the first team briefing for the Chester Creek murders. Ross, are you ready to take down notes?'

'One second,' he responded, jumping up from the reception desk with his laptop and hurrying over to a chair in front of the screens.

'Becky, let's start with you,' Maddie said.

Hudson faced Becky, watching as she flicked through some paperwork on her desk. She slid her glasses up onto the bridge of her nose, stood up and then began. 'So, admixture first,' she said, reading out the killer's approximate ethnicity percentages. She paused a moment while Maddie added the details with the red marker to the whiteboard.

'Thank you,' Maddie said. 'So, likelihood is that the attacker was white.'

'Probably,' Becky said, tapping on her keyboard. 'I'm just going to share my screen with you.'

Maddie stepped to one side, as Becky's computer display was mirrored on the digital whiteboard. In front of the team was an aerial map of Delaware County overlaid with a semi-transparent purple circle covering several streets. Within the circle was a scalene triangle comprised of thin red lines with a colored pin at each corner.

Becky stood up and walked over to the digital whiteboard. She pointed at the three pins on the map. 'These are the locations where the victims were likely picked up, if we base this on last sightings. It appears that the women were chosen at random and that the killer operated with a very basic set of requirements: that they were young and nice-looking. That, coupled with the time that it would have taken to get them—willingly or otherwise—into his vehicle, was all he appeared to be looking for. The fact that he bludgeoned at least one of them before assaulting her suggests that there is some doubt that he knew the victims personally. The likelihood here is that he knew the area very well and, when the mood took him, would go out on the prowl. And if luck was on his side, he would find what he was looking for. Here—' she pointed at one of the marker pins, '—is the location where he disposed of the bodies. As we heard from the detective earlier, the killer chose the same part of the Chester Creek on New Road, a location isolated enough for him to get the girls out of his vehicle and into the water without being seen.' She stopped and thought for a moment. 'I can't quite work it out, but there's something there to do with the water…why he chose this location.'

'He lives nearby?' Kenyatta offered.

'He most certainly did,' Becky confirmed. 'But my hunch is that there's something more than that; he'd have had to have driven—coming from either direction to this point—past plenty of isolated spots that would have been as suitable, if not *more* suitable places, to leave them. Better, too, if the goal had been either to hide the bodies completely or just to dump them as quickly as possible…'

'Do you think he *wanted* to be caught?' Hudson asked.

Becky shook her head. 'No, I don't think so. I think he was arrogant and assumed that he *wouldn't* get caught. He chose the victims randomly. He abducted them…and dumped them in a semi-isolated spot. There were no witnesses. He had no ties to the women and so thought that he was invincible.'

'And what about his possible address?' Maddie asked.

'So, based on the Circle Theory of Environmental Range, this purple area is highly likely to be where the killer resided at the times of the murders.'

'How likely?' Maddie quizzed.

'Well, in a study from the early 1990s, David Canter—a leading forensic psychologist—found this to be accurate in eighty-five percent of criminal cases. I mean, it's still a pretty big area,' she conceded. 'Here we're looking at a dozen potential streets. But the study also found that a serial killer can usually be found living within a triangle formed by the first three murders.' She pointed to the red-lined triangle contained within the purple circle. 'We only have three murders in total, but this does help potentially narrow the geographical area down considerably when it comes to building the killer's family tree. As you can see, we're down to seven potential streets.'

'This is great,' Maddie said. 'Anything else?'

'Well, using the FBI characterization of organized versus disorganized, the killer would appear at first glance to fall into the disorganized category: little preparation, random, unplanned behaviors, scant attempt to conceal evidence at the scene… But, if you look more closely, actually he *did* make plans. He decided to go out hunting for a victim. He knew exactly how he would overpower them…what he planned to do to them. Interestingly—and which the detective neglected to point out or hadn't realized himself—the murders were all carried out on a Friday night, although technically Terri was abducted in the early hours of the Saturday morning. But the point is that the killer *chose* to do this on a Friday night each time. He kept hold of the first two women for two days... Disposing of them on the Sunday, in other words.'

'Significance?' Maddie asked.

'Well, organized killers oftentimes live with a partner. It's possible that the partner worked or was away for some reason on weekends.'

'And what about the third victim, Sadie Mayer?' Kenyatta asked. 'The detective said she was kept for six days.'

Becky screwed up her face. 'Partner away on vacation or business trip?' She shrugged. 'I don't know...'

'Okay,' Maddie said with a nod. 'So, if we're looking at an organized killer, are there any other potential traits or characteristics?'

Becky nodded. 'Typically—although not always—a person who is socially capable, intelligent and who is sexually competent.'

'A regular guy on the surface, right?' Kenyatta said.

'Yes, but underneath that mask of normality is an unmistakable psychopath.'

'Would his partner *really* not know?' Kenyatta asked.

'She—it's most likely a woman—would certainly know of his anger issues. But know about his crimes? I doubt that very much.'

A moment of silence descended on the office, as the team considered what she had just relayed.

'That's all I've got at the moment,' Becky concluded, heading back to her desk.

'Fantastic start,' Maddie commended. 'Well done. Hudson, what have you got for us?'

Hudson picked up his notepad and stood to address the room. The first few times that he had been called upon to present to the team, a nervous grip had squeezed all the moisture from his throat and caused his cheeks to redden, but now that he was comfortable in his role and considered everyone currently staring at him as a friend, the task was rendered somewhat easier.

'No major revelations from the Y-DNA, unfortunately. His haplogroup is I-M253. Not a great deal of help knowing that the killer's patrilineal roots originated in Northern Europe and Scandinavia, nor that the common ancestor for this haplogroup is found around the Jutland Peninsula near the border of Germany and Denmark, since this was between two thousand and five thousand years BC.'

Maddie grinned at the useless details while adding the important element of the haplogroup to the board in red marker pen. 'Thanks for that. Anything *slightly* closer in time?'

Hudson leaned over his computer, sharing his screen so that the killer's Y-DNA matches appeared on the large digital whiteboard. 'As you can see, we've got seven surnames, one of which is *possibly* the killer's, but *possibly* not. Smith. Floyd. Findlay. Brown. Paris. Frost. Howley.' As he read out the names, Maddie wrote them in blue marker on the whiteboard. 'The closest match on his paternal side is one John James Smith, but we're looking at sixteen generations to reach the ninety percent bracket. So, again, not helpful.' Hudson threw his arms up. 'That's all I got on the Y-line.'

'No, that's great. Thank you, Hudson,' Maddie said. 'Gotta love a Smith.'

The team knew that it was very rare for a close enough match to appear in Y-DNA matches to warrant their investigation time, so when Hudson concluded this part of his initial research, having provided very little tangible evidence, he did so without feeling too bad.

'And phenotype?' Maddie enquired.

'Okay,' Hudson said, looking down at his pad. 'As usual, the statistics aren't conclusive. However, the strongest indications are as follows: the killer likely had brown hair, brown eyes and pale skin.'

'Great,' Maddie said, adding the details to the whiteboard. She gestured towards Becky. 'So, a very strong possibility that he's white.'

The team nodded in agreement, then Maddie faced Kenyatta. 'And last but not least is the lady who will have *all* the answers for us.'

Kenyatta rolled her eyes playfully, smiled, stood up and said, 'So, at GEDmatch I ran the kit through the homozygosity tool and, no, the killer's parents are not related in any significant way.'

Hudson scribbled a note on his pad. Knowing that the killer's parents were unrelated meant that genetic cousin matches could be ascribed firmly to distinct maternal and paternal branches in his family tree without fear of close overlap.

'So that's great news,' Kenyatta continued. 'I've also downloaded the cousins who share the killer's DNA. There appears to be nine distinct genetic networks—separate branches of the killer's family tree. Each of the nine clusters can be found in the shared drive, all ready for work tomorrow. That is all from me for now.' She smiled and sat back down.

'Great work, team,' Maddie said. 'Briefing over. Day over. Go home. Travel safely out there: it's looking pretty darn grim.'

A hum of organized busyness filtered around the office as they began to prepare to head out. Hudson put his computer to sleep, tidied the paperwork into one neat stack and carried his mug over to the sink where Becky was washing up.

'Ross and I are going to the Sun Trapp for a drink. Do you want to come along?' she asked.

'No,' he replied, his curtness drawing a look from Becky.

'Anyone can go there, you know,' she said, raising her eyebrows.

'I know. But, no,' he answered. 'I've got to get home.'

'Abigail's got you on a tight leash.'

Hudson sighed, placed his mug down, picked up his coat and headed back to his desk. He would wash the mug first thing tomorrow. Better that than have his personal life interrogated and used as office gossip.

'Hey, I was kidding,' Becky called after him. 'Jeez.'

'It's fine,' he said with a false smile as he pulled on his thick overcoat, slung his bag over his shoulder and called a general goodbye to the whole office.

Out in the corridor, Hudson sighed. He desperately wanted to go out with Becky and Ross, actually; to socialize with anyone, anywhere, in fact, rather than rush home.

He descended the stairs to the street level, pulled open the door and stepped out onto the sidewalk.

Instead of heading across the street and catching the tram home, he trudged aimlessly into the freezing snowstorm.

Chapter Eleven

'What's up with Hudson lately?' Becky asked nobody in particular as she tossed her cellphone into her yawning purse.

Ross shrugged.

'I think maybe he's a little sensitive about his home-life,' Kenyatta said from her desk, opting for office diplomacy. 'Maybe just don't talk about it—or Abigail—unless he brings them up.'

Becky exhaled, as though that was some great burdensome request. 'Maddie?' she called into her office. 'Do you wanna come for a drink?'

'No. I'll give it a miss this time, thanks. Although the kids *are* out tonight, I've got a bunch of other stuff to catch up on. You all go ahead.'

'Okay, then. See you in the morning,' she replied.

'Bye,' Ross echoed.

Kenyatta watched the two youngsters leave, then stuck her head around Maddie's office door. She was sitting at her desk, frowning at her computer monitor. 'Don't work too late. It's bad out there and you need to get home safe.'

'Yeah, I know,' Maddie agreed. 'I'll let the rush hour go, then leave.'

'Alright. See you tomorrow, honey.'

'Bye, Kenyatta. Have a good evening.'

Kenyatta zipped up her coat and left the office. Taking the elevator to the first floor, she pulled open the main door to the Kearns Building and flinched at the icy wind whipping the snow up around her in a directionless frenzy. 'Oh, my word,' she muttered, yanking a beanie hat from her pocket and tugging it down over her newly braided hair.

She looked down the street and caught sight of the tram headlights puncturing their way through the snowstorm. It was the Green Line tram that she needed to get home. From the shelter of the building doorway, Kenyatta watched the tram draw to a halt right in front of her. She sighed, deciding not to take it and stepped out onto the sidewalk instead. She headed half a block down the street where she turned right on 200 South, her footprints being quickly erased behind her as she walked. She inched her scarf down from her mouth, struggling to breathe properly. It was at moments like these that she knew she needed to lose weight and get fitter. One of these days she was going to fall down like a stone, dead. Just as had happened with both her parents. She was fifty-six years old and not in good physical health. Having spent most of her adult life looking after others, she'd had the perfect excuse of lack of time to take care of herself. Now, though, that defense held no sway.

After two blocks, Kenyatta slowed her pace and turned left on 200 West. Through the veil of snow, she caught sight of the word REDROCK in bright-red neon lights and she puffed out a quick burst of air.

She pulled open the doors and stepped inside the restaurant's warm embrace with great relief.

'Good evening, ma'am,' a bearded young man in a black shirt greeted. 'Do you have a reservation?'

Kenyatta shook her head, not quite ready for a conversation. 'Take out,' she mumbled.

The man handed her a menu and pointed to the bar that ran in an L-shape along one side of the restaurant. 'Place your order over there and the food will be right out.'

'Thank you,' Kenyatta said.

'You're welcome. Have a great evening.'

Kenyatta ambled over to the bar trying to normalize her breathing. She unzipped her jacket and then studied the menu. She ran her forefinger over the section with the wood-fired pizzas and made her choice.

'What can I getcha?' asked a young lady with a sleeve of complicated tattoos and an ear full of metal hoops.

'One wild mushroom and one Italian sausage pizza to go, please.'

The server punched the details into the cash register. 'Anything to drink at all?'

'Two large root beers, please.'

'Great. That'll be $31.50.'

Kenyatta settled the bill and took a seat at the bar. While she waited, she took out her cellphone. She touched the home button. The background wallpaper—a selfie of her and the three kids taken last summer—briefly illuminated the screen. Nothing from the boys. No missed calls. No text messages. The ill effects of her acrimonious divorce, granted three months ago, were being felt. Otis, having temporary legal custody of the kids, now seemed hell-bent on making life as hard for her as he could. She pocketed her phone and turned around on the barstool so that she was facing the windows. The storm had yet to abate. If anything, it had worsened since she had left work. She thought about Maddie and hoped that she wouldn't hang about the office too much longer. The woman worked too hard. But then, they all did. Some of the horrific images, which she had seen on the detective's presentation today, came to her mind. Those poor girls and their families left behind with no answers. But the chances of the Venator team finding the murderer were pretty good. Very good, in her opinion. She'd seen it before. Tomorrow, the whole team would be working on reconstructing those nine distinct family trees. Somewhere, linking all of those trees together, would be the name of the Chester Creek murderer.

Kenyatta hoped that the monster was still alive. Out there someplace, all smug and arrogant in the belief that he'd gotten away with his heinous crimes. But with some hard work and a little luck, justice would soon be catching up with him. Although Pennsylvania wasn't exactly prolific in carrying out death penalties, maybe they'd make an exception by getting off their asses to execute this guy. *Not views that she would be openly sharing with her church friends on Sunday, but they were her views, nonetheless.*

'One wild mushroom and one Italian sausage and two root beers?' a male voice called from behind the bar.

Kenyatta raised her hand as she spun around in her chair to the young, good-looking man with shoulder-length hair, holding up a plastic take-out bag. 'Thank you,' she said, taking the proffered food.

'Enjoy,' he replied.

She zipped her coat back up, raised her scarf and stepped out into the horrible evening. 'Jeez,' she muttered, as a freezing thrust of wind slammed against her. 'Good thing I'm built of stronger stuff.'

She continued along 200 West for a further block and a half until she came to a squat building that Kenyatta was always amazed to see continuing to stand. In its hey-day it had been a grand old bank. Now, it was in desperate need of either demolition or serious renovation. Through the smashed windows on the second floor, she could see the snow tumbling through the space where the roof had once been. The first-floor windows, boarded presumably to keep out vagrants and curious youths, were decorated in several layers of illegible graffiti and scarred with various failed attempts at arson. In the covered doorway was an unsightly assortment of canvas and trash bags, blankets and newspaper, and, protruding from somewhere in the middle of it all, there was a sleeping bag whose original color could no longer be reliably determined.

'Hey, Lonnie!' Kenyatta said to the pile of detritus. 'Lonnie!'

The stack started to move, and a toothless man with a long gray beard stuck his head out. 'Who's that?'

'It's me, Kenyatta. I've got you pizza.'

'Pizza?' he said. 'What kind?'

Kenyatta laughed. 'You're gonna be picky tonight, huh, Lonnie?'

He shrugged.

'Wild mushroom or Italian sausage. And a root beer.'

Lonnie huffed as he shuffled himself out of the pile of blankets. He was, as always, wearing the same filthy trousers, shirt, tie and jacket. Why he chose to be welded into that particular attire, she had never been able to establish. It hardly looked like the most comfortable of things to wear twenty-four-seven.

'So, what's it to be?' Kenyatta asked, holding the two boxes aloft once he had positioned himself beside her on the sheltered top step.

'Well, wild mushroom, I guess.'

She opened the first box. 'That would be mine,' she said, setting it to one side. 'And this is yours.'

'Thanks,' he said, lifting the lid and reaching in for a slice.

'Well, I figured you wouldn't make it to the kitchen tonight and might be hungry.'

'I'm always hungry, Kenny,' he said.

She smiled and began to tuck into her pizza. He was the only person in the world whom she had ever let shorten her name to *Kenny*. She couldn't help but think of Kenny Rogers every time he said it.

'Solved any murders lately?' Lonnie asked without pausing his eating or taking his eyes from the pizza.

'No. But we got ourselves a new case in, today.'

Lonnie glanced across at her. 'Is that so? Why don't you tell Lonnie all about it?'

And so, she did. She spared him all the unnecessary gore and violence, giving him the watered-down, cop-show version.

'Well, this guy sure sounds a piece of work,' Lonnie concluded when Kenyatta had finished. 'Hope you catch him for them ladies.'

'Yeah, me too. Do you know that neighborhood at all?' Kenyatta asked. In the two years that she had been volunteering at the SLC Homeless Kitchen, she had discovered next to nothing about his personal life or the backstory which had led him to the streets.

Lonnie looked blankly and shrugged. 'Don't think so.'

'Pizza good?' Kenyatta asked him.

'It's okay,' he said with a light sneer. 'It's a bit sweet for a pizza.

They need to lay off the caramelized onion. Tell 'em the next time you go there.'

Kenyatta laughed. 'I'll be sure to do that, Lonnie. Is there anything else you need?'

'A mask and gloves,' he replied.

'A mask? What like, Batman or something?'

Lonnie glowered at her and reached behind him with a groan. He pulled a crumpled newspaper out and handed it to her, jabbing a grimy finger at a story partway down the page. 'Read that.'

'I'll try,' Kenyatta said, angling the newspaper to catch a slice of the orange streetlamp light. 'Coronavirus?'

'Read it,' he instructed.

Kenyatta read the short story, then turned to face him. 'You want a mask and gloves because of some *coronavirus*?'

Lonnie nodded emphatically. 'Uh-huh do I. I've been looking in the city trashcans, but people know and aren't tossing them out—they're keeping them. They *know*.'

'Know what?' Kenyatta asked.

'Did you not read it, Kenny? Sixty-five countries now have the virus. More than thirty deaths in Italy. Iran's borders closed. Thirty-five people in Britain have it, the Paris half-marathon has been postponed and someone has *died* from in it in Washington State. It's creeping east, Kenny. Mark my words it'll be here soon enough.'

She smirked. 'I'll get you your mask and gloves, Lonnie, okay?' Kenyatta reassured him. 'But right now, I'm going to get on home.'

'Yeah,' Lonnie said. 'You've got your three kids to think of. Get them masks, too, while you're at it.'

'See you, Lonnie,' she said, standing up and touching his shoulder. 'You take care now.'

'Yeah. Thanks for the pizza, Kenny.'

'You're welcome.' She watched as he disappeared back into the tunnel of blankets and bags, then made her way towards the closest tram stop to head back to her empty home.

Chapter Twelve

Maddie approached her RAV4 in the underground parking garage beneath the Kearns Building. Her gaze, as it often did, settled on the bottom of the license plate. *Life Elevated*, it announced. Yeah, she agreed. Her life *was* elevated. For the most part. She unlocked the car, tossed her purse across to the passenger seat, started the engine and then crawled out of her parking space. At the top of a short ramp, a yellow barrier lifted automatically, and she proceeded forwards onto West Temple. As she approached the junction with 200 South, the lights turned red. She waited in the middle lane, reflecting on the day. It had been good. For day one of a serial-killer cold case, it had got off to a promising start. Unlike in some past cases, the detective had actually done as she'd asked and had come prepared. She stared at the stop light, remembering that he had kind of invited her for a drink. Where did he say he was staying? Hyatt House. That was it, she recalled, just as the lights changed to green. She thought for a second, not moving forwards. Her mind switched and, with the lane beside her empty, she took a hard right and drove on for two more blocks. Hyatt House Hotel was directly in front of her.

She pulled the car in beside the hotel entrance and looked through the windows of the first floor directly into the lobby area. People sitting in couches. A bar in the back corner. No sign of the good detective.

She took in a long breath. What *was* she doing? She was still married. Would one drink with an out-of-town detective, whom she would never clap eyes on ever again, change that, though? What if Michael waltzed through the hotel lobby and saw them talking? She'd introduce them, pull him up a chair and carry on chatting. It's not a big deal, she told herself. One lousy drink.

She drove slowly forwards into the hotel parking lot and found a spot for the RAV. She locked the car and walked to the hotel entrance. Becky's words suddenly pinged into her mind—'I think he was hitting on you'—causing her again to rethink her decision as the doors opened automatically. Sitting directly in her eyeline, slouched over a beer at the bar, was the detective. He waved.

Now she *was* committed.

She waved back and strode confidently across the lobby. 'Detective,' she greeted coolly.

'Well, hi, Maddie. I didn't think you'd come,' he said, seeming genuinely pleased to see her.

She shrugged. 'Yeah, I need a drink. Some cop showed up at my office today with a whole bunch of stomach-churning images and gruesome murder details.'

He grinned. 'He sounds like a real jackass.'

'No, no… He was okay, actually,' she said, taking a seat beside him at the bar. She caught the attention of the server. 'Could I get a white wine, please?'

The girl grimaced. 'I'm really sorry, you need to order food for me to be able to serve you alcohol.'

'O…kay. I'll get a bag of chips and a white wine, please.'

'I tried that one,' the detective muttered beside her.

Another grimace from the girl. 'It needs to be a *proper* meal.' She offered Maddie a menu. 'Here.'

'Okay, give me just a minute,' Maddie said, taking the menu. She turned to the detective. 'Have you eaten?'

'Not yet, I've just ordered barbecue pulled pork sliders.'

Maddie cast her eye over the menu. '*Sip and Snack*,' she mocked. One of the joys of living in Utah. She looked at the waitress. 'Okay, then. Can I get the Korean street tacos and a white wine, please?'

'Sure,' she answered. 'I'll tell the kitchen to bring the meals out together.'

'Thank you,' the detective said. 'So, Maddie… I'm curious how it went after I left?'

'Good. I mean, it's day one, so I haven't got you a suspect yet.'

He grinned. 'No, I wasn't expecting one.'

The waitress placed the wine down on the bar.

'Cheers,' Maddie said, raising her glass.

'Cheers,' he echoed. 'Here's to catching the Chester Creek killer.'

She drank some wine, enjoying the refreshing coldness.

'So, earlier on, when I asked how you go about identifying the killer, you said—what was it, now?—witchcraft and sorcery? Could you maybe be a *little* more specific?' he said, with a glint in his eye.

'Sure, why not?' Maddie answered. She didn't usually like to discuss ongoing cases but, since this was day one, she was happy to chat with him about their progress so far. She relayed the findings of each member of her team, pausing only when the detective needed clarification.

'Wow,' he said, once she had finished. 'All that in *one day*? Well, half a day, actually. Jesus, that's more progress than my department's made in twenty years.'

'Tomorrow the hard work begins,' Maddie said, sipping her drink.

The waitress arrived with two plates of food that she placed down in front of them. 'Is there anything else I can get for you?' she asked.

'Another beer for me, please,' the detective said. 'That is, unless I need to order another meal?'

The waitress humored him. 'No, you're allowed another beer.' She looked at Maddie. 'Another wine?'

'No. I'd better not, thank you. I have some left, here and I'm driving.' As the waitress left them, Maddie continued, 'Anyway, I've got to get back soon. The kids are out, but my mom's not.'

'Your mom lives with you?' the detective asked.

Maddie took a bite of her food before answering, 'Yeah.' She took in a protracted breath. 'She moved in with me a while back. Long story. My husband, Michael, disappeared a few years ago—in fact, it'll be five years ago on the eighth of this month—and my mom moved in to help out, be there for me and the kids.'

'Disappeared?'

'Yep. Vanished. Gone,' she said.

'Wow. I'm sorry to hear that,' the detective said. 'Can I ask what happened?'

'You can ask,' Maddie replied, picking at the tacos with her fork. 'But there isn't much to say. He went off on a fishing weekend down to Green River—as he did every now and then for as long as I'd known him—and just...never came back. The police found his truck in a parking lot. All of his stuff—tent, backpack, cellphone, rubber raft, fishing gear—all gone.'

'Was there any suspicion of foul play?' the detective asked.

'They don't know. His truck was found unlocked, which was very unusual for Michael. His cell had been switched off within minutes of his arrival at Green River, which was also very unlike him. A witness saw him parking and that was it. He and his belongings haven't been seen since.'

'That must be awful to...well...not know what happened to him.'

'It hasn't been easy with two kids who were under ten at the time.' Maddie drank some wine. 'It's the worst, actually.' She turned her wedding band. 'I mean...I'm married but I'm not. Did he walk out on us and is he out there some place, alive and well? Or is the more obvious scenario what happened? If that's the case, why haven't his body or belongings ever been found? Every day, without fail, my first waking thought in the morning is wondering what happened to Michael. Every day, I get no closer to the truth and can give myself no answers.'

'Is this why you set up Venator?' he asked.

'Yes…and no. I'm pretty sure a shrink wouldn't take long to join the dots together: my husband went missing and I have no answers, so I set up a company that provides answers to others in exactly the same boat. But in reality, I've been doing genealogy as a hobby for years and this was just a natural next step for me.'

'I can certainly see that you're driven by your work,' he observed.

Maddie nodded her agreement. 'What about you? I don't see a wedding band. There's got to be a story there: divorced, gay, both?'

The detective smiled. 'Divorced. Not gay. I'm the walking cop-show cliché. My wife left me because I was married to the job, blah blah blah.'

'Kids?' she asked.

'Wanted? Yes. Happened? No.'

'That's too bad. My kids are the bane and the sanity of my life all at once. To be honest, without them I don't know how I would have gotten through these past five years.'

'I can imagine,' he said. 'Maybe it'll happen for me one day but it's not looking too promising at the moment.'

'Stay positive,' she said. 'And on the note of kids, I'd better be getting back home.' She squinted through the window. 'Doesn't look like the storm's passing anytime soon.'

'You've barely touched your tacos,' the detective observed.

'Yeah, I'm not real hungry; I just wanted the wine.' She finished the last dregs of the drink and stood up, reaching into her purse.

'Hey, nice gun,' he commented upon seeing her purple CPX semi-automatic handgun. 'You got your license?'

'Yup,' she said. 'Right after Michael disappeared, I went and got my Concealed Pistol License and now that thing pretty well goes everywhere with me.' She placed a twenty-dollar bill on the bar.

'I'll get this,' he said, sliding the money back towards her.

'No need,' she replied, pushing it back to where it had been. 'It was good to talk to you, Detective. I'm glad I swung by.'

He smiled. 'I'm glad, too. I took a couple of days' leave, thinking it would be a good idea to explore Salt Lake City. I didn't figure on the weather, though. So, if you want to do this again?'

'I've got my work cut out these next few days, but it was really great to meet you.' Maddie extended her hand. 'Goodbye, Detective.'

'Bye, Maddie. Take care.'

Maddie strolled through the lobby, aware that he was very likely watching her leave. He was a nice guy and if circumstances had been different—*very* different—then she might well have taken him up on his offer.

She climbed into her RAV, started the engine and made her way home.

Chapter Thirteen

November 5, 1982, Aston, Delaware County, Pennsylvania

From this angle, with the narrow slice of light from the hall falling across her naked body, she looked just perfect. Like a sleeping angel.

He watched her for some time, not wishing to disturb her sleep. Then he went into the kitchen, where he took a pair of scissors from the cutlery drawer before creeping quietly back into the guest bedroom and sitting down on the bed beside her. He didn't want to disturb her, but he had to: it was Sunday.

He placed a hand on her hip, flinching at her coldness. 'Mary-Jane,' he whispered, reciting what he had read on her college ID card. 'It's time to go.'

She didn't respond.

'Mary-Jane, we've got to go.'

Repeatedly running his fingers gently through her hair, he paused when a short tuft was left protruding between his thumb and forefinger. Then, he took the scissors and carefully snipped it off. He held it up to his nose and inhaled, slowly and deeply. He was breathing in much more than the scent of Mary-Jane; he was also taking in the profound relief that released years and years of intolerable internal tension. He'd finally taken the step, crossed over that line which he'd fantasized about since his childhood; since watching his father holding the bag of kittens under the Chester Creek until their tiny, desperate cries had finally petered out. He could still hear the stark silence of the bag being pulled out of the water and his father just staring at him, as if willing or daring him to cry or protest, or something. But he had felt no inclination to do either. He had just wanted to hold on to that silence, to experience those long, long seconds of life gradually passing over to death.

He took the lock of hair and carefully placed it in a plastic sandwich bag, wanting to preserve the essence of her and this moment in some small but tangible way.

He rolled her onto her back, the light from the hall illuminating her fully now: the eight purple and crimson fingermarks shadowed around her larynx; her bruised and bloodied mouth; the hair matted and clumped together with caked, dried blood.

He held her hand and began to cry. He'd done it at last. She was here. He was here. But now he had to let her go, and after such precious little time together. He leaned his head on her chest and cried at their inevitable parting.

'Oh, God! Mary-Jane!' he screeched when he sat up, his neck in agony from having fallen asleep awkwardly on her cold body. He jumped up, rushed into the hall and looked at the clock: 2:34am. 'We *really* have to go now, Mary-Jane,' he called as he re-entered the guest bedroom. 'I'll be right back.'

He hurried down the hall, opened the internal door to the garage and switched on the light. He popped open the trunk of his red Dodge Coronet, then walked back through the house to the guest bedroom.

She hadn't moved.

He sighed as he kissed her forehead, then wrapped the bedsheet around her. Without much more effort than it had taken to overpower her when they had met, he scooped her up and carried her through the house to the garage.

'Okay, don't worry, Mary-Jane. You won't be in here for too long. It's just a short ride out, you hear?' He pushed the trunk shut, closed the door to the house and then opened the garage door.

As he started the engine, he studied the rear-view mirror. It was the first time he'd seen himself since he'd done it. Something was different. He looked at his brown cropped hair, his narrow face and his stubble. That wasn't it.

It was his eyes: they'd come alive…at last. After containing so much sorrow, he was finally happy again.

He grinned to himself as he backed out of the garage.

Chapter Fourteen

Tuesday, March 3, 2020, Downtown Salt Lake City, Utah

Maddie was sitting beside Kenyatta. The rest of the team were assembled at their desks, watching and waiting. She took a sip of her first cup of coffee of the morning, then logged in to the GEDmatch website. The entire right-hand menu of search tools was now available for the Chester Creek kit.

She clicked *One-To-Many* and watched as the killer's cousin matches loaded on the large digital whiteboard.

The silence from around the office spoke volumes.

24,243 people matched the killer. While the list looked impressively long, the reality was that, following several privacy debacles last year and a buy-out from a new company, Verogen, the entire database had drastically shrunk from its 1.4 million users to somewhere in the region of 200,000. Although the killer appeared to match with more than ten percent of the database, Maddie could see that they were unworkably weak connections.

She slowly scrolled down the list of matches. The highest was just thirty centiMorgans of DNA and the most distant a mere, insignificant seven centiMorgans. To try to connect the killer to someone with whom he shared 7centiMorgans of DNA was all but impossible; a common ancestral couple to a match this low could be as far back as seventh great-grandparents. Without endogamy reducing the number, the normal backward journey through a family tree involved the doubling in the number of ancestral couples at each generation, arriving at the absurd number of 512 seventh great-grandparents. And then there was the issue of false positives that occurred with such very low amounts of DNA.

'That's *not* a good list,' Kenyatta commented.

'Nope, it sure is *not*,' Hudson concurred.

Maddie confirmed their fears, when she adjusted the minimum quantity of centiMorgans to twenty, leaving a list of just 9 matches.

'Okay, I think the best way forward, here, is to prioritize our time with the genetic network clusters that Kenyatta put together for us yesterday from FamilyTreeDNA. Once we've made some progress there, maybe we can add some of these guys—she indicated the names in front of them—'to the family tree branches. So, Kenyatta, it's over to you.'

Kenyatta tapped some keys on her keyboard so that the digital whiteboard was displaying the Venator shared drive.

Maddie and the rest of the team watched, as she clicked the familiar folder labeled *ACTIVE CASES*, then a new subfolder that she had named *CHESTER CREEK MURDERS*. Within that folder were nine files, labeled *Cluster One* through *Cluster Nine*.

'These are the top nine closest cousin groups that we have connected to the killer—each one comes from one family branch, distinct from the other eight. Hudson, if you take clusters one and two, Becky, three and four, Maddie, five and six, and I'll take seven and eight. Nine is the hardest, so we'll leave that one alone for the time being. Beyond nine and we're looking at *very* low matches that are near-impossible to work with.'

'Okay, let's get going, team,' Maddie instructed. She trusted her team implicitly and knew that they all would do everything in their power to crack this case without her breathing down their necks and spoon-feeding them each step of the way.

She returned to her own office, keeping the door open in case they needed her. As much as she enjoyed their company, she needed her own space in which to work. Logging in to the shared drive, she clicked on the file named *Cluster Five*. A spreadsheet opened, containing a group of twelve men and women who all shared DNA with the Chester Creek murderer and with each other. With a workable fifty-nine centiMorgans of DNA—the highest of this group—a lady by the name of Aileen Moore had been designated as the lead name of cluster five. She was estimated to be the killer's second to fourth cousin and was, therefore, unlikely to be aware of his very existence.

Maddie sipped some coffee as she scrutinized each of the standard columns in the file: *Full Name. Relationship Range. Suggested Relationship. Shared centiMorgans. Longest Block. Email. Ancestral Surnames. Y-DNA Haplogroup. mtDNA Haplogroup.*

As was unfortunately all too common, not every column had been added to for each individual. Match names, estimated relationship ranges, precise quantities of DNA and an email address had been attributed to each cousin match, as usual; the remaining columns were sparsely filled at best. Only two of the matches had submitted any ancestral names with their DNA kits. Maddie picked up a piece of scrap paper and a pen, and walked into the main office, where she wrote down the seven possible surnames that Hudson had identified on the killer's paternal Y-DNA. Back in her office, she compared the names to the ancestral surname lists, helpfully provided by these two particular FamilyTreeDNA-users. No overlaps.

Maddie opened up the FamilyTreeDNA website. In the Family Finder Matches menu, she scrolled down to Aileen Moore. With no uploaded personal photograph, Aileen was represented by a pink female silhouette. Although their actual relationship might also be much closer, Maddie had no choice but to research every branch of Aileen Moore's family right back to as many of her thirty-two great-great-great-grandparents as she possibly could. One—possibly two—of those thirty-two people should be an ancestor shared between Aileen, the killer and the other eleven matches within cluster five.

Maddie took another mouthful of coffee. It was going to be a long day.

Situated just below Aileen Moore's name was a tree icon, optimistically colored blue, meaning that Aileen had added some kind of a family tree, though how extensive or accurate it was remained to be seen. Maddie clicked the icon and watched as a fresh tab opened onscreen. Disappointingly, the tree contained just three names: Aileen Moore and her parents, Marlene Patricia Gowing and William Charles Moore. It wasn't much at all to go on but, with a little luck and perseverance, it might just be enough.

Because Aileen hadn't provided her own personal information, the website had defaulted to *??? - ???* for Aileen's birth and death dates. For her parents, Aileen had included the genealogical data from which Maddie could begin her research.

Marlene Patricia Gowing born Nov 7, 1899, Pitt County, NC - died Aug 5, 1973, Richmond, VA
William Charles Moore born Mar 25, 1897, Pitt County, NC - died Oct 24, 1936, Hyde County, NC

The first step was to use that information to build as much of Aileen Moore's family tree as was logistically possible. Using the Ancestry website, Maddie clicked to create a new speculative family tree. She assigned the role of 'Home Person' to Aileen Moore, unable as yet to add any further biographical information about her. Next, she added her parents and the information provided on the FamilyTreeDNA website. The killer, of course, could be related to Aileen Moore via her maternal or paternal side, so both required systematic searching to ensure that the tree started accurately at its very roots.

'Now the fun begins,' Maddie said to herself, taking a sip of her coffee. She loved this part; the promise of solving an age-old, cold homicide case using simple genealogical research techniques.

By the time she had finished inputting Aileen's parents, her father, William Charles Moore, had twenty-two genealogy record hints that the Ancestry algorithms had determined might pertain to this man, while Marlene had thirty-five. Oftentimes they were correct, but sometimes they were so wildly inaccurate as to be worthy of sharing with the rest of the office for their comedy value.

Maddie slowly scrolled down the list of hints for Marlene Patricia Gowing. Ten Ancestry users apparently had her in their own family trees, which she would only check out once she had firmly established the facts for herself. Below that were several photographs that an Ancestry member had attributed to Marlene: some were portrait photos; others were documents submitted as photographs. Further down were census records, marriage records, WW2 Draft Cards, Social Security Applications and the place where Maddie, if at all possible, always liked to begin: burial information. Starting with a person's death often provided bountiful biographical detail of their life.

Maddie followed the link through to the Find a Grave website. In the top left of the page was a photograph of Marlene's grave with a bunch of fresh yellow roses laid upon it. Her name and dates of birth and death tied precisely to the information that Aileen had added to her limited tree on FamilyTreeDNA.

A mini biography brought a smile to Maddie's face.

Marlene P. Moore, widow at the time of death. Daughter of Daniel D. Gowing and Helen Whitehurst.
Marlene married W.C. Moore Feb. 23, 1918, Greenville, North Carolina. Mr. and Mrs. Moore had four sons, who all served our nation, and one daughter.

So far, the information was good, providing Maddie with suggested names for Marlene's parents, helping her push this line one generation further back. For the moment, she resisted saving the information to her speculative tree, wanting to find multiple sources confirming the same facts first; a mistake at this point would be enough to jeopardize the entire integrity of cluster five.

One of the photographs suggested as a hint for Marlene was

entitled *Marlene Moore obit* and appeared from the thumbnail image to be a newspaper clipping which Maddie hoped would be a full obituary.

Just as she had hoped, it was an extract from the *Richmond Times Dispatch* newspaper. Maddie read it through, making notes as she went.

Marlene Patricia Moore, age 73, died August 5, 1973 at her residence 3000 Chamberlayne Ave. She is survived by a daughter, Aileen Moore; four sons, William Jnr, Jack, Fred, Ramsey; and one brother, John Gowing. Mrs. Moore was a member of the First Baptist Church. Remains rest at the Bennett Funeral Home, 3215 Cutshaw Ave., where services will be conducted Monday 11am. Interment Riverview Cemetery.

Before adding the information to Aileen Moore's family tree, Maddie checked the details against the online *US Social Security Applications and Claims Index 1936-2007* on Ancestry, which confirmed what she had just read.

Name: Marlene P Moore
Gender: Female
Birth Date: Nov 7, 1899
Birth Place: Pitt Co, North Carolina
Death Date: Aug 5, 1973
Claim Date: Dec 9, 1966
Father: Daniel D. Gowing
Mother: Helen Whitehurst
SSN: 239-12-5436

She was now satisfied to add the new information regarding Aileen, her brothers and parents to the family tree. She was also happy to move back a generation further with confidence, having confirmed the names of Marlene's parents, Daniel and Helen.

Turning to the 1910 United States Federal Census, Maddie inputted Marlene's name, year of birth and added her parents' names to the *Father* and *Mother* boxes before hitting the search button.

Maddie could immediately see that the top result was correct. The family were living in Providence, Rowan County, North Carolina. She clicked to view the original census entry and located the family partway down the page. Once she had confirmed that the young Marlene was the very same as she whom Maddie was researching, she switched focus to Marlene's father, Daniel D. Gowing. She wrote down the pertinent details on her legal pad and then saved the census entry to Aileen Moore's family tree.

Daniel D. Gowing. Married approx 1895. 3 children born—all living. Birth place: NC, approx 1874. Father's birthplace: NC. Mother's birthplace: NC. Occupation: farmer.

Now that she had an estimated date, Maddie needed to try and locate the actual marriage of Daniel Gowing to Helen Whitehurst in the hope that *their* parents' names had been included, which would take the tree back a generation further still.

Opening the FamilySearch website in a new browser tab, Maddie typed in the approximate details of Daniel and Helen's marriage in the record search box. The second hyperlinked result in the list, which Maddie clicked, appeared to be correct.

She drank the last of her coffee as a scan of the original marriage certificate loaded onscreen. Her work had got off to a great start; if the others were having similar luck, then within days they might just have the name of the Chester Creek serial killer.

Name: Daniel Gowing
Date: Apr 2, 1895
Place: Goldsboro, Wayne, North Carolina
Age: 21
Ethnicity: American
Race: White
Father's Name: Jas. F. Gowing
Mother's Name: Fannie Gowing
Spouse's Name: Helen Whitehurst
Spouse's Gender: Female
Spouse's Age: 19
Spouse's Race: White
Spouse's Father's Name: T. H. Whitehurst
Spouse's Mother's Name: Cathryn Whitehurst

Maddie downloaded an image of the entry and attached it, along with all its various details, to Aileen Moore's speculative family tree.

Next, she opened up the 1880 United States Census and typed in Daniel Gowing's name, finding him as a six-year-old boy residing in Goldsboro Township, living with his parents. The census provided

Maddie with the ages of James and Fannie, as well as the fact that they, along with *their* parents, had been born in North Carolina.

After more than three hours' work, a low murmuring in Maddie's stomach made her look at the clock: 12:36. Time for lunch.

So far, she had managed to work her way backwards through the censuses and available vital records to identifying one pair of Aileen Moore's thirty-two great-great-great-grandparents. It was a good start.

She stood up and walked into the main office. 'How's everyone doing out here?'

'Good,' Kenyatta responded, 'Three pairs identified for my cluster lead.'

'Wow, that's good going,' Maddie replied, approaching Hudson's desk. 'And how are you getting on?'

Hudson looked up at her and pointed at the screen. 'Look who Kenyatta kindly gave me as the lead name for cluster one.'

Maddie grinned when she saw that he was trying to build a family tree for one James Jones.

Kenyatta theatrically threw her hands up in the air. 'What can I say? I'm a giver! *Someone* had to do him, and he *is* one of the highest DNA matches to the killer. So…'

'Needless to say,' Hudson continued, 'I've been concentrating on James Jones's *maternal* side which actually hasn't been so terrible, I guess.'

'There you go, honey,' Kenyatta said. 'You're welcome.'

'Becky, how about you? How are you getting on?' Maddie asked.

She nodded. 'Great—just started on my second pair of great-great-great-grandparents—Ellis Island immigrants originally from Germany, which could pose a few problems down the line.'

'Good work, everyone,' Maddie said. 'I'm going to brave the weather and head out for food—anyone want anything?'

Kenyatta pulled a sorrowful face, as she raised a box of salad. 'I'm good with my *leaves*, thank you.'

'Where are you going?' Hudson asked.

'Looking at that weather, I'd say not far,' she replied, nodding towards the veil of white outside the window. 'Probably Eva's.'

'Oh, good answer,' he said. 'I'd like *quelque chose de français et magnifique*.'

Maddie rolled her eyes. 'Or… Grilled cheese panini?'

'Yeah, that'll be great. Thanks.'

'Do you want me to go?' Ross asked as Maddie strode past him to the kitchen area and pulled on her coat and trilby hat.

'No, you're good. I need the air,' she said. 'Do you want anything?'

'I'm okay thanks,' he answered.

Maddie took the stairs down to the road and stepped out into the freezing Salt Lake City air. 'Jeez,' she muttered under her breath, wondering if this latest cold snap would ever end. Luckily, Eva's was right across the street.

She hurried to the crosswalk and waited impatiently for the lights to change as her exposed face began to sting from the driving snow. Finally, the walk signal flashed up and she strode towards the alluring bright-blue building opposite with the word BOULANGERIE emblazoned across the top. She tugged open the door, instantly grateful to be inside.

Joining the back of a small line, she took a look at the menu, tossing up the choice of a chicken pesto sandwich or a wood-fired pastrami panini, when she noticed someone staring at her in her peripheral vision. In the briefest of moments that it took for her to lower her gaze to see who he was—for the shape and appearance of the figure was unmistakably male—she wondered if the man could be Michael. It never was him, yet it was a common trick that her mind played on her on a rather regular basis.

'Hey there.'

'Detective,' Maddie said, finding that she was smiling in spite of the tormenting trick. 'What are you doing here?'

He held up a wrapped food parcel as he headed away from the counter. 'Getting some lunch. I had this damn-fool idea of taking a look around the city, you know, rather than sit in my hotel room watching movies. But, well, I'm starting to think it's not exactly the best weather for being a tourist.'

'No, it's definitely not that. Do you ski?'

'Never...and don't think now's the time to learn, either,' he responded.

'Shame—we have the best snow on earth, here.'

'Isn't snow snow?' he asked with a wry smile.

Maddie gasped. 'How dare you? That's such an insult to Utahns.' Then she laughed when she saw that he appeared to be taking her seriously. 'Sorry. Listen. If you're at a loose end, you're welcome to come up to the office and see what we're up to. I mean, we're nowhere near done and it might get a bit boring...'

'Sure, I'd like that,' he replied. 'Thank you.'

'What can I get for you?' the young lady behind the counter asked Maddie. 'Chicken pesto sandwich?' she guessed.

Maddie nodded. 'You got it. And a grilled cheese panini, please.'

'Sure. Anything else?'

'That's it, thanks. No. Wait.' She remembered Hudson's request and was caught by a sudden feeling of benevolence towards her team. 'Do you have anything typically French?'

'We've got these fresh French Macarons? Four flavors. That kind of thing?'

'Um…sure. I'll take 12…mixed.'

'Okay. That's fifty-one dollars, please.'

Maddie paid the bill, then stepped to one side, finding the line closer than expected behind her, which meant that she was now obliged to press momentarily against the side of the detective.

'You're a regular here, then?' he asked, apparently ignoring the contact.

Maddie raised her eyebrows, stepping out of the line. 'It seems so.'

'Listen,' the detective started, lowering his voice. 'There's something I wanted to say—not about the Chester Creek case—but I don't know if I'd be overstepping the mark, here.'

Maddie inwardly gasped as a chill ran down her spine: she was so *not* ready to date anyone. The very idea, all the while Michael's whereabouts was unknown, was horrific to her. But how to say it? 'Um,' was all she could manage.

'It's about your husband,' the detective added.

Maddie instantly calmed. 'Oh. Sure…ask away.'

'Well, I was just wondering if—'

'One chicken pesto, one grilled cheese panini and a box of Macarons,' the young lady behind the counter interrupted.

'Thank you,' Maddie said, taking the food and rejoining the detective as they moved towards the door. 'Sorry. Go ahead.'

He held the door open for Maddie and, as she walked past him, said, 'I was just wondering if you wanted me to see what I could find out about the case. I mean, when I think of the tower of work sitting on *my* desk back in Media…'

'It's probably no longer a priority,' Maddie finished.

'It doesn't sound to me like they've got much to go on. So, I guess it wouldn't be at the top of anyone's list, no.'

If she were being totally honest, Maddie knew inside that Michael's disappearance wouldn't have been actively researched for quite some time, but she had always hoped that every now and then the lead detective on the case had continued to work on it, exploring new avenues and revisiting potential oversights.

They headed in silence towards the crosswalk with Maddie deep in thought. Was it overstepping the mark if he did some digging? At this point, she just needed answers in order for her family to move on properly.

'Yes,' she said, barely audibly. 'Yes, please.'

'No promises but I'll take a look,' he said. 'I can probably also track down what happened to his vehicle and take it from there.'

'Well, that won't take much investigation: it was towed to my garage after he went missing and has stayed there untouched ever since. Trenton, my son, thinks he's getting it.'

'Oh, okay,' he said. 'That might make life easier.'

They crossed the street and entered the Kearns Building. 'Stairs or elevator?' Maddie asked.

The detective patted his free hand on his stomach. 'Better say stairs, I guess.'

'Have you told the families of the three victims that you're using investigative genetic genealogy on this case?' Maddie asked as they took the stairs to the fifth floor.

He shook his head. 'No, we decided that we didn't want to give them false hope. We'll go out to their homes once we've made an arrest or got something concrete to pass on to them. It's just not fair otherwise.'

'I agree,' Maddie said, opening the door to the office.

'Oh, hi again, Detective!' Ross said unnecessarily loudly, deliberately—in Maddie's opinion—drawing the attention of the rest of the team to their arrival.

She made a face, now certain from the telling looks currently passing between Ross and Becky that she and the detective had been a topic of conversation over their drinks last night. 'Look who I just bumped into in Eva's,' Maddie said, bizarrely finding herself trying to hide a sense of guilt over something which didn't actually exist. 'He's dropped in to see how we're getting on.'

'I won't stay long,' he added, holding up his packet of food, as if he would leave as soon as it were eaten.

Maddie took off her hat and coat and handed Hudson his panini. Then, realizing that her treat for them could serve as an ideal distraction, she held up the Macarons and said, 'And I've got a little…*quelque chose* for you all to boost your productivity levels.'

'*Fantastique*,' Hudson said.

Maddie asked him, 'Would you mind showing the detective what you've done so far and how you got there?'

'Oh, okay. Sure,' he replied, then turned to the detective. 'Grab a chair and I'll run you through it.'

Maddie quickly carried her sandwich off into her office. She wanted to close the door, to make a point to the rest of the team, but she couldn't actually bring herself to do it. Besides which, she didn't really *want* to close her door to the detective. If he had been old, married, gay or a woman, she would have invited him into her office and she would have been the one to demonstrate their work.

She unwrapped her food and stared at her computer screen, her mind elsewhere. She wondered what he might be able to turn up in the files on Michael's disappearance. Very likely, he would find nothing at all because the file was so scant. No witnesses. No body. No evidence of a crime's having been committed. No forensics. No suicide note. Nothing. Just a man who never returned to his truck and never returned to his family.

She took a few bites of her food, then set it to one side, having lost her appetite. Outside, she could hear Hudson giving an extremely in-depth and scientific explanation of investigative genetic genealogy; probably not at all of interest to the detective, or within his grasp. With a long sigh, Maddie stood up and walked back into the main office.

'So, while CODIS uses STR testing, or Short Tandem Repeat,' Hudson was telling the detective, '*we* use Single Nucleotide Polymorphisms, or SNPs for short—'

'Hudson,' Maddie interjected, 'That's probably a *little* more technical detail than the detective needs right now.'

'Oh, sorry; I can get a bit carried away.'

'No, it's great,' the detective countered. 'I had no idea that all of this existed; it's mind-blowing, really. And you already know the killer's ethnicity, eye color and hair color!'

'*Possible* ethnicity, hair and eye color,' Maddie corrected. 'Until we have our suspect list down to one, nothing is certain.'

'Why isn't every unsolved rape and murder given this treatment as standard?' the detective asked.

'Well, if CODIS were fit for purpose, you wouldn't need us half the time,' Maddie answered.

'True.' He looked at his watch. 'I guess I'd better shoot and leave you guys to crack on with the case. Thanks for the lesson, Hudson. Really, man.'

'You're welcome.'

Maddie walked him to the door. 'Goodbye.'

'See you. I'll let you know if I get anywhere with what we talked about earlier.'

'Thanks,' she said, shaking his hand and finding that she was inexplicably blushing in spite of herself.

Chapter Fifteen

'Two minutes, guys,' Maddie called from her office. She had had a productive afternoon once the detective had left and once she had broken her destructively cyclical thoughts about Michael. She bent down and took her wallet out of her bag and removed a twenty-dollar bill, which she carried with her into the main office.

'Here it is!' she declared, sticking the President Jackson to the top of the empty glass writing board. It was a light-hearted incentive for the first person who could identify the names of the one or two common ancestors that linked their entire genetic network cluster.

'I don't think *James Jones* is going to let me win it this time,' Hudson complained.

'It's mine, all mine!' Becky said with a great thespian emphasis.

Maddie stood beside the main digital whiteboard. On it was displayed a pedigree chart of Aileen Moore's family tree. 'Okay, is everyone almost ready for the briefing?' she asked, receiving nods and grunts of confirmation followed by silence. 'Good. I'll start. I've been working on cluster five'—she pointed to the screen beside her—'with the lead name of Aileen Moore. As you can see, I've managed four out of thirty-two ancestral lines. As is to be expected at this point, I've yet to look for the overlap with the rest of the names within the cluster. So far, this family is pretty rooted in North Carolina with no known connections to Pennsylvania. That's about it from me. Kenyatta?'

A mirror of Kenyatta's screen replaced Maddie's. She stood up to address the team. 'Well, I've managed to close up six of my thirty-two ancestral lines. No links to the rest of the cluster as yet and also no links to Pennsylvania, either. I've got Texas and North Dakota so far,' she said, returning to her seat.

'Thank you, Kenyatta,' Maddie said. 'Hudson?'

Hudson shared his screen and stood up. 'I've got four of James Jones's maternal lines closed. Interestingly, all four are from New Jersey and one of them hails from West Deptford which is literally across the Delaware River opposite Delaware County.'

'That is interesting,' Maddie agreed. 'What surname?'

'White,' he replied.

Maddie nodded, making a mental note of the name. 'Great. And Becky, what do you have for us?'

Becky pulled up her screen. 'So, *I* have closed down *eight* of my ancestral lines with one dead line at the grandparent level and am, therefore, one quarter of the way to winning the twenty bucks.'

'Well done,' Maddie said. 'Locations?'

Becky blew out a puff of air. 'Everywhere, but mainly west coast: California, Nevada, Arizona, Oregon...'

'Okay. Good work, team,' Maddie said. 'Hopefully, in a couple of days we might have the name of at least one of the Chester Creek murderer's ancestors. See you all in the morning. Take care out there.'

As the team began to close down their computers and pack up to go home, Maddie headed back into her office. She sat down at her desk, about to start work on Aileen Moore's next ancestral line. She was going to do another hour or so prior to heading home. Before she did so, she picked up her cellphone and saw that she had a text message from her son, Trenton.

Mom, Grandma's left the faucet running in the kitchen again

The message was punctuated not with a period or a heart but with the gritted teeth emoji. Three times. Maddie took in a deep breath and closed her laptop lid.

She texted *Coming home now* as she walked out of her office and shut the door. The rest of the team were also on their way out. She said goodbye to them all, waited for them to leave and then locked up the office. She took the elevator down to the parking garage in the basement and got into her RAV4 and drove home.

The I-15 had been plowed recently and Maddie arrived at her home in South Jordan in good time. She parked on her driveway in front of the garage and switched off the engine. She sat for a moment in the quietness of the cooling car, consciously working to shift her thoughts away from the complexities of Michael, as well as the current case at work, over to her role here, at home: mother and daughter.

'Jeez,' she said, as she stepped from the car and saw that the house was illuminated like some fully occupied hotel. In every room the lights were switched on and the curtains wide open. It seemed that her two teenagers were incapable of turning the lights back off before leaving any room.

She opened the front door and her feelings of annoyance instantly abated. Her home was her sanctuary and, when her kids and her mother were behaving, her sanity. She and Michael had bought the house fourteen years ago, right at the time that Nikki's adoption was going through. Given all that had happened with Michael, having the memory of bringing Nikki, and then later Trenton, back to this house was something of a stabilizing comfort to her. It was a big place—six bedrooms, a basement, four baths—in a great neighborhood with good schools; she felt safe here and couldn't ever imagine selling up, despite the bitter edge that had underlined the past five years here.

Maddie took off her hat and coat, pulled off her boots and walked down the hallway to the kitchen, where she received her usual welcome home: Trenton was sitting on the couch with unnecessarily large headphones on, animated by some kind of videogame he was playing on his tablet; Nikki was leaning on the kitchen counter, engrossed in her cellphone; her mother was nowhere to be seen, which was an instant worry in itself.

Maddie was confident that the kids would have been completely oblivious if the house had been burning down around them. 'Hello?' she said.

Without so much as a glance in her direction, Trenton raised a hand showing that he was wearing black nail polish: why? She had no idea. Nikki mumbled something incoherent, also without actually looking at her.

'Good day at school?' Maddie asked.

Nikki looked up and shrugged. 'It was okay. Got told by one kid to go back to China, which was nice.'

'What did you say back?'

Another shrug. 'That, if he was going to be racist, he could at least get his geography right because I was born a thousand miles away from China in South Korea.'

Maddie smiled. 'Good comeback. Do you want me to talk to your teacher?'

Nikki shook her head. 'Na, it's no big deal,' she answered, looking back at her cell.

'You'd tell me if you were being bullied, right?'

'You know I would.'

'Good,' Maddie replied, instinctively confident that she was telling the truth. She lowered her voice and asked, 'Where's grandma?'

Nikki rolled her eyes. 'In her room, I think. She keeps leaving the faucets on, Mom.'

'So Trenton said. I'll speak to her.' Maddie walked along the hallway and up the stairs to the second floor. 'Mom?' she called out as she approached her bedroom.

'In here,' her mom replied. She sounded cheerful, which was a relief. She'd always been a mild and placid lady, which was why Maddie had leapt at the offer of her moving in five years ago. Now she was as susceptible to mood swings as her two teenagers downstairs were.

Maddie pushed open her mom's bedroom door. 'Hi. How are you?'

Her mom was lying on her bed, reading a book that she set down beside her when Maddie entered the room. 'Okay, thank you. How was work today?'

Maddie sat at the end of the bed and placed her hand onto her mother's. 'Good. I think we're making progress on the latest case.'

'The what Creek murders?' she asked, frowning.

'*Chester* Creek in Delaware County,' Maddie answered. 'Three beautiful young women, horrifically raped and murdered… It sure makes me appreciate coming home, you know.'

Her mother squeezed her hand and smiled. 'We appreciate your being here. The kids need you.'

'How's your day been?' Maddie asked her.

'Pretty good. I went for a walk, watched an old Cary Grant movie—I do love that man, you know—and read lots of my book. That's about it.'

'Sounds like a great day to me,' Maddie said. She paused for a moment, trying to tread carefully. 'Trenton thought maybe you might have left the kitchen faucet running earlier?'

'Oh, did he now?' Her mother retracted her hand. 'He's just blaming me because I'm old, when it was actually probably *he* who left it running. Did you ever think of that?'

Maddie offered a comforting smile. 'It's okay if you did, Mom. I'm not here to fuss at you.'

'Well, I didn't. And it sure sounds like you are.' Her mom picked up her book and held it so that it obscured her face.

'I'll call you when dinner's ready,' Maddie said, heading towards the door. Her mom said nothing.

In the kitchen, Maddie pulled open the refrigerator, hoping to see something that inspired her to cook. The myriad of ingredients made no logical meal sense. 'Do you guys want to get a take-out?'

Nikki nodded and Trenton failed either to hear or to register the question.

Maddie exhaled. 'Trenton! Hey! Over here!'

Trenton pushed his headphones backwards. 'Oh, hi, Mom. How

are you?'

'Oh, hi, Trenton,' Maddie exclaimed. 'Should we do an UberEats?'

'Yeah, great,' he answered. 'Can we get the chicken fried steak from the Black Bear Diner?'

'Yes!' Nikki cheered. 'That is *exactly* what I need in my life right now.'

'Okay,' Maddie said. 'And I was thinking, given the current weather, how about on Saturday we go up to Park City?'

'Yes,' Trenton answered. 'Obviously. Do you even need to ask?'

'I was planning on meeting Stevie, going to the movies and whatever…but I'll rearrange,' Nikki said.

'Great,' Maddie said, thinking that that had been relatively painless. 'Now, what am I going to get Grandma for her dinner. She won't want chicken fried steak. That much is certain….' She looked at Trenton and added in a hushed voice, 'I asked her about leaving the faucet running.'

'And?' Trenton said.

'She blamed you.'

'Great,' he replied.

'What are we going to do about her?' Nikki asked.

Trenton rolled his eyes and Maddie couldn't help but take comfort from the fact that he knew that he didn't need to argue his corner. But the conspiratorial talk about her mom, as though she were some irritating burden, bothered Maddie somewhat. The truth was, she didn't know what she was going to do about her. 'Be kind,' she said. 'Be patient. Remember that the changes she's going through are no fault of her own. Be the loving grandkids that you've always been.'

Nikki nodded.

'And take the blame when she leaves the faucet running,' Trenton mumbled.

'Okay, I'm going to order this food. No cellphones or tablets tonight, okay?' Maddie said, but Trenton and Nikki were too absorbed in their cellphones and tablets to hear her.

Chapter Sixteen

Wednesday, March 4, 2020, Downtown Salt Lake City, Utah

'Is there a reason why you have a box of latex gloves and a face mask on your desk?' Becky asked with a giggle. 'Something you want to tell us, Kenyatta?'

Kenyatta raised an eyebrow and turned to face Becky. 'They're for my homeless friend, Lonnie.'

Becky screwed up her face. 'What on earth does a homeless person want with those?'

'He's worried about that virus thing,' Kenyatta replied, raising her hands in the air. 'I know it's ridiculous, but he's acting like it's one of the ten plagues of Egypt and I said I'd get them for him. I mean, he doesn't want vitamins or deodorant or shampoo or clean clothes; oh no, just gloves and a mask.'

'He's right to be concerned,' Hudson chipped in. 'It's spreading like wildfire. It's going to be real bad for this country, some are saying.'

Kenyatta frowned. 'Really? Isn't it just another SARS or Ebola that's going to blow over?'

Hudson shook his head vehemently. 'It *is* a kind of SARS but… They were contained and less infectious; this is out there now. A US epidemic is just a matter of time. Your homeless friend is really pretty insightful.'

'Well, maybe I'll get myself a box of these, then,' Kenyatta responded, tapping the box of gloves.

Returning her focus to the screen in front of her, Kenyatta wondered if she had just discovered a potential breakthrough with her cluster seven. As she had reported at yesterday afternoon's briefing, the ancestral lines, which she had closed, were based in Texas and North Dakota, but she had just discovered that one of her cluster-lead's great-great-grandfathers had been born in Lancaster County, Pennsylvania; twenty-seven miles from where the three murders had occurred. It could be a coincidence, or it could be a very critical lead. At this point, there was absolutely no way of knowing which it would turn out to be. Time and further research would hopefully provide the answer.

The lead name of cluster seven was Leo Ford, matching the killer with a paltry forty-nine centiMorgans of DNA. Within that genetic network cluster were eight other men and women who DNA-matched both Leo and the Chester Creek killer.

Kenyatta took a tiny sip of the bottled water that sat on her desk and that would barely reach the halfway point by the end of the day. She craved something fizzy. A root beer and a bag of M&Ms was what she needed right now. She looked at the unappealing daily box of salad on her desk, cursing her diet. No, not diet: regime. Her therapist encouraged her not to blame Otis for her depression and what had followed as a result of it, but she did blame him and that was that. Big-time blamed him.

'You okay, Kenyatta?' Becky asked.

'Uh-huh,' she replied. 'Just daydreaming of a parallel universe where Otis doesn't exist, I look like Beyoncé and I've figured out the identities of the Boys under the Bridge.'

Becky laughed. 'You could make some of that happen in *this* universe.'

'Yeah,' Kenyatta muttered. 'So my therapist would have me believe.' It was easy for Becky to pass judgement. She was a rich—very rich—young and beautiful, white girl with none of life's bigger problems to worry about.

'Theodore Scharder,' she said, forcing herself back into her work. Born, according to the census, in Lancaster County around 1799, where Kenyatta feared she would find the end of the line. She stood up and walked over to the bookshelves at the back of the room, pulling down the well-used copy of the *Red Book*: a guide to the available genealogical records by state, county and town. Carrying the book over to her desk, she thumbed through the thick tome, arranged alphabetically by state, until she came to Pennsylvania. Under the section headed *Vital Records,* she was disappointed to read, *Although a colonial law of 1682 provided for the recording of births, marriages and burials in Pennsylvania, few if any of these were ever entered in civil records.*

'Great,' Kenyatta muttered, reading on. She tapped her index finger on the page as she read, *John T. Humphrey compiled a series of* Pennsylvania Births *to 1800 for the counties of Berks, Bucks, Chester, Delaware, Lancaster, Lebanon, Lehigh, Montgomery, Northampton, Philadelphia.*

Maddie had a general policy of not bothering to clutter up the bookshelves with individual state, town or county records, when pretty well every genealogical resource was available—or else orderable—from the Family History Library just a couple of blocks away. So, Kenyatta logged into the FamilySearch website and navigated her way through the Wiki pages to Lancaster County. Sure enough, the volume existed on the library shelves. She jotted down the reference details on a piece of scrap paper and then stood up.

'Anyone need anything from that big wide world, out there?' Kenyatta asked. 'I'm headed to the FHL.'

'Good luck,' Hudson said. 'It's still pretty jammed with visitors lingering on after RootsTech.'

'Well, they'll just have to fight me for the book I'm after,' Kenyatta laughed, as she made her way across the room. Outside Maddie's office she said, 'I'm just going to the FHL. Do you need anything while I'm out?'

Maddie smiled. 'I'm good, thanks.'

Kenyatta left the office and took the elevator to the first floor. 'Oh, thank you, God,' she said upon seeing that no fresh snow had fallen since late last night. The sun was out, the skies were blue and she suddenly felt a jolt of optimism as she strode towards the Family History Library.

In just under ten minutes Kenyatta had reached the building. Hudson was right, there were more people here than usual. Over twenty thousand genealogists descended on the city for several days to attend RootsTech, the world's largest genealogy conference, and many stayed on afterwards to pursue their own family history.

Stepping into the elevator, Kenyatta rode up to the third floor where books pertaining to the US & Canada were held. She took out the piece of scrap paper and looked at the reference number as she approached the long lines of shelving.

974.815 K2h

'Here we go,' she said, a little too loudly, as she hurried down the aisle that promised to house the book for which she was searching. Plucking out the leather-bound volume, Kenyatta carried it over to the bank of dozens of desks and computers. She figured that the place was running at about eighty-percent occupancy but, despite this, managed to find a vacant desk and set down the book, finding that it was a hand-written index. If she needed to see any original documents, she would need to look at the microfilms that should also be located somewhere within the building.

Kenyatta took off her jacket and immediately set to work on the book, opening it at a helpful contents page. For Lancaster County there were several churches included: St James' Protestant Episcopal Church;

Holy Trinity Lutheran Church; Moravian Church; First Reformed Church; and St Mary's Roman Catholic Church.

Not knowing in which church Theodore Scharder might have been baptized, Kenyatta turned to the first in the list, St James' Protestant Episcopal Church. She let out a small squeal of delight when she discovered that within each church the baptisms had been indexed in alphabetical order, removing the need for a laborious search.

Thumbing through several pages to those children baptized under *S*, Kenyatta found a complete absence of anyone with the surname of Scharder. She moved on to Holy Trinity Lutheran Church and found the exact same thing. At the Moravian Church, two Scharder children had been baptized but way back in the 1760s.

Kenyatta made a note of their names, dates of baptism and the church, just in case the Scharder name became more pertinent to the case. At this stage it was simply another in a very long list of potential names.

In the index for the First Reformed Church there were no children with this name.

Thinking that she might have made a wasted trip and would have to return to the office without closing down this particular ancestral line of Leo Ford's, Kenyatta turned to the final church, St Mary's Roman Catholic Church.

And there he was.

Theodore, baptized April 4, 1799, son of Heinrich & Gertrude Scharder

Kenyatta couldn't help smiling, seeing herself waltzing into the office with her seventh ancestral line closed successfully. She copied down the details, not judging it as necessary at this point to see the original microfilm copy. Slamming the book shut, she pulled on her coat and replaced the index back on the shelf before heading to the elevator with a spring in her step.

'Any luck?' Hudson asked when she returned to the office.

'Oh, yeah!' Kenyatta replied, wafting in the air the piece of paper containing details of Theodore Schrader's baptism. 'That twenty bucks is almost mine…'

'I'm at *ten* ancestral lines closed,' Becky gloated with a mock-smug look on her face.

Kenyatta responded with a pretend sneer. 'Whatever, honey. It ain't over 'til it's over, is all I'm saying.'

She sat down and glared at the salad box goading her from the side of her desk. With a miserable sigh, she pulled open the lid and took out a none-too-indulgent carrot stick, holding it in front of her face. A carrot stick, of all things. She was actually going to eat a *raw carrot*…as a snack.

To try and distract herself from what she was eating, she pulled up the speculative family tree for Leo Ford, taking great pleasure in adding the baptism of his great-great-grandfather, Theodore Scharder, and the names of Theodore's parents, Heinrich and Gertrude.

Having eaten one of the three carrot sticks from her lunchbox, Kenyatta took a handful of cashew nuts and began to pop them one at a time into her mouth, finding it a little like chewing small pieces of flavorless wood.

She returned to Leo Ford's paternal grandmother to begin work on his ninth ancestral line. Joyce Hattie Hevenor, according to the 1940 census, had been born around 1882 in the state of Texas. With this in mind, Kenyatta turned to the 1900 US Federal Census and entered Joyce Hevenor's name and approximate year of birth in the search box. Fortunately for her, of the results suggested by the mystical website algorithms, there was only one that matched one hundred percent. She clicked to view the original census entry, finding that Joyce Hattie Hevenor, born in February 1882, had been living with her parents, Henry and Eliza Hevenor, in Johnson County, Texas.

Kenyatta saved the details to the master tree for Leo Ford. The entry gave the additional information that Henry and Eliza had been married for twenty-four years and had both been born in Alabama.

Kenyatta jotted *1876* on a piece of scrap paper, the approximate year of their marriage, then turned to the FamilySearch website and entered those details into the search engine. The marriage entry had been digitized and was available online. Kenyatta couldn't help but smile at the progress that she was making today as she clicked through to view a copy of the original marriage certificate. Henry Hevenor had married Eliza Miller on August 17, 1876. The entry confirmed their union and also provided a surname, albeit a common one for Eliza, but it failed to name Henry or Eliza's parents.

'Darn it,' Kenyatta muttered. She could try searching for their births in the same county but feared, in Eliza's case at least, that without knowing her parents' names it would be very easy to jump onto an incorrect line. For the lead name in her genetic network cluster, she needed to be able to apply the Genealogical Proof Standard which was the industry's five elements that allowed for a conclusion to be established with reasonable certainty.

She needed to think around the problem.

She put Henry and Eliza's details into the *US Social Security Applications and Claim Index 1936-2007* but failed to find anyone who matched. Did that imply that they had died prior to 1936? she wondered.

Returning to Ancestry, Kenyatta pulled up *Texas, Death Certificates, 1903-1982* and searched for Henry Hevenor, keeping all other search criteria open. Three results.

Henry Hevenor, born Dec 5, 1858, died Aug 8, 1927, Joshua, Johnson
Henry J. Havener, born Sep 20, 1849, died Sep 10, 1925, Wichita Falls, Victoria
Mack H. Heavener, born Jan 2, 1892, died Jul 25, 1972, Corpus Christi, Nueces

Kenyatta clicked on the topmost entry to view a copy of the original death certificate. She scrutinized the document, looking for detail that would confirm that she had the correct person.

Full name: Henry Hevenor
Sex: Male
Color or Race: White
Single, Married, Widowed or Divorced: Married
Date of Birth: Dec 5, 1858
Age: 68 years 8 months
Occupation: Farming
Birthplace: Alabama
Name of Father: Isaac Hevenor
Birthplace of Father: Alabama
Maiden name of Mother: Margaret Rhodes
Birthplace of Mother: Alabama
Date of Death: Aug 8, 1927
Cause of Death: Senile degeneration
Informant: Joyce Hattie Ford

Kenyatta clapped her hands together when she noticed the name of the informant. The death certificate was undeniably correct. She saved the document to Leo Ford's tree and then added the new biographical information of Henry Hevenor's parents.

Returning to the search index page for *Texas, Death Certificates, 1903-1982*, Kenyatta inputted Henry Hevenor's wife, Eliza, also finding the correct entry, which confirmed that her maiden name had been Miller. Once again, Joyce Hattie Ford had informed of the death. Now Kenyatta knew all four of Joyce's grandparents' names.

Opening up the *Red Book* on Alabama, Kenyatta read that, owing to poverty and political unrest, *In the 1860s and 1870s, 10 to 15 percent of the entire white population of Alabama migrated, with a third of these migrants going to Texas.* Just like the Hevenors and Millers, she thought, reading on. Under the section headed *Vital Records*, she learnt that births were not routinely recorded in the state prior to 1881 and that the digitization of church records was patchy at best. The most comprehensive collection was the *Alabama miscellaneous church records, 1807-1947* which were held on microfilm at the Family History Library. 'Oh, man!' she said, facing the prospect of returning quite so soon to that same building.

'What's up?' Becky asked.

'I gotta go back to the FHL,' she replied, standing from her desk with her pencil and legal pad in hand. She put on her coat, told Maddie where she was going, then left the building.

Kenyatta returned to the Venator office moments before the 4:30pm briefing. Breathlessly, she slumped down at her desk and took an unusually long glug of water.

'Any luck?' Becky asked her.

Kenyatta shook her head and eventually said, 'Nothing.' She set down her bottle and pulled up Leo Ford's family tree. She had now reached the end of her research into all of his paternal lines back to his great-great-great-grandparents.

'Okay,' Maddie said, striding into the office and positioning herself close to the digital whiteboard. 'Everybody good to go? Ross, could you take notes, please?'

Kenyatta looked up at the screen, noticing a big difference in the pedigree of the lead name for Maddie's cluster, Aileen Moore; many more ancestral lines had now been fleshed out. She set down her pencil and studied the surnames at the tops of each ancestral line, checking to see if any of the names appeared in her own genetic network cluster, which was the whole point in the sharing of screens during the briefing. She couldn't see any cross-over yet.

'So,' Maddie began, 'as you can see, I've managed to close down sixteen lines—all of Aileen Moore's maternal lineage. They're still predominantly North Carolina, but'—she picked up a digital pen and drew a green circle on the screen around the name of Caledonia Bennett—'*this* lady was born in Logan Township in Gloucester County, New Jersey…which is just a couple of counties across from West Deptford, New Jersey and, similar to the family that Hudson found, across the Delaware River from Pennsylvania.' She looked at him and asked, 'Remind me of the name you had from that area?'

'White,' he answered, jotting something down on his notepad.

Maddie snapped her fingers. 'White. Yes, thank you. Obviously we don't know yet if that's significant, but just keep it in mind. Hudson, do you want to go next?'

'Sure,' he said, displaying his computer on the large screen. 'James Jones's maternal lines are all closed down to the third-great-grandparent generation and I *think* I may have identified the common ancestors for genetic network cluster one.'

Kenyatta gasped in exasperation. '*Already?*'

Hudson moved out from his desk, picked up the green digital pen and drew a circle around the name of Harry White and his wife, Isabella Delaporte. 'This pair were both born in West Deptford. They are my cluster lead's great-great-grandparents via their son, Benjamin Joseph White. They are also the great-grandparents of *another* guy within cluster one via their other son, James.'

Maddie nodded approvingly. 'It looks like you're on your way to winning twenty dollars, Hudson.'

He grinned. 'It's still early days. I only discovered the link to the latest guy a half-hour ago, so it still needs much more work.'

Kenyatta raised an eyebrow and said, 'So, you get out of researching James Jones's paternal side, huh?'

Hudson shrugged. 'It looks that way,' he gloated, walking back to his desk with an exaggerated swagger.

Kenyatta chuckled. 'Good for you, honey. Good for you.'

'Kenyatta,' Maddie said, 'You've been in and out of the FHL all day: what joys do you bring to us?'

'Well, nothing as good as Hudson,' she said, nodding towards Hudson, as she stood up and shared her screen with the office. 'Leo Ford's paternal line is now back far enough. Unfortunately, I've hit an 1850s Alabama-sized brick wall for four of the surnames. So, I've got twelve out of sixteen names. Possibly of some significance is this guy,' she clicked on the name of Theodore Scharder to raise his profile up out of the pedigree. 'He was born 1799 in Lancaster County, Pennsylvania, just twenty-seven miles from the Chester Creek murders.'

'Okay,' Maddie said. 'That could be a *really* interesting lead, well done.'

'I think rather than starting work tomorrow on Leo Ford's maternal side, I'm going to concentrate instead on trying to link the rest of the cluster to the Scharder family.'

Maddie nodded. 'Yeah, I think that's probably a smart move. Anything else?'

'Nope,' Kenyatta said, sitting back down.

'Becky?' Maddie said.

'I'm up to eighteen ancestral lines but with three dead ends,' Becky said, standing up and mirroring the pedigree of the lead name of cluster three. She took a breath and then continued, 'Still no links to Pennsylvania or any names that cross over with the ones you've all highlighted so far. So, I guess I've got plenty of work still to do on mine.'

'Good job, everyone,' Maddie praised. 'I think we're getting somewhere. That's all for today. Have a good evening and I'll see you all tomorrow.'

Kenyatta put her computer into shut down, then put the half-touched salad box into her bag, along with the face masks and latex gloves.

'Anybody doing anything fun this evening?' Becky asked, talking to nobody in particular, as she packed away her things.

Hudson sighed. 'No. You?'

'Well, I had a date lined up for tonight, but he's bailed on me, so I'm going to take my frustrations out on the walls at The Front.'

'Where do you get all your energy from?' Kenyatta asked, tucking her chair under her desk. 'After a day at work, the last thing I'd want to do for *fun* is climb walls.'

Becky shrugged and smiled. 'I just love it. It relaxes me. What are your plans this evening?'

'Well, I've got the boys waiting,' Kenyatta said.

'Oh, that's great,' Becky enthused. 'So good to hear that.'

It took Kenyatta a moment to realize that Becky took her comment to mean that she would have her three sons with her this evening. She couldn't bring herself to correct her and quickly said, 'I've got to drop these masks and gloves off to Lonnie, first. So, I'd best be heading out. See you all tomorrow.'

'Have a good one with the boys,' Becky called after her.

Kenyatta nodded, said goodbye to Ross and Maddie and left the office, heading down to the first floor in the elevator.

Outside, the temperature had dropped dramatically since her last trip to the FHL, but thankfully there still had been no further snowstorms. She walked quickly through the busy streets until she reached the derelict building whose vestibule her homeless friend, Lonnie, called home.

'Hey, Lonnie. You in there?' she said to the piles of boxes, blankets and rubbish. 'Knock, knock. Delivery service.'

She waited a moment and then tentatively lifted a trash bag flap which served as the entrance to Lonnie's abode. She could see that his filthy sleeping bag was vacant; he was obviously out scavenging around the city. So, she took out the box of latex gloves and face masks and tucked them inside the dank tunnel where he slept. As she removed them from her bag, inside she noticed the half-eaten salad and placed that beside the gloves. Resetting the entrance flap, she walked to the nearest tram stop.

Kenyatta felt the familiar tightening in her chest as she pushed open the front door of her tiny house on 700 East Street. Inside was dark and unwelcoming; the same as it was each and every evening. She closed the door and switched on the lights, the orange glow from the overhead lamp only marginally lifting the gloomy atmosphere of the living room.

'Home sweet home,' she muttered, dropping her bag down beside the door and walking over to the kitchenette. She pulled open the refrigerator. Nothing but salads and stuff from the healthy shelves of Harmons. Nothing *nice*. In the freezer she found a burger-and-fries combo, which she took out and placed in the microwave.

While her dinner was cooking, Kenyatta wandered down the short hallway to her bedroom and changed into her pajamas. She passed the boys' bedroom door, which had stayed resolutely shut since Otis had got temporary custody three months ago: it was too painful a reminder to see their empty bunks on a daily basis. For the most part, she pretended that whatever lay behind that door had nothing to do with her, as though it led to someone else's apartment.

The microwave beeped its conclusion as Kenyatta re-entered the kitchen. Tipping the hot food onto a plate, she sat down on the couch and started her laptop up on the vacant place-setting beside her.

'My *other* boys,' she said, as she opened a Word document, entitled *The Boys Under the Bridge*. It was a forty-three-page dossier, the culmination of her pro-bono work for the National Center for Missing and Exploited Children. It was just one of 700 cases involving the unidentified remains of children, which were being revisited by the Center.

This case was deemed by many to be an impossible one to solve. The skeletons of two boys, estimated to have been around the ages of six and four, had been discovered in 1994 under a bridge on the Vietnam Veterans Memorial Highway in Penrose, Colorado. DNA had revealed them to have been brothers. And that was pretty much all that had been known about their identity, never mind who might have killed them, prior to Venator's agreeing to take on the case.

Kenyatta forked some fries into her mouth as she accessed the boys' files on GEDmatch and FamilyTreeDNA, hoping to see that a fresh cousin match might have popped up. If anything, there were now *fewer* matches than ever before. Their closest genetic cousin, matching with a meager fifteen centiMorgans of DNA, was with a kit, unhelpfully named *EN34*. With this pathetic quantity of DNA, the connection between EN34 and the boys could be as far back as their seventh great-grandparents. The rest of the genetic network cluster was much worse, quickly slipping below the normal cut-off point of seven centiMorgans, where false positives were much more likely.

Kenyatta had already established that EN34 was actually Elborn Nodecker, a sixty-seven-year-old man from Indiana, who had not replied to a single one of Kenyatta's emails or even the letters that she had sent to his home address, once she had tracked him down.

She took a mouthful of the burger, instantly regretting that she had broken her diet again. She cursed the random application of her willpower. When it came to maintaining a strict diet, it gave out on her in the first instance. Yet, when it came to her work, it supplied her with limitless stamina and patience. Such as on this case. Pending the magic arrival of a fresh DNA match, her sole focus was taking each and every line of Elborn Nodecker's family backwards to his seventh great-grandparents: all 512 of them.

Most nights after work, she would do a little more for the boys. Some nights she would achieve literally nothing at all, others she might get to add a whole bunch of names to Elborn Nodecker's family tree.

So far, she had traced lines back to half of the states in America, plus links to Italy, Germany, Britain and Ireland. But nothing yet back to Asia and that was the main problem. The boys had a very strong Asian ethnicity, which as yet had not been borne out in any of their genetic matches.

Kenyatta took another bite of the burger as she picked up on the ancestral line that she had been working last night: the Bearse family from Ohio.

From beside her on the couch her cellphone pinged.

Tears welled in her eyes as she read the message.

Hi Mom. Are you okay? Can we come over this weekend and hang out? Dad says it's okay. Jon

Chapter Seventeen

January 2, 1983, Aston, Delaware County, Pennsylvania

He wasn't going to make the same mistake as last time and allow her to seduce him into sleep. No chance. He watched her lying prone on the guest-room bed. On the nightstand beside her was a plastic bag containing a small swatch of her beautiful hair, the rest of which he had arranged so that it fell deliberately over the mess of her cheekbones. 'Sally...' he murmured, kissing her bare arm. 'Sally, it's really time you left.'

He didn't actually know her name. She had no ID on her and she had refused to tell him; so, he had named her Sally, as she had reminded him of a high-school friend whom he had liked: Sally Patterson.

The Dodge was ready and prepped, so he wrapped the sheet around her and pulled her into his arms. 'That's it,' he said encouragingly. 'Good girl. You've learned not to resist. It's a real shame you didn't learn that lesson Friday night.'

He carried her carefully through the house, tucking her feet down as he passed doorways so as not to hurt her. He placed her carefully in the trunk, stared at her quiet face for a few moments and then pulled the lid shut.

Opening the garage door as quietly as he could, he switched off the light and climbed into the driver's seat before firing up the ignition and pulling out of his driveway.

He drove the short distance with a big smile on his face, the sense of satisfaction somehow deeper now with Sally than it had been with Mary-Jane.

But his hunger for more had grown.

He quickly reached New Road, having not encountered a single other vehicle. He slowed down to a crawl as he neared the crossover point of the Chester Creek. He stopped the car, wound down his window and sat quietly. It was right here in front of him—thirteen years ago—that the skid marks had been etched onto the road.

The day that had started it all.

He convinced himself that he could still see the faint residue from those long black tire marks.

He lifted his gaze from the potholed road, looking all around him.

Not a sound.

Moving quickly, he opened the trunk and pulled Sally up into a sitting position. Then, he paused. Still nothing. Freeing Sally from the bedsheet, he placed his hands under her armpits and dragged her naked body from the car. He sat her down on the low concrete wall that topped the bridge over the Chester Creek.

Sally's head slumped forwards and, releasing one hand from her armpit, he pushed her forehead upwards. As he did so, her body slid sideways and out of his grip. Despite his best efforts to reach for her, she tumbled off the side of the bridge and down the twenty feet into the shallow water.

'Oh, Sally,' he gasped, raising a hand to his mouth. 'What have you done?'

No chance now to say goodbye.

He peered over the edge and could just make out an ill-defined pinkish shape in the river below.

He stared at the water, remembering the six kittens again. His father had thrown the sack into the trashcan when they'd reached home, but *he* had retrieved them and taken them off to the woods, where he'd given them names as he pulled their little bodies from the sack. He'd played with them, made them fight each other and then, over the next days, watched dispassionately as their bodies began to decompose.

As he closed the trunk and climbed back into the car, he tried to recall their names.

'Sooty, Jet...' he recalled with a grin, '...Ebony...'

Now, what *was* that black and white one called?

Chapter Eighteen

Thursday, March 5, 2020, Downtown Salt Lake City, Utah

Hudson Édouard was sipping a coffee at his desk in the main Venator office on his mid-morning break. Just like the rest of the team, though, he didn't really take a break at all; he used the restroom, stretched his legs, checked his cellphone, made a drink and simply carried on with his work. Kenyatta was sitting behind him, muttering something to herself as she glowered at her computer screen. Becky was in with Maddie, having made some discovery that she would no doubt be sharing at the briefing later on.

Following up on yesterday's discovery that Harry White and Isabella Delaporte, from West Deptford, New Jersey, were the common ancestors to two people within cluster one, Hudson was eager to try and link the rest of that genetic network to this couple.

First thing this morning, Hudson had chosen a woman from within the cluster, who, although only matching with thirty centiMorgans of DNA, had included a family tree which he now had open in front of him.

Mary Alice Hildebrand: related somehow to the cluster lead and the Chester Creek killer. Hudson had examined her tree carefully. It included all sixteen of her great-great-grandparents, which, provided the information was accurate, would save Hudson a great deal of time. However, none of the sixteen surnames were White or Delaporte. To achieve both of those names within the two further generations by which point the connection should have occurred, it strongly suggested that one of the eight women's mothers had been born a White, *her* parents being Harry and Isabella.

Having triaged the birth locations of Mary Alice Hildebrand's eight great-great-grandmothers, Hudson prioritized with the deliciously named Rose Sprunt, born in 1860 in Peapack, Somerset County, New Jersey. According to the family tree in front of him, Rose Sprunt had married a guy, named William Taylor, but the tree provided no information about their marriage.

Using the Wiki page on the FamilySearch website, Hudson pulled up *New Jersey, Church Records, 1675-1970* and inputted Rose Sprunt's name with a spouse, named William Taylor, and a marriage range of 1875 to 1925.

The third item in the results list looked promising. Hudson clicked to view a typed index page that had evidently been scanned from a microfilm. William Taylor, aged 22, had married Rose Sprunt, aged 19, on March 20, 1879 in the Reformed Dutch Church, Peapack, Somerset County, New Jersey. Although he had undoubtedly found the correct pair, Hudson had been hoping that Rose Sprunt's parents' names might have been included. He left the page open and then, in a new web browser, turned to Ancestry to search their census collection.

He finished drinking his coffee and set to work on finding Rose on the 1870 census. Thankfully for him, there was only one Sprunt family living in Somerset County at this time and it included a ten-year-old girl, named Rose.

Hudson zoomed in to get a closer view of Rose's parents, wondering if his hunch was correct. Peter J. and Phebe E. Sprunt, both forty-one years old and born in the state of New Jersey. No hint or clue was given as to Phebe's maiden name, so Hudson returned to the *New Jersey, Church Records, 1675-1970* tab that he had kept open, amending the search so that it was now for Peter Sprunt only.

1 Result for Peter Sprunt

Hudson didn't need to click through to see the full marriage entry: Peter's spouse was listed as *Phebe Elizabeth White*.

'Yes!' he declared. 'That twenty dollars is almost mine!'

'Nope!' Becky countered, standing up from her desk, holding a precious orange slip of paper that she now set about flaunting in the air above her. 'James and Jane Crowder from Amherst County, Virginia! *They* are the common ancestral couple for genetic network cluster three. Twenty dollars, thank you very much!'

'The one person who *doesn't* need the money,' Kenyatta commented.

'Oh, come on!' Becky said, shooting an incredulous look at her as she fixed the orange slip to the whiteboard and took down the twenty-dollar-bill prize. Taking the money in both hands, she kissed it lovingly.

'Well done,' Maddie said, leaning on the doorframe of her office and offering a quick clap of congratulations. 'The first direct ancestor of the Chester Creek murderer. Good job.'

'Thank you,' Becky said, placing the twenty-dollar bill down on Kenyatta's desk. 'For your homeless friend, Donnie.'

'Lonnie,' Kenyatta corrected. 'And you don't need to do that. I'm sorry. I didn't mean to criticize. You won that money fair and square. Here.' She picked up the money and offered it back.

'No, really,' Becky insisted. 'Give it to your guy.'

'Well, now I feel *real* bad,' Kenyatta mumbled.

'Don't. It's fine. Really. I'll take all the glory; your guy can take the money.'

Hudson quietly observed the exchange between the two women, then returned to his work. The full marriage entry in 1858 for Peter J. Sprunt to Phebe Elizabeth White gave no further useful information. No parents' names and no ages to help him narrow down her birth. But there was one simple way that he could find out who Phebe's parents had been.

Switching to the speculative family tree that he had created for the lead name in his cluster, Hudson pulled up Harry White's profile page. Under *Facts* he checked to see whether he had already found Harry on the 1850 census. He had. Hudson clicked to open the document to see who had been living in the household with Harry and Isabella.

Harry White. Age: 45. Sex: male. Occupation: Farmer. Place of birth: NJ
Isabella White. Age: 44. Sex: Female. Place of birth: NJ
Benjamin Joseph White. Age: 23. Sex: Male. Place of birth: NJ
James White. Age: 22. Sex: Male. Place of birth: NJ
Phebe Elizabeth White. Age: 20. Sex: Female. Place of birth: NJ
Louisa Jane White. Age: 17. Sex: Female. Place of birth: NJ

And there they all were, living together. Three people within the genetic network cluster whose ancestors had been siblings. Three people constituted sufficient evidence that the entirety of cluster one had descended from Harry White and Isabella Delaporte, including their Chester Creek serial killer.

With a great sense of satisfaction, Hudson pulled an orange slip of paper from the drawer below his desk and wrote on it:

Harry White and Isabella Delaporte from Deptford, New Jersey

'Another orange slip!' Kenyatta noted. 'Well done, *Monsieur*.'

'Thanks,' he replied, carrying the paper over to the whiteboard and putting it next to Becky's. He stood for a moment looking at the photographs of the three victims, then at the range of evidence and possible leads that their small team had generated in just three days. He looked meaningfully at each of the women in turn, confident that they would soon have the identity of their killer.

Back at his desk, Hudson closed the file pertaining to cluster one and opened that of cluster two.

The lead name for this cluster—and with the highest DNA match—was TAM962, who shared fifty-two centiMorgans of DNA with the Chester Creek killer. There were seven others in the cluster, who were also related to both of them.

Unfortunately, TAM962 had provided no information whatsoever apart from her email address that contained the same combination of cryptic letters and numbers.

Hudson copied the email address and, in a new web browser, opened up the BeenVerified website. He logged in using the company credentials and then, under the category *Email Search*, pasted in TAM962's email address.

Several boxes opened up on the page. Under *Potential Owner*, the name *Timothy Arthur Monk* appeared. So, not a *she* at all. According to this background check website, he had been born in August 1956.

Hudson scrolled down the page, noting details of Timothy's possible phone numbers and seven addresses that might pertain to him, all of which were to be found in Chicago. Further down the page were possible jobs held by Timothy. *Director of Nursing, Nyack Hospital. Surgical Nurse, Cinn.*

Next, came Timothy's relatives. Three family members were listed: a woman, Clara Monk, who was his own age and two men in their 30s, Simon and George Monk.

Finally, under *Social Media*, he received Timothy's Twitter handle, LinkedIn profile name and his Amazon username.

Hudson clicked the Twitter hyperlink and was taken to Timothy's profile page. Under *Media*, he quickly found a photograph of Timothy at a beach with his arms around a lady of a similar age. The tweet above the photo offered more information: *Thirty-five years today Clara and I said We Do! And we Still Do!*

'Thank you,' he muttered, noting down the date of the tweet, December 22, 2019. Hudson then began to search on Ancestry for a marriage between Timothy Arthur Monk and Clara unknown thirty years before, in December 1984.

Results 1-6 of 6

Hudson could immediately see that all of the suggested marriages were incorrect. So, he switched the same search over to the MyHeritage website.

7 records

Again, all of them were incorrect.

At FamilySearch, the promised 2,652 results presented were also not pertaining to the correct couple.

Undeterred, Hudson opened up the GenealogyBank website and typed in the same details.

'Gotcha,' he said, seeing Timothy's name highlighted in yellow over a thumbnail excerpt from a newspaper article out of Springfield, Illinois. He clicked to view the full page and then grinned at the genealogical data that it contained.

Monk-Schramm

Clara Schramm and Timothy Arthur Monk, both of Springfield, exchanged vows at 4pm December 22. The Rev. David Cessna officiated the ceremony at the Trinity Lutheran Church. The bride is the daughter of Mr. And Mrs. W.D. Schramm, 201 Bellerive. Parents of the bridegroom are Mr. and Mrs. Karl Monk of Lake Forest. Debora Forbes served as maid of honor, with Patricia and Daphne Schramm and Kristin Monk servicing as bridesmaids. Best man was Ken Monk, and serving as groomsmen were Ralph and Kurt Monk. Mr. and Mrs. Monk will reside in Chicago.

Hudson underlined all the members of the Monk family, then began to create a speculative family tree for them.

Within fifteen minutes, he had found an obituary for Karl Monk, which provided the names of two of his siblings and the date and place of his birth. Within thirty minutes, he had found Karl Monk on the 1940 US Census, living with his parents and siblings. Within an hour, he had traced the Monk line back to the early 1800s. By the time Maddie called the briefing, he had taken three of Timothy Arthur Monk's ancestral lines back to the great-great-great-grandparent level.

'Is everybody ready to share?' Maddie asked, breezing into the main office. The digital whiteboard was already displaying the pedigree of the genetic network on which she had been working. 'Ross, are you ready?'

'Sure am,' he said, picking up a notepad and pen.

'Ready and waiting,' Kenyatta responded, folding her arms.

'Yep,' Becky confirmed, putting her pencil down and spinning her chair to face the board.

'So,' Maddie began, pointing to the digital whiteboard, 'as you can see, I've closed down most of Aileen Moore's ancestral lines back to the third-great-grandparent level. Still the most prominent is this lady'—just as she had done in yesterday's briefing, she drew a circle around the name of Caledonia Bennett—'born in Gloucester County, New Jersey. I *think* I might have found a link between her and another person within the cluster, but I need to make a visit to the FHL to verify a birth record. So, keep your eyes open for Bennetts or her husband's family, Huffmans. Okay, Becky, over to you.'

Becky cleared her throat, mirrored her computer screen on the whiteboard and then stood up. 'Alright, then. *Vitally* crucial at this point—and in case anyone missed it—*I* won the twenty bucks for completing the first orange slip...'

'Shut...up,' Hudson interjected with a grin. 'You had an easy ride.'

Becky shot him a mock-incredulous look. 'As I was saying—before being so rudely interrupted—with hard work, I found that the common ancestors to cluster three were James and Jane Crowder from Amherst County, Virginia. Um, so far, though, no links to Pennsylvania...or New Jersey, for that matter. I'm having a few issues with my lead name in cluster four, so there's nothing to report yet on that front.'

'Great,' Maddie said. 'Hudson, what have you got for us?'

Hudson's computer screen replaced Becky's on the digital whiteboard, showing the profile page for Harry White. 'This guy and his wife, Isabella, from West Deptford, New Jersey, are the common ancestors for cluster one, so keep your eyes open for any Whites.' He minimized the tree and pulled up the nascent pedigree for Timothy Arthur Monk. The pedigree started with Timothy but, unlike a family tree, displayed only his direct antecedents. 'I've now moved on to cluster two and this is my lead name. As you can see, not bad progress so far but nothing yet to connect his family to the rest of the cluster and nothing in PA or NJ,' Hudson relayed, taking his seat.

'Great job,' Maddie said. 'Kenyatta?'

Kenyatta stood, showing her screen for the rest of the team to see. 'This, my dear colleagues, is the third person in genetic network number seven, who is descended from...' she paused, wide-eyed as she surveyed the room, '...Mister Theodore Scharder and Miss Carrie Escher from Lancaster County, Pennsylvania.' She wiggled her hips and picked up an orange piece of paper from her desk. 'And another pair of the killer's direct ancestors are *in* the bag.'

'Excellent work, everyone,' Maddie congratulated, watching as Kenyatta walked over to the whiteboard to fix up her discovery. 'We almost know the identity of a quarter of the Chester Creek killer's great-great-great-grandparents. So, good job. Have a relaxing evening, everyone. Hudson, could I see you for a moment, please?'

'Sure,' Hudson answered, following her into her office.

'Push the door the shut,' Maddie said quietly, sitting behind her desk.

Hudson was immediately nervous; it was rare for Maddie to pull anyone into her office and ask them to close the door. In fact, now that he thought about it, he couldn't remember its ever having happened. His thoughts began quickly running over his work and what might be the problem.

'You don't need to look so terrified,' Maddie said with a smile. 'Listen, I just wanted to ask if everything was okay with you? You seem a little… I don't know, not quite yourself. You know? Like there's something bothering you. I mean, you don't have to tell me anything, but if there's any issue here at work or something that I could do to help…?'

Hudson shook his head and mustered a smile. 'No. Everything's good, thanks. I'm a bit tired…but apart from that…'

'Yeah,' Maddie said, clearly not buying it. 'Is Abigail okay?'

'Uh-huh,' he replied. 'Actually, I should be getting back before I get into trouble.' He tried to laugh, but it came out sounding just as false as it actually was.

Maddie smiled. 'Okay. Well, I'm here…if ever you want to talk.'

'I know,' he said. 'I'll see you in the morning.'

'Take care, Hudson.'

He left her office and headed back to his desk, thankful that, apart from a curious glance from Ross, the other two had left already. He switched off his computer, packed up his bag and called an overly cheery goodbye to Maddie and Ross, and then left.

Outside, standing on the sidewalk, Hudson let out a long breath. He stood for a moment, absent-mindedly watching the city flitting past him. He looked at his watch: almost five o'clock. Like most nights, Abigail was out, so there seemed little point in rushing on home.

A hand placed on his shoulder startled him and he whipped around.

'You okay?' Ross asked.

Hudson nodded. 'Yeah, I'm just waiting for a tram.'

'Isn't *that* one heading your way?' Ross asked, nodding in the direction of the arriving din.

'Too crowded,' Hudson countered. 'I'll get the next one. See you tomorrow.'

'Sure,' Ross said, pulling on a set of headphones and wandering off down Main Street.

Hudson watched him go, wishing that he didn't always have to be so sharp with him; it wasn't intentional. Or maybe it was. He didn't know.

He drew in another long breath and turned to walk towards the Cheesecake Factory, having decided in that instant that that was how he would pass the next two hours. As he turned to head up Main Street, he walked directly into a middle-aged black lady who was standing motionless, seemingly staring right through him.

'Oh, I'm so sorry,' Hudson apologized, stepping aside.

The woman offered a weak smile and now began to hold his gaze. 'You're Hudson Édouard, right?'

Hudson took a better look at her. She was in her fifties, a thin, smartly dressed woman with curly black hair and crimson lipstick. He was certain that he had never met her before and yet, she seemed to know precisely who he was. 'Um, yeah, that's me.'

She smiled and extended her hand, showing perfectly manicured nails. 'Wanda Chabala.'

Hudson shook her hand, sensing that her name was vaguely familiar to him. 'Is there something that I can help you with?'

She nodded slowly and glanced around her. 'I don't want to talk out here. Could I take fifteen minutes of your time? Maybe get you a drink for your trouble?'

Hudson was curious. 'What's it regarding, exactly?'

'Investigative genetic genealogy,' she responded. 'A cold case.'

He looked at the Beerhive Pub directly behind them. 'Sure, let's go in here.' Hudson held open the door and watched as the stranger walked past him and into the confines of the dimly lit pub.

A long, dark, wooden bar ran almost the entire length of the narrow building. Around half of the stools were currently occupied by casually dressed office workers, taking a quick drink with their coworkers before heading home. Opposite the bar was a selection of tables and Wanda Chabala headed not to the first, which was vacant, but to the middle in a row of three empty ones further inside the room.

Hudson sat opposite her, still trying to work out how or why he had recognized her name. Perhaps he was just imagining that he found the name to be familiar; they continually worked with so many different names with varying degrees of importance. Her face certainly wasn't one that he recognized. 'Here,' he said, passing her the drinks menu. 'I already know what I'm going to have.'

Wanda smiled. 'And what would that be?'

'A glass of *Vieille Ferme Côtes de Rhône*,' he replied.

Wanda nodded, lowering her eyes from his to the menu, saying, 'You have French ancestry, right?'

'Yeah,' he answered, sensing that it was not simply his surname that had informed her of this fact. Whoever she was, she knew more about him than he knew about her.

'Hi guys!' a cheery young waitress with green hair greeted. 'What can I get for you, today?'

'Two glasses of *Vieille Ferme Côtes de Rhône, merci beaucoup*,' Wanda said with what sounded like an authentic French accent. 'And make it large.'

'Perfect,' the waitress said. 'And will you be eating with us?'

'No. Not this time,' Wanda answered.

'Okay. I'll be right back with your drinks.'

'You speak French *très bien*,' Hudson observed.

'*Ah, oui*. I lived in Paris for a few years,' she said, giving a dismissive wave.

'So, what was it that you wanted to speak with me about?' Hudson asked.

Wanda looked him in the eyes, knitted her fingers together above the table, and said, 'I want you to help me get a convicted murderer…out of jail.'

'Oh,' Hudson said, stuck for quite what else to say in answer to that unexpected statement.

'Brandon Blake. Ever heard of him?' Wanda asked.

Again, there was a flicker of recognition in his mind. He searched for a connection between Brandon Blake and Wanda Chabala. Yes, there was something there, but he couldn't quite force his tired mind to retrieve the information. An old news story, perhaps? 'It rings a bell, but I just can't quite place him,' Hudson finally conceded.

'He's two years into a life sentence in Minneapolis, having been wrongly convicted,' Wanda explained.

'Is he your...son? Brother? Husband?' Hudson ventured.

'He was convicted of murdering my daughter, Francesca.'

'Oh,' Hudson said again. *Now* he remembered the news story. 'And you want him released?'

Wanda nodded.

Hudson hoped to goodness that there was something more to this story than that she had simply searched and found inner forgiveness for her daughter's killer and felt that he no longer warranted punishment.

'I've done a lot of digging since the trial,' Wanda went on, 'and I don't believe for one second that he was responsible for what happened to my Francesca. Her murderer is still out there, still going about his business, still probably killing women. And all the while Brandon Blake is behind bars for a crime he did *not* commit.'

'Two glasses of...' the waitress said, returning, '...of that French wine. Enjoy!'

'Thank you,' Wanda said, pausing until the waitress had left before continuing. 'I've watched the tapes of his interviews: more than a hundred hours over ten interrogations; polygraph tests; and outright heavy bullying. Brandon changes his story five times, moving from having no involvement through to a total confession. The detectives implied that he might get full immunity, if he confessed. Just watch this,' she said, pulling her cellphone from her purse. She opened it up and handed it to Hudson. 'Go ahead. Click it.'

Hudson did just that, and a slightly grainy film, shot from a high angle, looking down onto a police interview room, started to play. A young black man with close-cropped hair, baggy jeans and a white t-shirt was seated facing the camera. Opposite him were two slightly overweight, white detectives.

'So, Brandon,' one of the detectives began, 'we know you did it. Every single lie-detector test you've taken, you've failed. Failed.'

Wanda leant over. 'Completely incorrect: he *passed* every test.'

'We know, Brandon. We know, okay?' the detective continued.

'We've given you a way out, haven't we?' the other detective asked. 'You won't go to jail, if you tell the truth. Tell us that you killed Francesca. If you don't...it's going to be serious for you. Really bad. There are a *lot* of people out there who want to do bad things to you. Do you understand? *Bad* things.'

'*Really* bad,' the other chipped in.

Hudson had been studying Brandon the whole while that the

detectives had been talking. He hadn't yet once stopped rubbing his hands up and down his legs, sobbing as he did so.

'Let's keep it simple, Brandon,' the first one said. 'Yeah? You just say yes to my questions. Were you with Francesca Chabala the night she was killed?'

Brandon nodded.

'You need to speak, Brandon. If we're going to save you, you need to actually say your answer aloud, 'yes'.'

'Yes.'

'Good. And you had sex with her, right?'

'Yes.'

'Good. And then... Well, things got out of hand, right?'

A painful whimper erupted from Brandon and he stammered, 'Look, will you actually leave me alone? No more tests and all of this, if I just say yes?'

'That's right, Brandon. All we need is a yes.'

'Yes,' he muttered.

'You killed Francesca Chabala, yes?'

'Yes.'

The film ended on a smug look between the two detectives.

Hudson passed back the phone and raised his eyebrows. 'Wow. That was uncomfortable viewing.'

'Yes, it is. And there's so much more of it.'

Hudson rode his thumb and forefinger up the stem of the wine glass, thinking. 'I take it there was no DNA left at the scene?'

'A perfectly testable semen sample was obtained.'

'And it matched Brandon?'

Wanda shook her head. 'No match to Brandon Blake. None.'

'What? How did this get past the jury?' Hudson asked incredulously.

Wanda drank some wine. 'Because they were told that Brandon had to have been there, else why would he have confessed. The jury were convinced by an argument put forward by the prosecution that someone else was also involved. And that if Brandon wasn't prepared to say who that other person was, then he would have to be convicted alone, based on his confession. It took the jury just ten hours to find Brandon Blake guilty of first-degree murder, rape and the use of a deadly weapon in the commission of a felony.'

'Wow,' Hudson said, trying to process the information. 'And I'm assuming that you want Venator's help?'

Wanda nodded. 'Well. No, actually.'

Now Hudson was confused. 'I don't understand. Why are you telling me all of this, then?'

'I want *your* help.'

Hudson realized then that Wanda must have had a distorted impression of his status within Venator. Wherever she had gotten her information about him, it was wrong. 'I mean, this sounds like the kind of thing we *could* do for you, but it's just not my call. You've picked the wrong guy here; I just work for the company and I have literally no sway over the cases we take on. You really need to—'

'Get law enforcement to approach Venator with the details of the case?' Wanda interrupted. 'I have tried. Repeatedly. I've even offered to pay for the cost of transferring the kit to your company and to fund all costs.'

'But?'

'But the cops got their man in Brandon Blake, so the District Attorney sees no need to revisit it unless any fresh evidence comes to light about this mysterious *other perpetrator.*'

Hudson sipped his wine. 'Listen, if it were possible and up to me, I'd take on the case. But it really isn't up to me at all. And even if I *could* convince my boss, our company simply doesn't have the authority to request DNA samples from law enforcement. This is a common misconception: it's not a bidirectional relationship. Law enforcement always approach us; *never* the other way around.'

Wanda nodded mechanically. 'What if *I* could get you the DNA sample?'

'There's no way my boss would get involved in that. No.'

'I'm not asking your boss, Hudson. I'm asking you,' Wanda said. 'Private employment.'

Now the picture in front of him had crystallized but the confusion had not lifted. Private work. The way in which he had been approached—and the way that Wanda was talking about getting ahold of state evidence—made it very clear that, if he undertook the task, it would have to be completely outside of the knowledge of anyone at Venator. Not just private work, but secret work. And that was something that he wasn't at all comfortable with.

'I'm…going to *have* to decline,' he finally said.

'Oh, I don't want you to decide right now,' Wanda countered. 'Think it over. Talk it over…with Abigail. And about what you might need to be spending the fifty thousand dollars on that I'm planning on paying you.'

'How do you know my wife's name?' Hudson asked, thumping down his glass and making a thin stream of wine slop over the side. It was one thing to have made enquiries about his role in the organization but not into his personal life.

'Hey, don't get upset, now. You and I both use the same methods for finding people, and for the same purpose,' Wanda said, sliding a business card across the table. 'Have a think, have a chat and then get on back to me.'

Wanda finished her wine, placed a twenty-dollar bill on the table and stood to leave. 'It sure was really nice meeting you, Hudson. I hope we can work together.'

Hudson nodded and silently watched her leave the building. As he drank more wine, he replayed what she had said moments prior to leaving: '…what you might need to be spending the fifty thousand dollars on…' She knew more about him and his life than that which she could have just looked up on social media or some type of background-check website. Much more.

The question now was whether or not he should or could take on the case. He picked up Wanda's business card, his mind running over the myriad of questions that her proposition had ignited, and then ordered another large glass of wine.

Chapter Nineteen

Friday, March 6, 2020, Downtown Salt Lake City, Utah

Becky Larkin was getting annoyed. It was past lunchtime and her progress today had been minimal. Heightening her anxiety was Maddie's arrival back from the FHL, having closed down one of her clusters, and Kenyatta's already confirming links between the families of her second genetic network.

She was getting nowhere with the lead name of cluster four, William Simmons. He matched the Chester Creek killer with what should be a very workable sixty-one centiMorgans of DNA, but, so far, Becky couldn't find anything more about him other than his name and his email address which she had run through BeenVerified, Spokeo, TruthFinder and Mylife background-check websites, receiving zero hits. Oftentimes, a failure to show up in these databases pointed to the person's not residing in the United States. Open searches for a William Simmons with no further identifying clues was a non-starter: far too many possibilities. With the clock ticking, Becky had no choice but to move to the next match within the genetic network cluster; a man with the much more illustrious-sounding name of Crispin Rivers, but who came with a much lower match of forty-seven centiMorgans of DNA.

Crispin had also only provided his email address to FamilyTreeDNA. Once Becky had checked against the background-check websites, she went on to find a corresponding LinkedIn profile which she now clicked to view.

The profile picture was of a man in his late twenties and who was categorized as a 'Retail Professional' from San Antonio, Texas. Becky jotted down the location and his approximate age, finally having something from which to work.

An open search for Crispin in Google and the main social media sites failed to find a match, so Becky turned to the GenealogyBank website and entered Crispin's name with a filter for the state of Texas.

An obituary for 2016 was the only result. It pertained to a Matthew Daniel Rivers and appeared in the *San Antonio Express-News*. Becky opened it up and read the article.

TSGT Matthew Daniel Rivers U.S. Air Force (ret.) passed away October 22, 2016 in San Antonio. He was born on January 14, 1947 in Philadelphia PA.

He was a loving father, grandfather and brother who will be dearly missed. Matthew was preceded in death by his wife, Maryann and brother, John Rivers. He is survived by his son, Nick Rivers and wife, Cath; daughter Alexis Kershner and husband, Antony; 4 grandchildren Raymond Kershner, Paul Kershner, Crispin Rivers, Austin Rivers; three sisters; nieces and nephews.

The obituary went on to talk about the funeral and burial arrangements, but Becky had harvested more than enough genealogical evidence to kick-start Crispin's pedigree chart. She now knew the names of his parents and those of one set of his grandparents. She drew a circle around the word Philadelphia, wondering if this could be the link.

Remaining on the GenealogyBank website, Becky ran an obituary search for Crispin's paternal grandmother, Maryann Rivers. She smiled as a lengthy recount of the woman's life appeared in front of her. The report detailed her early working life and the exact date and location of her marriage to Matthew. Of particular interest to Becky, however, was the opening paragraph, rich with genealogical information.

Maryann was born March 15, 1948 in San Antonio to Judson Archer and Carrie Lynn Carlton.

She added Maryann's maiden name and the names of her parents to the speculative family tree that she was building for Crispin Rivers.

'Oh, yes!' Hudson declared, taking one of the prized orange slips from his desk drawer.

'Already?' Kenyatta said.

Hudson nodded exultantly. '*And* it's a family from Pennsylvania.'

'What name?' Becky asked.

'Thomas Burbee and Margaret Wolfe,' he answered.

'I'll keep an eye open,' Becky said, yawning. 'I've got a family link to Philadelphia I'm working on.'

'That's where these two are from,' Hudson said, holding up the orange slip.

'Oh,' Becky replied. 'What's the name of your cluster lead? I'll see if my guy and yours are related.'

'Timothy Arthur Monk. But he's on FTDNA as TAM962,' Hudson explained, walking over to the whiteboard and fixing up his new information.

As Becky opened up the FamilyTreeDNA website, the office door opened. She heard Ross greet the visitor as if it were somebody he knew. Becky turned to see Detective Clayton Tyler lurking sheepish in the doorway.

'Hi. Is it possible to see Maddie, do you think?' he asked quietly, trying not to draw attention to himself.

'Hi!' Becky called over.

'Hey!' Hudson said to him.

'Just can't keep away, huh?' Kenyatta said with a grin.

'Come on through,' Maddie called from her office.

Becky raised her eyebrows at Kenyatta and smiled, receiving a reciprocal knowing look, as Clayton entered Maddie's office and directly shut the door behind him.

'Well, if he's expecting a name from us already, he's got a bit of a wait on his hands,' Hudson said, turning back to his computer.

'I'm not sure he's here for *that*,' Becky quipped, pulling up the autosomal DNA matches for the Chester Creek killer. She scrolled down the list until she found Crispin Rivers. She selected the check box next to his name, then clicked the *In Common With* filter. Sure enough, TAM962 was in the list. 'Hudson, this could be interesting: my lead guy, Crispin Rivers, *is* related to your Timothy Arthur Monk.'

Hudson nodded as he returned to his seat. 'So, maybe prioritize with the branch of the tree that came from Philadelphia and see if you can link it back to one of Thomas and Margaret Burbee's kids?'

'Yeah, good idea,' Becky agreed. First, though, she needed a drink and to stretch her legs. She wandered over to Ross's desk and asked, 'What are you up to, Rossy?'

Ross blew out his cheeks and stopped typing. 'Replying to various individuals who—since *The Winterset Butcher* case went viral—have been emailing in to ask if we can help work out who killed blah blah blah.' He leaned back in his chair and then lowered his voice. 'So, what do we think is going on in *there*?' he said, nodding to Maddie's closed office door.

'He *so* likes her,' Becky replied, 'but she can't or won't see it. But the way she says *Detective* like that, instead of using his name like she normally does with the law enforcement we're working with, there's *something* there. It's cute. I think it's time she...'

Maddie's office door opened, and Clayton strode out, beelining directly for the main door.

'No. I want to just stay home tonight,' Ross said loudly, quickly managing to save him and Becky from their otherwise obvious, self-imposed silence brought about by the detective's sudden re-appearance.

'Okay, then. We'll just stay in,' Becky agreed, playing along and watching as Clayton headed out of the office. 'Maybe catch something on Netflix...'

Strangely, he didn't turn and acknowledge the team but kept walking. Becky looked back over into Maddie's office, just catching a glimpse of her teary eyes before she closed her door.

'That was weird,' Becky whispered. 'Maddie was literally crying. I've *never* seen her cry.'

'Maybe he asked her out on a date? And it hit a nerve? I mean, that would be quite a tricky situation...' Ross suggested.

'Maybe.' Becky gazed at the closed office door. There was something more in it that she wasn't getting. Maddie would tell them all in good time, if it was anything that concerned them. She faced Ross. 'Do you really want to stay in tonight?'

Ross nodded. 'We can play on Tinder, find us a nice man each. Or one to share?'

Becky turned up her nose. 'I've right-swiped all the eligible bachelors in the Salt Lake area and left-swiped all the rest; there's seriously nobody left. I'm done with swiping.'

'Yeah, me too, actually,' he agreed. 'Do you think we're going to wind up as two lonely old spinsters, living alone together for the rest of our lives?'

Becky shrugged. 'I can think of worse things; like being married to an imbecile, for example.'

'There is that.'

'Plus,' Becky said, her eyebrows dancing a jig, 'I might just have found someone.'

Ross gasped. 'Who? When? What? How?'

'Jerome—a guy I met last week on the climbing walls at The Front. He seems sweet—or at least he did twenty-feet up in the air as we both simultaneously put our hands on the same sloper.'

Ross pulled a sickened face. 'I don't even want to *imagine* what a sloper is.'

'Anyway... He was kind of flirting, so we'll see,' Becky said, turning towards the kitchen area. 'I need a drink.'

'And I need to tell this guy that, as truly awful and sad as his sister's murder was, he needs to go through standard law-enforcement channels and not directly to us. I think people think we have some special access to the nation's DNA evidence stores.'

'If only,' Becky responded, pouring herself a glass of water.

She returned to her desk and let out a small yelp when she noticed the time. There were now under two hours until Maddie would call this afternoon's briefing. Everybody knew that progress always came in fits and starts, but that didn't take away the fact that she felt as though she had achieved very little today. She told herself to concentrate as she pulled up Matthew Daniel Rivers' profile within the family tree that she had created for his grandson, Crispin Rivers. He was going to be her priority.

As stated in the obit, Matthew had been born in Philadelphia, Pennsylvania in 1947. Becky opened a new web-browser tab and accessed the Wiki page on FamilySearch, navigating her way through to genealogical record listings for that state. She had a vague memory of a previous case that had occurred in Pennsylvania and recalled that birth records for this period were not in the public domain. Her fears were confirmed when she read that only births to 1905 were publicly available.

She needed another solution.

First, she searched for Matthew Rivers' marriage, hoping that it might mention one or more of his parents' names, but she could not find it in the various collections available online. Next, she searched for any families with the surname of Rivers on the 1940 U.S. Census: 153 people with that name were residing in Philadelphia alone. That was just not currently going to be a viable research option.

On the Ancestry website, Becky ran a search for Matthew Rivers in the *Public Member Trees* but found nothing pertaining to this specific family. She sighed as she conducted a similar search on the MyHeritage website.

And there it was. Bingo. She had a match.

Matthew D. Rivers
MyHeritage Family Trees
Rivers Web Site, managed by Alexis Kershner

Birth: Jan 14, 1947 - Philadelphia, Pennsylvania, USA
Parents: William Henry Rivers and Nellie Isabel Rivers (born Schenck)
Brother: John Rivers
Wife: Maryann Rivers (born Archer)
Children: <Private>Rivers, <Private> Kershner (born Rivers)

Becky clicked Matthew's hyperlinked name and then viewed him in the context of the extensive family tree that had evidently been created by Matthew Rivers' daughter, Alexis.

She followed the tree up the paternal side, finding that both of Matthew Rivers' parents had been born in Philadelphia, as had both of *their* parents. She jotted down the surnames of Matthew Rivers' direct line, looking to shortcut her research, if possible. *Rivers. Schenck. Arnold. Jarvis. Singer.* All, according to the family tree in front of her, born in Philadelphia.

Needing to cross-reference the list of names against those which Hudson had found, she opened up the Ancestry family tree that he had created for his cluster. Becky located the most recent common ancestral couple for this genetic network, Thomas Burbee and Margaret Wolfe, finding that Hudson had added some additional information to the couple's eight children.

Becky grinned. On Hudson's tree, she spotted that one of Thomas and Margaret Burbee's daughters, Grace, had married somebody by the name of Job Schenck. Switching to the MyHeritage family tree, she found that Crispin Rivers' great-great-great-grandparents were named Watson Schenck and Martha Trent. Their son, Job Schenck, had married Grace Burbee. Same date of birth and same location on both trees. Potentially, this was a fantastic development. If Becky could link further matches from cluster four to Watson and Martha Schenck, then she could complete an orange slip for this common ancestral couple. More excitingly, however, if she could also verify the family tree that had been compiled for Matthew Rivers, then she would have hit the double jackpot of discovering how two of the genetic networks overlapped.

Becky expelled a long breath of air when Maddie bound into the main office, giving two minutes' notice for the final briefing of the week. She was so close to having concrete information to give the team but no way close enough to achieve it in the time remaining. She picked up her pencil and took a clean sheet of paper from her legal pad, ready to take notes.

Maddie was standing with her back to the team, annotating something on the digital whiteboard. When Maddie turned around, Becky could see that all evidence of her earlier upset had vanished from her face. She met Becky's gaze, smiled—perhaps even knowingly—and then addressed the team.

'A very productive day, by all accounts,' Maddie began, drawing their attention. 'And, hopefully, a good end to the working week. You may have witnessed my happy dance upon returning from the FHL, where I confirmed a birth record that helped me to close down cluster five. The common ancestral couple, as I suspected, are George Huffman and Caledonia Bennett from Gloucester County, New Jersey. And, on the screen behind me is the pedigree for my cluster-six lead, which, as you can see, is looking pretty good, thanks to a well-sourced family tree that I've found online. The mirror tree that I've created is proving to be accurate so far, so it shouldn't be too long until I've got most of the lead's great-great-great-grandparents tracked down.' She spun on her heels and faced Kenyatta. 'What amazing discoveries have you made today?'

'Well,' Kenyatta said, rising from her chair and sharing her screen to the digital whiteboard. 'A pretty good one for me, too, actually. On the board we have a pedigree for the lead name of cluster eight. So far, I've managed to close down eight lines, *all* of them in Oregon. This pair, right here'—she pulled up the profile of Samuel Lacock and Joanna Hardy—'are the great-great-great-grandparents for two of the cluster. I'm fairly confident that I'm going to be able to confirm them as the common ancestral couple pretty soon.'

'Great job,' Maddie said.

'And that, ladies and gentleman, is all from me for today,' Kenyatta concluded, retaking her seat.

'Thank you, Kenyatta,' Maddie said. 'Hudson, go ahead.'

Hudson stood up once he had mirrored his screen on the digital whiteboard. 'Well, my main achievement today has been closing down cluster two by establishing Thomas Burbee and Margaret Wolfe as the common ancestral couple. Crucially, as you can see, they came from Philadelphia, so not far from Chester Creek—' he said, glancing over at Becky before continuing '—which, I think, Becky has more to say on. I have taken a quick look at cluster nine, which, as Kenyatta warned already, is a bit of a nightmare and, I think, is one we should probably abandon.'

Maddie nodded. 'Well, if we can each close down our designated two genetic network clusters, then we'll have identified half of the killer's great-great-great-grandparents. Then, it will be about trying to figure out how they interrelate. Okay, great. Becky?'

Becky smiled and stood up, her screen now overriding Hudson's. 'I didn't have the best of starts this morning. But, once I'd switched out the lead of the cluster, I made some pretty good progress. I'm literally on the verge of completing an orange slip for these guys,' she said, circling her mouse-pointer around the names of Watson Schenck and his wife, Martha Trent. 'If I'm right, which I'm fairly sure I am, then their son, Job Schenck, married Grace Burbee, the daughter of Hudson's Thomas Burbee and Margaret Wolfe.'

Maddie clapped. 'Well done, guys! Potentially our first connection at the great-great-grandparent level. Excellent. Okay, that's it for the day and for the week. I know I say it every week—and every time I get ignored—but *please* don't ever work on the weekend. *I'm* not going to, so neither should my team.'

Becky offered a sympathetic smile. There was a reason—a very good reason—why Maddie would not be working *this* weekend: Michael's anniversary.

Becky looked away, still feeling the low tremor of her guilt over his disappearance, which she guessed would never leave her until he was eventually found.

She started to pack up to leave, resolving that she *would* do some work over the weekend. She wanted to be able to return to the office on Monday and complete the orange slip for cluster four. She said goodbye to everyone, linked arms with Ross and left the office.

Taking a drink of her white wine, Becky placed the glass down on the table beside her. She was in her apartment, sprawled across the couch with her feet crossed at the ankles and her slowly overheating laptop resting on her thighs. On the computer screen was Watson and Martha Schenck's family tree, which she was attempting to connect to other members of cluster four. But her mind was elsewhere. She was staring out through the windows of her balcony doors at the black silhouetted outline of the Wasatch Range. It was the act of looking up at those mountains that had initiated the thoughts-snowball that had rolled from wondering if her parents would be staying up there this weekend, at their second home in Park City, to Maddie and what she would be doing this weekend. The link between the two—and one that she tried not to think of too often—was that Maddie's husband, Michael, had been working for Becky's father's financial firm at the time of his disappearance.

'Getting anywhere?' Ross called over.

Becky's eyes drifted from the window, across her spacious, open-plan home in the exclusive Sugar House Apartments, to where Ross was standing beside his younger sister, Alice, preparing dinner. 'I think so,' Becky replied, being pulled back to the task. 'I've just connected someone else from cluster four to the couple I think are the most common recent ancestors.'

'That's enough, isn't it? To close the cluster, I mean?'

'Yep,' Becky confirmed. '*And* I get to be the first to complete a *purple* slip for the next generation down, where two of the clusters meet.'

'I know, when you've explained your job before, I said that I understood,' Alice said, setting down her wine, 'but I…kind of didn't. I don't get how genealogy helps you to catch a serial killer from thirty years ago.' She turned to Ross and continued, 'I've asked him, but the explanation was about as clear as mud.'

'You weren't listening, you mean,' Ross replied, resuming chopping vegetables that he was about to turn into a stir fry.

'Well, it's like…' Becky stopped mid-sentence, put her laptop to one side, picked up her wine and walked over to the counter. 'Let me explain.' She picked up a handful of slivers of red pepper and laid them out vertically beside each other. '…fourteen, fifteen, sixteen. So, our serial killer—like almost all of us—should have thirty-two great-great-great-grandparents, each couple represented here by these sixteen red-pepper strips.'

Ross grinned and sipped his wine. 'Great analogy, Becks.'

'Thanks,' she said.

'With you so far,' Alice said.

'At the moment, we're trying to establish the names for as many of these sixteen couples as we can. In an ideal world, we'll be able to name all of them, but most likely that won't happen.' She picked up one piece of red pepper and held it in front of her face. 'This might look like an ordinary pepper to you, but it is not. Oh, no, it's actually Watson and Martha Schenck. Say hi.'

Alice waved. 'Hi.'

Becky took another piece of red pepper in her other hand and said, 'And *this* is actually Thomas and Margaret Burbee.'

Another wave from Alice.

'Now, Thomas and Margaret Burbee have a daughter, Grace, who gets married to Watson and Martha Schenck's son, Job. Okay?' Becky said, putting the red peppers down on the counter alongside the other fourteen pieces, and picked up a sliver of yellow pepper. 'Job and his new wife, Grace, are now represented here.' She wiggled the yellow pepper. 'And are the Chester Creek killer's *great-great*-grandparents.'

'Okay.'

Becky laid out eight slices of yellow pepper, directly below the red. 'If we can do this for all the red peppers, then we get down to just eight couples.'

'And then what?' Alice asked.

'Then we find all the children born to the yellow peppers.' She jabbed a finger at one of the pieces of yellow pepper and explained, 'The child of this couple over here might marry a child of that couple.' She repeated her finger-stabbing motion at different pieces of yellow pepper and then picked up four rings of zucchini, laying them down below the yellow peppers. 'Now we have four couples.'

'And you repeat the process,' Alice interjected.

'Uh-huh,' Becky said, enjoying this quite odd culinary demonstration. She now took two whole mushrooms and lined them up underneath the zucchinis. 'Now we have the Chester Creek killer's grandparents.'

Ross passed her a half-sliced red onion and, as she placed it beneath the mushrooms, Alice announced with excitement, 'His mom and dad.'

'Exactly.'

'Okay, I totally get it now,' Alice grinned. 'Thanks.'

'Easy, really,' Ross said. 'Now, do you mind if I fry your oh-so-neatly arranged clusters?'

'Go ahead,' Becky said, taking the wine and heading back to the couch. 'I'm just going to add the kids of Job and Grace Schenck to the tree, fill in a purple slip of paper and then call it a night.'

'Cold-case murder mysteries on Netflix?' Ross asked.

'Oh, yes!' she answered, placing the laptop back down on her legs.

'Don't you two have enough real-life murders to be going on with?' Alice asked.

'No,' they both answered together.

Becky pulled up the 1900 US Census for Job and Grace Schenck. They were living in Philadelphia with their five children, one of whom was likely to be the Chester Creek murderer's great-grandparent. She was about to save all the children to the family tree when she spotted something; or rather, someone. Living in the house with the family was a fifteen-year-old boarder by the name of Roland Crowder.

James and Jane Crowder from Virginia were the ancestral couple at the top of cluster three that had earned her the twenty-dollar reward. Was this surname a coincidence?

Becky's pulse began to quicken, as she scanned along the line of detail for Roland Crowder. His place of birth was given as Virginia, the same as his parents. There was a generation missing between James and Jane Crowder and Roland that Becky would need to establish before jumping to any conclusions. Directly above Roland Crowder on the census was one Rosanna Schenck, aged fourteen.

Could Roland and Rosanna have gone on to marry one another? she wondered.

It needed just a little more work, but it looked like Becky may have inadvertently discovered the identity of two of the Chester Creek killer's great-grandparents.

Chapter Twenty

October 30, 1983, Aston, Delaware County, Pennsylvania

They were on the guest-room bed together, naked. He was spooning her, gently running his fingers up and down the length of her body. She was quiet. The house was quiet. And the urgent voices in his head were once again stilled.

He rolled over onto his back and exhaled. The deep sense of calming satisfaction was slowly ebbing away, though. In its place that familiar feeling of agony of separation from her was returning.

'Sadie,' he said, almost inaudibly. But she didn't hear. Or didn't *want* to hear, more likely.

He grinned; it was fine. He felt the same. So, he would let her go on sleeping a little longer. Just a little, though.

He'd come to hate Sundays, marking, as it did, the end of his two days of total freedom. Tomorrow morning, bright and early, Fiona would breeze back in the house, unpausing their life that she had left on Friday afternoon, when she had driven up to Philly for work as usual.

He would wake most Monday mornings deeply angry, resenting the suppression of himself that inevitably accompanied the breaking of the day. At least, now, Fiona had learned to respect those two days. *His* two days. No more inquisitions about what he got up to. No more jobs or can-you-justs.

He rolled back onto his side, pressing himself into her cool skin. 'You're getting cold, Sadie,' he whispered, pulling the bed sheet across them. He would give her a few more minutes, then however much she protested, they would really *have* to go. He hadn't mentioned Fiona to Sadie. He hadn't wanted to. Why should he? It would only spoil an otherwise perfectly nice time.

'I'm going to get the car ready,' he told her, swinging his legs out of the bed and padding out of the guest room along the hall and into the garage. He covered his eyes for a moment, as the stark white strip lights flickered on overhead. He opened the trunk and began to head back to Sadie. 'One last thing,' he remembered, entering the guest bedroom, brandishing a pair of scissors.

Just then as he was about to cut out a lock of her hair, he heard a horribly familiar sound: a key in the front-door lock. Shit. He'd forgotten to deadlock it. He ran out of the room towards the door, but it was too late: it swung wide and Fiona stepped inside.

Her smile faded, as she looked him up and down. 'What's going on?'

'What are you doing home already?' he demanded.

'Why are you walking around the house like that?' she countered, closing the door behind her and setting her small suitcase down. 'Is there someone here with you?' She threw her keys to the ground and stormed into the house.

He grabbed her wrist. 'Get back here.'

In an unexpectedly sharp retraction, Fiona freed her arm and rushed towards their bedroom.

'Fiona!' he yelled, running after her.

Before she reached their bedroom, she stopped. She slowly turned her head and stared aghast into the guest bedroom, dropped her purse, then turned to look at him with abject horror on her face. 'Oh, God. No.'

Chapter Twenty-One

Saturday, March 7, 2020, Park City, Wasatch Range, Utah

'Come on, kids,' Maddie said. 'Finish up your pizza.' They were sitting in Cloud Dine, a restaurant near-as-damn-it at the top of the mountain above the Park City ski resort.

Nikki slumped backwards in the red plastic chair and exhaled noisily. 'I'm done.'

Maddie watched as Trenton reached over for Nikki's two remaining slices, shifting them over to his plate, having already finished his own pizza and half of Maddie's. He caught her rolling her eyes.

'What?' he asked. 'What's the big hurry, anyway? Have you got to be someplace else?'

Maddie forced a smile. 'Nope, nowhere on earth I'd rather be,' she said. It was true, partly. She did want to be here, spending quality time with the kids, but she was feeling restless. That pernicious ache of the anniversary weekend was lingering below the surface for all three of them; a shared but unspoken annual pain that such another previously inconceivable milestone could possibly have been reached. In many ways those five years had passed at an astonishing speed but, when she thought about it more deeply, it now had come to seem an eternity since Michael's presence had been felt in the house and in their lives. For a long time, she had kept everything of his exactly as he had left it and would find herself reacting angrily, if someone dared to move one of his possessions or perhaps to suggest making any significant alterations around the house. She had taken it quite badly last year, when her mother had gently floated the idea of using Michael's study as a crafting room or a hangout room for the kids. But, in the end, time itself had necessitated changes: food, which had been specifically purchased by or for him, had passed the various expiration dates and had to be discarded or eaten; the couches, which she and Michael had chosen together, had grown worn and tired and had had to be replaced; the kids' bedrooms, which he had decorated, had needed modernizing; gadgets, phones, music systems and other electrical devices had needed to be upgraded; new family portraits now adorned the walls, highlighting still further his continued absence. Some items, though, were so deeply personal to him that they remained untouched: his bedside table was exactly as it had been on his last day in the house;

and it would have to be a cold day in hell for her to toss his toothbrush into the trash. Dead or alive, that thing would be staying in their bathroom cabinet, right where he had left it five years ago.

'What's up, Mom?' Trenton asked, stuffing another slice of pepperoni pizza into his mouth.

Another hastily forced smile. 'Nothing at all, sweety.'

Maddie was fully aware of the sharp kick that Nikki sent under the table into Trenton's shin. She turned towards the window, knowing that her daughter would be mouthing something across the table at her brother along the lines of *'DAD*, dumbass!'

She stared out at the open expanse of untouched snow in the foreground, broken only by the occasional aspen, rising gray and skeletal into the sky. Beyond that were the pine-covered peaks of the vast Wasatch Range that appeared to run endlessly into the distance.

The silent mime-artistry passing between her two children had reached its conclusion and she turned to see Trenton forcing in a last mouthful of pizza.

'Done,' he barely managed to articulate around his current bolus.

'Trenton, close your mouth, for goodness' sakes,' Maddie scolded, picking up her ski helmet from the table. 'Ready?'

Nikki pulled on her jacket and strapped up her helmet. 'Yep. Good to go.'

Trenton groaned, clutched his stomach and stood up with a pained looked on his face, feigning—Maddie hoped—that he was on the verge of throwing up.

'It's your own fault,' Maddie said, fastening her helmet and putting on her jacket. 'I have absolutely no sympathy to offer.'

Trenton grinned, grabbed his helmet and coat and followed them through the crowded restaurant, dressing himself as he walked.

Outside, despite the azure skies, the temperature was bitingly cold. The three of them walked quickly over to the metal racks rammed with skis, poles and snowboards. Maddie took down her skis, snapped her boots into them, then pulled on her gloves. She waited for a moment for her kids to do the same, grateful to have long-since passed the days of having to help each of them in turn get into their apparel. She watched a nearby father struggling to assist his two children to do just that, while they stood gazing off indifferently into the distance.

'Which way do you want to go?' Maddie asked.

'Down,' Trenton answered, pushing past her and taking a lead toward the blue Snow Meadow run. Beneath her mask, Maddie smiled.

Trenton was an excellent skier and had only chosen this easy route for her benefit, knowing, as he did, that it had been a favorite of hers and Michael's.

They skied down the narrow track, one in front of the other, with Maddie already trying to keep up with her kids. Trenton took a left, as she knew he would, onto the blue Backstreet run and, also just as predicted, when the run widened, he spun around and started to ski backwards as he sang his dad's cheesy Backstreet Boys' favorite.

Maddie helicoptered her forefinger in the air, trying to encourage him to ski in the correct direction. After doing some odd wiggle-move, he turned around and they continued skiing through the aspen and fir woodland.

Maddie took in a long breath of the below-freezing air, grateful to be here with them, pretty much alone in this magical setting, one of her favorite places on earth.

'Mom,' Nikki called, slowing slightly and drawing up alongside her. 'Which one is Becky's parents' place?' She nodded her head over towards a stone-and-wood mansion not far from the edge of the ski trail.

Maddie shrugged. 'I'm not sure. Somewhere here in The Colony.' She and Michael had been invited to dinner one summer's evening when the kids had been small, but Maddie—for some reason that she could no longer recall—hadn't been able to make it and Michael had gone alone. What she did remember, though, was how much he had gone on about the size and expense of the place. 'Their *second* home,' he had said more than once that evening.

They passed more of the luxury properties, which flew off the real-estate offices' shelves for double-digit millions, until they reached the Daybreak three-person chairlift. With nobody in front of them, they skied into position and waited until the chairlift circled around behind them. Maddie was seated on the end beside Trenton. Was it a coincidence that he had taken the lead down the slopes and was now sitting in Michael's place, taking on his role of making sure everyone was in position before pulling down the safety bar?

'What?' he said.

'*What* what?' she asked.

'You're staring at me weird.'

Maddie smiled. 'Just seeing and appreciating what a fine young man my son is growing up to be.'

Trenton screwed up his face and turned away. 'Woah, did you see that?' he said. 'Snowboarder wiped out big time.'

Maddie sat back and relaxed, enjoying the ever-changing views opening up as the chairlift wound its way up the mountainside. Inexplicably, she felt more relaxed now. She knew exactly which routes Trenton would take them down, where they would stop for a drink and knew that he would get them back over to the parking lot in Mountain Village in good time before the lifts all closed. There was something comforting in knowing that the rest of the day would unfold on indubitable, defined tracks, the very antithesis of the occasion the weekend was marking.

Becky Larkin was resting her chin on her upturned palms, leaning on the veranda rail and watching a group of skiers go past. She had driven up to her parents' second home on White Pine Canyon Road first thing this morning to spend the weekend skiing with them.

'Ready?' her father's voice asked from behind her.

Becky turned to see her mother and father sporting the season's latest skiwear and strapping up their helmets. 'I'm ready.' She glanced over at the run and thought that she saw Maddie with Trenton and Nikki, skiing past the house. She looked more closely. It was them. 'Hey, Maddie!' she shouted, jumping up and down, waving. 'Maddie!'

They didn't hear and continued obliviously down the slope.

'That was Maddie and the kids,' she said to her parents.

'So we gathered,' her mother replied.

'Come on, we'll be able to catch them,' Becky said, making for the steps down to the trail. 'They're going quite slow.'

Her father reached for her arm. 'No…'

Becky looked down at his continuing grip, not understanding. 'What's the matter, Dad?'

'Let's leave them to it,' he said.

'What? Why? She'll be pleased to see you.' Becky glanced at her mother and saw the darkened way in which she was staring at the floor.

'We need to leave them alone, Becky,' her father insisted. 'Let's just go back inside.'

'What?' Becky stammered. 'But…we've come up here to ski! What's going on?'

Her father sighed. 'Think about it, Becky; they're here for some family time…together. It's five years since Michael disappeared. The last thing they want is the three of us invading their space like nothing's happened, you know?'

Becky was surprised by her father's attitude. She was even more surprised that he had remembered that this was the anniversary of Michael's disappearance. Despite the two of them having worked together, she clearly hadn't ever realized the closeness of their friendship being made apparent now by her father's reaction.

Her mother was already undoing and removing her helmet, when her father suggested that they all go inside.

'Can we go back out later, then?' Becky asked, following them to the front door.

'We'll see,' her father answered.

'Why don't I make us all a nice hot chocolate?' her mother suggested brightly, stepping inside the hallway and turning immediately into the spacious room on the right-hand side where all of their sports equipment was stored.

'Great idea,' her father agreed with sudden joviality.

A strange disquieting mood settled on the three of them as they silently hung their jackets and salopettes and placed their ski boots onto the warming rack, leaving Becky feeling as though she were being treated like a kid.

Her father—a well-built, athletic man with graying hair—grinned at her. 'Why don't we play a board game? Or watch a movie?'

Her mother emitted a stilted sound of excited agreement. 'Yes! Something we didn't get around to seeing over the holidays, like…*White Christmas*.'

Her father clapped his hands together, as though some great deal had just been struck. 'Perfect!'

Becky offered an uneasy smile as she followed them into the vast pentagonal-shaped hallway with its heated stone tiles and circular wooden staircase that wound up to the second floor. Her mother strode off to the kitchen, presumably to fix those hot chocolates, while Becky followed her father into the living room, going along with their performance.

She sat down on one of the couches with her legs folded under her and looked out of the tall windows at the blurred figures passing through the pine ski slopes over which the house looked. Her sense of unease continued to well inside of her, although she couldn't firmly attach a reason for it.

'There,' her father said, rubbing his hands together having added some logs to the open fire. He walked across the living room with its high exposed ceilings and rugged stonework on the walls. He could have sat in any one of the six couches that had been strategically positioned around the room by her mother, an interior designer, but he chose to sit right beside Becky. 'You know... I don't think I'll ever tire of that view,' he said, as if trying to intuit her thoughts.

'Hmm.'

'It's taken a lot of work and sacrifice to get us here,' he said, facing her. 'And we don't want to see that undone, now, do we?'

'Here we are!' her mother chirped, entering the room carrying a tray with three steaming cups of hot chocolate.

Becky tried to smile. She stood up, picked up one of the mugs and carried it over to a single armchair across the room. 'Thanks, Mom.' She sipped the drink, then added, 'I think I'll have this and then get back home.'

'Oh,' her mother said, showing disappointment. 'But I thought you were here for the weekend?'

Becky shrugged. 'I thought I was here to ski. Besides, I've actually got quite a lot of work to do.'

Her mother raised her eyebrows. 'She works you too hard, if you ask me.'

The façade—for Becky was certain that that was all it was, a façade—of normality persisted with her father making some syrupy comments about how the hot chocolate was the best he'd ever tasted. From her quiet corner of the room, Becky tried to interpret the unspoken conversation taking place in the looks and body-language exchanges between her parents. Something was amiss, but what that thing was, Becky did not know.

Kenyatta stood on her front path, sobbing. She pulled a tissue from her sleeve and dabbed her eyes as she watched Otis's car disappearing down the street. 'Oh, goodness me!' she said, trying to stifle her pitiful shudders of emotion. She blew her nose and took a deep breath, her eyes failing to see the car any longer. She turned back inside the house and closed the door. Another surge came over her, as the quietness of the house struck her with an almost-physical blow.

It had been the most wonderful Saturday morning that she had had in as long a time as she could remember.

Otis had, as promised, dropped the three boys off first thing and she'd gotten to spend most of the precious day with them. She'd anticipated their arrival with a nervousness that was both unfamiliar and upsetting: initially, she hadn't been sure how to interact with her own children. She had spent an inordinately long time choosing what to wear and a longer time still cleaning up the house.

The agitation had unsettled her bowels and she'd eaten more calories for her breakfast alone than she was permitted for the entire day.

But she needn't have worried. The boys were normal, behaving as though they'd only been gone a few minutes. It was Otis who had been different. He'd kept well back from the house, remaining on the sidewalk with an air of formal detachment; that man in a tan suit, impatiently adjusting his cufflinks, was not the man to whom she had been married for all those years. She'd thanked him genuinely and closed the door, wanting to spend every cherished moment with the boys. Their choice of how to spend those few hours had been 'to hang out,' and Kenyatta had been more than happy to oblige.

Now they were gone again, and the house had attained a new depth of emptiness; the happy cacophony of their laughter and gentle squabbling echoed noisily in her mind.

'Oh,' Kenyatta breathed, managing to bring her tears under control. A tightness across her forehead brought pain behind her eyes, something that she reasoned would be helped by a glass of cold Coke.

She slumped down in her couch with the drink, quite exhausted. She picked up the TV remote and channel-surfed for a while, not giving any one program more than ten seconds to prove its worth to her. Nothing. She switched it off, drank more Coke and took a look at today's *Salt Lake Tribune*. The main headlines were dominated by the state of emergency declared yesterday in Utah by the governor. Lonnie had been right all along; coronavirus *was* looking as though it might become a major problem. She made up her mind to get herself some gloves and masks. Maybe stock up on some essentials, too. She closed the newspaper, deciding to give the rest of her day to her *other* boys. There was something deeply cathartic and satisfying for her to end her day in this way. She went to her bedroom, put on her pajamas and returned to the living room with her laptop.

She opened up the file for *The Boys under the Bridge*, taking a moment to recall where she had got up to. 'That's right, the Bearse family from Ohio,' she muttered to herself. Then she remembered that it was the weekend, meaning that the rest of the team would be returning to work on Monday morning having usually developed their clusters in some significant way or other. Kenyatta inwardly cringed, knowing that it had been she who had initiated what was now seen as a weekly office competition. It had started three months ago, offering her a distraction from the deafening silence of her empty home and to prevent the return of the dark days of her depression. A depression which had been the catalyst for the breakdown of her marriage and had led to Otis' being granted temporary custody of the children. Maddie now even *started* the week with a briefing in the certain knowledge that the majority of the team would have pushed on with their cases sufficiently so as to necessitate a shifting of priorities or other such adjustments that would require a re-issuing of work tasks.

Reluctantly, Kenyatta closed the file for *The Boys under the Bridge* and opened up the speculative family tree that she had created for cluster eight. She had already confirmed that Samuel Lacock and Joanna Hardy from Oregon were the most recent common ancestors for two DNA matches within the cluster. She was confident that, with a little more work, she would be able to link someone else from the cluster to this couple and thus prove that they were another of the Chester Creek killer's great-great-grandparents.

Kenyatta took a swig of Coke and said, 'Alexa, shuffle music by Ella Fitzgerald.'

Alexa obliged with the soft piano tinkling and the opening lyrics of *Miss Otis Regrets*.

'Alexa, skip this song and never play it again.'

The song ended abruptly and the opening trumpet blast of *I'm Beginning to See the Light* filled the room.

'Better,' she said with a grin.

Maddie gasped as she pulled her car onto the driveway, doing an internal dance of joy at the sight of the blue Sedan parked in front of her, which belonged to her eldest daughter, Jenna. 'She's home! Quick!' Maddie said, hurrying Trenton and Nikki out of the car.

Maddie pushed open the front door of the house and called excitedly, 'Jenna! Where's our welcoming committee, for goodness' sake?'

Jenna appeared from the kitchen, rushing at Maddie with her arms spread wide. 'Hi, Mom!'

'Oh, it's good to have you home. You're early, though,' Maddie said, holding her eldest daughter's arms as she took her in. She was almost twenty-three years old and had never looked quite as grown up as she did right in that moment. She was tall with dark-brown eyes and Maddie's crazy blonde hair and curves.

'Surprise!' Jenna said to her, before hugging Nikki and lastly Trenton. 'It's so great to see you all again.'

'It's nice to have a normal sibling in the house,' Nikki said, with a sideways scowl at Trenton.

Trenton screwed up his face, pulled out his cellphone and wandered off into the kitchen.

'So, how was skiing?' Jenna asked. 'Where did you go?'

'Park City,' Nikki answered. 'Amazing as always.'

'I'm jealous as all hell,' Jenna replied with a sigh. 'I need a bit of Park City right now.'

Maddie threw open her arms. 'Then move back home to Utah. What's so great about year-round warmth in Florida, anyway?'

Jenna smiled. 'Well, there is also my boyfriend and my work to consider.'

'Let's go in the kitchen and you can tell me all about both of them,' Maddie said, grabbing her daughter's hand and towing her into the kitchen. 'Have you eaten? We had pizza at Cloud Dine, but now Trenton is starving to death…obviously.'

'I only had a salad at lunchtime.'

'Great, I'll rustle us up some pasta…or something.' As Maddie entered the kitchen, she noticed her mother sitting at the dining table, reading. 'Oh, hi, Mom. Are you okay?'

Her mother looked up from her book and arched one eyebrow. 'Why shouldn't I be?' She switched her gaze to Jenna. 'See what I mean?'

Jenna grinned. 'Grandma was just telling me about the fall she had last week over at Harmons.'

'What?' Maddie said, glancing from Jenna to her mother. 'You didn't have a fall, Mom.' She looked at Jenna. 'It was her friend Elaine who fell over at Harmons.' The moment that Maddie had finished her sentence, she regretted having said it at all; for everyone turned to look at her mom in an accusatory-but-worried fashion.

'I said no such thing,' her mom defended, scowling at Jenna. 'What I said was that my friend *Elaine* had fallen over at Harmons.' She rolled her eyes and said, 'That's the problem with young people today: they just don't listen to their elders.'

The worry was evident in Jenna's eyes, but she rescued the delicate situation and played along. 'You're right, Grandma. I mustn't have been fully concentrating, sorry. I blame the jet lag.'

'You see?' her mom said pointedly at Maddie. 'I'm not going mad.'

She set her book down on the table and removed her glasses. A rant was looming. 'Can either of you name your kindergarten teachers? Well, *I* can. Can either of you remember your first phone number? Because *I* can. Can you all describe your childhood homes, your best friends, the toys you played with? *I*...can.' She took a long breath, glaring at her accusers before resetting her glasses and picking up her book. But she wasn't done and off the glasses came once more. 'My sight and hearing isn't what it once was, I've got some teeth that aren't my own and, yes, I'll admit I'm not as sure-footed as I once was. But up here,'—she tapped her temple with the arm of her glasses—'up here is all in good working order; you don't need to indulge me.'

'It's okay, Mom,' Maddie said. 'Nobody's indulging you.'

'I should hope not,' she answered, placing her glasses back on her nose and resuming her reading.

Maddie shot a knowing look to the kids but dared say nothing. She pulled open the refrigerator. 'Dinner... Pasta and garlic bread, I think?' She pulled out some vegetables and said, 'Tell me about your job, please, Jenna.'

'What is it you *actually* do, Jenna?' Maddie's mom asked.

Jenna grinned. 'I'm a forensic anthropologist, Grandma, specializing in cranial reconstruction.'

'Well, that's as clear as mud to me.'

'So, basically, I work with the University of Florida to help identify unknown remains by reconstructing what the face of a deceased person might have looked like.'

'Oh my... That's a *horrible* job,' her grandma replied.

'It can be, yes,' Jenna agreed with a laugh.

'Where did you two get this unhealthy obsession with death that you both seem to have?' she asked, eyeing Maddie and Jenna suspiciously.

Maddie laughed, beginning to prepare the vegetables. 'It's not an obsession, Mom.'

'Um, yes, it is,' countered Trenton, peering up from his cellphone.

'Okay. Well, maybe it is a little,' Maddie was forced to agree. 'We just both want to help, I guess. What are you working on right now?'

'A difficult one, actually. Half a human skull was discovered in a storm drain a few months back and at the moment we're working to stick it back together again before attempting a digital reconstruction.'

'*Half* a skull?' Nikki asked incredulously.

Jenna nodded. 'We've only got eleven of the twenty-two bones we should have.'

'I think I've had just about enough of all this morbid conversation,' Maddie's mother interjected, standing up from the table. She shuffled from the room, muttering, 'And in front of the kids, too. No wonder…'

'Whoops,' Jenna whispered. 'Should I go after her?'

Maddie shook her head. 'No, leave her. She's really just annoyed that I—stupidly—called her out about telling you she'd had that fall. I've just got to work out how to be more subtle about these things.'

'That would be a first,' Trenton mumbled.

'Have you heard anything back from your insurance company yet about whether they'll cover Grandma's Alzheimer's?' Jenna asked.

'Not yet, no,' Maddie replied, hacking into an onion. 'I've got this horrible feeling that it's just going to be left to us to deal with.'

'Great,' Trenton said, wandering out of the kitchen. 'Guess I should get used to taking the blame for everything around here for a long while yet, then.'

'I'm going to go get changed and grab a shower,' Nikki said.

'Okay, honey. Dinner won't be for a while.'

Once Nikki was out of earshot, Jenna said, 'Grandma definitely did say that it was she who had the fall—she described the bruises on her legs and everything.'

'I'm sure,' Maddie said. 'There's been a definite change in the last few weeks—a fuzziness in her memory.'

'It must be tough for her,' Jenna said.

'Yeah, and on top of that, this weekend is quite an emotional time for us all.'

'How are Trenton and Nikki feeling about tomorrow?' Jenna asked quietly.

'Um, well, you know what they're like; they don't exactly say much. I think it's bothering them a whole lot, though.'

'And…what about you?'

Maddie set down the knife, rested her hands on the counter and stared at her eldest child while she processed the question. 'I don't know,' she finally answered.

Jenna moved towards her and placed a hand down on hers. 'Don't take this the wrong way, Mom, but I've asked Judy, a lawyer friend of mine… And, well, under Utah law you can have Michael declared legally dead, now. It doesn't mean—'

'What?' Maddie interjected, that familiar surge of defensive emotion rising inside. 'No. I'm not going to have Michael declared dead, when I don't have the first clue that he actually *is* dead. He may be out there someplace—'

'I know, fell and banged his head and have amnesia, or run away from home or been kidnapped...' Jenna parroted, mimicking the oft-used phrases by many from the past five years. 'Having him declared dead doesn't mean he actually is.'

'Then what's the point?' Maddie pushed, tears welling in her eyes.

Jenna squeezed her hand. 'To be able to move on.'

'And you think having a piece of paper that says he's *presumed* dead will do that, Jenna?'

'Maybe, yeah.'

'Maybe not,' she muttered. She started cutting a pepper but stopped immediately and met Jenna's eyes. 'There's something I need to tell you. I had a detective guy—someone I'm working with—pull up Michael's file, and yesterday, he told me about a couple of things in there that I was never told at the time of the initial investigation; or at least I don't remember them.'

'Like what?'

Maddie lowered her voice. 'Michael received a phone call just *after* he was last seen pulling into the parking lot at Green River. The call lasted twenty-four seconds, just before his cell was switched off.'

'From who?' Jenna asked.

'From someone at his work.'

'Why didn't they tell you this back then? Did the police try and find out who it was that made the call?'

'I don't know. There's nothing in his file at the National Crime Information Center. But the biggest thing that this detective told me was that no prints were found on Michael's car.'

'Yeah, we knew that already.'

'No. *No* prints were found on his car. As in *none*. Not even Michael's own or any of ours.'

'How's that even possible?'

'It isn't. That's just it. The detective says the car has to have been intentionally wiped clean.'

'Oh my God. But why?'

Maddie shrugged. 'I don't know.'

'So, now what?'

'This detective has suggested getting Michael's car checked again for prints, DNA, whatever.'

'And are you going to do it?'
'I haven't made up my mind yet,' Maddie answered.

Chapter Twenty-Two

Sunday, March 8, 2020, South Jordan, Utah

'Does anybody want something to drink?' Maddie asked, having only just finished her coffee seconds before. She was sitting at the table in the living room, her gaze shifting from her mother to Jenna, to Trenton and finally to Nikki.

Jenna was the only one to offer an answer, the rest merely shook their heads. 'I'm still drinking mine, thank you.'

Maddie nodded, taking in each member of her family, enveloped as they were in a shared cocoon of anticipation, as though Michael might have been biding his time and had chosen today of all days—the fifth anniversary of his disappearance—to reappear magically. The mood was heavy, as though they were sitting in a hospital waiting room, expecting the worst news of a loved one's plight.

'What about food? Anyone hungry?' Maddie asked, trying to sound normal.

'I'll have a cookie,' her mother said, looking up momentarily from her sewing.

Maddie stood up with great enthusiasm for the basic task of walking into the kitchen and getting her mother a cookie. 'Trenton? Do you want anything?'

He silently shook his head.

While in the kitchen, Maddie looked for something else to do. The counters were clean and tidy, thanks to Jenna. The dishwasher had been loaded and the floors were vacuumed. It was too early to think about dinner, plus she presumed that everybody was experiencing the same churning of their insides, as was she. She tried to think back to this time last year. What did they do? She had a feeling that it had gone unmentioned in the run-up to the actual day and life had continued awkwardly through it. It was peculiar, she thought—as she labored over opening up the box of cookies and neatly arranging them on a plate—that the fifth anniversary should hold a greater significance than the fourth, sixth or seventh; the next big one would be ten. God, that would really be a grim milestone to reach without any new information.

It hadn't helped that she'd slept terribly. She'd spent the entire night ruminating over what the detective had told her in her office on Friday. 'No. I don't think you get it, Maddie,' he'd said. 'There were *no* prints found on the car. As in, none whatsoever; zilch. Someone wiped the car clean and did a good job of it, by all accounts.' And then there was the mysterious phone call, just before his cell was switched off. For the past five years various narratives had played out in her mind about what might have befallen him, but they all started with him arriving at Green River, parking—as a witness had reported—switching off his cell and then…

In none of her fantasy imaginings did she see someone remove all trace of themselves and him. Why would they do that? The answer left her feeling nauseous because it removed the improbable but benign possibilities to which the family had been clinging: Michael could not have suffered a head injury and now be living in some state of amnesia unaware of his real identity; he could not have upped and left his old life, for there was nothing to be gained in this scenario by removing his own fingerprints from his own car; it also removed the chance of his having been the unfortunate victim of an accident, like drowning or slipping from a rock or his boat getting into difficulties in the rapids of the Green River. The only possibilities that now remained were wholly and terrifyingly sinister.

'Shall I take those through to Grandma?' Jenna asked from the doorway, startling her.

'Oh. Yes, thank you,' Maddie said, sliding the plate of cookies over to her daughter.

'Do you think you should tell Trenton and Nikki?' Jenna said quietly, correctly intuiting the matter dominating Maddie's thoughts. 'About the new information, I mean.'

Maddie blew a puff of air from her cheeks. 'I don't know. I don't know how.'

'Do you want me to do it?'

Maddie shook her head. 'I'll do it, but not right now.' She met Jenna's eyes. 'Could you watch them today, if I went somewhere?'

'Sure. Where do you want to go?'

'Green River,' Maddie answered. She'd never dared go there since his disappearance, having never had the desire or the mental capacity. Now, though, a shift had occurred in her mind. Whether it was this new information or the significance of the anniversary, something was compelling her to go and visit the site.

'That's like…three hours' drive,' Jenna pointed out.

'Yeah, I know.'

'Do you really think it's a good idea?' Jenna probed. 'I mean, what are you going to do when you get there, anyway?'

Maddie shrugged. She honestly had no idea.

'Why don't we all go?'

Maddie considered Jenna's suggestion. 'I don't think the kids will want to spend three hours in the car just to go and see the place where their father disappeared, then spend another three hours driving home.'

'Maybe ask them?'

Maddie straightened up and entered the living room.

'Were you all that time baking them, or what?' her mom asked.

'What?' Maddie replied.

'The cookies. Oh, thank you, Jenna,' she said, taking one from the plate. 'I only wanted one, not the whole box. You can leave them just there.'

'Kids,' Maddie began, shoving her hands into the back pockets of her jeans and raising her shoulders almost to her ears in discomfort, 'Um… I was wondering. I would maybe like to take a drive down to Green River today. You're welcome to come along or… I don't know, stay here. It's probably a dumb idea, but—'

'It's a great idea, Mom,' Nikki interrupted, her expression and demeanor visibly lifting from the melancholy of the occasion so far.

'I'll come,' Trenton agreed, snatching two cookies from the plate.

'Green River?' her mother parroted. 'What on earth do you think you're going to do down there? Look for him?'

'No, Mom. I'm not going to look for him.' She shrugged. 'For the first time, I just want to see the place. I've imagined it, Googled pictures of it, but never actually been there. But I… I actually think now might be the right time.'

'Seems like a big *waste* of time…and gas, if you ask me.'

'Let's go,' Trenton said, standing up.

Hudson Édouard was strolling along North Temple with his wife, Abigail, at his side. She slipped her arm through his and said, 'What's up, Huds?'

He smiled. 'Oh, nothing. Just daydreaming.'

She squeezed his arm. 'Come on. You've been quiet for the past few days, now. What's wrong? What's going on with you?'

'A work conundrum… An ethical thing,' he replied cryptically.

'Tell me,' she said, pulling him to a stop.

'It's complicated.'

'How about I buy us lunch at the Red Iguana, and you tell me all about it?' she pushed, pointing at the restaurant just ahead of them.

Hudson took in a breath. It probably was time to bring her into his confidence. Ever since Wanda Chabala had accosted him outside work on Thursday, their discussion had dominated his thoughts but without producing any kind of a resolution to the matter.

They sat at a quiet table at the back of the restaurant and ordered two chicken burritos. Hudson folded his arms and began, 'So, do you remember seeing a case in the news a few years back: a guy, Brandon Blake, being convicted of murdering Francesca Chabala in Minneapolis?'

Abigail looked blankly at him. 'Should I?'

'No. He was convicted based on a confession that he gave, despite DNA evidence not linking him to the crime.'

'Right,' Abigail said.

Hudson was aware that she was watching passers-by outside the window, not fully engaged in what he was telling her. He needed to cut to the chase. 'Francesca's mom came to see me after work on Thursday, wanting me to get Brandon Blake out of jail.'

Abigail stared at him, open-mouthed. 'What? The person who killed her daughter?'

'She's watched all the police interviews. And...with the DNA sample not matching Brandon, plus the fact that he's since recanted his confession, she wants me to help her find out who it was who *did* kill her daughter.'

'Okay,' she said, anticipating more.

'She wants me to do it personally. Not Venator,' he clarified. 'Which is the crux of the problem that I'm having real trouble resolving.'

'Does it matter if you undertake private work? I mean, if you did it at home and didn't use your work time? What's the big deal?'

Hudson lowered his voice. 'The big deal is that the police aren't going to simply hand over the DNA sample. She's getting it via some other...non-legal method. Anything I find, therefore, will also have to be outside of law enforcement. So, I find the guy's name and hand it to her. Then what?'

'I see,' Abigail said. 'Don't take it on, then.'

Hudson looked at his wife, confident that she now understood the problem: he could potentially be providing some shady hitman with his next job. There was more to tell, though, to help her to understand why his indecision was weighing on him so. 'She—Wanda Chabala—

has offered me good money to help her.'

'Okay,' Abigail ventured. 'I'm going to ask: how much money?'

Hudson took a breath, lowered his voice to a whisper and said, 'Fifty thousand dollars.'

'What?' she shrieked, her eyes widening at the thought of the luxuries that the money could afford them, before realization kicked in and settled her mind onto the one thing on which they both knew the money would be spent. 'That would cover the cost of adoption.'

Hudson nodded, still finding it a striking coincidence that Wanda Chabala had offered him that sum, when the average cost of adopting a child stood at forty-three thousand dollars.

'Wow. Hudson,' she said, squeezing his hand across the table.

At that moment a waiter brought out their food. 'Two chicken burritos? Enjoy!'

They managed to thank him but sat in silence, looking at each other as the gravity of the decision swelled between them; an alternative universe, which had existed only in shared fantasy, was now presenting itself as a real, tangible possibility.

'Come on, already!' Trenton said. 'I'm bursting, here.'

'Maybe you should have gone at the gas station like we all did, instead of sleeping the whole way here, then,' Nikki scolded.

'Well, we're here now,' Maddie said, pulling into the large parking lot of the Flaming Gorge Visitor Center. She slowed the car to a crawl and stopped directly outside the Visitor Center building. Before she had even switched off the engine, Trenton leapt out of the back and was making a desperate dash for the long oblong building.

'I'm going to stretch my legs,' Nikki said with a yawn, stepping out of the car.

'Three and a half hours,' Maddie said, with a sideways glance to Jenna. 'And what for, exactly?'

Jenna shrugged. 'I think it was the right thing to do, though, if only to have something meaningful to help pass the day. Come on,' she said, patting Maddie on the thigh. 'Let's get some air, too.'

Maddie got out of the car and stretched as she took in her surroundings which, she had to admit, were pretty stunning. The parking lot overlooked the wide expanse of the Green River and, on the opposite side, hills of rolling deep-red rock. She could see why Michael had liked to come here. Not that he'd been seen in this actual place, but why would he need to stop at the Visitor Center? He'd made this trip dozens of times previously—he was hardly likely to go in to pick up a map and ask for information about the area.

The journey here had passed in easy conversation punctuated by long spells of silence: they had talked about Jenna's boyfriend's having moved in with her, despite Maddie's having yet to meet him; about the picturesque scenery through which they had passed; and about Maddie's mom's slowly deteriorating condition. They had talked about everything except for Michael, his disappearance and what they were going to do when they finally got here. Maddie had thought about picking up some fresh flowers from the gas station to lay at the spot but thought better of it, convincing herself that such a gesture would only amplify the effect of the new information that she had yet to impart to the kids.

An email alert sounded from her cellphone and Maddie pulled it out to take a look. She smiled when she saw that it was from the detective.

Hi Maddie. Just wanted to say that I hope today goes as well as it can under the circumstances. Clayton

She smiled and pocketed the phone just as Trenton reappeared, shielding his eyes from the sun, as he watched a light aircraft coming in to land at a small airfield nearby. 'Just looked at a map. The spillway is just across the dam, then first right down to the water,' he informed them.

'Great,' Maddie replied. 'Shall we?'

The family got back inside the car and Maddie pulled out, turned left onto the road and crossed over the Flaming Gorge Dam, arcing around until they passed a small brown sign with white writing that read RIVER ACCESS with an arrow pointing to the right.

With an unsettled nervousness in her stomach, Maddie indicated, pulled off the road and then began the winding descent to the water's edge.

'Wow!' Nikki said, as the road reached a hairpin bend, facing directly towards the base of the dam from where a tumult of bubbling white water was spewing.

Maddie took a hard left turn and descended further into the ravine. She slowed the car down, seeing the small parking lot that signified the end of the road drawing nearer. Her heart began to thump as she parked in the very spot that she recalled seeing in the photographs from the initial investigation. A man, hiking with his young son, had remembered seeing Michael parking his car here and stepping out of the vehicle. After that, he had apparently taken a phone call, then vanished into thin air.

'Is this it?' Nikki asked quietly.

Maddie nodded. 'Yeah, this is it.' She opened her car door and slowly stepped out. They were surrounded on all sides by the dark green pines that rose impossibly from the cracks and crevices of the carmine-red rocks.

The four of them formed a loose group, moving instinctively down to where the road narrowed and seamlessly became the boat slip, finally disappearing beneath the Green River. Michael's talk of having to navigate the rapids here must have been referring to much further downstream, for Maddie could not perceive that the wide river was even moving at all.

As they reached the water's silent edge, Jenna placed her arm over Maddie's shoulder and Trenton, with one arm threaded through Nikki's, held her hand.

'Kids,' Maddie said, holding back her tears, 'there's something I need to tell you about your father's disappearance.'

Chapter Twenty-Three

Monday, March 9, 2020, Downtown Salt Lake City, Utah

'Good morning, everyone!' Maddie said, striding into the main Venator office with a brightness that took even her by surprise. Considering the significance of the weekend that had just passed and a late one last night, she had slept well and woken with a surge of positivity. The team greeted her from their desks as she took center stage in front of the three investigation boards. 'I hope you've all had a restful weekend and *not* been working on the Chester Creek case,' she said. 'But'—she glanced at each of the team's desks—'I can see some orange slips…and a purple one, wow! Well done, Becky! Ross—are you ready to take notes?' He nodded and pulled up a chair beside Becky, with a pen and pad resting on his crossed legs. 'Good. Okay. So, who wants to start the ball rolling?'

Hudson raised his hand. 'I will.'

'The floor is all yours,' Maddie said, taking a step to the side.

Hudson shared his computer screen on the digital whiteboard. It was the top of one branch of a family tree. Following a dramatic sigh, he ran his cursor around the two names and said, 'These two lovely people, John Minchin and Caroline Marsh, are the common ancestors for cluster *nine*.' He waved the orange slip of paper that he had completed for the couple in the air above him.

'Woah,' Kenyatta said. 'Cluster nine looked pretty-well impossible—well done, Hudson. Bravo.'

'Yeah, it wasn't easy,' he continued, 'but Abigail was working all day Saturday and I just kinda got lost in it. Stayed in my PJs all day.' Hudson pointed at the speculative family tree being shown on the big screen. 'What's interesting about these two is that they lived in Pennsylvania—about fifty miles out from Chester Creek.'

'Good work, Hudson,' Maddie said. 'That looks promising.'

'Thanks,' he replied, walking over and fixing the orange paper to the whiteboard alongside the others.

'Kenyatta?' Maddie said, having seen a similar slip on her desk.

Kenyatta stood up, displaying her screen for the team. 'So, as I thought on Friday, this couple, Samuel Lacock and Joanna Hardy, are the common ancestors for cluster eight. So far, though, I don't have any links for them outside of Oregon state.' She held aloft her orange slip. 'But, it's another one of these completed. So, it's all good.'

'Well done,' Maddie congratulated. 'So, we've now identified *half* of the Chester Creek killer's great-great-great-grandparents. Not bad for a week's work, guys. Becky, did you listen to me and take the weekend off?'

Becky stood up and shook her head. 'I did work a little,' she said, while she squeezed an inch of air between her thumb and forefinger. 'I couldn't *not* after what I said at the briefing on Friday afternoon, where I thought I'd found that Watson Schenck and Martha Trent were the common ancestors for cluster four. Well, that *was* correct. So, they're now on an orange slip.' Becky clicked to mirror her screen on the whiteboard, showing Watson, Martha and their children. She moved over to the board, picked up the green pen and drew a rough circle around their son, Job Schenck. 'This guy, right here, married a Grace Burbee who was the daughter of Hudson's Thomas and Margaret Burbee. So,' she continued, holding up a purple slip of paper for the investigation, 'we now have the first of the Chester Creek killer's great-great-grandparents in the bag.'

Maddie offered a small clap, resuming control of the briefing. 'Well done, Becky. Great work. This is amazing. So, I need to confess something: I didn't actually do *any* work this—' she paused, as she noted the fact that Becky was still standing by the whiteboard, hand on hip, with a look of mock-outrage. 'Becky?'

'I hadn't quite finished,' she said with a cute smile, holding up a blue slip of paper.

'What?' Kenyatta gasped.

'No way!' Hudson exclaimed.

'Please,' Maddie said, 'continue. My *sincerest* apologies for interrupting prematurely.'

Becky cleared her throat dramatically. 'It was actually a sort of accidental luck, to be honest. I was filling out the children of Job and Grace Schenck from the 1900 Census, one of whom was a fourteen-year-old girl by the name of Rosanna.' Becky touched the screen to bring up the family. 'And…living in the same house was a boarder, going by the name of Roland Crowder, from Virginia.'

'Ah!' Maddie said, spotting the link.

'Yes,' Becky confirmed. 'So, I did a little more digging and found that Roland Crowder married Rosanna Schenck and, consequently, they are one of four of the Chester Creek killer's great-grandparent couples.'

'That's amazing, Becky,' Maddie enthused. 'It's a game-changer for the week ahead. Go stick the *three* pieces of paper up on the board.'

'Two great-grandparents down, six to go,' Kenyatta commented.

Maddie watched as Becky stepped to the whiteboard and stuck the purple slip below the run of orange slips and the blue one below that. With more work and a bit of luck, those slips of paper would create an inverted pyramid, hopefully terminating with the name of the Chester Creek killer.

'Our investigation has now reached the tipping point,' Maddie began, 'where we move into the reverse-genealogy phase. Becky, since you found them, I want you to continue working on Roland and Rosanna Crowder—fill them out, find their kids, grandkids and great grandkids. Hudson—' she strode over to the whiteboard containing the completed slips of colored paper '—I want you to continue with finding as many descendants as you can from your cluster one, Harry and Isabella White. They're in West Deptford, literally across the water from Chester Creek. There *must* be a link coming pretty soon. Kenyatta—' Maddie turned back to the whiteboard and studied it for a moment, before spinning back to face her '—I'd like you to pick up with Theodore and Carrie Scharder. Again, they're close by in Lancaster County. How many miles away did you say that was from Chester Creek?'

'Twenty-something,' Kenyatta answered. 'Not far.'

'I, however, will be working on cluster six, since I'm the only one who has not closed down both of their genetic networks. I'll be in my office, if anyone needs me. Great work, everyone.'

The team instantly got on with the task in hand as Maddie returned to her office. She pushed the door closed and slumped into her chair with a deep exhalation: really, the weekend had taken its toll on her. She clicked to open her emails, scrolling down to the one sent by the detective, yesterday.

Hi Maddie. Just wanted to say that I hope today goes as well as it can under the circumstances. Clayton

She hadn't replied yet. She looked at the screen, thinking.

Dear Detective,

No, that sounded too formal. That was the language she used in her work. Delete.

Hi Clayton, Thanks for your thoughts. Yesterday was tough, but we got through it, thank you. The kids and I headed down to

Too much information. Delete. Delete.

Clayton, Thank you for thinking of us. It was a hard day and I'm glad it's over, to be honest. After much late-night deliberation with my eldest daughter, I've decided to go ahead with your suggestion of getting Michael's truck re-analyzed for fingerprints and DNA. Please could you advise of how to proceed? The Chester Creek case is progressing well; we have identified the first pair of his great-grandparents. Will be in touch. Kind regards, Maddie

She reread the email and removed the reference to the case, not wishing to get his hopes up. She hit send and it was gone.

What she had written in the email had been true: she and Jenna had stayed up late, discussing Michael, once Nikki and Trenton had gone to bed. Whether it was Jenna's age or the fact that she wasn't Michael's daughter, something made the conversation less laden with emotions than with the younger two present. They talked about the possible repercussions of having his truck checked again. The only negative that they had been able to come up with was the impact on Trenton and Nikki, having to have everything potentially dredged up all over again. The more Maddie thought about it, though, the more she accepted that there was no way that she could rest in light of the new knowledge that had come from the detective.

Even though her emails were set to automatically download to her inbox, Maddie clicked refresh to see if the detective might have replied already. He hadn't. So, she pulled up the file of names compiled for cluster six. The lead name for this genetic network was Keith Spencer, a man who shared forty-two centiMorgans of DNA with the Chester Creek killer. There were just five others within the cluster, who all likely shared the same ancestral couple. Just one of these five people had a limited family tree, but none of the names on it linked to anyone that the team had thus far identified. A well-sourced mirror tree, which Maddie had copied from one online, had proven to be very accurate so far, helping her to quickly identify all sixteen of Keith Spencer's paternal great-great-great-grandparents. Halfway there.

Now Maddie needed to focus on Keith Spencer's maternal side.

Assuming that his mother, Marsha Klein, had been born around the same time as his father, Maddie estimated the date of her birth to have been around 1945. A short newspaper report into Keith's marriage had stated that his parents had resided in Newport, Rhode Island. So, Maddie selected *Rhode Island Town Clerk Vital and Town Records 1630-1945* from the FamilySearch website, entering the known details for Marsha Klein.

0 Results

Nothing.

Maddie pulled up Keith Spencer's family tree that she was working on, clicking on the information for his parents' marriage. She realized at that moment that she hadn't actually run a search herself for Keith Spencer's parents' marriage. She opened up Newspapers.com and looked for mention of their 1963 wedding.

1 Match

She read the article in the *Newport Mercury*, making notes on the family names mentioned therein.

The marriage of Miss Marsha Klein, daughter of Mr. and Mrs. Joseph Klein of Cumberland Hill, to Gregory Spencer, son of Mr. and Mrs. James Spencer of 50 Lee Ave., Newport, took place today in St Joan of Arc Church in Cumberland Hill.

Given in marriage by her father, the bride had her younger sister, Miss Lucille M. Klein, as maid of honor...

Maddie skimmed over the details of the groom and his family, transcribing two more pertinent details.

...ushers were Terrence Klein and Raymond Klein, elder brothers of the bride...

Maddie added the names of the two brothers to the tree and then opened the BeenVerified background check website, running a person search for Marsha Spencer, adding her approximate age and the location of Rhode Island.

We found 1 name match for Marsha Spencer

She scrolled down the page, scribing the personal details of Marsha as she went but not yet certain that she had found the correct person. The website provided Marsha's phone numbers, home address, email address, the car she drove and then a list of her relatives; her husband being listed as Gregory Spencer. The correct addendum to his name in red lettering *Deceased at age 63 on May 03, 2008* informed Maddie that she had categorically found the right person. Under the *Social Media* tab, there were two entries: Facebook and Rivoters.com. Maddie clicked the latter link. The website was for *Registered voters in the State of Rhode Island and Providence Plantations, USA.*

Maddie followed the link through to the details presented.

June 28, 2019: Marsha Spencer was born March 13, 1945 and she registered to vote, giving her address as 32 Commonwealth Ave, Newport, Rhode Island and Providence Plantations. Party affiliation: D

Although the website didn't help Maddie to push backwards in her family tree, it did provide a precise date of birth and further confirmation that she was indeed the correct person.

Next, Maddie went to the suggested Facebook profile page for Marsha. She could instantly tell that it was seldom used. However, after a couple of minutes spent mining the page, she had found one of her brothers, Raymond Klein, among her friends list. Raymond's profile, thankfully open to the public, was very active and it only took Maddie twenty minutes of sifting through his timeline to find a selection of old family photos that he'd scanned, uploaded and shared with the world.

Maddie grinned as she opened a photograph of a small gathering of people, clustered around a central couple with their hands clasped around a knife that had evidently just been plunged into a cake. The caption provided by Raymond Klein was *Mom and Pop's golden wedding party, April 13, 1985.* Below the caption he had added a who's who of the featured guests, naming his parents as Joseph and Jayne Klein.

Maddie downloaded the photograph, added it to the family tree that she was building and then added their wedding date of 1935.

In a new tab, Maddie opened the 1940 US Census, running a search for the Klein family by using the information that she had just obtained. She quickly found Joseph and Jayne, living with their two sons, Raymond and Terrence, in Newport, Rhode Island. She saved the information to the tree, then began to wade backwards through the various censuses and vital records, easily pushing the Klein family back into the nineteenth century.

A few hours later, being lost in the task, there was a gentle knock at Maddie's door. It was Kenyatta, pulling on her jacket. 'I'm heading out to get some lunch. Want anything?'

'No. I'm good, thank you,' Maddie replied. 'How are you getting on out there?'

Kenyatta smiled wryly. 'I don't want to speak too soon, but good, I think. Are we having a briefing this afternoon?'

Maddie thought for a moment. She didn't usually hold one on a Monday morning *and* afternoon unless something significant had arisen that necessitated a change in direction for the investigation. She hadn't been made aware of anything pressing. Besides which, she wanted time to play catch-up to the rest of the team, which she was unlikely to do in the few hours left before she would need to hold any briefing. 'I don't think so at this point, no,' she answered noncommittally.

'Okay, see you shortly.'

'See you in a while.' Maddie stood up, stretched and then wandered out to the kitchen area. She set the machine to make her a fresh coffee and, as it was being made, took a leisurely walk around the office. 'Ross,' she said with gusto, leaning on his desk.

'Yes, ma'am!' he answered.

'Have you got anything for me?'

'Um…' Ross frowned at his screen. 'Yes, actually, an enquiry from a detective in Twin Falls, Idaho, has just come in. I don't think it's one you'll want, though: it's a *live* case.'

'What do you mean, *live*?'

Ross pushed his face closer to his computer screen and read the details. 'Detective Maria González has been working on a homicide that has just turned into a serial-killer case. It's not cold; his most recent victim was…two weeks ago.'

'Jesus,' Maddie muttered. 'Forward it to me, would you?'

'Done,' Ross confirmed.

'Thank you. Anything from Detective Tyler?'

Ross shook his head, taking a confirmatory glance at his inbox, just to be sure. 'Are we expecting something more?'

'No.' Maddie shook her head and wandered over towards Hudson, resolving to give the detective a call, if he had not emailed back by the time she returned to her desk. 'How's it going?' she asked Hudson, resting against his chair.

'Oh,' he said, clearly taken aback. He minimized the browser in which he had been working, but not before Maddie had caught sight of the fact that he had been using his personal Gmail account.

'It's okay. It's lunchtime,' Maddie felt the need to say, touching his shoulder. 'You can do whatever you want. It's your time. Goodness knows, Venator takes enough of yours.'

'No, it's just…' he began. 'I… Yes, I've made some progress but not enough to call a briefing over.' He must have realized that he sounded bullish and quickly added a fake titter to the end of his sentence.

Maddie gave a smile as she headed towards Becky, all the while wondering how it was that she knew the name Wanda Chabala, whom Hudson had been in the process of emailing. 'Becky, how's your morning been? Ready to complete a *green slip* of paper yet?'

Becky laughed. 'Not quite. I've got most vital records for Roland and Rosanna Crowder's kids; *ten* of them, would you believe? Typical. I'm now working down each of those kids, finding their marriages and *their* kids. No familiar names, as yet.'

'You've done really well on this case, Becky. Well done,' Maddie praised.

'Thank you.'

Maddie headed back over to the kitchen area, calling generally, 'Does anybody want a hot drink? Speak now or forever hold your peace.'

Becky, Hudson and Ross declined the offer, so Maddie picked up her freshly made coffee and returned to her office, pushing the door closed behind her. She refreshed her emails. Nothing from the detective, so she picked up her phone and dialed his number. Voicemail. She considered leaving a message but thought better of it and ended the call. At the top of her inbox was the email that Ross had just mentioned from a Detective Maria González. Even though Ross had given her the case in a nutshell, she read the email carefully, then sat back in her chair, cradling her coffee, mulling. Venator had never been offered a live case before, so Maddie had never had cause to consider the implications of this. Her initial reaction was that, yes, they could help. But what about her team? None of them had had any law-enforcement training and she was concerned, too, about what the pressure of a live case might do to them; they already worked ridiculous hours outside of the office of their own volition. They'd never sleep.

She decided that the decision shouldn't be hers alone: once Kenyatta had returned, she would seek the opinion of the rest of the team.

She took a drink of her coffee, momentarily distracted by Hudson's laughing at something outside. She remembered his defensiveness just now. What was the name of the person whom he had been emailing? Wanda Chapala? Chabela? She typed the name into Google.

Did you mean Wanda Chabala?

Yes, that was what she had meant. She began to recall the details of the high-profile murder case, as it appeared in front of her. The only thing making it high-profile, set against all the hundreds of other daily murders that occurred in the US, was that the murder victim's mother, Wanda Chabala, was currently fighting to get the man—found guilty of her daughter's rape and murder—exonerated. Why was Hudson emailing *her*? As she had told him, what he did at lunchtime was his own business. And yet, there was something about his contacting her that was troubling. He'd never mentioned her or the case before and she doubted very much that they were friends or even acquaintances. And his behavior had been odd. For now, she decided to do nothing but sit tight.

From the main office came Kenyatta's incredulous high-pitched voice. 'No hand-sanitizer left in Walgreens, no face masks and no gloves! Nothing!'

Maddie strolled out, clutching her coffee.

'Maybe your homeless guy will share the ones you got him?' Becky suggested.

Kenyatta shrugged off her coat. 'He was right, though, wasn't he? Look at what's happening in Europe right now. Honestly...'

Maddie waited until Kenyatta was sitting at her desk with her rant over, then addressed the team. 'Could I have a moment, please? I've had an inquiry from a detective in Twin Falls, Idaho, who wants us to consider taking on a *live* serial-killer case. And...I wondered what your thoughts might be on the matter?' She briefly outlined the email and then asked for their feedback.

'I'm *really* up for that,' Becky said eagerly. 'Count me right in.'

'Me too,' Hudson agreed. 'That would be amazing.'

'Absolutely!' Kenyatta added. 'We'd be like *real* detectives.'

'I thought you'd all say that,' Maddie said with a wry smile. 'Thank you.'

Maddie drank more coffee, then returned to her office. She opened the email from Detective Maria González and replied with the standard Venator response that she used when she declined to take on a case. The team's reaction had been exactly as she had anticipated: they would doubtless work tirelessly, putting the case above everything else in their entire lives, until it was concluded and the perp was captured, but Maddie wasn't prepared to shoulder that level of responsibility.

Finishing her coffee, she returned to her work on cluster six. So far, she had identified twenty-four of Keith Spencer's thirty-two great-great-great-grandparents. She clicked on Keith's maternal great-great-grandfather, a man with the delightful name of Stanley Sydney Stables, born in Nevada in 1873.

On the FamilySearch website, Maddie found birth records for the state, covering the approximate year of his birth. Typing in his details, she received one hit:

Nevada State Board of Health
Bureau of Vital Statistics

Name: Stanley Sydney Stables
Place of Birth: Carson Valley, Douglas Co., Nevada
Date of Birth: Nov. 16, 1873
Father Full Name: Elwood Sydney Stables
Mother Full Maiden Name: Mary Fredericka Valentino

Maddie paused. Valentino. She'd definitely come across that name during the research into this case. Accessing the shared drive on the computer, she opened the list of associated names that Ross kept up to date from each briefing. The names were arranged in various ways, but Maddie scrolled directly to the alphabetized version. Nothing for Valentino. If she *had* come across the name, then it must have been through her own research that she hadn't shared with the team.

She thought for a moment, her mind insisting that the name had appeared in a family tree somewhere. She returned to the FamilyTreeDNA website and filtered the cousin matches so that it was only displaying cluster six. Just one of the cluster members had included a family tree. She clicked to view it and, sure enough, found that the person's great-great-grandmother had been named as Mary Fredericka Valentino.

Yes! She had just found the probable common ancestors for cluster six.

Before she set to work confirming that the Stables family provided one half of the common ancestral couple, by linking one other person from the cluster to that family, Maddie wanted to add the rest of Elwood and Mary Stables's children. If she was right, then one of their children would have to be the killer's great-great-grandparents.

Fortunately for Maddie, there were only four other children to work up. She started to look at the hints, suggested by the Ancestry algorithms, for one Samuel Thomas Stables. She paused when she saw a possible suggestion for whom he had married: Sarah Emily Minchin.

Maddie stood up and marched out into the main office, heading over to the whiteboard, hurriedly scanning the names on the orange slips of paper. *John Minchin and Caroline Marsh from Pennsylvania.* Hudson's weekend discovery, she recalled.

'Hudson,' Maddie said. 'I've got a Minchin appearing as a possible link to cluster six. Samuel Thomas Stables married to a Sarah Emily Minchin. Ring any bells?' She looked over at him to see that he was partway through completing a purple slip of paper. 'Sorry to interrupt this important moment.'

'That's okay. Just filling it in for Darnell Garrick and Louisa Jane White from New Jersey,' he said, finishing up and then typing something into his computer, which he shared on the digital whiteboard behind Maddie. 'Okay, so that's the family.'

Maddie scrutinized the family tree. John and Caroline Minchin had had three children: George Joseph, John Jr. and Sarah Emily. 'And there she is!'

'Is that a purple slip, as well?' Kenyatta asked incredulously.

'If I can confirm it all, yes,' Maddie answered with a grin, hurrying back to her office to try and substantiate her findings.

Waiting unread at the top of her inbox was an email from Detective Clayton Tyler...with URGENT typed in the subject line.

With a slight uncharacteristic tremble affecting her hands, Maddie clicked to open the email.

'Well, nobody's touched it since it was towed back here,' Maddie said, hours later, standing in the stark, white strip-lighting in her double garage. With her hands on her hips, she was staring at Michael's black Ford Explorer.

'Then I guess it should be easy enough to re-check it for prints,' Jenna commented, standing beside her.

'I don't know why, but I'm feeling pretty nervous about having it done.'

'It's understandable, Mom. It does have the potential of providing an answer.'

'And…not necessarily one we want to hear,' Maddie muttered. 'I guess that's the problem: at least the purgatory we've been living in these past years left us some room for hope.'

Jenna placed her arm around Maddie. 'We'll get through it, whatever happens.'

Maddie closed her eyes and wrestled with her emotions so as not to cry. 'It's been so great having you home, you know. I really wish you didn't have to leave tonight.'

'I know but I've got to return to my life in Florida; to Rick and to my job. But I'll be back and I'm always at the end of the phone. And you should totally come visit—with or without the kids. Take a break.'

Maddie laughed. 'Oh, yeah. I could leave them with Grandma.'

Jenna laughed and squeezed her shoulder. 'So, when are the CSI coming to sweep the truck?'

'Tomorrow. I'm going to be working from home in the afternoon while they're here… Well, trying to, at least.'

Maddie gazed at the truck, willing it to give her some answers. Thanks to the detective, just maybe, after all these years, it would finally offer something up and reveal what had happened down there at Green River.

Chapter Twenty-Four

Tuesday, March 10, 2020, Downtown Salt Lake City, Utah

Becky Larkin was feeling positive as she bounced into the Venator office, holding the decaf latte that she'd just picked up from across the street at Eva's. Outside, the snow had pretty much melted and the sun was shining, all of which had enabled her to run the four and a half miles to work this morning.

Ross shook his head as she entered the office. 'You've got just too much energy, Becks. It's really not normal.'

'I've got to stay in shape,' she answered, removing her backpack. 'Do you remember that guy I was telling you about that I met at The Front; Jerome?'

'Sure. I remember. What was it, now? Let me see. Oh yeah, that's right. You touched his sloper?' Ross said with a laugh.

Becky made a *not-funny* face. 'Well, he's texted me and wants to go out on a date.'

Ross's eyebrows performed a small dance of excited curiosity. 'Details, Miss Larkin. Details.'

She pulled out her cellphone. 'We're going out tonight, which, as first dates go, could be the best of my entire life. Get this: he suggested we go to The Front for a climb and then—'

'Wait. He wants to go *climbing* on your first date?' Ross interjected.

Becky nodded emphatically. 'Hell, yes. And then dinner. I mean, is that not just—'

'Weird.'

'Perfect. I was about to say,' Becky countered. 'Anyway, you're just jealous.'

Ross turned his nose up. 'Of a fit, athletic, good-looking twenty-year-old..? Yeah, I am, actually.'

Becky pouted and headed over to her desk. 'Morning, Kenyatta,' she greeted.

'Good morning, honey,' Kenyatta replied.

Becky fired up her computer and sat at her desk, sipping her drink as she thought with nervous excitement about her upcoming evening. But first, as her awakening computer reminded her, she had a lot of work to achieve in the meantime.

'Morning,' Hudson said, arriving at his desk. 'No Maddie, yet?'

Becky swiveled in her chair, not having realized that Maddie was not already at the office.

'Not yet. I guess she's stuck in traffic,' Kenyatta said. 'I opened up this morning.'

'That's not like her,' Becky said.

'Yeah, but with all that's going on…' Kenyatta said with a shrug.

'What *is* going on?' Becky asked. 'With the Michael situation, I mean? I just feel like something's happening.'

'Yes, something *is* happening.'

The voice came from behind Becky, making her flush with embarrassment. She swung her chair around again to be confronted by Maddie. 'Sorry. It's really, so none of my business. I was just concerned for you is all.'

Maddie smiled. 'I know that. It's fine. I'll just get myself ready, and I'll come back and tell you all what's going on with me.'

Becky watched with embarrassment as Maddie walked off into her office.

'Awkward,' Hudson whispered.

Becky nodded, thinking it probably best not to say anything else. She opened up the family tree that she had been working on for Roland and Rosanna Crowder and their ten children. So far, she had also identified twelve of Roland and Rosanna's grandchildren, one of whom could be the killer's father or mother. Always, without fail, when she reached this point in a case, the reality of the situation re-presented itself. After the initial debrief by the detective in charge of each case, where the victims' demise was always explained in graphic detail, the process of genetic genealogy was necessarily detached and almost clinical in its undertaking, as the team sieved through hundreds of potential names; knowing the majority of them to have nothing whatsoever to do with the killer. But here in front of her were the names—some with photographs—of twelve people who could have created the child that went on to rape and murder at least three young women.

'Okay, if I can just have five minutes,' Maddie said, entering the office with a coffee. She took a breath and ran her fingers through her wild blonde hair, as though she were searching for the right words. Another sharp intake of breath and then she spoke, staring at the floor as she did so. 'So, I mentioned Michael to Detective Tyler last week and he offered to take a fresh look at the file. And…um…he did just that and found a couple of things that I was previously unaware of, or had overlooked, or…I don't know. But the news came as a bit of a shock to me. Basically, Michael took a call from work just after he arrived at Green River'—Maddie directed her eyes briefly over towards Becky—'then he disappeared. The fingerprint check of his truck found no prints, which I had always taken to mean *no suspicious* prints, but actually, it meant no prints *at all*; including Michael's or anyone else's.' For the first time, she looked up, taking in each member of the team. 'As you can imagine, it's come as a pretty big shock. I'm going to leave at lunchtime today because Michael's truck is going to be tested again for prints and DNA.'

'Why don't you take some time off, Maddie?' Kenyatta said quietly. 'We can cope here just fine.'

Maddie smiled and sipped her coffee. 'Thanks, but I'll be okay. I mean, nothing has actually *happened*. It's just, you know… I just wanted to keep you guys updated.'

'Well, you go right on and do what you gotta do,' Kenyatta said.

'I will. And right now, that's putting up an orange slip for cluster six, Elwood Sydney Stables and Mary Fredericka Valentino from Nevada, *and* a purple slip for Samuel Thomas Stables and Sarah Emily Minchin.' Maddie took the two pieces of paper from the back pocket of her jeans and added, "Where did Samuel and Sarah Emily live?', I hear you cry. Well, I will tell you: they lived in Cochranville, Pennsylvania.'

'How far away from Chester Creek is that?' Hudson asked.

'Thirty…short…miles,' Maddie revealed with a big smile as she began to stick the pieces of paper onto the whiteboard.

Outwardly, Becky was mirroring the fresh sense of enthusiasm that had come from Maddie's discoveries, which she could also see on her colleagues' faces and discerned in their eagerness to get back to work. But inwardly, her mind was churning over the implications of what Maddie had just relayed about Michael's disappearance and the look that she had given Becky when she had mentioned that he had taken a work call just before he'd disappeared. She couldn't help but sense a tenuous link forming in her thoughts between this and what had happened with her parents up at Park City on Saturday. Their reaction had been…weird. *Very* weird, in fact. She couldn't ever recall a time in her adult life when her father had suggested playing a board game. And even to consider watching a movie, when there had been near-perfect skiing conditions right outside the house, was unheard of. Both her mom and dad's demeanors had visibly altered, when Becky had told them that she'd seen Maddie skiing past the house. Something was amiss.

Maddie passed by her desk with her usual warm smile, saying or betraying nothing, as she headed back into her office. Becky finished her latte as she stared absent-mindedly at her computer, hoping that Maddie wasn't somehow linking her by association to whatever 'call from work' Michael might have taken right before he had vanished.

Becky consciously arrested her errant trains of thought and parked them to one side, forcing her mind back onto the case. Specifically, back to the twelve men and women who could be one of the Chester Creek killer's parents. She pulled up the list of surnames that had shown up in the killer's Y-DNA matches: *Smith, Floyd, Findlay, Brown, Paris, Frost, Howley*. None of the twelve potential parents had any of these surnames.

'Hudson,' she called over. 'Could I borrow you for a moment?'

'Sure,' he said, paddling his feet to propel his chair around the desk to arrive at Becky's side.

'I've got these twelve individuals who are potentially the killer's parents. Am I correct in thinking, though, that actually we're looking at just the females, since none of the males have the surnames brought up by the Y-DNA results?'

Hudson pulled an uncertain face. 'Technically, yes, but—'

'NPE. Right. I'm there with you,' Becky concluded.

'Exactly. The killer, his dad, grandad, great-grandad and so on could have been the result of a non-paternity event. I mean *prioritize* with the females and have that as your current working assumption, but just don't ignore the men.'

'Oh. I would *never* ignore the men,' she said flippantly. 'Thanks.'

As Hudson scuttled back off to his desk, Becky opened up the profile page for the first of Roland and Rosanna Crowder's granddaughters, one Vera Wolsey. She had been born in Philadelphia in 1937.

All Becky could remember about the age of the potential suspect, identified by a friend of the third victim, was that it was a very broad range. She opened the fact file provided by the detective and scanned down the page until she found the description. *Long face. Short hair. 'Scary' eyes. Ethnicity unknown. Approx. age 20-50.*

If the killer had been fifty years old at the time of the murders, then he would have been born five years *before* Vera Wolsey. However, if he had been twenty years old at the time of the murders, then he would have been born in 1962 and Vera Wolsey could easily have been his mother. Another potential possible maybe.

The only information, which Becky had so far confirmed about Vera, was what the 1940 US Census had revealed.

She clicked on the *Hints* tab to see which records Ancestry had suggested might pertain to her. The first was a possible memorial reference on Find a Grave. Becky clicked the *Review* button and a page opened with a brief description of the interment.

Name: Vera Sterns
Birth Date: Dec 11, 1937
Death Date: Mar 23, 2008
Cemetery: Cedar Hill Cemetery, Philadelphia, Pennsylvania
Burial or Cremation Place: Philadelphia, Pennsylvania
Has Bio? N

Becky clicked through to the Find a Grave website to see if there was any further detail. Sometimes lengthy biographies, photographs and memories of the deceased were shared. Other times, such as this, only the barest of detail had been included. She saved the information to Vera Wolsey's profile, then ran an open search for her in various online repositories. At Newspapers.com she found a brief reference to Vera's divorce from Eldred Sterns. At MyHeritage she found a family tree stating that Vera and Eldred had had three sons together: Joe, Carl and Wayne.

By lunchtime, Becky had developed the profiles of all seven of the women who were potentially the killer's mother. Frustratingly, none of them had yet produced links to any of the names that the team had so far connected to the Chester Creek killer.

'Are you okay, honey?' Kenyatta asked softly, stooping down beside Becky's desk. 'You're awful quiet today.'

'Um, yeah. I'm—' she began, stopping mid-sentence, as Maddie called over from the main office door that she was leaving for the afternoon. She looked so fragile and vulnerable to Becky as she headed home to face goodness only knew what. As the chorus of goodbyes had been returned to Maddie, an idea struck Becky. She turned her attention to Kenyatta and said, 'No, actually. I don't feel so good.'

'What's up?' Kenyatta asked.

'Head. Stomach,' Becky lied, rubbing her temples for extra effect.

'Why didn't you tell Maddie? She would've given you the afternoon off.'

'I don't want to let people down,' she muttered pathetically.

Kenyatta stood up and folded her arms. 'Well! Now I'm in charge, and I'm telling you to go home and get some rest.'

'I can't do that. I—'

Kenyatta raised her index finger. 'Ah, ah, ah! Don't make me pull the plug on your machine. 'Cause you know I'll do it,' she said, placing a hand on Becky's computer power cable.

Becky offered a weak smile. 'Thanks, Kenyatta. If I feel up to it later, I'll work from home.'

'No…you won't,' Kenyatta instructed with a roll of her eyes as she made her way over to the kitchen area. Becky switched off her computer and packed up her bag. She hated lying, but the sight of Maddie standing at the door, so helpless and stranded-looking, was just eating her up.

She walked over to the front desk and was met with Ross's inquisitive gape. 'I'll tell you later,' she whispered. 'If anyone asks, I'm home in bed.'

'What's going—'

'I'll tell you later,' she repeated quietly. 'See you tonight.'

'Your date?' he reminded her.

'Shit,' she said, pulling out her cellphone and leaving the office. She opened up the text thread between her and Jerome and typed out a message to him.

Hi Jerome. I'm really sorry but I'm going to have to take a rain check on tonight. I've been sent home from work sick. I'm bummed. I was so looking forward to it and hope we can reschedule? Becky

Well, it wasn't exactly the best of starts to any possible relationship that she might have with him. But she could hardly be sent home from work sick at 1pm and then be scaling walls at The Front at 6pm. Besides which, she didn't know how long it would take to achieve doing that which she had planned.

Becky was back in Park City, trying to do some more work on Roland and Rosanna Crowder's descendants while she waited for her parents to arrive back home, presumably from the slopes. But trying to work was useless. Her thoughts were repeatedly drawn back to Michael

Barnhart and a feeling of dread would paralyze her cognitive ability. She closed her laptop lid with a sigh and stood from the couch, ambling over to the huge living-room windows that offered a widescreen view of the Wasatch Range. Normally, it was a view that could settle, soothe and stimulate her mind. Today it did nothing but emphasize the fact that this stunning vista was only afforded her by her father's work, which pulled her full-circle back to Michael Barnhart.

'Becky!' her mother exclaimed, dashing into the room and kissing her on the cheek. 'What a wonderful surprise.'

'Hi,' her father greeted. 'What brings you back up to the mountains? Not that you ever need an excuse, of course.'

Becky couldn't look at them, struggling to retrieve the lines that she had rehearsed on the drive up here. The words tangled, overlapped and were squashed by her parents' impatient stares. 'I came here because something is bothering me.' She looked at her father before she continued, preparing to capture and gauge his reaction. 'Why didn't you want to see Maddie on Saturday?'

Her father held a poker face, but she noticed the quick flick of her mother's eyes onto her father, as if reaching out for guidance on how best to respond.

'What do you mean?' her father said, clearing his throat.

Becky could feel her anger rising but was determined not to show it. 'On Saturday, when I came up here to ski with you both, I told you that Maddie Barnhart was out on the ski trails. At that point you decided that we wouldn't ski; and you sure didn't want me to go find her.'

Her father laughed. 'Oh, that. My God, Becky. You came all the way up here to ask us *that*?' He looked at his wife and laughed again. 'God, I thought you were going to tell me you were pregnant or had some terrible illness...'

She waited for him to answer her question but, when he didn't, she opened her hands, as though his answer had not been an answer at all.

'What? She's going through a tough time and I thought we needed to give her a little space with her family. That's it. It's really no big deal,' he explained.

'How did you know she needed space?' Becky pushed.

'Because I knew it was Michael's...fifth anniversary. You're really gunning for me because I wanted to give your boss some space? Becky, come on. What's going on, here?'

'But how did you know it was the fifth anniversary of his

disappearance? It seems a strange thing for you to remember, when you forget your own wedding anniversary most years.'

Her father gestured toward her mother for some support or encouragement. 'Can you believe this? Do *you* understand it?'

Her mother shook her head and gazed out of the window. She turned to face Becky. 'Let's have a nice cup of coffee or—'

'Do *not say* hot chocolate,' Becky warned.

'Becky!' her mother said. 'What's gotten into you?'

'Why don't you just go ahead and tell us what's really going on in that head of yours. Something is clearly upsetting you,' her father suggested.

'Michael Barnhart received a phone call moments before he was never seen again,' Becky spelled out, carefully studying her parents for a sign of betrayal in their body language or a misalignment between their words and comportment. 'That call came from The Larkin Investment and Finance Group.'

From her father, nothing. From her mother, a definite but almost imperceptible widening of her eyes and an inability to meet Becky's gaze.

'And?' her father said.

'And I'm asking you if there's a connection between that phone call, his disappearance, your amazing memory for his anniversary and the fact that you were acting very strangely on Saturday, when I suggested we ski with Maddie.'

Her father shook his head. 'This is really quite unbelievable, Becky. Is that what happens when you work at playing detective twenty-four seven? Everything becomes a big conspiracy? *Everyone*—even your close family—become villains, rapists and murderers? I mean, come on. Is that what you're saying, here, Becky? That someone at the office phoned Michael Barnhart? And then what? Killed him? That's deranged.'

Becky didn't quite know what she *was* suggesting. She was simply reacting to her instincts that something wasn't right. She turned and walked out of the living room, with her mother calling after her and her father saying to 'let her go'.

She climbed into her car and clutched the steering wheel tightly, as the adrenaline charged around her body. Even though he had denied all knowledge, Becky knew him well enough to know that her father had been trying too hard to cover something up.

Chapter Twenty-Five

Wednesday, March 11, 2020, Downtown Salt Lake City, Utah

Hudson strolled along Main Street, weaving his way around a great deluge of commuters who had just poured out of the red line tram. It was a bright morning and the snow had been cleared from the sidewalk into dirty, gravel-peppered snowbanks along the roadside. He was walking purposefully, yet, without his usual sense of urgency to get into the office. He didn't know whether his reticence was due to a profound sense of guilt or a deeper worry that Maddie might have seen him emailing Wanda Chabala on Monday, despite her having said nothing further to him about it. Certainly, he was nervous about receiving Wanda's reply. After much deliberation with Abigail over the weekend, he had emailed her on Monday lunchtime—typically, just as Maddie had been passing his desk—to say that he had decided to agree and take a preliminary look into the case for her. He'd tried to sound vaguely aloof and detached in his email, not fully committing to the project of trying to exonerate Brandon Blake by obtaining the DNA of the real perpetrator, all using highly questionable methods. The tone of her reply had been friendly and informal, but the attached contract had been anything but, instantly dispelling any sense of control or disassociation that he had been hoping to achieve over the job. He and Abigail had each read over the contract several times before he had signed and returned it late last night. So far, he'd heard nothing in response and that, truth be told, was the source of his anxiety and lack of desire to rush in to work and apply his thinking elsewhere.

A sudden slap on his left shoulder startled him and he shot an annoyed look to his side to find nobody there.

'Hey!' came Ross's voice from his right-hand side, grinning at having successfully accomplished a prank that Hudson had last found vaguely amusing back in seventh grade.

'Hi,' he replied flatly.

'How are you?' Ross asked.

'Good thanks. How's Becky doing? Is she better?'

Ross nodded emphatically. 'Back to bouncing around the apartment, drinking her low-carb, high-protein, organic, vegan shakes. Back to running into work. Yeah, I'd say back to normal.'

'Good,' Hudson said, stopping outside of the Kearns Building and waiting for the automatic doors to open. He gestured for Ross to step forward into the lobby area first, which he did, heading for the elevator. 'See you up there,' Hudson said, instead taking the stairs.

Pointlessly, he wanted to beat Ross to the fifth floor and took the stairs two at a time, quickening his pace at the sound of the *ping* that signaled the elevator's arrival on the first floor.

Out of breath, he got up to the Venator office, finding Ross feigning relaxedly sitting at his desk and apparently typing at his computer. 'You sure took your time,' Ross commented, without looking up at Hudson.

'It wasn't a race,' he said, casually strolling past him to hang up his jacket. 'Morning!' he called generally. Maddie responded from inside her office. She sounded cheerful enough, but they had yet to hear what had happened with the fresh sweep of Michael's truck. She hadn't returned to the office yesterday afternoon.

'Morning, honey,' Kenyatta responded with a wave. Becky was sitting beside her and said, 'Hi.'

Hudson went to his desk and started up his computer. 'Glad you're feeling better today, Becky.'

'Yeah. Back to normal, thank you.'

'Yes, so Ross said,' Hudson replied. In those *exact* words, actually, he thought with some suspicion.

Hudson opened up the family tree file that he had been working on since Monday. Yesterday afternoon, he had discovered the link between two of the genetic networks with the marriage of Thomas Garrick to Rosie Huffman. By completing a blue piece of paper for the couple, the team were now in possession of the names of four out of eight of the Chester Creek killer's great-grandparents. Hopefully, today, by systematically working through each of the couple's four children, he would be able to link up with another genetic network to reveal a second of the killer's four grandparents.

Hudson looked over at the whiteboard containing all the combined information pertaining to the investigation, his eyes settling on the police suspect sketch of the killer. He might well be out there someplace, alive and completely unaware of how close the Venator team was getting to naming him and revealing his identity. Time, anonymity and freedom were no longer on his side. The photos of the three victims caught his attention and for a moment he purposefully took in each of them in turn, gaining from their frozen stares a fresh impetus to close the case.

He flipped his attention to what was on his computer screen: Thomas and Rosie Garrick on the 1920 US Census. They were living in a rented property with their four children in Gloucester County, New Jersey. These people didn't like to stray too far from their childhood homes, he observed; this being the third generation to live in the same county. At some point soon, however, at least one family member would cross over that water into Delaware County, Pennsylvania.

Hudson was pretty sure that vital records for this period in this county were not available online but checked the Wiki page at FamilySearch to be absolutely certain. He was right, which was going to make his searches even more labored.

Returning to the US Federal State Census collection, he typed the Garrick family names into the 1930 Census, finding that two of the four children had still been residing at home with their parents. For the time being, those two children were not his priority and he spent some time trawling the same census for any signs of the two who were absent: Alexander and Marion Garrick. For the latter, there were multiple possibilities but none about which he could be completely certain. Alexander he easily located, living just across town with his own young family. The census did not provide the maiden name of Alexander's wife, which would be crucial if Hudson were going to identify which of Thomas and Rosie Garrick's grandchildren was one of the Chester Creek killer's parents. To achieve this, Hudson needed to run open searches across every online archive to which he had access. The information that he needed was out there someplace.

It took fifty-five minutes of searching for Hudson to find and confirm that Alexander Garrick's wife's maiden name had been Wren, making it unlikely that Alexander Garrick was the person for whom he was searching.

Switching to the 1940 Census, Hudson repeated his search for each family member, starting with Thomas and Rosie Garrick. Nothing was forthcoming for the couple. Wondering if they had died, he ran a search for each of their four children. First, he found Alexander and his family, then he looked for Marion. Again, as with the previous census, he was faced with several possibilities. One result in the list for West Deptford stood out and he clicked to view it.

He'd got it.

Brown, Walter, head, married, 31 years old, born New Jersey, Farmer
Brown, Marion, wife, married, 30 years old, born New Jersey, Farmer

Brown, Wallace, son, single, 11 years old, born New Jersey
Brown, Harry, son, single, 9 years old, born New Jersey
Brown, Edith, daughter, single, 6 years old, born New Jersey
Brown, Enoch, son, single, 3 years old, born New Jersey
Garrick, Rosie, mother-in-law, widow, 61 years old, born New Jersey

The entry gave rise to a wide grin on Hudson's face. With Rosie Garrick being listed as Walter Brown's mother-in-law, Hudson knew that he had found the correct Marion. But what was most exciting was the fact that Marion had married someone with the surname Brown, one of the surnames identified in the Chester Creek killer's Y-DNA.

He forced himself to calm and not to race ahead and announce to the rest of the team that in Wallace, Harry or Enoch Brown he had potentially discovered the killer's father. After all, Brown was hardly the rarest of names.

He rubbed his hands together in excitement as he saved the census data to the growing family tree.

'Monsieur Édouard!' Kenyatta said, eyes narrowed. 'What's going on over there? You look like the cat that got the cream.'

Hudson smiled. 'Oh, maybe something; maybe nothing. You'll find out in—' he looked at the clock '—just under three hours' time.'

Kenyatta raised her eyebrows in response to his nebulous but tantalizing answer.

'Enoch Brown,' he muttered to himself, pulling up his profile page. As he did so, a message notification from his personal Gmail account pinged in at the top right corner of his computer screen. The name of the sender, in bold letters, was *Wanda Chabala*. Hudson took a quick glance behind him this time before opening up the email.

Dear Hudson,
Many thanks for signing and returning the contract. The account details for the DNA kit of my daughter's murderer are attached. As agreed, half of the fifty thousand dollars has been transferred to your bank account; the remainder will be sent upon finding a successful DNA match. Just a reminder of the contract's strict non-disclosure stipulations and to be clear that you report to me and me alone.
Wanda

Hudson hovered his mouse over the attachment but dared not open it. Not here. He closed the email, logged out of his Gmail account and closed the tab inside which it had been open. He took out his cellphone and opened up the app for his bank account. Just as she had said, the money really was there. Half of what he and Abigail needed to be able to adopt a child. 'It's a win-win-win situation', Abigail had repeatedly asserted in their discussions. A murderer would get taken off the streets, Brandon Blake would get his rightful freedom back and they would get to have a child. 'Hudson, there are literally no downsides to this,' she had insisted, ignoring his profound unease at how the DNA sample had come to be obtained. No matter how it was framed and how much he agreed with her about the upsides of taking on the case, it still felt wrong to be doing it in this way and he couldn't stop himself from wondering what would happen to the perpetrator, once Hudson had handed over his name; it would be impossible for the police to be pulled in at that point. But he'd signed the contract and accepted the money; he was now past the point of no return.

The afternoon briefing arrived astoundingly fast. Maddie called for their attention and stood with her arms folded in front of the three boards, looking frazzled. She'd kept to her own office pretty well all day, having revealed nothing about how it had gone yesterday with the CSI sweep of Michael's truck. She sort of smiled, but it didn't convince Hudson.

'So, what have you all got for me?' Maddie asked. 'I feel a bit out of the loop what with all that's been going on at home and, today, dealing with a mountain of admin. Have you guys made any significant discoveries?'

'Shall I start?' Kenyatta suggested, rising from her chair and giving her burgundy skirt a gentle downward tug.

'Go right ahead,' Maddie encouraged.

'Okay,' Kenyatta began. 'I've been pushing down on the Stables ancestral couple that you found, Maddie.' She paused and brought up Elwood Sydney Stables and Mary Fredericka Valentino on the digital whiteboard, then made her way over to it. She pointed at Elwood and Mary's son, Samuel Thomas Stables. 'This guy here,' she said, clicking his name so that his own profile appeared, 'he and his wife, Sarah Emily Minchin, had a daughter together, one Henrietta Stables.' She clicked on Henrietta's name. 'Henrietta went on to marry a guy by the name of Richard Wolsey. I carried on down with *their* kids and found that their son, Richard Wolsey Junior, winded up marrying a lady by the name of Minnie *Crowder.*'

'Ah, the Crowder connection,' Maddie said. 'So, let me get this straight. Does that mean that Richard Wolsey Junior and Minnie Crowder are the Chester Creek killer's *grand*parents?'

Kenyatta nodded. 'It sure does, yes.'

'Wow,' Maddie said, clapping. 'That's great work. You'd better fill in a *green* slip, then.'

'I'll pass you over to Becky, now,' Kenyatta said, taking a curtsy before sitting down and retrieving a green slip of paper from her desk drawer.

Becky pushed her glasses up onto the bridge of her nose and walked over to the digital whiteboard. Once there, she touched the screen to open up the children of Richard Wolsey Junior and Minnie Crowder, where Kenyatta had left off. 'Okay, so here we have three girls and one boy: Vera, Sally, Claudette and Jermaine Wolsey.' Becky paused for dramatic effect, pointing at the names onscreen. 'One of these four is very likely to be a parent to the Chester Creek killer.'

'Wow,' Maddie said again. 'This has come along so quickly. It's getting real. Any time for geo-profiling the suspected parents yet?'

'No time so far, but it's my next job,' Becky replied with a grin.

'I have a question,' Hudson said. 'Did Vera, Sally or Claudette marry into the Brown family?'

Becky shook her head. 'No. Vera married a Sterns, Sally married a Hankel and Claudette a Davis.'

Something wasn't right.

'Why? What's up, Hudson?' Maddie asked.

'Do you mind if I share my screen?' he asked.

'Sure, go ahead.'

Hudson shared the profile of Walter Brown, then stood up and said, 'So this guy here, Walter Brown, his great-grandparents were Theodore and Carrie Scharder.' He clicked to show Walter's wife. 'Marion Brown's maiden name was Garrick and her grandparents were Harry and Isabella White.'

'Hang on,' Maddie interjected. 'So, you're saying that Walter and Marion Brown are the killer's *other* set of grandparents? Another green slip?'

'Uh-huh,' Hudson confirmed. 'Which is where we have a problem.' He clicked to view Walter and Marion Brown's four children. 'Wallace, Harry, Edith and Enoch Brown. One of these four is potentially the Chester Creek killer's *other* parent and, as you can see, there's no overlap with what Becky and Kenyatta have found, comparing against what I've found.'

'That *is* a problem,' Maddie agreed. 'Eight names with no overlap…'

The team fell silent.

'The money's in!' Abigail yelled the moment that Hudson opened the front door to their apartment. She jumped up and down on the spot and then threw her arms around him. 'We're actually going to be doing this, Hudson!'

'Provided I can find the perpetrator's name, yes,' he agreed.

Abigail clasped her hands together. 'Come on, then, already. Get on with it!'

'Now?' he said, slipping off his shoes.

'Duh. Yeah. Come to the kitchen and I'll fix us some dinner while you get on with it.'

Hudson narrowed his eyes. 'You *do* realize this will probably take like…dozens of *hours*? Four of us in the office have been working for over a week non-stop on our current case and we've still yet to ID the killer.'

'You can do it,' she said with a dismissive wave, leading the way into the kitchen.

Hudson's laptop was already helpfully waiting for him on the kitchen counter. Onscreen was the log-in page for FamilyTreeDNA. He looked at her as if to say, '*Really*?' He sat in front of it, pulled out his cellphone and accessed the email containing the kit number and password. He glanced up at Abigail and warned, 'Don't touch a dollar of that money, you hear? We'll move it into our savings account, just in case we need to pay it all back.'

'Pay it back? We're not paying it back, Hudson. We are where we are. And I won't be spending it, either. We both know where every bit of that money's going.'

Hudson raised his eyebrows as the dashboard for the kit appeared in front of him. With some degree of reluctance and uncertainty, he clicked on *Matches* for the Autosomal DNA.

'Well?' Abigail asked, her hands clasped together at her chest.

Hudson nodded. 'His closest match is four hundred and twenty-two centiMorgans *and* an X-match.'

'I've no idea what any of that means. Something to do with a Marvel comic superhero?'

Hudson laughed. 'It means that the man who killed Francesca Chabala can only be related to this—' he glanced at the name of the match '—Jennifer LaFleur via his *maternal* side.'

'And that's good?'

'Yeah, that's very good.'

Abigail moved around to his side of the counter and, in a rare display of affection, encircled him in her arms. He could feel her sobbing onto his shoulder. 'Despite—you know—everything,' she said quietly, 'we're going to have a child.'

Hudson took her hand in his and gently squeezed it. He had no idea if any of this—including adopting a child with Abigail—was the right thing to do or not.

Chapter Twenty-Six

Thursday, March 12, 2020, Downtown Salt Lake City, Utah

Kenyatta Nelson was at her desk, nibbling carrot sticks and taking notes, while Maddie opened a special morning briefing.

'So,' Maddie said, pointing to the eight names that she had written on the whiteboard under the heading *SUSPECT'S PARENTS*. 'Vera, Sally, Claudette and Jermaine Wolsey and Wallace, Harry, Edith and Enoch Brown. Two of these people are the Chester Creek killer's parents.' She paused, presumably for dramatic effect. 'They were all born in the 1930s, so the Chester Creek killer is likely to have been born at some point between the late 1940s and the 1960s. But…there's something we're not getting here, people. Assuming that we've not made an error, we have four women who could have given birth to him, and four men who could have fathered him, but so far there's no obvious overlap between the two families. There doesn't appear to have been a marriage between a Wolsey and a Brown, so we need to look hard for that connection…or oversight or error, of course. I think—given the Y-DNA situation—we're good to assume, or at least prioritize, with Wallace, Harry and Enoch Brown as being the potential fathers and Vera, Sally or Claudette as being the potential mothers. We can't completely rule out Jermaine and Edith at this stage, but I don't think we'll put them to the top of the priority research pile. So, Kenyatta, I'd like you to continue with the Wolsey women. Get *everything* you can on them saved to their profiles, including any sons they may have between them. Hudson, you keep digging on the Brown family. Again, get everything you can on them and all of their kids. Becky, I want you to concentrate on geo-profiling; at least one of them has to have lived in or near Chester Creek. I'm going to be around and pitch in as and where and when it's needed. It's possible—with a bit of luck—that we could get a name by the end of the day. Any questions?'

Silence.

'Then let's get to it.'

Kenyatta popped another carrot stick into her mouth as she set to work bringing up the Wolsey siblings on her computer. Her first job was to triage them, working on them in order of most likely to least likely. As Maddie had already suggested, Jermaine Wolsey was probably not the killer's father, so he dropped straight to the bottom of her list.

Becky had already completed some work on the eldest child, Vera. She had had three sons, Joe, Carl and Wayne with Eldred Sterns from whom she had later divorced. From what information Kenyatta could see, Vera had lived and died in Philadelphia, so she too dropped lower in the priority list, leaving Sally and Claudette Wolsey. Save for the names of their spouses, there was little information in the two women's profiles, so it was a toss-up as to with which one she should start.

For no particular reason, Kenyatta picked Claudette, beginning by inputting her name into various background check websites. She quickly found a probable candidate living in Redlands, California, now aged eighty-two. According to BeenVerified, she had resided at her current address for the past thirteen years. Prior to that, different addresses were given for the Redlands area back to 1974. Listed under the *Relatives* tab were her husband, Steven Davis, and two potential children, Teri and Robert Davis. This Claudette Wolsey fitted with the information that Becky had already found and Kenyatta was certain that she had discovered the correct person, meaning that her son, Robert Davis, was a potential suspect as being the Chester Creek killer.

Kenyatta clicked through to view a background report on him. He was now sixty years old and also currently living in Redlands, California. She worked out that he would have been twenty-eight years old at the time of the murders, so perfectly possible.

She scrolled down to the *Jobs* section of the background check and could see that Robert Davis had a long history of working in schools as an art teacher. *Redlands East Valley High School. Redlands Unified School District. Redlands Teachers Association.* Below that, under *Social Media*, was a link to his Twitter account. Kenyatta clicked through and came face-to-face with his profile picture. She enlarged it, the circular image around his face centered on her screen. He didn't fit the police sketch image. Although, she had to remind herself that the drawing had been done thirty-seven years ago, produced from a description of a person of interest on a dark night, who wasn't even necessarily the killer.

She studied him carefully. He had a soft round face and warm green eyes. There was no clue as to his original hair color, the top of his head being completely bald and the short tufts just visible above his ears being light gray in color.

Kenyatta flicked through the small stack of paperwork and notes on the side of her desk, wanting to remind herself of the killer's possible phenotype: brown hair, brown eyes and pale skin. Robert Davis was the polar opposite, she thought, saving his photograph and attaching it to his profile.

He didn't quite fit the bill physically or geographically and certainly didn't *look* like a serial killer, but then she recalled Becky's assessment of the crime when the detective had first introduced the case: she predicted that the guy would likely be socially capable and intelligent. Besides, phenotyping was only currently running at around seventy percent accuracy, so Robert Davis could in no way be dismissed from potentially being the killer.

Kenyatta spent some time trawling his Twitter account for additional information. She found occasional photos that he had shared from his youth, which she also saved across to his profile. There were pictures of his parents and also references to his sister, Teri, who, Kenyatta learned from his tweets, had died in an automobile accident in 2018. Her obituary, which she easily found on the GenealogyBank website confirmed Robert to be the only surviving sibling.

The more Kenyatta found out about Robert Davis, the less likely she felt that he was the Chester Creek killer. Although she could not completely eliminate his mother, Claudette Wolsey, as being the killer's mother, it was, in her opinion, improbable.

Following normal procedure, Kenyatta printed out a single sheet of paper with Robert Davis's name, photograph and a short biography, which she attached to the glassboard under a new heading of *SUSPECTS*.

Robert Davis was their first on the list.

She turned her attention to the whiteboard, where Maddie had written the eight potential names of the Chester Creek killer's parents. She picked up a black marker and wrote the new subheading, *Unlikely*, under that list of names. Below that, she wrote Claudette and Jermaine Wolsey's names before rubbing them out from the suspect list.

'While you're there, Kenyatta, can you demote Edith Brown to the unlikely list for me?' Hudson called over.

Kenyatta obliged, leaving five names as potential parents.

She returned to her desk and brought up the profile for Claudette's sister, Sally Wolsey. Born in January 1940, she had married a Julian Hankel in 1959 in Philadelphia. That was the sum total of their knowledge on her so far.

Searching for Sally Hankel on background check websites produced just a single hit.

Sally Hankel
Age 77 years old

Born January 1940
Deceased at age 77 in November 2017 in PA
Location Media, PA
Aliases Sally Wolsey

'Woah,' Kenyatta said.
'What's up?' Becky asked.
'Oh, sorry. I just found that Sally Wolsey died in 2017 in Media, PA.'
'Oh, wow,' Becky said. 'Do you have an address? Did she have sons?'
'Give me half a minute,' Kenyatta said, opening up a new tab in her browser and putting *Sally Hankel death Media 2017* into Google. 'I'm just pulling up an obit on Legacy.com.' She skim-read the article that included a photograph of Sally. 'Um, you guys might need to hear this. Maddie!'
Maddie hurried out of her office and stood behind Kenyatta.
'Sally Wolsey's obit,' Kenyatta said, pointing to her computer.
'Share it,' Maddie instructed.
Kenyatta obliged and the team silently read Sally Wolsey's obituary on the digital whiteboard.

Sally Hankel, age 77 of Media, PA, passed away peacefully on the night of November 7, 2017.
Sally was born January 8, 1940 to Minnie (nee Crowder) and Richard Wolsey Jnr. She is pre-deceased by one son, Paul, one sister, Vera and her only brother, Jermaine. Sally met her future husband, Julian Hankel while attending Darby High where she graduated in 1958. They were married October 2, 1961 and Sally became a full-time mother and homemaker, remaining in Delaware County her whole life. Sally was the devoted and loving wife of her late husband, Julian and the loving mother of Kenneth and the late Paul. Services and interment are being planned for a later date.

'Remaining in Delaware County her whole life...' Maddie read aloud. 'Kenyatta, can you prioritize with getting what you can on Kenneth Hankel, preferably a full address history to pass on to Becky. I'll work on finding out exactly how *late* the late Paul Hankel was. Everyone okay with that?'
After universal agreement, Hudson rose from his chair and headed over to the whiteboard. 'I've just eliminated Wallace Brown.'

Maddie watched him add Wallace Brown to the *Unlikely* list and said, 'So now we have just two potential fathers in Harry and Enoch Brown and just two potential mothers in Vera and Sally Wolsey. We've almost got him. Let's do this.'

Kenyatta attached the obituary and photograph to Sally Wolsey's profile page, then returned to BeenVerified, scrolling down to view Sally's relatives. Her husband, Julian, was listed first with the immediate addendum as having been deceased since 2015. Next was her son, Paul. Kenyatta looked at his report, which was notably brief, then called out the little information that it did contain to Maddie, 'BeenVerified has Paul Hankel deceased in April 2001, but really not much else about him.'

'On it. Thanks,' Maddie replied from her office.

The last associated relative of Sally Wolsey was her other son, Kenneth. She clicked his name and the information held on him appeared onscreen. Born 1962, he had an early address history in the environs around Delaware County. According to the report, between 1983 and 1985, when the murders had been committed, he had been living on Dutton Mill Road, Aston Township, Delaware County.

Kenyatta gasped when she pulled the location up on Google Maps: Dutton Mill Road ran directly over the Chester Creek. 'Becky. I've got an address for you and it's good...*real* good.'

'Go ahead,' Becky responded, pen poised over her legal pad.

Kenyatta read out the address, adding the pertinent fact of its proximity to the Chester Creek.

'Let me take a look,' Becky said, tapping the information into her computer.

After 1989, the report listed addresses for Kenneth Hankel all over the US, his current residence being given as a suburb of Los Angeles. Kenyatta stared at the information, wondering if his transient nature explained the apparent cessation of murders at Chester Creek, following Sadie Mayer's death in October 1983. She jotted down the information, saved a screenshot of it to Kenneth's working profile and then continued to read his background report.

She raised her eyebrows when she reached *Criminal & Traffic*: eight convictions were held against him.

'That's a pretty big rap-sheet,' she muttered to herself as she began to scrutinize the crimes for which Kenneth had been prosecuted. *Drug possession*—two counts. *Receiving stolen goods*. *Assault*—two counts. *Traffic Infraction*. *Robbery*.

Other than the state in which they had occurred, the report didn't provide any additional information about the crimes that Kenneth Hankel had committed, so Kenyatta jotted down the details and then switched to Newspapers.com.

The first of Kenneth's drugs charges were cited in the *Asbury Park Press* of New Jersey in the edition of February 4, 1986 in a long list of sentences passed by the then Superior Court Judge.

Kenneth Hankel, Munroe Avenue, Neptune, one-year probation and a $500 fine for possession of drugs in Neptune May 11, 1985.

After taking a screenshot of the story and adding it to Kenneth's profile, she noted the dates and locations of his crime in order to build a working timeline of his movements.

She found Kenneth living in Baltimore in July 1989, his crime there being reported in *The Baltimore Sun*.

Kenneth Hankel, of the 8000 block Eastdale Avenue, receiving stolen goods, three years suspended, two years probation and $1,000 restitution to the State Police.

Having saved the information against his profile, Kenyatta searched for the assault crime, which she found had taken place in Iowa and had been recorded in the Cedar Rapids publication, *The Gazette*, in September 1992.

Kenneth Hankel, 3455 C Ave. NE, was fined $150 after pleading guilty to a charge of assault. He also was fined $50 after pleading guilty to a charge of speeding in relation to an incident on April 11.

Kenyatta spent the rest of the morning conducting searches for Kenneth Hankel's reported criminal activities. By lunchtime, she had built up a comprehensive dot-to-dot map of crimes that he had committed across the US. The list started to amount to many more than those given on the background check websites. He was a career criminal, that much was certain, but the crimes for which he had been apprehended were never more serious than assault. Was he the Chester Creek killer? Kenyatta wasn't sure. More research was needed.

She typed Kenneth's name into Classmates.com, which specialized in high school yearbooks, and selected his home state of Pennsylvania.

Four results.

She viewed the first link, which was a scanned entry from the Sun Valley High School yearbook of 1977. A black and white image, containing the photographs of eighteen ninth graders loaded in front of her. Kenneth Hankel was the center-bottom image.

Average. That was how Kenyatta considered the image of Kenneth as she zoomed in to get a closer look. He was smiling directly at the camera and looked like any other ninth-grader kid. Frustratingly, because of the tone and color of the image, it was hard to gauge anything against which she could compare the phenotype predictions. She slowly scrolled up the page, studying the pictures of the other children around him. A girl with much lighter hair and lighter eyes than Kenneth's, a black man with very dark hair and an Asian girl all helped by offering reference points, suggesting that Kenneth was probably light-skinned with brown hair and dark eyes: a complete match with the phenotype prediction.

Kenyatta looked at the second recorded image, which had been taken from the same high school in the following year. Again, Kenneth just looked ordinary. She repeated her check of his classmates and drew the same conclusion about his skin, hair and eye color.

In 1979, his junior high school year, Kenneth had begun to take on a more mature, grown-up look. His twelfth-grade photo, taken in 1980, was the one that Kenyatta saved to both his profile page and also to the suspect sheet containing his biographical detail. She printed it out and carried it over to the glassboard. Before she pinned it up, she compared it to the police suspect sketch. Not similar. Not dissimilar.

She fixed the piece of paper onto the board, beside that of Robert Davis, and gazed at the pair of them. Of the two, Kenneth, being local at the time of the murders and being a criminal, was obviously a much more likely suspect than an art teacher who lived thousands of miles away in California.

'Here's another one,' Maddie announced, shuffling in beside Kenyatta and holding up a suspect sheet for Kenneth's younger brother, Paul Hankel. 'I've completed this for Paul, but there's practically zero chance of his being the killer. It appears he went traveling after high school and then lived for most of the 1980s in South Africa. He's got a pretty strong alibi...at least for the second murder. Plus—as you can see—he has mousey hair and blue eyes, just like his father.'

'Hmm,' Kenyatta agreed, looking at his photograph. 'Whereas this guy—' she pointed at Kenneth '—has a *long* list of criminality all over the States and he was in Delaware County at the time of the murders. I'm hoping Becky might be able to tell us more at the briefing.'

Becky grinned. 'I'll have a detailed report by four thirty,' she said, standing up. 'But, right now, I'm going out to pick up some lunch. Anyone want anything? I'm going to Eva's, but I am willing, if the price is right, to actually walk past the end of the block.'

Kenyatta huffed. 'I would literally sell my soul right now for a panini from Eva's, but I've got a *delicious*—yes, I'm trying to convince myself, here—quinoa and tuna salad in the refrigerator. So, I'll pass. But thank you for asking.'

'I would love a grilled cheese panini, merci,' Hudson said, without glancing up from his computer. 'I'm down a Harry-Brown rabbit hole and won't be back up for some time.'

'Now, *this* is exactly why I've turned down the live serial-murder case from Twin Falls,' Maddie suddenly revealed.

'What?' Becky said, stopping on her way toward the door and spinning right back around.

'You turned it *down*?' Kenyatta stammered.

'Yes,' Maddie confirmed. 'Look at you all. It's two o'clock and *none* of you has stopped for lunch.'

'I did!' Ross called over.

'Good,' Maddie replied.

'I'm surprised at you,' Kenyatta said. 'And a little disappointed, to be honest.'

Maddie seemed taken aback.

'I thought Venator was established for the express purpose of helping law enforcement with identifying remains and perpetrators of homicides, sexual assault or abduction. Why does it matter how far in the past the crimes have occurred?'

'The Chester Creek murder case,' Maddie tried to explain, 'has gone unsolved for thirty-seven years and, yet, you three can't stop yourselves for even a half-hour lunch break. Imagine the pressure of thinking that, if you wouldn't solve the case quickly enough, another woman could be murdered… I'd never be able to get you to leave the office.'

Kenyatta shrugged. 'Don't you think that's partly our prerogative?'

Maddie opened her hands. 'It's irrelevant. I've informed the detective in charge that we won't be taking the case. Now, I would like you all to *please* take a break. This is a crucial moment in the case, and I need you all to be functioning at your very best: we cannot get this wrong.'

Becky, out of sight from Maddie, made a face to Kenyatta and Hudson, suggesting a shared surprise at Maddie's decision to turn down the live case in Twin Falls. It *was* a surprise to Kenyatta and she intended to speak privately with Maddie about it later on. But she was right, they did need to take more regular breaks and step back from the work now and then. With that in mind, she walked over to the kitchen area and took her Harmons salad from the refrigerator. She had been about to head back over to her desk with it, when she watched Maddie returning to her office. 'Lunch date?' Kenyatta suggested.

Maddie smiled. 'Come on in,' she said, gesturing with her hands. As if intuiting her thoughts and intent, Maddie pushed the door closed behind them.

Kenyatta sat down and opened her unappealing salad.

'That looks amazing,' Maddie observed. 'I've just got a cheese sandwich from home, today.'

'I would love to swap but I'm being good,' Kenyatta said, forking some lettuce into her mouth.

'Is everything okay with you?' Maddie asked her.

Kenyatta nodded. 'Yeah, I think so. I had my boys come over on Saturday and we just had ourselves such a blast. It was so good to have them back…even just for a few hours.'

'How was Otis?'

Kenyatta made a face. 'Stood on the sidewalk with his arms folded like some kind of prison guard or some such. But it was okay.'

'Good, I'm glad. You so don't deserve to be separated from your sons like that.'

'Let's hope the courts agree with *you* next month. What about you? How did it go on Tuesday with Michael's truck?'

Maddie took a bite of her sandwich, seeming to mull over the question as she chewed. 'Three guys arrived from CSI—wearing their space-suit get-up—swept the car for prints, blood and DNA and whatever, then promptly left again.'

'And did they find anything?'

'They think they may have gotten a partial print from the trunk catch,' Maddie revealed, gazing downwards. 'And I can't decide if that's a good thing, or not.' She shrugged, then met Kenyatta's stare. 'I mean, great if they can find someone involved in Michael's disappearance but… What *does* it imply, when this person attempted to wipe the car clean of all prints and who had also opened the trunk?'

'Well, even with this information, you know so little about the picture of what happened down there. Finding a partial print doesn't have to indicate that something bad went down. That print might come back from someone…I don't know…at the service station, or some person who helped Michael unload his boat from the car, or one of the kids. I think you've just got to try to assume nothing about it, which I know is easier said than done. Hell, in my head I'm never going to see my kids again and they'll hate me forever, but I don't think that's a helpful way of looking at things, you know? You need to re-frame it. And, yes, that is my therapist talking.'

Maddie smiled. 'At least we can be doing some good to help others here. I feel like we could have an ID for the Chester Creek killer by the end of play, today or tomorrow, if we keep up this level of progress.'

Kenyatta nodded her agreement as she tucked into her food. 'Listen. I know you've made the decision about this Twin Falls case and that's fine, but, for the future, don't be so hasty to withhold our assistance. Look at what we can achieve in ten days, here: we're such a good team together. So, put us out there to make the best use of our talents.'

'Maybe,' Maddie replied. Then, after a short pause, continued, 'Tell me about what you got up to on Saturday with the boys.'

'Nice change of subject,' Kenyatta said wryly. 'But I'll tell you, anyways.'

'This is the most significant briefing of the case so far,' Maddie announced, upon opening the meeting at four thirty. She was standing in front of the glassboard, looking slightly apprehensive and more serious than usual. 'Kenyatta, do you mind starting us off?'

'Okay,' Kenyatta said, standing up. She talked through her initial triaging of the four Wolsey siblings, carefully going through each point and her rationales underpinning the decisions that she had made. At this stage in an investigation, it was absolutely crucial not to overlook or to dismiss an important fact or procedural step. She explained her basis for not believing Robert Davis to be a likely contender for the Chester Creek murderer. Then, she spoke at length about Kenneth Hankel, his crimes and their geographical anchoring. On the digital whiteboard, she shared images of both Robert and Kenneth.

'What's your gut on this?' Maddie asked.

'My gut reaction is that Robert Davis is not in the frame. I don't have any evidence that rules him firmly *out*, but I just don't feel it against what I've found. Kenneth, on the other hand is still a suspect. But the crimes—only those where he was actually caught—had no sexual element or real endangering of human life; and he *was* in the right area at the right time. I think Becky has something more to say on all of that.'

'Okay, Becky?' Maddie said.

Becky stood up and addressed the team. 'So, first to Robert Davis. I *really* don't think he's our guy at all. He doesn't fit any kind of profiling. As Kenyatta said, we can't eliminate him completely, but I would say there is a one-in-a-million chance that we're looking at its being him.'

'And Kenneth Hankel?' Maddie asked.

'Well, geographically speaking, he's in the right county but his address at the time is outside of the Circle Theory of Environmental Range *and* outside of the triangle formed by the first three murders. Look.' On the digital whiteboard Becky displayed the map that she had shared of the Chester Creek area following her initial assessment of the killings' locations. The map now had the addition of a green drop-pin around which she ran her cursor. 'The house that Kenneth Hankel lived in at the time of the murders is *very* close to Chester Creek. Like just a few yards away. But, given that the belief is that he kidnapped the women, took them back to his house and then left them in the creek, if he lived here, the location the bodies were found in makes little sense.'

'But I thought you said he drove past possible places to leave the bodies, choosing that location specifically,' Hudson said. 'In which case, he could live anywhere.'

'Yes, but I would have expected that to have occurred somewhere *within* this purple circle, not without.'

'But it's not impossible, right?' he pushed.

'No, of course not,' Becky responded. 'But there's also the fact that Kenneth Hankel was living at home with his parents at the time of the murders. Again, that's not an impossibility if maybe he lived in the basement, had his own access points… But the way the house currently appears online, I can't see any basement or outhouse. I'm working on trying to get some older photos or maps of the property to double-check that. Remember, the victims were probably alive at the point of entering his house, so if his parents were living there, they would have known about it.'

'Unless they were both away on weekends,' Kenyatta reminded her.

'Yeah, there is that possibility, too,' Becky agreed.

'Okay,' Maddie said, 'Let's take a look at the others. I've also added Paul Hankel to the list of suspects, but I feel he's way down the possibility list, as it appears that he was in South Africa at the time of the murders. I can't rule out the chance that he flew back home to see his mom and dad and, while back in the US, decided to kill three women.' She shrugged. 'It's possible but not probable. Hudson, have you got anything for us?'

Hudson stood up, sharing his screen. On the digital whiteboard appeared a black-and-white photograph of a young boy in a wheelchair. 'This is Harry Brown, one of the suspect's potential fathers. He caught polio as a young boy and was confined to a wheelchair his whole life. Although we can't know if he unofficially fathered any children, he certainly didn't marry or have any acknowledged, documented offspring.'

'That's another one pushed down the list,' Kenyatta muttered.

'Yeah,' he agreed. 'I would say he was way down the list of being the killer's dad. But what I did find was that, at the time of Harry Brown's death in 1965, his brother, Enoch, was living in Delaware County, and look what I discovered.' Hudson tapped his keyboard and, seconds later, a portrait photograph appeared on the large screen in front of them, zoomed in on a young man, labelled as Enoch Brown. 'This is the yearbook photo for 1956. Guess which high school?' When nobody was forthcoming in suggesting an answer, he revealed, 'Darby High.'

'Wasn't that the same school that Sally Wolsey went to?' Becky asked.

'Yep,' Hudson confirmed. 'Not just Sally, but *all* of the Wolsey kids.'

'Hang on,' Kenyatta uttered, 'I thought the Wolseys lived in Philly?'

'Darby High is in Delaware County…but it's practically West Philadelphia,' Hudson replied.

'And I thought the Browns were last seen in West Deptford?' Becky questioned. 'On the 1940 Census?'

'They moved across the river sometime after the war,' Hudson responded.

'So, this is highly likely to be the link between the two families,' Maddie said, folding her arms and gazing pensively at the floor.

'Yes,' Hudson agreed. 'Because look at this.' He slowly zoomed out from Enoch's photograph, revealing the other eleven students in the image. In the row directly below Enoch was a girl, labeled as Vera Wolsey.

'Sally's sister was in his class?' Maddie said, staring, as was the rest of the team, at the two images above one another.

'Uh-huh,' Hudson said.

Maddie said, 'So, one theory could be this: Enoch Brown meets Sally Wolsey at Darby High; they get together and produce Kenneth, although he's recorded as actually being Sally's husband's—Julian Hankel's—child.'

'It's possible,' Kenyatta agreed.

'How does this all work, date-wise?' Maddie asked.

Kenyatta answered, 'Sally Wolsey married Julian Hankel in 1961, Kenneth was born 1962.'

'Maybe she married him while pregnant?' Maddie mused.

Kenyatta could see from Becky's face that she wasn't convinced. 'Could Kenneth be in that fifteen percent of people who don't fall into the geo-profile? He did live right by Chester Creek, after all.'

'As I said before, yes, of course he could,' Becky confirmed. 'And I agree that he does look like a very strong suspect.'

Maddie folded her arms, then pointed to the photo on the whiteboard screen. 'Let's park Kenneth Hankel to one side for the moment. Based on what we now know about the two families' attending the same school, what have we got on Vera Wolsey? Any sons?'

'Three boys,' Hudson answered, 'Joe, Carl and Wayne.'

'Any more about them as yet? Location? Criminal checks?' Maddie asked.

'Not yet, no,' Hudson replied.

'Okay,' Maddie said. 'So, we're down to just six suspects, the most likely of whom—so far—is Kenneth Hankel, but we need to do more work on this. Great effort, everyone. I think we'll wrap up there and pick it up tomorrow. Have a good evening.'

As the office packed up around her, Kenyatta walked over to the whiteboard and stared at the names of the suspects. Robert Davis. Paul Hankel. Kenneth Hankel. Joe Sterns. Carl Sterns. Wayne Sterns.

One of those six men was the Chester Creek serial killer.

Kenyatta arrived at the old bank, carrying a take-out bag from RedRock. She bent down at the once-grand entrance doorway and gazed into the piles of boxes and rubbish, listening to see if he was home. 'Hey, Lonnie!' she eventually called. 'Lonnie, you in there?'

From inside came the groan of someone unhappily disturbed from sleep.

'Lonnie, it's Kenyatta here. I got you pizza.'

'Not that mushroom shit again,' he mumbled.

'No, just cheese and tomato. It's plain.'

She heard him huff and grumble something about wanting to be left alone.

'It's getting cold,' she warned, taking a seat on the bank steps. 'And so am I for that matter.'

There was another audible sigh and a shuffling of fabric before he poked his head through a curtain fashioned from plastic garbage bags.

Kenyatta couldn't help but grin at the sight of him. Same old unwashed shirt, tie and jacket but now accessorized with a pristine surgical face mask and a pair of the latex gloves that she had bought for him. 'I see you got the mask and gloves I left for you, Lonnie.'

'Yeah, I did.'

'I picked up some for me today, too,' she told him, gesturing to the bag slung over her shoulder.

He stared at her, dumbfounded. 'Well, then, why in the hell ain't you wearing them? Have you seen this pandemic, Kenny? Have you, though?'

She'd never seen him so serious before. 'Alright, alright,' she conceded, reaching into her bag and opening the packet of masks and gloves and putting them on. 'That better for you?'

'Better for *us*,' he answered.

'Here,' she said, handing him the take-out bag and a twenty-dollar bill.

'Smells better than the last one,' he commented, dragging out the pizza box. 'What's the money for?'

'My friend at work, Becky, wanted you to have it.'

'Hmm,' Lonnie said, pocketing the money. 'Another do-gooder. Make sure you thank her, so she can go into the weekend feeling great about herself on account of her act of benevolence.' He took out a piece of pizza, noticing that Kenyatta wasn't eating. 'Are we supposed to be sharing this one pizza?'

Kenyatta shook her head. 'Nope. I'm not eating, today.'

'Suit yourself,' he said, opening the box, lowering his mask to his chin, and yanking out a slice which he folded in half and rammed into his toothless mouth.

'Are you keeping okay, Lonnie?' she asked.

'Trying to stay away from the pandemic,' he said around the mouthful of food. 'How's your case going? You found your guy yet?'

'Almost. We've gotten down to the last few names,' she revealed, summarizing the current position of their Chester Creek murder investigation, explaining about Kenneth Hankel, his slew of crimes across the country and the fact that he was currently their prime suspect.

'Hmm,' Lonnie muttered. 'You check any of them prison records?'

'Pardon me?'

'I said… You check prison records for this Kenneth guy?'

Kenyatta stared at him, amazed at her own oversight. 'Lonnie!' she said, pulling her cellphone from her bag.

'What?' he barked.

She held up her hand. 'Just give me a minute.' She opened up an internet browser to access the Federal Bureau of Prisons website which maintained a list of inmates who had served time in Federal prisons since 1982. How had she not thought of this? She typed Kenneth Hankel's name into the search engine.

Kenneth Hankel
Register Number: 07592-001
Race: White
Sex: Male

Released On: 11/25/1983
Sentence: 6 months

Kenyatta turned to Lonnie and said, 'Kenneth Hankel was in Federal prison at the time of the third murder.'

'There you go, you see. He ain't your guy, then.'

Chapter Twenty-Seven

November 3, 1983, Aston, Delaware County, Pennsylvania

He entered the guest bedroom, saddened. The time had come…in the end. He switched on the light, his eyes being immediately drawn to the putrid stains on the white linen. The dark fringe of the misshapen discoloration had imperceptibly crept outwards and was by now nearing the edge of the bed.

He watched her for a while, until he could no longer bear the persistence of the half-dozen blowflies that were passing in and out of her nose and mouth.

Poor Sadie was changing. Her purple-gray skin now had an odd marbled glow and, as he stepped forward to stroke her leg, he found that her skin rippled beneath his fingers like a layer of clothing, separate from the body on to which it clung.

He sat down on the bed beside her. There was no point telling her that it was time to go: she knew it. He watched a blowfly land on her thigh and whacked it hard with his hand. The fly escaped, but he found that, in doing so, he had torn her skin open.

'Oh, my God. I'm so sorry, Sadie,' he said, lifting the flap of skin back into place. 'There.'

From the garage, he could hear the sound of the engine running. Without thinking about it any further, he pulled the bedsheet over her, scooped her up in his arms and carried her through the house while holding his breath. He placed her down in the trunk and quickly closed the lid.

He switched off the light, standing for a few seconds while his eyes adjusted to the darkness, ahead of moving around to the front of the garage to lift open the door. Again, he just stood, watching and listening. It was past three in the morning and the street was expectedly deserted.

Climbing into the Dodge, he slowly crept forward onto the driveway, then got out and closed the garage door. Moments later, he was on his way.

He drove slowly, not wanting to reach his destination. Now that Fiona was home and had discovered his secret, things would have to be different. Very different. He would have to leave. Move away someplace.

His mournful contemplation was pierced by a set of oncoming headlights. He straightened in his seat, when the light from a passing streetlamp revealed the car to be a police patrol vehicle. He could feel the weight of the stare from the officer behind the wheel but kept driving and kept his cool. He watched as the taillights slowly receded in his rearview mirror and passed out of sight.

He grinned. 'That sure was close, Sadie,' he called behind him.

He reached the point on New Road where his father's car had come to a screeching halt thirteen years ago. He had visited the site the very next day to find that, to his surprise, the only clue as to what had gone on there had been the long skid marks on the road. He remembered bending down and touching the tiny flecks of black rubber, ground into the road's surface. He had run his hand along the full length of the tracks; the spot from where his father had slammed on the brakes to where the car had finally come to a full stop. He had sat on the wall which overlooked the creek, wondering what exactly had killed him. The fall onto the rocks? Or had he drowned in the shallow water? He had returned again to the spot the following day and repeated those actions, this time sitting on the wall and closing his eyes as he imagined his father's death. The event had been simultaneously a great relief from his tyranny and a reawakening of the fascination that had started way back with the drowning of the kittens. Water and death. He went back to the spot most days for a very long time, facts smoothly yielding to fantasies.

He switched off the engine, climbed out of the car and took in a long draw on the night air. He could smell and taste the creek as he walked around to the rear of the auto and popped open the trunk. The smell hit him right away. He was forced to cover his mouth and nose with the sleeve of his sweater.

'Sadie,' he said, half-chastising and half-lovingly. He took a sharp intake of breath, holding it as he cradled Sadie in his arms, and carried her to the low wall alongside the road. His lungs were aching, but he knew that he was able to hold his breath for longer still. He'd timed himself in the bath. Two minutes and thirty-two seconds was his record.

'Bye,' he blurted on his outward breath, releasing her over the edge of the bridge and down into the darkness below. The replying sound was a dull thud and a light percussive splash of water.

He returned to the car, shut the trunk and climbed back into the driver's seat. Switching on the radio, loud, he joined in with the second verse of *Take Me Home, Country Roads*, as his took him home with a smile on his face.

He pulled up on his driveway, opened the garage and drove the Dodge carefully inside. He dropped the door and entered the house. It was still dark, just as he had left it.

'I'm home,' he grunted, entering the dark living room. In a narrow chink of light coming from the neighbors' property, he could just make out Fiona's silhouette. She was still sitting in the same chair, having apparently not moved.

Chapter Twenty-Eight

Friday, March 13, 2020, Downtown Salt Lake City, Utah

Maddie parked her RAV4 in the garage beneath the Kearns Building. Under her coat, she was wearing a pair of khaki trousers, one of Michael's old lumberjack shirts and one of his way-oversized sweaters; a comforting tribute, borne out of the murky realms of her subconscious. She switched off the engine and stared through the windshield. The results of the CSI sweep of Michael's truck could come back any day now, a thought that had disturbed her sleep last night and had continued to dominate her mind on the drive to work. Closing her eyes, she took in a series of long breaths, trying mentally to compartmentalize her preoccupying thoughts and anxieties.

After a few moments, she opened her eyes, ready to take the Chester Creek case to its looming conclusion.

She got out of the car, locked up and headed over to the elevator. As she stepped out on the fifth floor, she couldn't help but laugh. Becky and Hudson were waiting impatiently outside the Venator office. 'You're eager,' she commented, pulling out her keys as she walked towards them.

'We're *so* close!' Hudson said in reply.

'We want to get this guy,' Becky said.

'Morning!' Kenyatta called, appearing at the top of the stairs.

Maddie shook her head as she opened the office. 'Well, since pretty well the whole team seems to be assembled here before 9am, let's get coffee, or whatever, and then what? Should we say…briefing in five minutes to plan the day?'

'I need to speak first,' Kenyatta insisted, raising a finger into the air. 'I have some news.'

'Intriguing,' Maddie said, hanging up her jacket and trilby hat, and switching on the coffee machine. In her office, she turned on her computer and hoisted up the blinds. Outside, the sky was leaden and heavy with what looked like an imminent fresh flurry of snow. She sighed as she gazed down at the sidewalk, desperate to get out for some physical exercise. A long run. Maybe on the weekend she could get out, if the snow didn't turn out to be too bad.

In the kitchen area, she made herself some coffee, watching as the team all settled in at their desks. When Ross arrived, she moved into the main office, ready to start the day. Nursing her mug in both hands, she propped herself up on Hudson's desk and said, 'When you're ready, Kenyatta. I think we're good to go.'

Kenyatta stood up, just as a screenshot from the Bureau of Prisons appeared on the digital whiteboard. 'See if any of you can spot my tiny, little lapse of attention to detail yesterday,' she said, folding her arms.

Maddie read the detention information for Kenneth Hankel. She got it. 'Oh.'

'That's great, Kenyatta,' Becky enthused. 'It definitely rules him out, then.'

'Well, it's great *now*,' Kenyatta agreed, 'but it might have been even greater to know *yesterday* that Kenneth Hankel couldn't have been the Chester Creek killer because he was locked up in Federal jail at the time of the last murder. The time we spent debating—'

'It's okay, it's okay. You got there in the end,' Maddie reassured her, stepping over to the glassboard. She unfastened the mugshots of Robert Davis and the Hankel brothers, Kenneth and Paul, reattaching them at the bottom of the board; the team's research had strongly suggested that these three men were not the Chester Creek killer.

The names of Joe, Wayne and Carl Stern remained under the SUSPECTS heading.

Maddie looked at the two names remaining under the SUSPECT'S PARENTS title, then said, 'We must have missed something here. We're left with Enoch Brown and Vera Wolsey as the killer's parents'—she turned and tapped their names with a marker pen—'which gives us a problem: there is no recorded child to this couple. The way I see it is we have three possible scenarios: one, as we suspected with Kenneth Hankel, one or more of Vera Wolsey's sons were not biologically Eldred Sterns's, but rather Enoch Brown's; two, they had a child together, who was raised by a family member as their own; three, that the child was adopted away. Does anyone have any alternative ideas?'

Becky shook her head.

'Nope,' Hudson said.

'No, Kenyatta said. 'Which means we've got our work cut out again.'

'Exactly that,' Maddie agreed, unable to take her eyes off Enoch Brown and Vera Wolsey. 'With regard to the third option, I'm going to get in touch with Detective Tyler to see if he can access records that are unavailable to us, regarding possible adoption scenarios. We need to build up as detailed a picture of Enoch, Vera and Vera's three boys' lives as we possibly can. So, Hudson, if you continue with your work on Enoch… Becky on Vera… And Kenyatta, if you take the three boys. We need *everything* we can get our hands on right now—social media, obits, newspaper stories, yearbooks, criminal histories, background checks, work, photos—to crack this one: *anything*. Are we all good with that?'

The team murmured, nodded their agreement and immediately began work.

Maddie sipped her coffee and strode to her office, pushing the door closed. Sitting at her desk, she picked up her phone to call the detective. An unnerving sour feeling in the pit of her stomach was inhibiting her from dialing him. She drank more coffee, looking awhile at the phone in her hand. Finally, she dialed the direct number to his office. He answered almost immediately.

'Detective Tyler speaking,' he answered gruffly.

'Detective, it's Madison Scott-Barnhart here,' she said, instantly cringing at herself for formally using her full name. 'Maddie,' she quickly added.

'Oh, hi there. How are things in good ol' snowy Utah?'

She spun her chair around to see outside. 'Well, it had pretty well cleared up, actually, but now it's just started again,' she laughed. 'How are you?'

'Uh, well… I can't see my computer anymore because of the pile of cases I'm working on and I've gained ten pounds in the last two weeks. That kind of sums things up at my end.'

'But apart from that, you're good?' she asked with a laugh.

'Yeah, just perfect,' he replied. 'I don't have the results back from the truck analysis yet, I'm afraid.'

'Oh, that's fine,' she said dismissively, as though it had completely slipped her mind. 'I was actually calling about the Chester Creek case.' Before he could jump in with an expectation of the case's conclusion, she quickly added, 'I need you to look something up for me.'

'Okay, go ahead,' he encouraged.

Maddie took great care to give as much detail as she could about Vera Wolsey and Enoch Brown, but without any fanfare and even without discussing the fact that any potential child, after whose possible existence she was currently enquiring, could very well be the killer.

But it was obvious and when she'd finished, he immediately asked, 'And you think their child could be our guy?'

Maddie took a moment to answer. 'It's just one theory we're working on.'

'Are you close?'

'I think so, yes.'

'Wow, what's that been? Like eleven days? Jesus, you can have *all* my cases.'

'Let's not get ahead of ourselves, now, Detective,' she warned. 'How soon do you think you can look up that potential adoption for me?'

'Oh, not long at all. Give me an hour, tops, and I'll email you the answer.'

'Great. I'll let you get to it. Be in touch. Bye.'

'Bye, Maddie,' he said.

She ended the call and sat drinking her coffee, watching the gently tumbling flakes outside. She liked the detective, she had to admit. In another time and place, they might just have dated. She gazed at her wedding ring, wondering what it really meant, being married to a man whom she hadn't set eyes on in five years. What if one of her best-case scenarios—that he'd been injured and lost his memory—came true, and he suddenly remembered his old life and walked right back in? Then what? Could they really just pick up where they'd left off? The idea was absurd, but it was a hope onto which she and the kids had been clinging all this time and, without evidence to the contrary, onto which she was certain they would continue hanging indefinitely.

She finished her coffee and stood to leave her office; now really wasn't the time to be maudlin about Michael. She started to helicopter around her team, beginning with Ross. 'Anything of interest come in?'

Ross grimaced. 'Apart from the continual stream of emails from people suggesting that you look into this murder or that set of unidentified remains, no.'

She wandered over to Hudson. 'How's it going?' she asked, placing her hand on the back of his chair and taking a look at his screen. She still had no idea why he had been emailing Wanda Chabala last week and even less certainty about whether it was even any of her business to ask, since it had been during his lunchbreak.

Hudson sighed. 'There are literally gazillions of Enoch Browns out there. Social media, Spokeo, TruthFinder, BeenVerified, MyLife are producing nothing obvious. I mean, look at this.' He clicked on one of maybe fifty open internet-browser tabs at the top of his screen. This one was for Newspapers.com, where Hudson had typed in Enoch's name.

1,034,633 results

'A million,' he complained, with a pained look on his face. 'Even if I narrow down the search,' he said, selecting Pennsylvania from the map of the United States, 'it still leaves me with over one hundred and eleven thousand.'

Maddie watched, as he narrowed the search field down to Delaware County, displaying a much more manageable results list of 124 articles. 'There you go,' she soothed, patting him on the shoulder.

'Yeah, so we'd better hope he did something newsworthy in Delaware County, or he's off-radar.'

'They're not Sternses!' Kenyatta suddenly yelled, making Maddie jump.

'My goodness. What?' she said.

'Joe, Carl and Wayne. Vera's boys. Sterns is *not* their surname; it's *Wolsey*!' Kenyatta exclaimed. 'They had Vera's surname. The tree I found them listed on must have been based on somebody's incorrect assumption, or something.'

Maddie slid around behind Kenyatta's desk, seeing the family tree that she was working on. 'But that's still the wrong surname…Y-DNA-wise, I mean.'

'Yeah, it is,' Kenyatta agreed. 'But it leaves it much more open as to the three boys' parentage.'

'Okay, so one possible narrative,' Maddie said, gazing up at the ceiling as she composed her thoughts, 'is that Vera and Enoch got together at high school—they were in the same class, after all—but never married. Too young, parents disapproved, or whatever. One, two or all three of the boys were fathered by Enoch Brown but they never took his name.'

'That would fit, yes,' Becky agreed.

'Let me see if I can get a yearbook photo of the boys,' Kenyatta said, opening up MyHeritage.

'Good idea,' Maddie said, watching over her shoulder as Kenyatta inputted Joe Wolsey's name into a yearbook search. They looked at the top result and then at each other.

1972. Chester High School. Born 1957.

Kenyatta clicked to view the entry and a grainy yellow image loaded. 'Oh, my!' Kenyatta said, gazing up at Maddie.

'Zoom in,' Maddie instructed, glancing quickly at the police sketch on the whiteboard.

Kenyatta pulled the image full screen. Joe was around the age of sixteen, with pale skin, short dark hair and with a long, thin face staring out, unsmiling.

Despite the lingering traces of youth, Joe Wolsey looked remarkably like the police sketch image for the Chester Creek killer. Neither Maddie nor Kenyatta spoke; they silently alternated their gaze between the yearbook image and the suspect sketch.

'He was born the year after Vera and Enoch's senior year at high school,' Maddie observed.

'Yeah,' Kenyatta said, saving the image to Joe's profile page. She then adjusted the yearbook search criteria for Carl Wolsey.

1972. Chester High School. Born 1958.

The image that appeared for Carl left Maddie in no doubt that he was Joe's sibling. He too had short dark hair and those same dark, haunting eyes. And, just like his brother, he seemed to stare out of the photo with a vacant, cadaverous expression.

Kenyatta repeated the search for the final brother, Wayne, who had been born 1960, then displayed the three pictures side-by-side.

'Pull it up on the board for everyone to see,' Maddie instructed. 'Take a look at this, guys.'

Hudson and Becky looked over as the photos of the three Wolsey brothers appeared on the digital whiteboard.

Hudson stood up and moved towards the screen to get a closer look, unable to suppress a gasp. As he reached the whiteboard, he looked from the three boys to the suspect image on the adjacent board. 'Wow.'

'They're pretty damn identical to the police sketch,' Becky said, voicing everyone else's thoughts. 'God. It's the eyes, isn't it? I can see why that witness described them as 'scary': they're terrifying.'

'Unless we can prove otherwise,' Maddie began, 'ten years after these pictures were taken, one of those boys went on to brutally kill three women.'

'At *least* three,' Becky said.

Maddie couldn't force her eyes away from their faces, couldn't stop herself from imploring from them the simple question of *why*? What had tipped them over the edge to perpetrate something so barbarically brutal? What she had learned from the past cases, with which she had been involved, was that it usually wasn't a single trigger, but rather a slow path of deviancy that often started with a defective childhood or some other sort of adverse childhood experience. Becky was always keen to remind the team that environmental factors contributed an estimated eighty percent of causation in creating a serial killer, leaving twenty percent to possible defective genetics.

'Good work,' Maddie said, finally drawing her eyes away from the whiteboard. 'Kenyatta, can you get those printed out and up on the suspect board?'

'Sure, will do.'

Maddie returned to her office to check whether she had received an email from the detective. She had.

Dear Maddie
There are no official recordings of an adoption by either Vera Wolsey or Enoch Brown to anyone else. Hope this helps. What does it mean for the case?'
Best,
Clayton

Maddie walked straight back out into the main office, announcing as she passed through, 'No official adoption, guys.' She could tell, though, that they were distracted. Hudson was sharing his screen. A newspaper article. Maddie moved in closer in order to read it.

Lebanon Daily News, Pennsylvania. September 21, 1970

Chester Man Drowned in Creek after Chase
Chester, PA
A man identified as Enoch Brown, 33, of Chester was found drowned in Chester Creek Saturday night, within an hour after he led police on a 25-block auto chase with his fourteen-year-old son, Joe Wolsey in the back of the car. Several shots were fired by police.

Brown was spotted shortly afterward on New Road with his son, where he apparently fell from the bridge into the water, while his son, Joe looked on.

An autopsy was slated.

'The bridge on New Road was exactly where the bodies were

dumped,' Becky said, barely audibly.

Chapter Twenty-Nine

Friday, March 13, 2020, Downtown Salt Lake City, Utah

'...*his son, Joe looked on,*' Maddie read again.

The team had fallen silent, work had paused, as they all took in the news that Joe Wolsey had been in the back of his father's car during a police chase, had had shots fired at him and had watched his father apparently fall from a bridge into the Chester Creek at the precise location where the three victims' bodies had been disposed of twelve years later.

Kenyatta broke the silence by standing up and collecting the three biographical sheets for Joe, Carl and Wayne Wolsey from the printer and sticking them up beneath the SUSPECTS heading.

'Maddie,' Ross called over. 'Phone call. It's urgent.'

Maddie didn't turn but raised her hand by way of acknowledgement, and to signal that she would be just a moment, before offering some parting comments to the team: 'We obviously can't eliminate Wayne and Carl at this time, but Joe Wolsey is looking like a very strong candidate to be the Chester Creek killer. Hudson, can you see if you can find any other references to this story. It says that an autopsy was held: see if that's reported. Work with Becky on getting an address. Kenyatta, keep going with finding anything and everything on the other two—'

'Maddie...' Ross insisted.

She walked over to Ross's reception desk.

'Trooper Antoniewicz wants to speak with you. He says it's urgent,' Ross said.

'Patch it through to my office,' she directed, worried and not familiar with the name. She pushed the door closed with her foot as her phone began to ring. 'Madison Scott-Barnhart.'

'Good morning, Ma'am. This is State Trooper Santiago Antoniewicz. Could you please confirm your mother's name for me?'

Maddie's heart went cold. Her *mother*. God, what had happened? Her throat instantly dried as she sank down into her office chair. 'Is she okay? What's happened?' she managed to ask.

'She's fine...but I need you to confirm her name for me, please,' he persisted.

'Pat...erm...Patricia Scott,' she answered. 'What's happened?'

'We picked her up after she was trying to force entry into a property. The owners called the police and we now have her in the back of the car.'

'What?' Maddie stammered. 'Trying to…*force entry* into a property? *My* mother? Sixty-two years old, gray hair…'

'Uh-huh, that's correct,' he confirmed.

'Sorry, Officer, I'm just a little confused, here. Why exactly was she doing that?'

'Your guess is as good as mine. She said it was her house and was quite rude to the current owners when they wouldn't let her inside.'

'I can't believe it,' Maddie said. 'She's not been arrested, has she?'

'No, she hasn't this time,' he said.

'Look, she doesn't make a habit of this sort of thing,' Maddie said. 'What are you going to do with her now?'

'We can take her home if it's nearby.'

'Where are you?' Maddie asked. 'I'm currently downtown, but she lives with me in South Jordan.'

'We're right in the neighborhood on Horseshoe Circle.'

Maddie exhaled. It made sense, now. 'Number twenty-two?'

'Yeah, that's right,' the trooper confirmed.

'It's her old address. She's got mild Alzheimer's. I'm sorry.'

'Right, okay. Sounds like you need to get her some help. You know, she can't just go wandering back to her old property like that and trying to force her way inside.'

'Yeah, thanks for that,' Maddie said, noting his tone. 'Let me give you my address and I'll see you there.'

Maddie gave him her address and ended the call. 'Patronizing jerk,' she muttered. But he had a point: it was no longer safe for her mom to have the freedom to come and go as she pleased.

She opened her office door, showing a mask of normality as she reached for her jacket and hat. Last, she turned casually to the team and said, 'I have to run home real quick. Any major problems you can get me on my cell; anything else, Kenyatta is in charge. I shouldn't be too long.'

The drive home on the I-15 was pretty much a blur for Maddie. Considerations for Michael or the Chester Creek case didn't even get a thought. She agonized over her mother the whole way, trying to formulate a resolution to their painful situation, one that would be satisfactory for all concerned. But every potential solution wound up circling right back to the start with the distressing plain truth of the matter: she couldn't personally look after her mother, she couldn't afford a full-time caregiver and she couldn't bring herself to put her into a home, either.

The patrol car was waiting in the drive when she reached her house. As she parked outside, Maddie was expecting to find her mother angry, indignant and defiant, with some fanciful story that she had concocted to explain away why she had been trying to get into her former home. But the woman climbing out of the back of the squad car was a broken-spirited waif. Tears were streaming down her face and she averted her gaze, wholly unable to look Maddie in the eye.

'Oh, Mom,' Maddie said, rushing up and hugging her. She turned to face the police officer and said a short, polite, 'Thank you for bringing her home,' before ushering her mother towards the house.

'You're lucky the homeowners didn't want to press charges,' the policeman called after her.

Maddie glared at him, then unlocked the front door.

Inside, with the door closed, her mother caught her reflection in the oval hallway mirror. 'I'm...scared,' she said timidly.

'We'll get through this,' Maddie tried to reassure her, though she had nothing to offer that could substantiate her declaration of positivity.

'Here,' her mom said, handing Maddie her set of house keys. 'I don't think I want to go out alone, not ever again.'

Maddie took the keys, thankful to have a short-term solution to the problem. 'Do you want a drink or anything to eat?'

She shook her head. 'I'm going to lie down. You can get back to work. Lock me in. I'll be fine.'

Maddie had already reached the harrowing conclusion that, for the time being, the safest thing would be not to let her mother out of the house alone; but to hear those words coming from her mouth chilled her blood. 'I'll get Nikki to come home straight from school,' Maddie said, watching her mom sloping off towards her bedroom with tears in her eyes.

She left the house, locking the door behind her and reassuring herself that her daughter would be there momentarily.

An hour later, Maddie was riding the elevator to the fifth floor of the Kearns Building. She stared at the gray walls as she nervously tapped her bunch of keys into her thigh. The door pinged open and she forced herself to achieve a smile, striding confidently back into the Venator office.

She noticed immediately the strange atmosphere in the room. The team was throwing furtive glances her way and Hudson appeared to be trying to stifle a grin. She felt as though she had just crashed her own surprise birthday party. 'What's going on?' she asked.

'What do you mean?' Kenyatta replied innocently.

Maddie saw the playful twinkle in her eyes. 'Something's going on...'

Kenyatta's eyes widened and she shrugged.

Becky turned her face from Maddie as she approached their workstations. Perhaps they had discovered something, she reasoned, looking up at the digital whiteboard but finding it to be on standby. Then she caught the glassboard in her peripheral vision. Under *SUSPECTS* were just two people; one of the brothers was no longer present, but she couldn't make out from this distance which had been eliminated in the time that she'd been gone. She rushed over to find out and emitted a small gasp. Turning to face the team one at a time, she said, 'Joe's out?'

'Uh-huh,' Kenyatta confirmed with a smile. 'Just Wayne and Carl Wolsey left.'

'Well, what did you get on Joe?' Maddie asked.

Hudson woke the digital whiteboard, revealing a short newspaper story, dated September 20, 1982.

Man found hanged in garage
A 25-year-old man from Chester was found hanged in the garage of his mother's home yesterday afternoon. Joe Wolsey of New Road, Aston, had suffered a history of mental illness and had recently been released from the county psychiatric hospital. Mr. Wolsey was pronounced dead at the Delaware County Memorial Hospital.

'Notice the date?' Hudson asked her.

Maddie looked to the top of the paper. 'Yeah, a good six weeks *before* the first murder.'

'And?' Hudson pushed, elongating his question.

'And...' Maddie scrutinized the date again, 'I don't know.' She looked at him for clarification, seeing that Becky and Kenyatta were also staring at her.

'Joe Wolsey took his own life on September 19; twelve years *to the day* after his dad drowned in the Chester Creek.'

'Jeez,' Maddie commented. 'What a sad story. And New Road. That's where the bodies were left, right?'

'Uh-huh,' Kenyatta confirmed.

'This is the house they lived in,' Becky said, her computer screen overriding Hudson's.

A view of a quiet sidewalk-less, single-track lane appeared on Google Street View. Superimposed on the road were the white words, *New Road*. Maddie presumed the Wolsey-Brown family had resided in one of the small homes to the right of the lane, but Becky pulled the view sharp left, revealing a tiny derelict property.

'Oh,' Maddie uttered. The house—if it could be described as such—was two-story and just one room's width. On the first floor were a set of rotten garage doors and above it, the house itself. Three glassless windows were set into a tired beige wall with a center-pitched roof. '*This* was the family home?'

'Yeah,' Becky said. 'And take a look at this.' She began clicking her way down New Road, past a church and a bunch of regular homes. After five or six clicks, she stopped. 'This is the bridge where Enoch Brown died—as witnessed by his eldest son, Joe—and where the Chester Creek serial killer left the bodies of his three victims.'

'Are we thinking that Joe or Wayne lived here, and this is where the crimes were committed?' Maddie asked.

'I don't think so,' Becky answered. 'Take a look at this.' Becky tapped her keyboard and brought up the original map of the area that she had created, with a large, semi-transparent purple circle within which was contained a scalene triangle with the three abduction sites at each of its apexes. 'As you can see, their address on New Road is *outside* of the Circle Theory of Environmental Range *and* outside of the triangle formed by the three murders.'

'But it's pretty close,' Maddie ventured, having taken a spare chair at Kenyatta's desk. 'And like a lot of the stuff we do here, it's not always one hundred percent.'

A frown settled on Becky's face as she thought for a moment. 'I don't think the killer was living at that address in New Road at the time of the murders. Nearby, for sure, but not in *that* house. It just doesn't fit the geo-profile, never mind the logistics of bringing abducted girls back to that tiny property, with his mom living there.'

Maddie nodded. 'So what we're potentially looking at here is a young couple, Enoch and Vera, who got together in high school but didn't marry and who probably struggled to raise their young family in a'—she pointed to the whiteboard—'well…*shack*, for want of a better word. Enoch Brown seems like he's getting in trouble with law enforcement. He dies in Chester Creek after a violent police chase with poor fourteen-year-old Joe looking on. Joe goes on to suffer mental health problems and then later takes his own life. When does Vera's new man, Eldred Sterns, turn up on the scene?'

'So, they marry in 1972,' Kenyatta reported, 'but they divorce five years later, with Vera claiming that he was abusive towards her. At some point after Joe's death, she moves back to Philly—where she was born—and appears to have stayed there for the rest of her life.'

'Presumably leaving Wayne and Carl behind in Delaware County,' Hudson added.

'And do we have anything on the pair of them yet?' Maddie enquired.

'Only a little so far,' Kenyatta replied. Neither one of them is currently residing in Delaware County. Address history for both on background check sites only begins in 1988, by which point they're both out of the area. The current address for Wayne is in a town, called Oxford, about forty miles west of Chester Creek, although he has moved all around the country in the intervening years. So far, no sign of a marriage or kids for him. For Carl, three wives and six kids scattered around the US. Current location is a small town in Ohio.'

Maddie raised her eyebrows. 'Interesting. Any criminal history for either?'

'I haven't got that far, as yet,' Kenyatta said.

'Shall I take that on?' Maddie suggested.

'Sure, go ahead.'

Maddie looked up at the clock: 1:39pm. 'We've got three hours, guys,' she said, striding towards her office. She paused in the kitchen area and made herself some coffee. While it was brewing, she thought of her mom's forlorn expression as she had lumbered off to her bedroom earlier. Maddie pictured her mom's reaction at hearing the door being locked up from the outside, as though she were some sort of a sequestered, high-risk psychiatric patient. Maddie was tempted to call her but quickly reasoned that, knowing her mother as she did, it would be better to leave her alone with Nikki for the time being. Whatever happened here today in the office, she was going to be getting home on time and attempting something close to a normal family dinner together.

She carried her coffee into her office and sat down with a

meaningful sigh.

The simplest method of checking the brothers' criminal history—since it was unknown where, when or even if they had committed any crimes—was through newspapers, background check companies and the Bureau of Prisons. More specific detail could often be accessed from individual prisons, but such information usually came with an associated financial and time cost.

Maddie inputted Wayne Wolsey's name into the background check websites. He had a lot of previous addresses around the US; it was a long list. As she looked at the associated map, which displayed all the locations as red marker pins, she wondered if he was the Chester Creek killer and whether, as Becky had suspected all along, there would be a slew of other murdered women close to each of those places. She hoped that Becky was wrong as she moved down the page to *Criminal & Traffic* on the BeenVerified website, seeing the number 0 marked against it.

Despite its being fairly conclusive, Maddie returned to the top of the page and sent Wayne's address history to her office printer. She collected the sheet, placed it next to her on the desk and opened up Newspapers.com. She began a systematic cross-checking of his name and the locations where he had lived against the dates he had lived there.

In just over an hour, she had concluded the list, finding no attributable crimes for Wayne Wolsey. In fact, he had failed to show up in any newspaper story at all. Returning to BeenVerified, Maddie looked curiously at Wayne's work history.

Rogers & Jones - bricklayer
Crandles - laborer
Wyo-Build - bricklayer
Bo's Bricks - assistant

Maddie added the detail to Wayne's biography and updated his profile page with the new information. Next, she turned her attention to Wayne's brother, Carl. Editing the background search entry and switching it to his name, she scrolled down to check any convictions recorded against him.

Criminal & Traffic 5

With great interest, Maddie clicked to view the report.

Failure to pay toll
06/1/2019
La Crosse County, WI
Guilty. Paid fine.

Speeding 90/70
07/28/2012
Bingham County, ID
Guilty. Court fines $18,000

Sex A-V CH
08/11/2001
Harris County, TX
Non-Adjudication of guilt. Court fines $100,000

Sex A-V CH
10/10/2000
Harris County, TX
Probation Revoked. Court fines $89,925

Sex A-V CH
08/30/1999
Jefferson County, MO
Guilty. Court fines $100,000

'Wow,' Maddie muttered flatly, as she copied and pasted the list of crimes across to Carl's biography page. Three convictions for aggravated sexual assault. It was this kind of sexual criminal history that Becky was certain would have existed prior to and alongside the Chester Creek killer's known three victims' cases, also.

Maddie looked at his profile photo, the one Kenyatta had found from his high school yearbook. Things were starting to fall into place.

Returning to her newspaper search, she began to run a check against each of the dates of Carl Wolsey's crimes to see if they had been reported locally. She had just an hour and a half left before this afternoon's briefing would bring this working day to an end and send her home to her family. Although she intended to investigate each of Carl's crimes, she started with the most serious and most apparently relevant to this case: the aggravated sexual assaults. The first, appearing in the *Jefferson City Post-Tribune*, was easy to find.

City of Herculaneum
LEGAL NOTICE
Carl Wolsey, a forty-one-year-old, has registered with the Herculaneum Police Department as a convicted sex offender at 999 Peggy Drive, Herculaneum, MO for a conviction or adjudication of Sexual Assault of a Child. The victim was a female, seventeen years of age. A photograph is located at the following internet address: https://www.mshp.dps.missouri.gov/CJ38/searchRegistry.jsp.
The registrant was assigned risk Level 2 using Static 99 guidelines.

Maddie took a screenshot of the article and pasted it into Carl Wolsey's biography page, once she had scribbled down the internet address which would provide more information and a photograph. Before she visited the site, she needed to remind herself of the Static 99 guidelines. They had been created to give an actuarial assessment of adult male sex offenders over the age of eighteen, placing them on a scale of negative three to positive ten. She looked up the Nominal Risk Levels, finding that Level 2 meant that Carl Wolsey had been deemed, in August 1999, to be of average risk.

Typing in the web address from the newspaper, Maddie was taken to the Missouri State Sex Offender Registry page. In front of her were two options for tracking down offenders: address search or name search. Maddie inputted Carl Wolsey's name and year of birth, then hit *Search*.

A screen loaded with Carl Wolsey's mugshot in the top left of the page over a turquoise backdrop. He was unshaven, overweight and, although he had clearly aged since his high school yearbook photo that had been taken twenty-seven years before, he still bore the unmistakable gaunt appearance shared by his two brothers. The dark shadows beneath his eyes made him appear all the more terrifying to Maddie.

Having checked that the image had saved, Maddie read down the appended biographical detail.

Name: Carl Wolsey
Gender: Male
Race: White
Date of Birth: 1/26/1958

Primary Address:
999 Peggy Drive, Herculaneum, MO
County: Jefferson

Physical Description:
Height: 5 Ft 11 In
Weight: 200lbs
Hair Color: Brown and partially gray
Eye Color: Brown

Switching to Google Maps, Maddie ran a search for his address. In satellite mode, she could instantly see that he had been living in a trailer park, surrounded by dense woodland. She dragged the little orange man onto the map and found herself looking at the joining of Peggy Road and Michael Drive. Number nine hundred and ninety-nine was situated right on the elbow joint of the two roads. It was a typical size for a trailer and, like those neighboring it, fairly run-down. Maddie returned to the satellite aerial view and noticed something. She zoomed in to twenty meters above the property. Behind that particular trailer—unlike any other in the park as far as she could see—was a path leading off to a clearing in the woods, which appeared to be dirt and rocks. From that small clearing, another narrow path wound further through the woodland to a river of some kind.

Maddie pulled in tighter so that the name of the river appeared: Joachim Creek.

Carl Wolsey, a thrice-convicted sex offender, lived in the only trailer with direct and apparently private access to a creek.

Maddie shuddered as she looked up at the clock: 4:15pm. She moved over to the doorway and called into the main office, 'I've got something. Let's do the briefing now.'

'So have I,' Kenyatta said. 'And it's pretty big.'

Chapter Thirty

November 4, 1983, Aston, Delaware County, Pennsylvania

The grief of losing Sadie had trashed the remainder of his night's sleep. He gave up trying and swung his legs over the side of the bed, resting his head in his hands. Dawn was just beginning to push light through the thin curtains. He looked at the digital alarm clock with a sigh: just before six. The space beside him in the bed was empty; it didn't look slept in at all. He ran his hand under the blankets up to the pillow. Cold. Another sigh, then he got up and walked, naked, into the kitchen, where he switched on the radio and fixed himself some coffee.

With the drink in his hand, he headed toward the door but then stopped and listened. The local radio was giving the *News at Six*. He turned up the volume.

'The body of a young female has been discovered this morning in Chester Creek. It is believed to have been found by a man walking his dog in the exact same location as the bodies of Mary-Jane Phelps and Terri Locke, although police have yet to confirm that the county is facing the possibility of having a serial killer in its midst. Police are...'

He switched off the radio, walked down the hall and entered the living room. He pulled open the curtains, the nascent morning light barely illuminating Fiona. He sipped his coffee and looked scornfully at the way her hair was sagged forward, covering her face.

He put his cup down on the coffee table, walked over to her and grabbed a handful of her hair, yanking it backward. A guttural noise—half-snore, half-belch—erupted from her throat, making him take a step back. Her head instantly flopped to the left, toppling her entire body down over to the side. He slowly moved his eyes up over her flaccid body to her throat where the deep red bruising glowed against her pasty skin. Her mouth was open and her face expressionless, just the way he had seen her on countless mornings just before she had woken. But now she wouldn't be waking up, he realized as his gaze came to settle on her hair and the matchbox-sized rectangle of it that he'd cut out.

'Well,' he finally said to her, 'it's your own fault for coming back so early. You know the weekends are *my* time; not *yours*. So...' He shrugged.

Think, he told himself as he began to pace the room. He glanced outside, the light bringing Fiona's Chevrolet out of the shadows. He had to move the car. And fast.

He gulped down the rest of the coffee on his way to the bedroom. He flicked on the light, grabbed his discarded underwear, pants and shirt, then found his Phillies baseball cap. Returning to the hallway, where Fiona had dropped her purse, he took out her car keys and then stealthily left the house through the front door. For a moment, he just stood and listened. No sign or sound of any of the neighbors. He got into Fiona's car, released the parking brake and allowed the vehicle to roll off the drive.

Only after he was clear of the house, did he switch on the ignition and begin the drive to Philadelphia.

He took his time getting back home, not wanting to leave an obvious trail. He'd left Fiona's Chevrolet in the parking lot not far from her work, as she herself would have been expected to do. He walked some distance, eventually deciding to hop on a bus. Finding himself deposited by the station, he took a train out to the airport. Merging in with the chaos and busyness of the arrivals terminal, he took a cab-ride from there into Chester and then walked the rest of the way home.

He arrived back to find the phone ringing. He dithered about whether or not to answer, but then picked up. 'Hello?'

'Oh, hi, there. I'm calling from TJW Accountancy in Philadelphia. I'm trying to reach Fiona Gregory. Is she home?' the female voice asked.

He wasn't ready for the question. In a split-second, he weighed the decision of which would be the best lie to tell: Fiona's never having come back home from work Friday night or her having left as usual first thing this morning?

'Um, no. She's not here, I'm afraid. Um, she left for work this morning,' he said, trying to sound sincere. 'Wait. Are you saying she didn't get there?'

'Well, I don't mean to worry you, sir, but… Well, no. The fact is, she hasn't shown up today yet. You know… I'm sure there's a very good explanation,' she said.

'Like what?' he asked, enjoying the role and hearing the woman on the other end, squirming in her predicament.

'Like maybe her car broke down or something.'

'But she would have called me,' he insisted. 'And you, for that matter. This isn't like Fiona at all.'

'Well, if it's out of character, maybe you should call the local hospitals and notify the police.'

'Yeah, I'm going to do that right now.'

'Okay, good luck.'

'Thanks,' he said, hanging up. He took in a long breath, then dialed the local hospital. When they told him that nobody fitting Fiona's name or physical description had been brought in over the past twenty-four hours, he phoned the police in Media.

'Sir, you need to wait until she's been missing for at least twenty-four hours,' the duty officer informed him. 'In most cases, missing people show up. My advice is to not worry but spend the rest of the day contacting Fiona's closest friends and relatives. You know, the people she'd go to if she was in any kind of trouble or who might have called on her because they're sick... That kind of thing.'

'But it's just so out of character,' he pushed, simultaneously gazing at Fiona's body on the couch. 'She would *definitely* have called me.'

'You don't know how many missing persons reports I've filled in during my time in the police. Almost always there's a good reason why they were missing.'

'*Almost* always,' he mimicked.

'Listen, buddy. Give us a call tomorrow morning if you haven't figured out where she's gone to, okay?'

'Sure,' he said.

'And try not to worry.'

He hung up. He wasn't worried. Not at all.

Chapter Thirty-One

Friday, March 13, 2020, Downtown Salt Lake City, Utah

Carl Wolsey's rap-sheet was displayed on the digital whiteboard for the whole team to see.

'I've only had a chance to review one of the three aggravated sexual assaults so far,' Maddie explained, standing in front of the board, moving on to show the satellite view of his address in 1999, 'but if we take a look at where he was living at the time of the first assault, you can see that he's in a trailer park. His unit, conveniently, is the only one to have its own'—she threw her hands in the air, then pointed to the clearing in the woodland—'*whatever* this might be which, in turn, also happens to lead down to…a creek.' She paused a moment in thought. 'It might be a smart move for us to run a search for any girls or women who have been murdered in the area and dumped in the creek for the dates that Carl Wolsey was living there.'

'You think he's got a thing for creeks?' Hudson asked, looking at Becky.

'Yes,' Becky confirmed. 'There's likely a maintained, significant psychological link to where Enoch Brown was killed. Maybe he became fixated with the spot…'

'So, like a ritual?' Maddie asked.

Becky nodded. 'Maybe. Sort of, yeah.'

'Then why stop and move out of the area?' Hudson probed.

'As I said, he's probably a smart guy and realized that he was coming ever closer to getting himself caught?'

The room was quiet for a moment, each of them mulling over what they had just learned.

'And what about Wayne?' Hudson asked. 'Any criminal activity for him?'

'None found in background checks,' Maddie relayed. 'Clearly, at this time he's not eliminated, but Carl Wolsey ticks all of our boxes.' She took a breath, folded her arms and looked at Kenyatta. 'What's your big discovery, Kenyatta?'

She raised her hand, studying whatever was on her computer screen. 'Give me one more minute…'

Maddie knew her well enough to know that it would have to be really important, if it meant that she was not giving the team briefing her undivided attention; even for one more minute. 'Okay. Hudson, do you want to go next?'

Hudson stood up and began, 'I've been concentrating on Enoch Brown, especially the years between the three boys' births and his death in 1970. These'—he clicked to share his screen—'are just some of his crimes. As you can see, he was in and out of jail throughout the sixties. Everything I've found so far has been theft related. Money, cars, goods and a couple of assaults thrown in for good measure, but nothing else. One report also stated that he was an alcoholic who couldn't hold down a job. I think it's safe to say the Wolsey boys had a pretty rough time of it during their upbringing.'

'History repeating,' Maddie muttered.

'And I found why he and Vera never married: Enoch didn't ever get a divorce from a very short-lived marriage right after college.'

'Interesting,' Maddie said as Hudson sat back down. 'Good job. Kenyatta, are we ready yet?'

'Oh, yes,' she said with a big smile. 'Take. A. Look. At. This.' With a click, her computer screen was mirrored for the team to see.

Maddie stared hard at the whiteboard. On it was a selection of family photographs contained within a Flickr account.

Kenyatta stood up, walked to the front and said, 'These pictures have been uploaded by one of Carl Wolsey's daughters.' Drawing her finger down the scroll bar a short way, she selected a single image, bringing it up full screen.

Dominating the foreground were the two surviving Wolsey brothers, easily identifiable from their yearbook photos, grinning at the camera relaxedly. Wayne's hand, holding a can of Budweiser, was draped over Carl's shoulder. In Carl's left hand was a rifle of some kind. Below the image was the caption: *uncle waynes place, august 99*. It was an interesting image to a point but didn't quite live up to Kenyatta's hype. Maddie looked at her for clarification.

'Do you see what's behind them?' Kenyatta said.

With that nudge, she saw it immediately: right behind the three men was a red Dodge Coronet.

'It's Carl,' Hudson commented quietly.

Maddie was sitting at the head of the kitchen table. It was the first time that she had sat in Michael's place at a family dinner and she had expected it to draw comment from one of the kids. But it hadn't happened. They had both gone to their usual seats and, if they had even noticed—which she very much doubted—they hadn't mentioned it.

They silently ate the mac and cheese that Maddie had prepared, a strange atmosphere hanging in the air. She sensed that perhaps it was caused by what had happened with her mother earlier that afternoon. Out of some sense of protecting her mom's dignity, Nikki and she hadn't told Trenton anything about it, but he had guessed that something was up, when he had seen her forlornly refuse to leave her room for anything, including dinner.

'When are we going to hear the results of the CSI check on Dad's truck?' Trenton asked, revealing in that moment the true cause of the disquietness.

'Any day,' Maddie said, tugging a forkful of stringy macaroni from her plate. 'But it might not tell us anything.'

Nikki looked at her and asked, 'Will the police do something about it, if they find evidence?'

'If they find something that wasn't picked up five years ago, I guess so, yes.'

'And then will you have him declared legally dead?' she asked.

'No, I'm not. Why would you even ask that?'

Nikki shrugged. 'I heard you talking to Jenna about it. I mean, maybe it's the right thing to do. Are we just going let another five years pass, hoping that he might come back to us?'

'Listen. Let's just take it one step at a time, okay?' Maddie said.

'Do you think you'll start dating?' Trenton asked.

'Wow,' Maddie said, setting down her cutlery. 'Where did *that* come from?'

'I'm not saying you can't or shouldn't…' he defended.

Maddie faced Nikki and said, 'I'm not planning on taking the legal steps you just mentioned'—then turned to Trenton—'and I'm certainly not planning on dating. I'm married. The fact that my husband isn't here right now is beside the point as far as I'm concerned. Okay?'

The kids nodded their heads and Maddie, shaken by the conversation, took in a long, quiet breath. What struck her the most, she realized upon reflection, was the kids' growing maturity.

'I'm sorry,' she eventually said.

'What for?' Nikki asked.

'For not including you sometimes in discussions about your dad.'

'We might actually be able to help,' Nikki responded. 'Well, *I* might be able to help.'

Trenton made a face as he shoveled a mass of macaroni cheese into his mouth.

'I know,' Maddie conceded. 'He'd be very proud of you both.'

A somber atmosphere descended over the table as they silently ate their dinners.

A few minutes passed and then Nikki asked, 'Have you solved the case that you're working on yet?'

Maddie took a moment to consider the question. 'Almost. I think by Monday morning I'll be passing a name to the detective in charge of the case.'

'Cool,' Nikki said. 'Well done. Another bad guy off the streets.'

'It's a team effort,' she said, despite the team's not being especially pleased with her for throwing them out of the office directly after the briefing today. Each of them had wanted to stay on, being so close to nailing the Chester Creek killer. She knew that they would have gone home and carried on working, and she had warned them against spending their entire weekend on it.

'Monday's going to be a great day all round, then,' Trenton enthused.

'Why? What else is happening on Monday?' Maddie asked.

Trenton smiled widely. 'Oh, you didn't hear the news today?'

Maddie shook her head. 'I had just a couple of things on my plate... So, no.'

'Drum roll, please,' he said, putting down his knife and fork and tapping his fingers on the edge of the table. He took an inordinately long breath and then revealed, 'The governor announced that, because of coronavirus, all school districts in the state will close for two weeks from Monday. It's party time!'

'He said *what?*'

Chapter Thirty-Two

November 5, 1983, Aston, Delaware County, Pennsylvania

'Godammit,' he shouted, bringing his fist down heavily on his alarm clock to end the horrendous racket. It was two in the morning and he had a blinding headache. As much as he wanted to continue sleeping, he forced himself out of bed. With a long yawn that ached his brain, he stood up and stretched. He picked up the heap of clothes from the floor and dumped them on the bed. Pitch-darkness and semi-drunkenness contrived to make getting dressed nearly impossible; he stumbled twice trying to pull on his socks and had to use the dresser to steady himself while he pulled on his pants. Once he'd achieved it and passed by the bathroom to urinate, he continued his drunken stroll along into the kitchen. Pulling open the refrigerator, he took out a can of Coke. Standing in the cold light, he downed the drink, belched and then walked down the hall to the garage.

Without switching on any lights, he pressed his ear to the garage door and listened. Nothing but the running of his own heart. He pulled open the garage door and stood quietly for a moment, taking in the sounds from outside. Once he was satisfied that nobody was about, he climbed into the Dodge and, as he had done with Fiona's car, released the parking brake and silently rolled the car out onto the driveway. He got out and closed the garage door behind him, and again rolled the car down the hill before firing up its engine when he felt far enough away from the house.

Needing air, he wound down the window as he drove west out of Delaware County. After pacing the house for most of the day, he at last had a plan: plans for tonight; plans for the morning; and then plans for his future outside of this damned county.

He'd seen enough cop shows and was smart enough to know that, if Fiona wound up in Chester Creek like the other girls, he'd have the cops on his doorstep arresting him within hours. He needed a different state and a different M.O. It was *always* about the M.O. Were people really so stupid?

He'd started by pulling out a whole bunch of old hiking maps, taking a long time to scour them for a suitable spot. He'd eventually found it about fifty miles west from his home. With the site chosen, he'd got himself blind drunk on Budweiser and then gotten Fiona ready for the ride.

As hard and vomit-inducing as it had been to achieve, not even the smartest detective would be able to prove a *modus-operandi* link between Fiona and his other girls. Except for the water, of course. There *had* to be water. There was always water.

He thought back to that day, when he had been ten years old, walking home from school along New Road when a car had skidded to a halt right beside him. His dad had been driving, with Joe crying his eyes out in the back and begging to be let out. Bullet holes in the side of the car.

'Get in!' his dad had shouted. He'd been drunk, of course. He was always drunk.

He'd refused. Although, seeing Joe so messed up like that—covering his face and screaming that he just wanted it all to stop—had really gotten to him.

His dad had climbed out of the car and grabbed him by his hair, dragging him round to the back.

He had managed to wriggle free of his grip somehow and, with his dad standing beside the low bridge wall, had given him one long, hard shove in the chest, sending him backwards down into the Chester Creek.

A pitiful cry, barely audible splash and the low thud of his father's skull cracking on a rock, and it was all over.

In other ways, that was when it had all started.

The best part was, Joe had been covering his face at the time, so had no idea of how their father had fallen.

As he traveled down the near-empty Baltimore Pike, he looked in his rearview mirror, imagining that he could see Fiona. He'd miss her, for sure. But now *his weekends* had just become *his weeks*. Hell, his weeks, his months. *His life.*

He caught sight of himself in the mirror and smiled back.

He kept to the speed limit the whole way there, crossing the state line into Maryland after three-quarters of an hour behind the wheel. He stayed on the same road for another fifteen minutes, then began to ease off the gas as the woodland, which had enclosed the freeway for the past few miles, ended. A neat line of small orange lights curved round to the mid-distance, illuminating the Conowingo Bridge.

The bridge—all 1,334 feet of it—was perfectly straight. Once he got on the bridge, he would be able to see any traffic for miles around. But there was nothing in either direction, so he stepped on the gas, knowing that he needed to get beyond the shallows to the deeper water, where the current would pick Fiona up and take her out to the Atlantic, if she made it that far. It amused him to wonder where she might wind up. Bermuda? The Bahamas? She'd always wanted to go there. She was fascinated with Cuba; maybe she would end up there.

He slowed down, trying to look beyond the streetlamps into the inky waters of the Susquehanna River. He'd driven far enough. He stopped the car and waited. He looked in his rearview mirror: nothing. Then, he looked through the windshield: nothing.

He jumped out, hurried around to the back of the Dodge, popped the trunk and took one final look around. He hauled the suitcase out, much heavier than it looked. He dragged it across the highway to the concrete barrier, bent down to scoop it up and then launched it clear off the side of the bridge.

'Bye, Fiona,' he said flatly.

A rather paltry splash replied that Fiona had hit the water. Correction, her torso had hit the water. Now all he needed to do was dispose of the rest of her.

Chapter Thirty-Three

Saturday, March 14, 2020, Salt Lake City, Utah

It was daylight when Becky Larkin woke. Her hand fumbled on her bedside table for her glasses in order for her to take a look at the time: 10:14am. She sat up and yawned, noticing a dull ache across the front of her head. That would be the four bottles of white wine, then, she reasoned, managing to stand up and walk across her bedroom to the door.

She found Ross curled up on the couch under a blanket, watching Saturday morning trash TV, she imagined. Judging by his screwed-up face and inability to look up at her, he was in a similar state as was she.

'Morning,' she said, slumping down beside him.

He made a low groaning noise, still not looking at her.

'What are you watching?' she asked.

Another moan and then, 'Some news thing about the coronavirus. We're basically all going to die...'

'Cheery,' she said, realizing that she needed water. She sat up and wandered over to the kitchen. 'Drink?'

'Coffee,' he muttered. 'Very strong. Not any of your decaf crap.'

Becky knocked back the glass of water for which her body had been yearning, wished she hadn't in equal measure, then set about making Ross some coffee from her fancy machine. 'What are your plans for the day?' she called over.

A weak, E.T.-like finger protruded from under the blanket and pointed at the TV.

'Oh,' she responded. 'Want to go on a run later, or do—'

'No!' he interrupted.

'I feel like I need to expend some energy,' she said.

'Go skiing,' he suggested.

'Yeah...' It *was* perfect conditions for skiing: a hundred and fifty percent snowpack and clear blue skies. 'My parents are still up at Park City, making the most of it. Rumor has it, they'll be closing down any moment, but I don't think I want to run into them right now, to be completely honest.'

'Take a ride out to Alta or Brighton, then. What is it with you and your parents, anyways?' he asked. 'Why are you so down on them at the moment?'

Becky carried the drink over to him, setting it down on the coffee table. She craned Ross's legs off the side of the couch and sat down beside him. So far, she hadn't told anyone about her suspicions regarding her father and Michael Barnhart.

'What is it, Becks?' Ross pushed, his legs promptly reappearing on her lap.

'So, you know how Maddie has had this detective guy we're currently working for look into her husband's disappearance?'

'Uh-huh.'

'And it turned out that Michael received a phone call from someone at my dad's work moments before he was last seen? Well, I spoke to my dad about it.'

'And?' Ross asked, sitting up and muting the TV.

'And he and my mom acted like…*really* weird. You know when you just know there's something up?'

'Maybe they're just feeling sorry or feeling guilty because he was working for him at the time,' Ross suggested.

'No, there's definitely something more to it than that. But I don't know what it is or how to find out.'

'Hmm,' Ross said. He thought for a moment, then said, 'Lois Strange?'

Becky blew out a puff of unimpressed air. Lois Strange had once been her father's PA and later became one of her closest friends. That had ended three years ago when Lois had brought a sexual harassment suit against Becky's father. 'I can't ask Lois,' Becky concluded. 'It ended so…messy with her. Trying to maintain a friendship with her and a relationship with my father, all while they were on the verge of a court case, was pretty much impossible. I can hardly turn up and start asking questions as if I *now* believe everything she says.'

'Did you not believe her back then? With the harassment case, I mean?' Ross asked, picking up his coffee and cupping it between his hands.

Becky sighed. It was complicated. 'Let's just say they were both very convincing in their arguments. The fact that I didn't outright disown my dad and take her side, though, was enough for Lois to break off our friendship. And I don't blame her, either.'

'Is it not worth a shot, though?' he asked.

'I don't know,' Becky replied, picking up her cellphone and opening Facebook. Lois had unfriended her a long time ago but not fully blocked her, meaning that Becky was still able to view her page.

She looked at Lois's smiling profile picture, wondering whether or not she should try to reestablish contact.

Hudson Édouard was sitting at home in his pajamas at the kitchen counter, working on his laptop. Abigail had left for work early this morning, so he was intending to spend the time pursuing his private work for Wanda Chabala.

He had begun research on the case three nights ago, when he'd first accessed the DNA kit of the person who had raped and murdered Francesca Chabala in Minneapolis in 2005. He'd been presented with a pretty decent match of 422cMs of DNA by a woman, named Jennifer LaFleur. FamilyTreeDNA had estimated that the relationship between Jennifer and the killer was somewhere around the first-to-second-cousin mark, although other permutations were also possible. Crucially, Jennifer had also matched the killer on his X-DNA, which meant that Hudson only needed to look at the killer's maternal side in order to find the connection.

A background check on Jennifer LaFleur revealed that she had been born in New York city in 1950. She had worked as a sonographer for several years at the New York Presbyterian Hospital and at the Manhattan Diagnostic Radiology company. Her current address was given as Quenzer Street, Nesconset, New York, where she appeared to live alone. Hudson followed a link to her open Facebook account. Her profile photo showed her to be a black woman with a gray afro, green eyes and a warm smile. Her friends list had provided Hudson with a list of potential family members whom he had yet to attach to her tree. He'd easily found out the name of Jennifer's mother by looking at the comments below an article that Jennifer had shared back in January, entitled *When You Have a Strong Mother, You Grow Up to Be a Strong Woman*. Mary B. LaFleur-Gagliano had commented: *Aawww. You are a strong woman. So proud of you, darling daughter. Thank you.*

Hudson's next step was to find the name of Jennifer's father in order to identify any potential siblings and then trace *their* children; these being among the most likely ways in which the killer could be related to Jennifer LaFleur on the face of it.

Knowing that Jennifer had been born in February 1950, Hudson worked on the assumption that her parents had married at some point prior to that date.

He ran a check for New York vital records on FamilySearch, finding that marriages for this period were not available online. Then he remembered something. The not-for-profit activist group, Reclaim the Records, had successfully taken New York City to court to force them to release records that should be in the public domain, but which were not. Hudson was pretty sure that these records included marriages for this period. He was also pretty sure that Reclaim the Records had won their case.

Opening a new web-browser, Hudson accessed reclaimtherecords.org. From a drop-down menu of states under *Record Requests*, he chose New York. He was right: a link was offered to the *NYC Marriage Index 1950-2017*, covering some 4,757,588 licenses filed in the city.

In the search boxes, he typed *Mary* as Spouse #1 with no surname and *LaFleur* as the surname of Spouse #2 with no forename, then hit enter.

Spouse #1: Mary B. Dinota
Spouse #2: Raymond LaFleur
Borough: Manhattan
Date: License issued 1949
Status: Public Document

Hudson hovered his mouse over the legal status, which informed him that—as the document was more than fifty years old—he would be able to obtain a copy via the New York City Clerk's Office. However, in this case it wasn't necessary. The entry had provided him all the detail that he needed: the full names of Jennifer LaFleur's parents.

Returning to the wiki page on FamilySearch, Hudson found that birth records for New York City were available on the vitalsearch website, for which Venator had registered log-in details. He went to enter the company credentials but stopped. What if Maddie questioned what he had been doing? It had never happened before and she knew that the whole team worked on their cases from home, but what if she made the link between this and having seen him emailing Wanda Chabala on Monday?

He decided against using the Venator credentials and paid the twenty-nine ninety-five for his own ninety-day credits. Once he had paid, he was able to access their archives. He found that the search period ran to 1965, covering the Manhattan, Brooklyn, Bronx, Queens and Staten Island districts.

Besides Jennifer, the search revealed just one additional child to Raymond and Mary LaFleur—Velveta LaFleur—which made life much simpler for Hudson. She being female, it also accentuated the possibility that the killer could be one of Velveta's sons, upon whom she had conferred her X-DNA.

Hudson returned to Jennifer LaFleur's Facebook friends list, finding one Velveta Mercaldo. He clicked on her profile, finding that it was a private account, giving no access to friends, photos or her timeline. So, he returned to Jennifer's page, slowly scrolling down her timeline and viewing the comments attached to each and every photo or story that she had shared. He didn't have to go back too far to find a photograph of two women smartly dressed, standing outside a theater. One was clearly Jennifer and the other was tagged as Velveta Mercaldo. The caption read, *My lil sis and I ready for the show!*

Three male Mercaldos were listed in Jennifer LaFleur's friends list, but, given the gravitas of the case, before he pursued them, Hudson wanted something more substantial to confirm that Jennifer LaFleur and Velveta Mercaldo were definitely siblings. A *My lil sis* caption under a photo hardly constituted the Genealogical Proof Standard.

Hudson stood up, made himself a coffee, then began to run background checks on Velveta Mercaldo.

Kenyatta Nelson was clapping her gloved hands together to keep warm. She was standing with three of her colleagues from the SLC Homeless Kitchen in Pioneer Park in the city center. She was standing behind a long trestle table on which were three soup urns and a large basket of bread rolls. A gathering of a half-dozen homeless men and women loitered around the table. They primarily came for the hot food, but, once a week on rotation, a variety of services were on offer from hairdressers to dentists and doctors, providing free basic health and hygiene care. Tonight, it was the turn of the podiatrist who was currently working on Lonnie's filthy feet. Kenyatta watched with admiration; she hated feet at the best of times, but the ones that this brave young woman got to see once every six weeks were something else altogether.

Kenyatta walked over to them. 'Hey, do you want more soup, Lonnie?'

'No,' he snapped from under his face mask. 'And keep your distance; you might be infected.'

'Okay, Lonnie,' she said, taking a step back. He'd arrived inebriated and in a foul mood. The bread rolls were too hard and the soup too salty for him. 'Did you ever cook, Lonnie?'

He glowered at her, turning swiftly back to continue his admonishments of the lucky lady cutting his toenails. 'Damn it, that's too close! It hurts! Are you even trained to do this?'

'Lighten up, Lonnie,' Kenyatta said gently, sensing the young woman's nervousness. 'She's just here to help you out.'

'Yeah, you're all here just to help, aren't ya?'

'Yes, we are.'

'Is that why you swing by my place with pizza every week? Huh?' he demanded.

'You're my friend, Lonnie,' she said.

'Well, you're not mine,' he countered.

Kenyatta shrugged. 'Friendship doesn't have to be bilateral, Lonnie. I want you to be safe. I want you to be well.'

He scowled at her. 'Well, Kenny, if it makes you feel good about yourself, you go ahead.'

'I will,' she said defiantly, walking slowly away from him. He clearly needed his own space right now.

'Just ignore him,' her colleague Jim told her, squeezing her forearm. 'It's really just the booze talking.'

'Yeah, I know,' Kenyatta said. 'It's fine.'

'Did you have a good morning?' he asked.

She smiled, fully aware that he was trying to change the subject. She was grateful for that. She liked Jim. He was a big bear of a man and someone whom she was glad to have around. 'I did some work on a cold case. Two little brothers murdered and dumped under a bridge in Penrose, Colorado in 1994.'

'Oh, that's awful,' he commented. 'Did you get anywhere?'

'Well, progress on this one is slow—real slow, actually—but I'm not ever going to give up on those two mites.' She had been about to add the specific detail of what little progress she had made this morning but quickly realized how pathetic it would sound. Working on the boys' closest genetic match, Elborn Nodecker, Kenyatta had managed to successfully identify another two sets of his seventh great-grandparents, leaving just another four hundred and ninety-six to be identified. It was, by all accounts, a hopeless situation.

'Good on you, Kenyatta,' Jim praised. 'Someone needs to not give up on these people…'

Kenyatta wasn't sure if he was still talking about the two brothers, or Lonnie who was now ranting at the podiatrist, or maybe just people in general.

'I've got my sons visiting for the day tomorrow,' she said, 'so, you see, all is good in the world.'

Jim touched her arm. 'Hey, you deserve that, Kenyatta; you're a good person.'

Becky was sitting in Nordstrom's eBar, drinking a pomegranate iced tea. She had taken a brown leather chair in the corner of the cafe and sat waiting, constantly glancing at the door every time a customer came or went. The place was modern, clean with ochre walls and terracotta floor tiles and a view out over the water fountains right in the heart of the Nordstrom City Creek Center.

She told herself to slow up a little; she'd been here just a couple of minutes and her drink was almost gone. She looked at her watch, then back at the door, still not even certain that this was such a good idea. After a lot of encouragement from Ross this morning, she had sent a message to her former friend, Lois Strange. She'd been upfront and honest in the message, telling her that she wanted to ask her a favor, adding, too, that she had missed their friendship. Lois had almost immediately replied, saying that it was great to hear from her and she would be happy to meet up today.

Her cellphone beeped with an incoming text message that Becky half-hoped was Lois canceling their meeting. She pulled it out of her jeans pocket, only to see that it was from Jerome.

Hi. How would you like dinner at St Bernard's tomorrow night?

Becky smiled and replied that she would indeed like that very much. She hit send and was drawn to the sound of the door opening. There she was. Her old friend, Lois Strange. She took a quick look around the cafe, spotted Becky and smiled as she strode towards her.

Becky set her drink down, stood up and embraced her. The anxiety build-up from waiting and the uncertainty of meeting her were dispelled in a protracted out-breath as she hugged Lois. 'I've missed you,' she whispered.

'Me too,' Lois agreed, eventually pulling back. 'Do you need a drink? I'm gasping for coffee.'

'Yeah, I'll get another of these. That'd be great,' Becky said, lifting her near-empty drink. 'Pomegranate iced tea.'

'Iced tea…in *this* weather?' Lois stammered. 'I see you're still a fitness freak, then.'

'I try,' Becky said with a smile. 'Although the empty bottles of wine from last night would suggest otherwise.'

'I'll be back in two shakes,' Lois said, grinning at their old in-joke saying, and headed over to the counter.

Becky smiled and finished the last mouthful of her tea, watching Lois as she ordered. She hadn't changed at all, at least not physically. But what about emotionally? What had the case done to her? Lois's lawyers and Becky's father's lawyers had agreed to an out-of-court settlement, the finer details of which Becky had never been able to glean. The case had been brushed under the carpet and dismissed from conversation at the family home.

Lois returned with two drinks. She handed one to Becky, then sat down opposite her. 'So, how are you?'

'Good, thank you,' Becky answered. 'And what about you?'

Lois nodded. 'Yeah, good. It's taken a while, you know, but I'm working as a PA again to a CEO in a big tech firm in the city,' she said, quickly adding, 'a *female* CEO.'

Becky pretended not to have noticed the barb in her comment. 'Oh, I have one of those. That's great to hear. And are you still living at the same place?'

Lois shook her head. 'No, I moved in with my boyfriend—sorry, *fiancé*—last year. Bigger place, outside of town. It's nice. How about you? What are you doing these days?'

'I work for an investigative genetic genealogy company right here in the city,' Becky replied.

'A what?' Lois asked with a laugh.

Becky grinned. 'You've heard of *The Winterset Butcher*, right?'

Lois frowned. 'Yes.'

'Venator was the company that identified him through genealogy and DNA. That's who I work for.'

'Oh my God,' Lois said. 'That is *so* interesting. So, that's what you do: solve cold cases?'

'Pretty much, yeah.'

'Wow—cool job.'

'Well, I love it and my boss is pretty cool. She's kind of who I wanted to speak to you about, actually: Maddie Scott-Barnhart.'

Lois's expression didn't change. If she recognized the name, she gave no glimmer. 'You're looking at me like I should know her.'

'Her husband was Michael Barnhart who vanished five years ago.'

'Oh, yeah… He worked for your dad, right?'

'That's right. It's come to light in the last few days that, right before his cellphone was switched off and he was never to be seen again, he received a phone call from The Larkin Investment and Finance Group.'

'Oh,' Lois responded. 'Who made the call?'

Becky shrugged. 'That's what I was hoping you could help me with.'

Lois smiled. 'I literally know nothing at all about that, Becky. I'm really sorry.'

Becky fleetingly perceived something in Lois's eyes, along with a subtle shift in her demeanor. She knew more than she was letting on. Becky lowered her voice and said, 'I know you weren't treated well and helping any member of the Larkin family isn't exactly going to be on your bucket list… But it's not really for me, it's for Maddie and her two teenage kids who haven't seen their dad for five years and want…need answers. Whatever you say to me now, I promise won't get back to my dad.'

Lois looked uneasy. 'I can only tell you two things, Becky. One, if the call was made internally from the main building, then it would have been patched through the switchboard, meaning that it would be completely untraceable; there would be no way of knowing from which office the call had come. Second, after the police started making enquiries at the office, the company's lawyers sent out a gag order.'

'What do you mean?' Becky asked, incredulously.

'Every single employee was told in no uncertain terms that they were legally prohibited from cooperating with the police,' Lois said.

'Could they do that?'

'Sure. They *did* do that. We were all told that unless we were subpoenaed by a Grand Jury, we would lose our jobs if we talked. Of course, no detective from Salt Lake City Police Department looking for a missing man is going to have the resources to issue subpoenas.'

Becky was in shock. 'And my father was presumably also gagged by this order? Maybe still is?'

'Becky… Your father *signed* the order.'

Chapter Thirty-Four

Sunday, March 15, 2020, Salt Lake City, Utah

Keeping with the theme of the weekend so far, Hudson had once again failed to get dressed. Today, he had even failed to get out of bed. Abigail had gone to work. Under normal circumstances, she wouldn't have let him get away with staying in bed or working on a Sunday at all but, when she'd arrived home from work yesterday and he'd told her how fast he was moving through his private investigation, *she* had suggested that he stay home today to get the job done.

Up to now, luck had been on his side. Small families, good vital records, open-access social media accounts and detailed background checks had all helped him quickly to work out that the connection between Jennifer LaFleur and the man who had raped and murdered Francesca Chabala was through Jennifer's sister, Velveta Mercaldo. By bedtime last night, Hudson had reduced the suspect list to one of Velveta's two sons: Jackson and Warren. He'd gone to bed and dreamed of the case pretty much all night long. In his nocturnal imaginings he had seen one of the brothers—in his ensuing wakefulness, he could no longer recall which one—being shoved handcuffed into a jail cell as Brandon Blake rushed out of it, flinging his arms around Hudson in pure gratitude for his freedom. But it wouldn't be like that, Hudson reasoned, sitting back in his bed. He was simply being paid to hand over the name of a suspect to Wanda Chabala. The involvement of law enforcement or a final CODIS check had never been mentioned, which troubled him deeply. What if he were wrong? All he could think to do was *not* be wrong; be absolutely certain that the man, whose name he would give up, had been guilty of the rape and murder of Francesca Chabala.

With his laptop resting on his thighs, Hudson began to investigate the two Mercaldo brothers. He started with the eldest, Jackson. Born 1972, he would have been thirty-three at the time of the crime. Hudson brought up a background check page for Jackson, making a note of his telephone numbers and email addresses before continuing a slow scroll down the screen. The address history stopped him.

10106 Emerson Ave S. Minneapolis, MN
Apr 1997 - Jul 2006

In a new browser tab Hudson ran a Google Map search for the address: Jackson Mercaldo had been living two blocks away from where Francesca Chabala had lived at that exact time. He took a screenshot of the map and added it to the profile page that he had created for each of the two potential suspects.

Returning to the background check, he found a wife for Jackson along with possibly two sons and a daughter.

Opening the DNAPainter website, Hudson inputted the amount of DNA, 422cMs, into the Shared cM Project tool to check whether it was theoretically possible for one of Jackson's or Warren's sons to have been the perpetrator, in addition to them.

This set of relationships is just within the threshold for 422cM, but has a zero probability in thednageek's table of probabilities

Coupled with the fact that Jackson's two boys would have been twelve and thirteen at the time of the crime, Hudson was now contented not to include them as suspects.

Continuing with Jackson's background check, Hudson found no criminal, traffic or bankruptcy entries against his name and no associated job history, either. He followed a link to Jackson's Twitter account which provided a small insight into the guy's mind, seeming to be an endless stream of posing the same question to various female celebrities: *hi! how are you today? i'm a big fan!* Taylor Swift, Hayden Panettiere, Britney Spears, Halle Berry and Salma Hayek seemed not to have replied. The Cooking Channel had also failed to respond to his tweet, *I like the coooking channel it is fun to watch people cook.*

He'd reached the end of the background check for Jackson. His address certainly put him at the right place at the right time. Hudson had more research that he wanted to do into Jackson Mercaldo, but first wanted to run a check on his brother, Warren. Again, the address history for the period in question was potentially of great interest.

983 Fremont Ave. S. Minneapolis, MN
Jan 2004 - Nov 2006

Google Maps quickly confirmed that both siblings had been living within a quarter of a mile of where Francesca had been killed.

Hudson found himself staring at the screen as he imagined passing the two names to Wanda Chabala, wondering what her next move might turn out to be. She clearly had a plan.

Hudson needed a break. He set the laptop to the side of his bed and got up. He wandered through to the kitchen, taking a cursory glance into Abigail's immaculate bedroom on the way. He fixed himself some coffee and switched on the TV. He skipped across the channels through college football, a cooking show, and a *Law & Order* special before pausing on a round-up of the local news. He watched an attractive young presenter in a cerise suit deliver the headlines.

'In Summit County yesterday, Utah recorded its first community transmission of the deadly coronavirus, which is currently sweeping the globe. The virus is also responsible for the closure—with immediate effect—of many of the region's top ski resorts...'

'What joyful news,' Hudson muttered to himself, switching off the TV and carrying his coffee back to his bedroom. Getting back into bed, he pulled his laptop onto his legs and resumed Warren's background check. The next available data after his address history was *Relatives.*

'What?' Hudson gasped when he saw the only name listed as a relative to Warren Mercaldo. It couldn't be.

But it was.

Maddie was pushing herself harder than she had done for a long time. Under a cold but clear azure sky she ran her usual route along the Utah and Salt Lake Canal Trail. The narrow dirt track, sandwiched between the backyards of the properties on South Jordan Farms Road and the canal, ran for miles in either direction. So far, the only people, whom she had encountered, were two other runners who had ignored her existence as they passed by, which was fine by her. She was seeking anonymity...solitude. She was pushing against Lewis Capaldi's *Someone You Loved* rasping loudly in her Air Pods.

She ran faster, the muscles in her calves screaming and her lungs struggling to pull in enough oxygen to keep her going at this pace for much longer. Anger, fear, worry and frustration pressed down on her chest and shoulders. She suddenly stopped, panting for breath, hands pushing into her thighs, trying to shake the tight clenching in her head.

Fighting back against her own emotions, she thought about the email that she had just received from her insurance company.

...Your insurance does not cover long-term custodial care... Your insurance does

not cover limited care in a nursing facility…

Custodial care. It made it sound so institutional but actually was just a fancy way of saying that nobody was going to be there to help, when her mom entered the middle stages of the disease and needed assistance dressing, eating, washing and with basic home-living. They would only cover medical treatments; the rest would be down to Maddie to figure out.

Her mom had been very subdued since the incident on Friday and had so far refused to talk about it. The longer it went on, the less Maddie knew how to deal with it. Should she *not* talk about it? Should they discuss it as a family? Should she wait until her mom brought it up, with the risk that that might never happen? Michael would have had the right answer; he would have known exactly what to say and do.

She felt his absence every day, usually in subtly different ways. Sometimes she would wake and turn to his vacant side of the bed, wish him good morning and then not explicitly think of him again for the rest of the entire day. Other times, her grief felt as raw and as fresh as the darkest days that had grown out of his failure to come home, leaving just getting through the daily chores and dealing with the kids feeling like a monumental undertaking. In times of crisis, such as she was now feeling about her mother's situation, she just wanted someone to talk it over with, someone to hold her and tell her that everything would be okay; someone to guide her forward toward an answer.

Maddie was finally able to gather in a long breath and quell the shifting, formless anxiety. Everything would be okay…because it had to be.

But that wasn't what was bothering her mind. At least, that wasn't *all*.

Reigning herself in to a gentler pace, she jogged back home, trying to pinpoint the locus of the problem. Was it the kids' being home from Monday unsupervised and the idea of their squabbling for fourteen days and not noticing their grandma and all that she might be getting up to? Nope, that wasn't it, either. Not completely.

She jogged along the trail some more, wondering if perhaps it was a work-related problem, but there was nothing resonant that she could put her finger on. She arrived home fifteen minutes later, none the wiser.

The house was eerily quiet. Maddie kicked off her sneakers and entered the kitchen for a glass of water. Her mom was quietly doing a jigsaw puzzle, Trenton was happily blowing people's heads off in some war-based video game, and then the warm sight, which threatened to resurrect Maddie's current delicate emotions, was that of Nikki, casting a maternal eye over her brother and grandma as she fixed the lunch for everyone.

Maddie leaned in, gave her a sideways hug and kissed her on the cheek.

'Yuk, you're all sweaty. Get off,' Nikki complained.

Maddie looked at the chicken salad piled onto four plates on the counter. 'You're going to make someone such a good wife one day, you know?'

Nikki turned around, incredulous. 'Really? Did you actually just say that?'

Maddie laughed. 'Sorry.'

'Yeah, who's going to want to marry *her*?' Trenton chipped in, not missing a beat and without taking his eyes from the screen for a second.

Nikki picked a piece of marinated chicken from one of the plates and tossed it, hitting Trenton on the side of his head before it dropped to the floor.

He scowled as he touched the slimy spot on his temple, saying, 'Well, that was disgusting.' He bent down—still without looking away from his game—and danced his fingers around on the floor until he found the piece of chicken and then promptly popped it into his mouth.

'No. *That* was disgusting,' Nikki countered.

'Okay. That's enough, you two,' Maddie said. 'Have I got time to grab a shower before we eat?'

'Sure,' Nikki responded with a smile.

Maddie kissed Nikki on the cheek again. 'Thank you.'

Nikki squirmed under the kiss and gave her a look of disgust. 'In fact, *definitely* go and shower before we eat. You take as long as you need to stop being so disgustingly sweaty.'

'Love you,' Maddie said as she left the kitchen.

Becky was in her apartment, gazing out of her balcony doors at the distant Wasatch Range. She was wearing a pair of jeans, a loose shirt and had her hair tied back. She had been trying to work but couldn't concentrate. Her mind kept going back over Lois Strange's words yesterday: 'Your father signed the order.' Becky had responded to that by asking if that was common practice at The Larkin Investment and Finance Group. 'That was the only occasion during my whole time there,' Lois had responded. Becky didn't know what to do. Ross's advice had been to confront her father about it. Yesterday, because of the spread of coronavirus, Park City had abruptly ended the ski season way ahead of schedule, meaning that her mother and father would soon be headed back home. She thought about going to see them, to confront him with what she now knew, but the truth of the matter was that she didn't think she could bear to look her father in the eye as he lied to her, squirmed and gave some politician's answer about the gag order or, because it had come from Lois Strange, completely decried it as an attempt at revenge. Becky believed Lois and was certain that her father did know something about Michael Barnhart's disappearance. What that something could be, however, she could not imagine.

She walked over to the open-plan kitchen area, took some juice from the refrigerator and sat back down at her laptop that was open on the countertop. She was looking for Wayne Wolsey's address at the time of the three murders, which hadn't shown up on various background check websites. But it was no good, she just couldn't clarify or coalesce her thoughts around the case. She had to speak with her father. Not knowing if her parents had left their Park City home or not, Becky decided to call his cellphone.

He answered right away with a cheery, 'Hi sweetie. How are you?' It sounded as though he was in the car. Maybe they were headed back home after all.

She took a quick breath. 'Not great, to be truthful.'

'What's the matter?' he asked, sounding genuinely concerned.

'Something I have in front of me,' she lied. 'A gag order, signed by you, telling your employees not to cooperate with the police about Michael Barnhart's disappearance. What did—'

The line went dead.

Had he ended the call? Or maybe he had driven through a bad spot for signal? Becky tapped *Dad cell* in her recent calls list. It rang until the voicemail kicked in. Becky hung up and tried her mom. Same thing.

'Damn it,' she said, slamming her phone down on the counter.

She took off her glasses and massaged above her eyes and over her temples. She composed her breaths, put her glasses back on and then tried to return to the work-task in hand. She was going to give the case another few minutes and then stop, wanting to spend the afternoon relaxed and slowly getting ready for her date with Jerome tonight. The restaurant—St Bernard's—was out at the Solitude Mountain Resort, a place she sometimes liked to ski. It was a good choice. Great food and a beautiful mountain location. She was quietly confident about the date.

Becky opened up *U.S. Public Records Index, 1950-1993, Volume 1* on Ancestry. These records were compiled from various sources, including postal change-of-address forms, public record filings, historical residential records and White Pages. She typed in Wayne's name, year of birth and a date range of 1980-1984, then hit search.

Name: Wayne Wolsey
Residence Date: 1983
Phone Number: 342-5586
Address: 210 Crozerville Rd
Residence: Aston, PA

Becky opened up a fresh browser tab and copied the address across to Google Maps, watching as the red pin plopped down on Crozerville Road, a wooded street to the left of the west branch of the Chester Creek.

She took a swig of her juice, then carefully began to overlay the locations of the three abductions onto the map, testing her theories about where the killer likely lived. As she was almost done, her cellphone began to ring. Her father.

'Hi,' she said, strolling over to the balcony as she spoke.

'Becky, listen up,' her father began, 'If you push me on this, it won't go well, okay? I have to make literally dozens of decisions a day to do with the businesses. I will *not* discuss this with you. It's your choice how this goes from here on in.' He ended the call before she could speak.

Becky was deeply wounded. She'd seen her father's venomous eruptions before, usually reserved for his subordinates, but it had never been directed at her before now.

She had no idea what to do next. One thing was certain, though, she didn't want to arrive at her date with Jerome all worked up and stressed out. It was time to stop working, to take a bath and try to put things out of her mind for the time being.

As she went to close her laptop lid, she took in fully what she'd been doing at the moment when her dad had called. Wayne Wolsey's address at the time of the murders.

She sat back down at the kitchen counter. 'Oh, my goodness.'

'That's it!' Maddie cried. She was standing in her shower, right in the middle of washing her hair, when she realized what had been bothering her all morning: the photo that Kenyatta had discovered on Friday. Something hadn't felt right with her, but she hadn't known what exactly that could be. She turned off the water, hurriedly dried herself, pulled on her robe and then padded downstairs to Michael's study.

She fired up her laptop and hurriedly accessed the Flickr account for Carl Wolsey's daughter. Skipping past several images, she sought out the picture of Wayne and Carl posing in front of the camera, the incriminating red Dodge visible in the background behind them. She found it.

Maddie clicked to enlarge the photo, then zoomed in. Blurred by its distance in the background of the shot was that which she had originally assumed to be the side of a building. But, just as she had suspected moments earlier in the shower, it wasn't a building at all: it was a trailer.

She studied the image carefully for some time, then pulled up Google Maps and entered the address for Peggy Drive in Herculaneum, Missouri. When the map loaded, she dropped the little orange man onto the approximate position of the trailer, seeing the view as it was when taken in September 2013. She spent a little time altering her position until it was as close as she was going to get to the photograph of the two Wolsey brothers. The trailer had changed but the trees in the background and the road surface in the foreground were identical. The picture of Wayne and Carl had been taken on Peggy Drive. The same address that Carl Wolsey had been registered at in 1999 following his conviction for sexual assault. What else had Carl got up to, there?

From outside the study, Trenton yelled, 'Before I get the blame, I just want to make it clear that the water—or urine, or whatever it is—out here on the hallway floor is nothing to do with me...'

Maddie craned her neck to see that her dripping hair had created a small puddle behind her on the floor. She should go get dressed, but first she wanted to take a look for any unsolved female murders in the area around Herculaneum, Missouri in the late 1990s.

In Newspapers.com, Maddie conducted a search in the *St Louis Post-Dispatch* for a ten-year window around 1998 with the filter of *dead body*.

25,463 matches

She slowly moved the cursor down the list of results, checking the yellow highlighted strip running over the words which had matched her search criteria. Most, she quickly discerned, related to the '90s TV show, *Over My Dead Body*.

Maddie edited the search parameters from *dead body* to *murdered* and *water*.

The sixth result caught her attention and she clicked to read the story dated October 21, 1998.

Remains are Identified as Herculaneum Woman's

Before she read on, Maddie looked at the grainy image beside the headline. The victim was a young, pretty girl with long blonde hair; someone Maddie considered comparable to the three Chester Creek victims. She started to read the article but was quickly interrupted.

Nikki poked her head around the door. 'Mom, are you coming in for lunch? Trenton claims he's starving to death and I can't hold him back much longer.'

Maddie rolled her eyes. 'That boy… Yes, I'll be right there.'

'Okay,' Nikki said. 'Oh, and I've cleared up your Hansel and Gretel water-trail through the house.'

'Ah, thank you so much, Nikki.'

'You're welcome,' she replied, disappearing from view.

'Hey, go ahead and start. Don't wait for me!' Maddie called after her, unable to resist reading the article first.

The skeleton of a woman found Tuesday in Jefferson County has been identified through dental records as that of 18-year-old Tandy Howard, a receptionist who disappeared eight months ago.

The Missouri Division of Criminal Investigation office said positive identification was made Wednesday night after Miss Howard's dental charts had been obtained.

Tandy Howard has been missing since February 4, when she disappeared after walking home from a friend's house.

The skeleton was discovered Tuesday afternoon in a rural area of Herculaneum by four boys who found a partly buried skull beside Joachim Creek—

Maddie stopped and shuddered. A young, attractive female,

abducted walking home at night and found beside a creek at a point in time when Carl Wolsey was living in the very near vicinity. But how near? The Joachim Creek ran for miles on end and was a tributary to the Mississippi River. She read on.

The boys were stopped to rest from a day's bicycling and spotted what they thought was a stone. They dug up the object and discovered that it was a skull. The youths carried the skull home, where their parents called the police. The boys led investigators to where they had made the gruesome discovery, where the rest of the skeleton was uncovered.

Herculaneum County Coroner, Stephen Aramowicz said the body appeared to have been left in the location in which it was discovered, close to the Herky Horine Road, rather than having floated there in the creek.

Maddie paused her reading and opened up a Google Maps search for Herky Horine Road. Just as she had feared, it was just a few yards away from Carl Wolsey's trailer.

Although she only had circumstantial evidence, there was little doubt in Maddie's mind that Tandy Howard was another victim of the Chester Creek killer. She looked at Carl's long address history, wondering how many more victims were out there.

She intended to continue her search, but first, she needed quickly to go and get dressed and eat lunch with her family.

'Just coming,' Maddie called as she darted from the study up to her bedroom. She sat down on her bed and hurriedly shook a towel across her hair as her cell phone pinged a message. It was from Becky on the Venator WhatsApp group.

Guys…Hate to spoil your Sunday, but…I don't think Carl Wolsey is the Chester Creek killer…

Maddie gaped at the screen, utterly confused and half-wondering if Becky could be messing with them. It would be very unlike her to make such a risky joke.

Becky Larkin is typing…

Her recent discoveries played through Maddie's mind, while she apprehensively waited for the follow-up message. Given how long it seemed to take to type, she was surprised by its eventual brevity.

I think it's Wayne.

Maddie sent an immediate reply: *How?! Why?!*

The slamming of the apartment door startled Hudson. He waited, staring in anticipation. Moments later, Abigail walked in with a big smile on her face.

'How was work?' he asked.

'Alright,' she answered. 'It was the…' She stopped mid-sentence and stared at him. 'Wait, what's up?'

'I've kind of hit a major problem with my research,' he answered.

'The Wanda Chabala case or the creek case?' Abigail asked, sitting down beside him.

'The first,' he confirmed.

'Well, what kind of major problem?'

'I've narrowed the likely suspects down to two brothers and I don't think there's much more I can do to work out which one it is.'

'Right,' Abigail said. 'So, Wanda will need to do that thing—what's it called, trash DNA testing?— to find out which one it is. That's not such a big deal, is it?'

'*That* isn't the major problem,' Hudson clarified.

'What is, then?'

'Take a look at this,' Hudson said, spinning his laptop so that it faced her with the details of Warren Mercaldo's only listed relative, his wife.

Wanda Chabala
Age 54
Lives in Minneapolis, MN

'But isn't she the mother of—' Abigail said.

'Uh-huh.'

'You're kidding me?'

Hudson shook his head.

'So…he raped and killed his own daughter or niece?'

'No, no. Warren wasn't Francesca's biological father. Wanda married Warren when Francesca was sixteen years old.'

'Wow. What are you going to do?' Abigail asked him.

'What can I do? Tell Wanda that either her husband or her brother-in-law killed her daughter? Hand back the money and tell her it wasn't possible, all the while knowing fully well that an innocent man is serving time and the real killer is someone she sees regularly? I don't know, Abigail... This whole thing is turning into the ethics nightmare that I'm now realizing I already sensed it would be.'

'Oh,' Maddie said, finally entering the kitchen to find the lunch eaten and only her mother in the room, loading the dishwasher.

'Your lunch is there,' her mom said, nodding towards the one remaining plate on the table.

'Where are the kids?'

Her mother shrugged. 'I think Trenton said he was going out on his bike.'

Maddie was disappointed in herself and knew that she would need to make it up to Nikki later.

Her mom closed the dishwasher door and then turned to face Maddie. 'Could I talk to you, while it's quiet?'

'Of course, let me fix us a nice drink and we'll have a chat. What would you like? I'm going to have a glass of red. I know it's early but...whatever.'

'I'll join you.'

Maddie poured out two glasses and carried them over to the table, where her uneaten lunch was waiting. Her mother sat herself down opposite her. 'Cheers,' Maddie said, chinking glasses with her mom across the table.

'Cheers.'

'We haven't done this in a while. So, are you feeling okay?' Maddie started, picking at the chicken salad.

'Just about over the humiliation of being brought home in the back of a police car, if that's what you're asking,' she said with a gentle laugh. 'You know, as I walked up to the house on Horseshoe Circle, I was utterly convinced that it was my home. I was. I got my key—your key—out of my purse and tried to put it into the lock. It went in okay, but it just wouldn't turn. Something—' she paused and frowned, effortfully recalling her perceptions '—something in my head told me that it wasn't *quite* right. Like the impairment you feel after too much alcohol. Yet, I just couldn't resolve what the problem was exactly. I thought maybe I'd brought the wrong key with me or that one of the kids had bolted it from the inside, or something. The house was, of course, utterly familiar—I described to the policeman the layout of the house to prove that it really was mine—but I knew someplace deep down that there was a sensible reason why my key didn't fit in that lock. Just something, out of my reach, you know?' She paused but was not done. 'And…it wasn't the first time it happened, either.'

'Really? Mom, you should have told me.'

'How could I?' she said, sipping her wine. 'It didn't matter *that* time. As I was making my way toward the house, a switch flicked and I knew right away, clear as day, that that was my *old* house. I just had a good old laugh to myself, turned right around and headed on home. I just put it down to regular old age and forgetfulness.'

'Oh, Mom…'

'It's getting worse, though, isn't it?' she asked. 'Generally, I mean.'

'Well, I wouldn't necessarily—'

'Maddie,' she interrupted. 'It's getting worse. Isn't it?'

Maddie nodded. 'I think you might be moving into the middle-stage.'

Her mom's face fell. 'I need to get my affairs in order, while I still can.'

'Mom, this isn't a death sentence. You know that. This stage can last for many, many years.'

Her mom began to sob quietly. 'I so wanted to be a help to you after Michael went but I'm just another burden now.'

Maddie stood up and went over to comfort her mother. 'You'll never be a burden, Mom. We've got some tough times ahead, sure, but we'll get through them as we always have.'

'Will the insurance help out?' she muttered through her tears.

'Yes,' Maddie lied. 'And there's a support group down in Draper that you and I can go to. It'll be okay.'

'I think I'm going to go to my room.'

'Okay, Mom,' Maddie said, kissing her on the top of her head.

Maddie watched her leave as tears could now be permitted to well in her own eyes. She took a long breath and then an even longer drink of wine. Realistically, it wouldn't be long until her mom required an increasing amount of extra care. With the kids and her job, Maddie would quickly need more help, but she wouldn't be able to afford a full-time caregiver. That is, unless…she could get Michael's life insurance.

She stopped herself short, unable to follow that thought through to her having him declared legally dead.

She stood up and carried the wine and salad to Michael's study. Her laptop woke to the profile page that the team had created for Wayne Wolsey, which Becky had just updated. Specifically, she had recreated the map of Delaware County which she had shown to the team in the first briefing, with each of the abduction sites forming the apexes of a scalene triangle. Around the triangle was a purple translucent circle. Within both shapes was a red drop-pin and the annotation, *210 Crozerville Road.* Below the map Becky had typed some notes:

Wayne Wolsey was living at 210 Crozerville Road, Aston from 1981 to 1984. The address falls within the Circle Theory of Environmental Range (purple circle) and also falls within the triangle of the first three murders. Carl Wolsey <u>was not</u> living in Delaware County at the time of the murders.

Maddie's previous conviction that Carl had also been responsible for Tandy Howard's murder was suddenly thrown into doubt. She was confused and pulled up his profile page, locating the reports, which she had discovered, into his criminal past. He had been added to the Missouri Sex Offenders' list at the end of August 1999. Tandy Howard had disappeared in February 1998. One thing Maddie didn't know was the date of Carl Wolsey's conviction.

Running a specific newspaper search for Carl's crime, she quickly found a short report that stated that he had been sent to jail for eighteen months in January 1998; one month before Tandy Howard had been abducted.

Carl Wolsey could not have been responsible for Tandy Howard's murder.

Maddie brought up the photo of the two Wolsey brothers outside the trailer on Peggy Drive, catching sight of the caption afresh, *uncle waynes place, august 99*.

It *was* Wayne's trailer.

Maddie realized then that Carl had obviously given his brother's address upon release from prison in August 1999.

Which left only one conclusion: Wayne Wolsey was the Chester Creek killer.

Just as she was adjusting to this new information, another message came in from Becky. It was a screenshot of a newspaper article from the *Delaware County Daily Times*. Maddie zoomed in and read.

Police Use Roadblock in Search for Missing Woman

Police set up a roadblock this morning in their continuing effort to discover what has happened to a 22-year-old woman from Aston, who has been missing for two weeks.

State Troopers and Delaware County police stopped all motorists traveling on Crozerville Road and asked if any had seen Fiona Gregory on Friday, November 4, the day she disappeared. Her boyfriend, Mr. W. Wolsey, with whom she shared her home, reported that on that morning Miss Gregory had left for work as usual. Police said that she never reached TJW Accountancy, her employers in Philadelphia, although her auto was found nearby. Troopers began checking motorists about 6:30am, the earliest they think the woman would have started out for work.

Maddie looked again at the date that Fiona Gregory had gone missing: November 4, 1983. The exact same day that Sadie Mayer's body had been found.

Opening her emails, Maddie sent Clayton a message with URGENT in the subject line.

Clayton, could you please check the National Crime Information Center for Fiona Gregory. There should be a Missing Adult Seek to Locate entry for her. Was she ever found??

Maddie attached a screenshot of the newspaper report, then sent the email.

Chapter Thirty-Five

Monday, March 16, 2020, Downtown Salt Lake City, Utah

Maddie parked in her usual spot in the garage below the Kearns Building. She stepped from her SUV, feeling a gathering, consuming dread. The schools had shut for at least two weeks because of the pandemic and so the kids were home with her mom, but she had no idea who was looking after whom. She guessed that Nikki would assume the role of parent, organizing her brother to get on with his home-learning while also taking care of her grandma. It bothered Maddie, but there wasn't much she could do about it, at least not today; this was one of the most important days for the Chester Creek cold case investigation. Achieving their goal of identifying the name of a single suspect wasn't the end of the process. They now had to stress-test their findings to make absolutely certain that they were pointing the finger at the right person.

She entered the first floor of the building and smiled when she saw Becky walking toward her. 'Good morning,' Maddie greeted. 'Ready for today?'

Becky returned her smile. 'Very much so.'

'Good,' Maddie said, accompanying her on the climb up the stairwell. 'You certainly threw us a curveball, yesterday. I mean, wow.'

Becky grinned. 'Yeah, I'm certain that Wayne is our guy.'

'Did you manage to do anything *besides* work?' Maddie asked.

'Yeah. Something's been bugging me all weekend that I'd like to talk to you about, later. In private?'

'Sure thing, of course.'

'Thanks. And…I went out to Solitude on a date last night.'

Maddie's face lit up. 'And how did that go?'

Becky nodded, mulling over the question. 'I think really well. I've been on *a lot* of first dates and this felt, well, better than most, actually. He seems like a really nice guy.'

Maddie touched Becky's elbow. 'Good. I'm really pleased for you.'

'We're going out again tomorrow, climbing, and then out somewhere for a meal after.'

'He sounds right up your alley,' Maddie commented as they reached the fifth floor. She pulled her keys out of her purse and unlocked the door to the Venator office. 'Here we go,' she said, hanging up her hat and jacket. Becky helped her to go around the office switching on the computers and the digital whiteboard that would become pivotal in reaching the outcome of today. In her office, Maddie turned on her own computer and checked her emails. Still nothing from the detective about the sweep of Michael's truck, which was further compounding her feeling generally unsettled. He had replied to her question regarding Fiona Gregory's disappearance, however.

She went to make some coffee and saw that Kenyatta and Ross were just walking in together through the door. 'Morning! How are we today?'

'Great, thanks,' Ross answered.

'Just swell, thank you, Maddie,' Kenyatta replied, pulling off her coat. 'And your good self?'

'Braced, I think, is the word,' Maddie said, taking her coffee.

Hudson entered the office moments later and Maddie gave the team five minutes to get themselves ready for the Monday morning briefing.

She pushed her office door shut and just stood motionless with her eyes closed, holding the cup to her chest, mindfully noticing her breathing. She was trying to close down the extraneous thoughts that were weighing on the edges of her mind. The detective would get in touch when the results came through; there was little to be gained by ruminating and constantly checking her emails. And Nikki or Trenton would text or call, if there were any issues at home. She had to assume on all fronts that no news was good news.

Time pushed forward as it always did.

Maddie did three long belly-breaths and left her office. 'Are we ready, guys?' she said, waltzing over to the digital whiteboard. 'Kenyatta, could you pull up Wayne Wolsey's profile page from the shared drive?'

'With pleasure,' Kenyatta said, tapping her keyboard.

Moments later, the page, headed with Wayne's photograph, appeared in front of the team.

'Thank you,' Maddie said. 'So, first things first. Let's bring in any new information that's come up over the weekend; you know, those two days when you're not supposed to work at all. Anyhow, as you all know from the WhatsApp messages exchanged yesterday, Becky made a pretty big discovery.' She pointed to the photo on the board behind her. 'This guy is now our number-one suspect. Wayne Wolsey.' Maddie scrolled her finger down the board. 'She also found that Wayne's girlfriend, Fiona Gregory, disappeared from their shared home on November 4, 1983 which, coincidentally, is the exact same day that Sadie Mayer's body was found in the creek. Detective Tyler confirmed early this morning that Fiona Gregory was never found—she remains on the missing persons database.'

'Another victim,' Kenyatta mumbled.

'I think it's fair to consider her as another potential victim, yes. What's also interesting is that another report into her disappearance stated that she worked away from home in Philadelphia…and didn't come home on weekends.'

'Which is clearly when he would go out looking for his victims,' Becky chipped in. 'The fact that he kept Sadie for longer suggests that she, Fiona, could have arrived home early, or unexpectedly at least, and found him with Sadie in the house.'

'And he then killed *her*,' Hudson said.

'Yeah, that's the likely conclusion I reached, too,' Maddie confirmed. 'But obviously we'll leave law enforcement to connect those final circumstantial dots together.'

'But why didn't the police link her death to the Chester Creek killer at the time?' Kenyatta asked.

'I asked myself the same question,' Maddie began, folding her arms. 'I guess after a few days, when her body didn't show up in the water and she didn't seem to fit the pattern seen across the other cases, they assumed that it wasn't the same guy.'

'How many more are out there?' Hudson asked.

'Now, there's a question,' Becky replied.

'I did spend some time yesterday compiling a list of unsolved murders that had occurred within a ten-mile radius of the various locations where Wayne Wolsey lived, which I'll also be passing along to Detective Tyler to take into consideration,' Maddie explained.

'And how many did that run to, dare I ask? Kenyatta asked.

'Six,' Maddie answered.

'Wow.'

'Yeah,' Maddie agreed. 'But at this point, that's purely speculative and way beyond the scope of our remit.' She drank some coffee and then turned to the whiteboard, picked up the red marker pen and wrote *WAYNE WOLSEY* under the heading of *SUSPECT*. She turned to face the team. 'Based on everything we've discovered, does anyone *not* agree with this assessment?' she asked, jabbing the marker at Wayne's name.

'I know I say it every time. We *have* to know if there are any doubts whatsoever for any of us.'

When nobody spoke, she turned around to look over some of the other likely facts about the perpetrator that they had discovered early on. 'So, the killer's predicated phenotype was brown hair, brown eyes and pale skin. Wayne Wolsey has all of those. The Y-DNA suggested the surname Brown in the killer's paternal ancestry. We believe that Wayne Wolsey's father was Enoch Brown.' She turned back to the team. 'But we shouldn't be complacent. Even though the final suspect will have to go through CODIS, we still need to be one hundred percent confident that the name we're handing over is correct and we've not been blindsided by confirmation bias or any prejudices. We're going to pull apart everything we've found. Look for flaws, gaps, inconsistencies and whether or not we can apply the Genealogical Proof Standard to each and every one of our findings. Start with the DNA: now we know who he is, do the number of centiMorgans match correctly and perfectly with the lead names in each genetic network cluster and are the chromosome overlaps correct? Kenyatta and Becky, I want you to cross-check and verify each other's work. Hudson, you and I will do the same.' She glanced at the wall clock. 'It's almost nine twenty. Let's meet again at twelve thirty. Any questions?'

The team understood the process well and confirmed this via shakes of their heads and muttered agreements that they had no questions before getting down to work.

Maddie returned to her desk and immediately opened the file labeled *Cluster One* in the shared drive for this case. James Jones had been designated the lead name for this genetic network. Hudson had found that James Jones's great-great-grandparents were Harry White and Isabella Delaporte. According to the DNA evidence, Wayne Wolsey and James Jones shared 52cMs of DNA. Maddie inputted that figure into the DNAPainter website, receiving several possible ways in which the two men could have been genetically related.

Next, Maddie opened up the pedigree file for Wayne Wolsey and counted the generations back to the shared ancestors, Harry White and Isabella Delaporte. If Hudson's research was correct, then Wayne Wolsey and James Jones were third cousins once removed. According to DNAPainter, that option was one of the most likely, given their shared amount of DNA.

On the FamilyTreeDNA website, Maddie opened up the *Chromosome Browser* and ran a comparison search between Wayne

Wolsey and the closest six matches with cluster one. The segment data showed sufficient and expected overlaps of DNA that had derived from their shared ancestors, Harry White and Isabella Delaporte.

Maddie smiled, shut down the file and then repeated the task for cluster two. Once she had done that, she checked the killer's Y-DNA, confirming again that which Hudson had found. She also cross-checked the killer's phenotype, reaching the same conclusion that Hudson had reached.

With the DNA seemingly water-tight, Maddie moved on to Hudson's research into Enoch Brown. She read his file and then began working through his references, opening up background check websites, newspaper articles and social media accounts to scrutinize his work.

It was just after midday when Maddie finally sat back in her chair, completely satisfied with Hudson's research. She sent a short email to Becky, telling her that she was free if she wanted to come and talk to her. Seconds later, Becky entered the office and shut the door behind her. Something serious, then, Maddie thought.

Becky sat down in front of her. 'I don't know how to say this...' She stared at the floor in a very un-Becky-like way: none of her usual sparky confidence or enthusiasm. Without looking up at Maddie, she found a way to begin: 'I asked my father about the call that Michael received to his cellphone down in Green River. He didn't tell me anything at all, but I know he knows something.' She finally met Maddie's eyes.

'Becky, I don't—'

'I haven't finished,' she interrupted. 'It's been bothering me a lot. So, I got in touch with an old friend who used to work at The Larkin Investment and Finance Group. She told me that a gag order was placed on all employees after Michael disappeared and the whole firm were told *not* to cooperate with police. My father was the one who signed that gag order.'

'God...' Maddie uttered in disbelief.

Tears were pooling in Becky's eyes as she shrugged. 'And I don't know what to do. My father made it very clear to me that, if I keep asking and pushing him, it will be the end of our relationship. I really don't think I can get any more out of him, Maddie.'

'Do you have any ideas about why he would put a gag order on his own employees?' Maddie asked.

Becky shook her head. 'None at all. I also asked about the

possibility of tracking the phone call, but it would have gone out through the switchboard, which means it could have been from any phone in the entire building.'

'But what could Michael have been doing there that needed this level of…whatever is going on? I don't understand.'

'I don't know, Maddie. I'm sorry. I'm still trying but I don't know where else to turn to look,' Becky said, her tears at last spilling.

'It's not your fault, Becky,' Maddie tried to soothe. 'And thank you for coming to me. It means a lot and I know it can't have been easy.'

'It doesn't help, though, does it?'

'It's another piece of the puzzle,' Maddie said, trying to sound appreciative and diplomatic.

A stolid silence surrounded them.

'What do you want me to do?' Becky finally asked.

Maddie stared at her, trying to untangle her feelings about what she'd just been told. The wife and mother in her desperately wanted answers and didn't care if getting them ruined Becky's relationship with her father. But Becky was more than just her employee; she was her friend and the last thing, which she would want, would be to risk her coming to any harm. From what she had said, that now didn't seem out of the realms of possibility.

'I don't want you to do anything more,' Maddie said, finally. 'Hopefully something will come back from the CSI sweep which, as you know, is imminent.'

Becky ran her index finger up her left cheek to her eye. 'Are you sure?'

'Very,' Maddie said, completely not sure. 'Don't mention it again to your dad. Go back to being normal with him.'

Becky raised her eyebrows. 'I don't know if I can. Not knowing is somehow just as bad—or worse.'

'Tell me about it,' Maddie said. It was time to move this on. She sat up with a smile, as though she had just swept everything to one side, and asked, 'Are you ready for the final briefing?'

'Yes… Although, I might just run to the bathroom.'

'Go ahead and then we'll get started. Hopefully it will be a short and simple one.'

Becky stood up and turned to leave.

'Thank you, Becky. I know it can't have been easy coming to talk to me about that.'

Becky smiled and left the office.

Maddie had literally three minutes in which to process the information before she would find herself standing back in front of the team for what she hoped would be Venator's conclusion to the Chester Creek cold case. While it was still fresh in her mind, Maddie typed what Becky had just told her into the Notes app on her cellphone. She reread it several times, hoping to elicit some substance, but it made no sense whatsoever.

When she heard Becky return to the office, she closed her cellphone and walked on out, hoping that her bearing didn't betray her inner turmoil. She stood at the front of the room, Kenyatta, Hudson and Becky falling silent and giving her their full attention.

'This is *possibly* the final briefing in the cold case investigation into the Chester Creek murders. You know how it goes. I'm going to start.' Maddie fired a quick glance at Hudson: 'I've found no flaws, inconsistencies or anything that casts doubt over the name of the suspect or the processes and documentation that got us to his name. Hudson, you found anything in my work?'

He shook his head. 'Nothing. It all checks out.'

'Becky?'

'Nothing from me.'

'Kenyatta?'

'Same. Nothing.'

Maddie inhaled at length, stood tall, and looked at each member of her team. 'I want to thank you all for your hard work and dedication in getting us to this point in the investigation so quickly. You've all worked really amazingly…as always. I can now compile the file and call Detective Tyler and tell him that we have identified the Chester Creek killer as being one Wayne Wolsey.'

A short bubble of suspenseful silence was burst by a spontaneous round of applause.

Chapter Thirty-Six

'Detective MacRory,' a brash voice came from the other end of the phone.

'Oh. Hi, there,' Maddie said, slightly taken aback. 'Could I speak with Detective Clayton Tyler, please?'

'He's not in the office right now. Who's calling?'

'This is Madison Scott-Barnhart from Venator. We've been doing some work on—'

'Ah, sure. The genetic gynecology people,' he snorted. She could almost hear his sneer down the line.

'Genetic *genealogy*,' Maddie corrected. 'When will he be back?'

'I don't know. He's in the building someplace. I'll get him to call you right back.'

The line went dead. Maddie stared at her phone, incredulous. 'What a nice guy.'

The morning—perhaps the weekend…or longer, even—had exhausted Maddie. She slumped back in her chair for a moment. In the stillness of her office, she noticed her hunger and leapt up and asked the team, 'What do you all want from Eva's? It's on me; I'm buying. We're going to have a long lunch break together to celebrate the closing of another case.'

'Great! But what did Detective Tyler say to the news?' Kenyatta asked, obviously bemused by Maddie's not relaying his reaction straight off.

'Oh, I didn't get to tell him yet. He's not at his desk right now.'

Kenyatta sighed. 'Disappointing.'

'So, let's get some lunch. What'll it be?'

'Grilled cheese panini, *pour moi*,' Hudson replied. 'Merci.'

'No surprise, there, then. Brunch flatbread, please, Maddie,' Becky said.

'Ross?' Maddie asked.

'I'll get the grilled cheese, too, thanks.'

'Chicken salad for me, thank you,' Kenyatta said. 'Do you need a hand?'

Maddie shook her head. 'You all relax. And I mean *relax*.' She pulled on her hat and jacket and headed out of the office.

Outside, it was one of those days that Salt Lake City does best: big, beautiful blue skies but cold as the mountain stream. She stood in front of the doors to the Kearns Building, enjoying the warm sun on her skin for a moment. She walked up and down for a few seconds to empty her mind, then she crossed the street to Eva's and joined a short line to order the food. She was enjoying that familiar sense of unbridled freedom that she knew her colleagues also all felt when a case was finally closed. She ordered the food, then returned to the office, armed with a paper carry-out bag in each hand.

'Any calls?' she asked Ross.

'Nope, nothing,' he answered, hungrily accepting his panini from her. 'Thank you very much.'

Maddie distributed the rest of the lunches. 'Enjoy, everyone.' She sat beside Kenyatta and ate her food, relishing the ability to chat with her colleagues in a much more convivial manner for once. It happened from time to time but maybe not often enough.

'So, what's next?' Kenyatta asked.

'Well, after lunch, I'd like us to take another look into some of our open-active cases, ones where we've not made much progress; see if any new matches have come up. I've got a few enquiries come in from various detectives around the country, but I've not accepted anything as yet.'

'*Boys under the Bridge*?' Kenyatta asked, her eyes wide with supplicant anticipation.

'I know. Listen. We can take a look, but I'd also like to review the *Cleveland Cannibal* and the *Mount Vernon Serial Killer* cases.'

'Sure thing,' Kenyatta said.

Once she had finished her lunch, Maddie returned to her office and dialed the detective once more.

'Detective MacRory,' came the curt voice on the other end.

Maddie opened her mouth to speak and promptly hung up, turning instead to her emails.

A light tapping came from her office door. Hudson. 'Hi, come in.'

He entered the room, closing the door behind him. 'Can I have a minute?'

'Of course, you can. You know that,' Maddie replied, having flashbacks to Becky's similar question just a short while ago, and this new visitor to her office now rekindling that same sense of dread.

'I've got a problem,' he revealed. 'Quite a big problem, actually.'

'Okay, what sort of a problem?'

'So, here goes. Abigail and I are hoping to try adoption.'

'Oh, okay. That's really great,' Maddie said, surprised. 'I had no idea you were going down this route. Well…it was all a while back, now, but sure, I'm more than happy to tell you all about how the process went for us. Of course, it's probably not exactly the same—'

'Thanks,' he interjected, 'but that's not what I wanted to talk about. As you know, adoption is like off-the-charts expensive and, um, well, in order to pay for the adoption, I may have taken on a private job.'

'Okay,' Maddie said, having no idea where this was leading. 'What kind of a private job?'

'Ever heard of Francesca Chabala? Raped and murdered in Minneapolis in 2005?'

Maddie nodded. 'Yeah, I know it. Brandon Blake was convicted but denies all knowledge. DNA doesn't match.'

'That's the one. Francesca's mom, Wanda Chabala, asked me to take on the case to try and find the real killer.'

'But how did you do that without the involvement of law enforcement?' she asked.

Hudson went quiet, eventually saying, 'Wanda Chabala got hold of the DNA sample somehow.'

'But how?' Maddie pressed.

Hudson shrugged.

'*Hudson*,' she chastised. 'That's *completely* unethical. We get so much flak from people—including many from within our own genealogical community—who already think we're misusing DNA and overstepping a privacy line, and you've done *this*?'

'I know, I know,' he mumbled.

'And did you find the perp?'

He nodded slowly. 'I've got it down to two brothers.'

'And you're worried about what's going to happen when you hand those names over?' Maddie surmised. 'Because you know it's probably going to render the fact inadmissible as law-enforcement evidence, don't you?'

'Yeah, that's part of the problem,' he agreed.

'Part? There's *more*?'

'Yeah,' he said. 'A pretty big 'more': Wanda Chabala is married to one of the two suspects.'

'Jesus, Hudson! I don't even know what to say to this. You've come for my advice?'

Another forlorn nod.

'Wow. I'm going to need to—'

Maddie's desk phone began to ring. She could see that it was Ross.

'I need to take this.'

'Sure,' Hudson said, standing and making his way out of the office. 'Sorry,' he muttered as he closed the door.

'We'll talk later, Hudson.'

Ross said, 'Maddie, Detective Tyler is on the line for you.'

'Put him through,' she said, straightening in the chair and preparing to deliver her message, finally.

'Maddie?'

She smiled at his voice. 'Hi, Detective. How are you?'

'Good, thank you. You?'

That simple question completely threw her, as she desperately searched for an honest response to offer him. She had no answer, so she simply said, 'I tried to call earlier.'

'Yeah, I just got back to my desk and MacRory gave me your message.'

'He's a real charmer, isn't he? You might want to switch around who takes the calls on outside lines in your office,' she offered helpfully.

'I hear you. Nothing I can do, I'm afraid. The CSI results are back. That's what I was chasing. I've got something for you.'

Maddie let out a small, shallow gasp. 'And I've got something for you, too.'

'His name?' the detective asked eagerly.

'Uh-huh. I'll email you over the complete report, including his current address,' Maddie informed him. 'He's still alive and living in Pennsylvania.'

'Jesus. Do you realize that that's been exactly two weeks? Wow, just wow. Well, what's his name, then? Come on, this is killing me!'

'His name…is Wayne Wolsey.'

'Never heard of him,' the detective said flatly, which, under any other circumstances, she would have taken to be dismissive. But she knew that tone well from other lead investigators of cases: he was utterly bemused.

'And you've got something for me?' Maddie asked, gripping the desk.

Chapter Thirty-Seven

Thursday, March 19, 2020, Oxford, Pennsylvania

The pre-dawn sky above Detective Clayton Tyler was a solid ceiling of black cloud with no stars and no moonlight. Standing in a clump of dense bushes, he could barely see his own hands in front of him as he raised the binoculars and trained them on the property. Getting to this point had taken three days of co-ordination with the Oxford Borough Police Department whose detectives had just confirmed over the radio that they were in position.

'I barely got any sleep in the car and now I'm freezing my ass off out here,' complained MacRory, the only member of staff from Clayton's own department available to accompany him. He sniffed the air. 'Every time I come to Pennsylvania it stinks of manure; it's too damned rural for me. Do you see anything?'

Clayton stared at the trailer, unblinking. 'Nothing yet.'

The trailer was rundown, painted blue long ago and standing in its own sizeable and private grounds. The area around them was rural, fields and woods dominating the landscape for miles in all directions. The property was on Old Creek Road to the east of the town of Oxford.

Immediately following his conversation with Madison Scott-Barnhart on Monday, a detailed and lengthy report had been sent through to his email. He had been—and still was—staggered at the level of detail that a small genealogy company had managed to achieve in fourteen days. The name of the suspect—Wayne Wolsey—would have sufficed, but it had been accompanied by photographs, occupations, family history, crime scene analysis, psychological reports, geo-profiling, newspaper articles and, lastly, his present address which was where Clayton's binoculars were currently trained.

'Do you really think he's our guy?' MacRory said, picking his ear. 'I'm reserving my judgment on this until I see his name as a complete match in CODIS. And they think there are other victims, too?'

'Uh-huh,' Clayton confirmed. 'His former partner, Fiona Gregory, disappeared from their home the very same day that Sadie Mayer's body was discovered. They also have an incomplete list of female victims who've been murdered and who've wound up in water close to where he's lived over the years.'

'So, the Feds take over and it runs on forever,' MacRory scorned. 'I thought the idea behind this was that it would be a quick and easy win.'

'Well, let's get him charged with our three murders and take it from there.'

MacRory went quiet for a few seconds, before saying, 'So, this guy has a thing for water, huh?'

Clayton shrugged at his inanity, not that MacRory could have seen in this darkness.

'I mean, his place right here backs onto the Big Elk Creek and that report these amateurs put together shows him pretty well constantly being by creeks and lakes. Some weird water fetish, I don't doubt.'

'I think they thought it more of a psychological issue stemming from childhood traumatic experiences.'

MacRory laughed. 'Ain't it always?'

Clayton elbowed him. 'Shut up. Something's happening at the trailer.'

'What?' MacRory whispered.

At the far end of the trailer, a light had been switched on and the silhouette of a single figure moved in the room. 'Lights on at the property,' Clayton spoke into his radio.

'Copy that,' came back the voices of the four officers stationed in unmarked Ford Explorers at either end of the Old Creek Road.

'I'm going to go in closer and try to confirm it's our suspect,' Clayton said quietly. 'Watch my back.'

MacRory raised his own binoculars and focused them on Clayton who silenced his radio and broke cover from the shrubbery at the far west edge of the property. He took out his SIG Sauer P227 semiautomatic pistol and clamped it between his hands as he stooped down and slowly crossed the long grassy expanse that led down to the trailer, grateful for the darkness of the lingering night. He noticed a variety of sheds and outbuildings dotted around the property that would need a thorough search, if this guy really did prove to be the Chester Creek killer. As Clayton made his way towards the back end of the trailer, where he had seen the figure, he hoped to God that Wolsey didn't have a vicious dog. That was the only thing that the report from Venator had failed to disclose about the guy.

When a security floodlight suddenly lit the entire area around him, Clayton threw himself to the ground. With bright-white light shining directly on him, he crawled on his belly as quickly as he could to the trailer's side, flattening himself against it below the illuminated window.

He removed the safety catch from his pistol, pointing it upward and expecting trouble.

'Shit,' he mouthed to himself, as the floodlights switched off, leaving just the amber glow from the inside of the trailer shining out. In the center of the light directly in front of him was the black outline of a figure, staring out of the window, trying to see what had triggered his floodlight sensor. Clayton was holding his breath, not daring to move an inch.

The figure remained at the window.

Time slowed down as silence wrapped itself around Clayton, amplifying the only sound for miles around as far he could tell: his own heartbeat.

It seemed to take several minutes but, in reality, just a few seconds passed before the figure inside the trailer moved back away from the window, leaving a clean rectangle of light on the grass directly in front of Clayton's position.

Still, he didn't dare to move, in case the person inside had decided to come out and investigate further for himself what had activated the security lights. Gingerly, he touched the trigger of his weapon, the cold metal providing some degree of reassurance and its latent protection calming him slightly.

He heard a low-level thump from further back inside the trailer and decided to take a chance look. Slowly, he turned around and peered up through the window. The inside was in a real state with trash strewn around the damaged furniture. A man with his back to the window was bent over at the far end of the room, pulling on a pair of jeans.

Clayton took a couple of slow steps backward so that he still had a good view of the inside but with a reduced chance of his being spotted.

The man put on a red and black lumber shirt and ran his hands though his shoulder-length, lank hair.

Clayton judged him to be in his late fifties or early sixties; roughly the age of Wayne Wolsey. Finally, he turned around as he pulled on a pair of boots, and Clayton got to see him face-on.

It was him.

'Suspect identity confirmed,' Clayton whispered into his silenced radio. 'Appears to be alone and possibly preparing to leave. Stand by.'

Wayne began to move toward him. Clayton tucked himself back against the trailer again as Wayne's silhouette moved across the room. He could hear Wayne talking to himself, as he opened and banged closed a series of cupboard doors.

The shadow moved away. Clayton could feel a gentle rocking, as Wayne's heavy boots thudded through the trailer. The lights went out inside, plunging Clayton back into darkness. He heard the door unlocking and what sounded like Wayne stepping out onto some metal steps.

He held his breath and listened to the trailer being locked up. Wayne coughed a long rasping cough as he lit up a cigarette and thankfully moved in the opposite direction from where Clayton was hiding.

Clayton peered around the edge of the trailer, confirming that Wayne Wolsey was alone and headed in the direction of a truck parked on a dirt driveway that ran from the trailer out to the road.

The truck lurched to life with a noisy growl. Headlights washed the track with yellow light.

The moment that the truck began to move down the drive, Clayton said into his radio, 'Target on the move, alone. Driving a black Ford F-150. Stand by to tail.'

With the vehicle far enough away from him, Clayton switched his radio from silent, hearing confirmation that the two units at that end of the road were ready to follow the suspect.

'He's turning down towards Little Elk Creek Road,' Clayton confirmed, watching the truck disappear from his view. Two unmarked cars were parked out-of-sight off-road and waiting in either direction of the street, ready to shadow at a distance.

Clayton holstered his gun and ran back across the grass.

'Jesus, he was standing right over you,' MacRory said, when Clayton rejoined him.

'Yeah, I know,' Clayton said. 'Come on, let's get to the car.'

The pair pushed through the periphery of the woods, back to their Mustang which was hidden off-road.

'Target is south-bound,' came a female voice that he recognized as Detective Olson who was heading up the local team. 'Cigarette in hand.'

'Sweet,' MacRory said, jumping into the passenger seat beside Clayton.

Clayton turned the car around and sped southward in the direction of Wolsey and the trailing unmarked police car.

'I've never been a smoker,' Clayton said. 'How long does it take to finish a cigarette?'

'Five minutes, give or take,' MacRory answered.

'So, this could be a pretty short pursuit, then,' Clayton mumbled, stepping on the gas.

'Let's hope so.'

'Target has taken a left onto Hickory Hill Road,' Olson relayed.

'We see you up ahead,' MacRory replied.

'I'm going to drop back—the roads are pretty deserted, and he'll spot a caravan of unmarked cars a mile off,' Clayton said as he reached the junction and turned left onto Hickory Hill Road. Just up ahead, he could see the pursuit vehicle.

A minute later, Olson called excitedly over the airwaves, 'He just flicked out! He just flicked out!'

'Yes!' Clayton said, hammering the steering wheel with his fist as he accelerated towards them. Up ahead, he could see the brake lights of the Explorer, pulled over at the side of the road.

Clayton parked up behind them just as Detective Olson bent down and, wearing a pair of latex gloves, picked up the cigarette butt and dropped it into an evidence bag. 'Wayne Wolsey's DNA,' she said, handing it over with a wide smile.

'The smoking gun,' MacRory commented.

'Good job. Thank you so much,' Clayton said, taking the proffered bag.

'Are you sending it off to Greensburg?' Olson asked.

Clayton shook his head. 'I'm driving it up there myself, right now.'

'Oh, okay,' she said, surprised. 'Well, good luck.'

'Sure, thanks for your help. I'll be in touch when we need to make an arrest.'

'I'll hear from you soon, hopefully. Goodbye,' Olson said, returning to the Explorer.

The Pennsylvania State Police Bureau of Forensic Services was located in Greensburg, a four-hour drive from Oxford. Despite the case taking over thirty-seven years to solve, Clayton was not about to waste another minute in trying to bring it to a close. 'Come on,' he said to MacRory as he buckled up. 'Let's get this DNA processed.'

Clayton took a parking spot directly outside the Pennsylvania State Police Bureau of Forensic Services building on Willow Crossing Road. It was located in the suburbs south-west of the city in a nondescript, two-story brick structure with no external clues as to what went on inside.

Despite spending just under four hours in the car, MacRory opted to stay put, leaving Clayton to go in alone. He had called ahead. So, once he had signed in at reception, a young lab assistant came down to meet him.

'Detective Tyler?' she asked, shaking his hand.

'Yeah, hi,' he said.

'You've got a cigarette you want DNA-testing, right?' she said, eyeing the evidence bag in his hand.

'Yeah, please. What's the turn-around going to be?'

'If there's sufficient material on the cigarette, I'll have the results to you within twenty-four hours.'

'Perfect,' he said. 'Thank you so much.'

'You're welcome. Have a good day.'

'If the results come back positive, I will have the *best* day,' he replied, strolling out of the building.

He got in the car beside MacRory and exhaled.

'Wanna go get a burger and beer?' MacRory asked.

'Sure. Why the hell not.'

Chapter Thirty-Eight

Friday, March 27, 2020, Oxford, Pennsylvania

Detective Clayton Tyler drove the unmarked Mustang along Market Street, heading into the center of the small town of Oxford. On either side of the wide street were small buildings showing off a couple of hundred years of history. It looked to Clayton like a decent place to live as he gazed out through the passenger window across the bulky frame of MacRory who was focused on where the black Ford F-150, two cars ahead of them, was headed.

Clayton had just taken over the lead from one of the local teams who had been tailing Wayne Wolsey from his house to this point. The plan was to catch him off-guard and away from his property. Sufficient DNA had been extracted from the cigarette by the Pennsylvania State Police Bureau of Forensic Services and, as required by the Department of Justice, the results entered into CODIS. Wayne Wolsey's DNA was a one-hundred-percent match for the Chester Creek killer. Even though Clayton had developed total faith in Maddie and the team at Venator, the confirmation still blew his mind. As he continued following the F-150 down Market Street towards the intersection, he thought of the rows and rows of cold case files stored in the basement of the police department that could be solved using genetic genealogy. Hell, if every police department handed over all their cold cases, where a decent DNA sample had been obtained, it would significantly improve the current success rate of one percent of cold cases that ever got solved in the US.

'He's taking a left at the lights,' MacRory told him.

Clayton signaled to turn left, but the traffic light suddenly changed to yellow and a horse-drawn Amish buggy in front of him pulled to an abrupt stop. 'Damn it.' He could switch on the sirens, but that was completely not the way that they had agreed to bring Wolsey in. They had to let him go and hope that they could catch him up.

'Target heading south on Third Street,' MacRory said into the radio. 'We don't currently have eyes on.'

'We're four vehicles behind you,' came the reply from Detective Olson who was leading the local team again.

The lights changed and Clayton took the left turn. 'Do you see him?'

'Nope,' MacRory replied.

Right in front of them the road split. Clayton scanned both directions but couldn't see the F-150. 'Tell the other team to take a right on Locust and I'll head straight on.'

MacRory picked up the radio and directed the other unmarked car as Clayton had suggested.

'There!' Clayton said, moments later. 'I think I just caught the back of his truck. Is that him three cars in front?'

MacRory pulled a pair of binoculars from his lap and raised them to his eyes. 'Yep, that's him. He's signaling left.' MacRory lowered the binoculars and looked at the GPS display on the dashboard. 'Target turning left onto Broad Street.'

'He's parking,' Clayton said, arriving at the intersection and watching the Ford F-150 slide into a roadside parking spot. A gap in the oncoming traffic allowed Clayton to turn in and park directly behind Wolsey's auto.

Clayton saw the driver's door open and quickly reached across, shoving the binoculars and radio that were in MacRory's lap precipitously to the floor. 'Don't look at him,' he said, pulling out his cellphone and pretending to study it as Wolsey got out of his truck. He stood right beside Clayton's window while he lit a cigarette. Clayton fiddled with his cellphone, catching MacRory slowly drawing the binoculars and radio backwards with his feet. Having lit up, Wolsey strode up the sidewalk and entered Napa Auto Parts, the building next to which they were parked.

Clayton turned to MacRory as he inched the Mustang forward so that it was almost touching the back of the F-150. 'Tell the back-up team to park in front of him to box him in. I'll go in. You wait right outside the door.'

Stepping out of the car, Clayton walked to the entrance of the gray building. Wayne Wolsey was the only customer inside, leaning up against the counter, laughing at something with the young female assistant. He handed over a bill, picked up a small box and turned back toward the door.

For the first time, Clayton got a good look at him face-on. He had shoulder-length gray hair pulled back over a balding scalp. His cadaverous face was dominated by a wiry gray mustache. And then there were the eyes. Just as Sadie Mayer's friend had described them, the eyes were hauntingly dark, holding Clayton's gaze as he drew alongside him.

'Wayne Wolsey?' Clayton said, stopping him in his tracks.

'Who's asking?'

Clayton pulled out his badge. 'I'd like you to come to the station with me and answer some questions, please.'

Wolsey twitched his mustache, glanced at the door and saw MacRory's hulking body filling the window. 'Regarding what, exactly?'

'Regarding the murders of Mary-Jane Phelps, Terri Locke and Sadie Mayer.'

'Is that so?' Wolsey said with a snigger. He shrugged. 'Sure, I ain't got much else to do for a coupla hours.'

'Good. As I'm sure you know, the station is just a couple of streets away. You can either leave your truck here and come in our vehicle, or I can ride with you,' Clayton said.

'You don't trust me to drive by myself, huh?'

'It's procedure,' Clayton replied, not trusting him one bit.

Wolsey snorted. 'Well, I ain't walking across town to fetch my truck when I'm done with your questions, so I guess you'd better get in with me.'

'Let's go,' Clayton said, directing him to the door.

Outside, MacRory had been joined by three other detectives, including Olson.

'Wow, you sure brought the beef in,' Wolsey said, then spotted Olson and added, 'and a pretty tag-along.' He noticed then that his truck was tightly sandwiched between the two police vehicles. He squinted and crouched down to get a better look. 'I'm a pretty good driver, Officer, but I ain't *that* good.'

'Get in your truck and they'll move them,' Clayton said, moving to the passenger door and waiting while Wayne opened the truck and climbed inside. Clayton got in and watched while Wolsey fired up the engine. The F-150 stank of stale nicotine and, just like Wolsey's trailer, was filled with dirt and rubbish. 'Know the way?'

Wolsey grinned. 'Course I do,' he replied, nodding an acknowledgment to the detective behind the wheel of the Explorer, which was practically kissing the F-150, as he pulled back slightly. He turned the car around and began heading towards the Oxford Police Department building.

'Am I allowed to smoke?' Wolsey asked.

'It's your vehicle,' Clayton said, winding down his window.

Wolsey lit up and began the drive to the police station.

Clayton stared the whole time at Wolsey's profile, saying nothing, but all the while keeping a peripheral eye on the road to make sure that they were headed in the right direction. If Wolsey was bothered or worried about the encounter so far, then he was doing a damn good job of concealing it. He acted as though he were alone in the car, drumming the wheel, muttering to himself about the lights changing to red, and brazenly ogling a pair of teenage girls in short skirts.

Clayton's inner tenseness abated when Wolsey pulled into the parking lot in front of the Oxford Police Department.

Wayne switched off the engine and finally turned to acknowledge Clayton. 'Now what? I hope this ain't gonna take too long.'

Clayton was ready to pull his weapon, if needed. If Wolsey was going to spring an opportunistic move, it would be now. 'Wait right there.'

MacRory pulled up alongside them in the Mustang and jumped out, opened the driver's door of the F-150 and ordered Wolsey from the car. Clayton got out, too, just as the other two unmarked cars pulled up. The Oxford detectives piled out and led the way into the single-story brick building.

'Just through here,' Detective Olson said, leading them through to a small windowless interview room.

'Take a seat,' Clayton directed.

Wolsey sat down on the hard plastic chair to which Clayton had pointed. Wolsey stared impassively at the floor as the three detectives sat across the table from him.

'You want a drink? Hungry?' Clayton asked.

Wolsey screwed up his face. 'Na. Let's just get this over with, and I'll go home and eat by myself, if it's all the same to you.'

'Okay,' Clayton said, leaning his elbows on the desk and scratching his chin. He took a moment, just staring at Wolsey, wanting to go in slowly. 'You know what, the Chester Creek murders happened when I was just a kid. I don't really remember too much about them and I never heard any of the grim stuff until I got to high school.' He looked at Olson and smiled. 'Us kids used to accuse the poor old janitor of being the killer, saying that he chopped up little kids before tossing them into the creek.' Clayton laughed. 'I distinctly recall having the figure of Freddie Kruger in my mind, when I thought about the Chester Creek murderer. Did you ever hear of it up here in Oxford?' he asked Olson.

She shook her head. 'Never.'

Clayton pointed his thumb at MacRory. 'This guy, right here, he was on the original investigation.'

'Yup,' MacRory agreed. 'A real long time ago.'

Clayton continued, facing Wolsey, 'It became like some urban legend, passed down through the school from class to class. Hell, maybe it still does to this day, for all I know.' Clayton paused, staring at Wayne's calm manner, wondering how he would fare under a polygraph test. 'But, when I came to review the cold case files of this *urban legend*, I got to see the stark reality that I'd never seen before. I saw the photos of the three young girls, bludgeoned, strangled and raped. And then their bodies tossed like garbage into the Chester Creek. I read the statements of their families, locked terminally inside thirty-seven years of grief and uncertainty, never knowing who had killed their precious daughters.'

Still no reaction from Wolsey.

'Thirty-seven years this guy got away with it. I guess he thought himself as some clever guy who'd never be caught. Like a modern-day Jack the Ripper.'

Wolsey stared at him impassively.

'Lucky for me, the detective reviewing the case, the Chester Creek murderer wasn't clever at all.'

Wolsey exhaled. 'He can't be so dumb…if he got away with it all this time.'

'Yeah, but you see, he wasn't smart, Mr. Wolsey; he left his DNA at each of the three scenes,' Clayton said, noticing Wayne's eyes flick up briefly to his.

A long silence stretched out with the three detectives staring hard at Wolsey.

'What do you want me to say?' Wolsey eventually asked, alternating his gaze from one of the detectives to the another. 'You just spoke at me with some nice little story from down Chester way.' He sat up in his chair, thumping his hands down on the table. 'Detectives, you need to ask questions. If not, I'm about ready to get on outta here.'

Clayton nodded. 'Yeah, you're right,' he said, looking up at the ceiling. 'I do need to start asking questions. Um. I guess my first to you would be this: how would you explain that the DNA of the Chester Creek killer—the man who raped and murdered those girls—matches one hundred percent to your DNA?'

For the first time, Wolsey appeared a little uneasy. He chewed his lower lip.

Clayton waited patiently, staring at Wayne.

The silence in the tiny room grew heavier.

Eventually, Wolsey sat up. 'DNA you say?'

'That's correct, Mr. Wolsey. A DNA sample was taken from each of the three girls, which matches you and you alone.'

Wolsey narrowed his eyes and leaned forwards on the table with a grin. 'Here's the thing, Detective: I don't believe a word you say. I ain't committed no crimes or taken no DNA-tests, so how come you suddenly wind up with my personal DNA in your possession, huh?'

'Witchcraft and sorcery,' Clayton replied.

'And what's that supposed to mean, exactly?' Wolsey asked.

'Ever heard of The Winterset Butcher?' Clayton asked him.

'Everyone has.'

'Hear how investigative genetic genealogy was how he got caught?'

Wolsey nodded and Clayton was certain the reality of the situation had just dawned on him.

Wolsey glanced uneasily at Olson and MacRory, then back to Clayton. 'Well, Detective, I don't believe you and, as is my constitutional right, I ain't saying nothing more about nothing.' He stood up. 'So, if you're done, I'd like to leave.'

Clayton sighed, glanced to his left and said, 'Detective MacRory, you were on the original investigation; would you like to do the honors?'

'With tremendous pleasure,' he began, then with a gravitas that Clayton had never heard emanate from him before, said, 'Wayne Wolsey, I am placing you under arrest for the murders of Mary-Jane Phelps, Terri Locke and Sadie Mayer. You have the right to remain silent. Anything you say can and will be used against you in a court of law. You have the right to an attorney. If you cannot afford an attorney, one will be provided for you. Do you understand the rights I have just read to you?'

'I understand,' Wolsey muttered.

'With these rights in mind, do you wish to speak to me?'

'No. I do not,' Wolsey replied. 'I don't believe you've gotten my DNA.'

Clayton grinned. 'Oh. Believe me.'

Chapter Thirty-Nine

Friday, March 27, 2020, Downtown Salt Lake City, Utah

Emmanuel Gribbin. Maddie had run his name through every background check company to which she had access, but nothing had come up. She stared at his name, jotted down on a pad beside her computer keyboard. His fingerprint, and his alone, had been discovered on Michael's truck in the recent CSI sweep.

Maddie had started up a fact file and profile page on Ancestry for him, but it was sparse to say the least. Emmanuel Gribbin had died in Washington DC in 2018 at the age of fifty-four. Background had found nothing to add and, thus far, she had not been able to locate a corresponding birth for the man.

Emmanuel Gribbin.

Detective Tyler had said that the partial print had been found on the trunk catch, implying that Emmanuel Gribbin had opened or closed the trunk at some point. The detective had added that the only criminal activity, which he could find against the guy, was a DUI in Washington DC in 2014.

Maddie had given the kids and her mom Emmanuel's name but had only informed Jenna of the precise location of the fingerprint, since the only conclusion that she could reach as to why it had been found on the trunk catch was not a good one.

She ran her finger over his name. *Emmanuel Gribbin.* It sounded simultaneously pious and sleazy to Maddie. *Emmanuel* the savior. *Gribbin* the mass murderer.

A knock at her office door rattled her back to reality. It was Hudson.

'Come in,' she directed.

He entered the office. 'You might want to take a look at the mayor's Twitter feed,' he said with a grimace.

'Okay…' Maddie said, elongating the word as she pulled up the mayor of Salt Lake City, Erin Mendenhall's Twitter feed. The most recent tweet was a one-minute-and-forty-two-second video, posted eleven minutes ago. Maddie watched the full video and said sarcastically, 'Oh, fantastic.' In it, the mayor had explained that she had just signed an Executive Order, directing all people living in the city to stay home, except for essential travel, with immediate effect. Maddie raised her eyebrows and asked Hudson, 'Do you think investigative genetic genealogy counts as *essential*?'

Hudson smiled. 'I'm not sure about that. And Governor Herbert has also issued a directive for Utahns to stay home.'

'Great. Push the door shut,' she said. With the door closed behind him, she asked, 'What did you decide to do with regard to Wanda Chabala?'

Hudson looked sheepishly down at his feet. 'Abigail is desperate for a child. We need that money…'

'Oh,' Maddie replied. Her advice had been to hand back the money and to make an anonymous tip-off to the police and Brandon Blake's lawyer about the DNA match. 'So, what did you do, then?'

'Nothing so far. Wanda asked me yesterday for an update and I said I was still working on it.'

'Hudson, you can't hand her those two names, when you have no idea what will happen next,' Maddie insisted.

'But Brandon Blake is currently behind bars for a crime that he didn't commit,' he countered.

'That's unfortunate but it's not your job to use illegal methods to get him off. And, actually, illegal methods which may well render your discoveries inadmissible, by the way. Why don't you just bust him out of jail, if that's your main concern?' She could see that he was wounded by her candor, but he needed it. 'What are you going to do, Hudson?'

'I don't know,' he replied. 'I keep hoping I've made some mistake, but I've gone back over my work and I'm a hundred percent sure that Warren or Jackson is the guy. Why should he keep walking the streets? He's done it once; who's to say he's not done it again or might not in the future? What if it happened to Jenna or Nikki—'

Maddie raised a hand. 'Don't you dare do that, Hudson.'

'Sorry. Sorry, it's just not at all simple.'

'Do you know how much damage this would do to our field of work? We'd be torn to pieces, and rightly so. CODIS has many, many flaws, and our legal system is far from perfect, but getting hold of someone's DNA like this is totally unethical. You can't even completely verify the source of the sample. You've seen what lack of trust did to the database at GEDmatch; what if that were to happen across the board? Well, I'll tell you exactly what would happen: no more cold cases getting solved using investigative genetic genealogy and you're out of a job. And while we're talking about your job, you might want to spare a thought for Venator's reputation and the livelihoods of your dear colleagues in the event that this thing blows up in your face.'

'But the adoption is going to—'

Maddie shook her head and argued, 'No, that's not a good-enough excuse, Hudson. Are you absolutely sure your insurance won't cover the medical bills to investigate where a biological problem might be? It could be something so simple. If not, you do what most people do— including Michael and I—you get a loan.'

'We don't…it…' Maddie's phone began to ring. 'I'd better let you get that,' he said, scarpering from the office this time.

Maddie was riled by the conversation and didn't really want to talk to anyone, but she could see that the call was coming from the reception desk. 'Hi, Ross,' she said, trying but failing to sound normal.

'Detective Tyler is on the phone for you.'

'Patch him through.' The line went quiet for a moment, then she heard him clearing his throat. 'Hi, Detective.'

'Hi, Maddie,' he greeted. 'How are things down there?'

'Uh, well, let's see. I've just heard the mayor declaring that only essential businesses are to remain open, so…'

'Well, I for one think you should be given special dispensation to stay open as a *bona fide* branch of law enforcement.'

Maddie laughed.

'I'm serious. Anyway. I've got some news for you about the case.'

'Oh, yeah?'

'After wasting a while denying it, Wayne Wolsey has just admitted to the three murders and has been charged.'

'Wow. That's awesome,' Maddie enthused. 'What about those other murders that fit his M.O.?'

'He's intimating that there might be others but he's playing us to see what we know. I threw in the name of Tandy Howard and he looked at me with a grin, asking where the DNA evidence was.'

'God… He knew he had to be more careful with the ones after Sadie Mayer,' Maddie said.

'Uh-huh,' he agreed. 'But he's overlooking some pretty major evidence.'

'The hair?' Maddie guessed.

'Yep, the hair. Wanna know how many little plastic bags of different locks we found in his trailer?'

'No…but yes,' she answered.

'Eleven.'

Maddie gasped. 'Oh my God, that's insane.'

'Each hair sample is being DNA tested, now. There's a specialist scientist guy who's pretty good at extracting DNA from hair without follicles. So, it looks promising. We're taking samples from Fiona Gregory's brother to test against Wolsey's souvenir collection, then we'll work on those other names you found.'

'I'm so relieved that he's off the streets at last.'

'Yeah, me too,' the detective agreed. 'And it's all thanks to you.'

'And my team.'

'And your team. Please pass on my sincere gratitude to them.'

'I will,' she agreed. 'Thanks for letting me know, Detective. What a great result.'

'You're welcome…um…'

A small lull in the conversation, and his not ending the call on that point, made Maddie realize that he still had more to say.

'If ever you're over this way, give me a shout. It's legal in Pennsylvania to *just* drink in hotel bars.'

She laughed. 'I'll do that. I've got a friend in Philly who I see from time to time, so I might just take you up on that offer.'

'Yeah. Yeah, do. I really mean that, you know?'

'Well, it's been great working with you, Detective, and thanks for your help with my domestic problem, too. I'd better go deliver the good news about the case to the rest of the team. And then tell them to pack up and head home to hunker down until this pandemic passes over.'

'Good luck with that. Thanks again. Bye, Maddie.'

'Bye, Detective,' she said, ending the call. Sweet guy. On the computer screen in front of her was the final frame from the Salt Lake City mayor's video which had effectively announced the closure of the city. She stood up and entered the main office. 'Guys,' she said, making her way to the three boards at the center of the room. 'I have fantastic news: Detective Tyler has just called me to say that Wayne Wolsey has admitted to the three murders and has been arrested and charged.'

Kenyatta, Becky and Hudson spontaneously clapped and cheered at the result. Maddie waited for their jubilation to subside. 'They're also testing the locks of hair he kept as souvenirs—all *eleven* of them.'

'What?' Kenyatta gasped.

'Woah,' Hudson said.

'I thought there might be more victims,' Becky said, 'but I did not think it would be *that* many. Wow.'

'Yes, exactly. It's a horrific number. Well done, everyone. You all worked really hard. Good job.' She paused a beat to breathe. 'On a different note, as I'm sure you're all aware, the mayor has issued a proclamation. Effective immediately, it directs people to stay at home for all but essential travel and work. Given that we are *not* an essential service, the office will be closing today until further notice.'

The team greeted the news with gasps and murmurs of disbelief.

'Don't worry. Your jobs are safe, and we can all still work the cases from home. I'll be opening a business account with Zoom that we can use for videoconferencing. So, I think today we're pretty well done. Let's go out on a high. Shut down your workstations when you're ready and take anything home with you that you might need. When you're done, you're free to go.'

'How long's it going to be for?' Kenyatta asked.

Maddie shrugged. 'Your guess is as good as mine.'

'Maybe ask your friend, Lonnie,' Becky suggested. 'He sure seemed to have the lowdown and grasped the urgency of it all before the rest of us.'

'Yeah, he was right all along,' Kenyatta said. 'Unbelievable.'

As the team began to close down their computers and pack up to leave, Maddie turned to face the three boards containing their work on the Chester Creek murders. She looked at the results of their hard work that all distilled down to that one single name: Wayne Wolsey. She removed his photo, screwed the paper into a ball and erased his name. She turned and looked pensively at the faces of the three victims, each after the next. Mary-Jane Phelps. Terri Locke. Sadie Mayer. 'We got him for you,' she whispered. 'We got him.'

Maddie cleaned the boards of all but those girls' names and pictures.

An emotional Kenyatta was the first to leave the office. She hugged everybody, sobbing goodbye, as though she were leaving and never coming back. 'You won't shut down Venator, will you?' she asked.

'No, Kenyatta,' Maddie assured her. 'I have no plans to close the business.'

'And you're sure there's nothing else we can do to help around here?'

'Nope. I'm almost ready to go, myself.'

She hugged Maddie again and then shuffled out towards the elevator like a poor lost soul. Hudson went next. He too hugged everyone. 'Think very carefully about what you do next, my friend,'

Maddie whispered as she held on to him. Becky and Ross left together with far less drama, behaving more as though they were simply going on vacation for a week or so.

Maddie was left standing in the office alone. She double-checked that all the computers had been switched off at the sockets and that the window locks had been fastened. In her office, she stood for a moment, making sure that she also had everything that she might need. She gazed out of her office window down onto Main Street. It was snowing again. Heavily now. Great. The ride home on the I-15 would be a crawl at best, but at least once she was home, she would be staying there for the foreseeable future. Given what was going on with her mom currently, that might not be such a bad thing at all.

Maddie locked her office and turned into the main room. She took one last lingering look around, switched off the lights, then stepped out into the hall. As she locked the office, she looked at the brass *VENATOR* nameplate on the door with a mixture of pride at what they had just achieved and trepidation about when she might next be returning here. With her head fogged with uncertainty, she headed for the elevator which she noticed was already on its way up.

The doors opened and a beautiful young Latin-American woman smiled at her as she exited the elevator. Maddie went to step inside but stopped when she saw the woman heading towards the Venator office. She backed out and asked, 'Can I help you?'

The woman turned. 'Maybe? I'm looking for Madison Scott-Barnhart.'

'That's me.'

'Oh, hi,' she said with a smile. She walked back towards Maddie with her hand extended. 'Detective Maria González.'

The officer from Twin Falls. Maddie shook her hand. 'I'm sorry, I've just closed up the office—indefinitely—because of the virus. I'm headed home right now.'

Detective González appeared deflated, yet Maddie could see that she wasn't going to go quietly. 'Ma'am, I would *really* appreciate it, if you could just spare me maybe fifteen-to-twenty minutes before you leave? I'll get you some coffee or something nearby?'

Maddie thought for a moment and then nodded. 'Sure, okay. They serve a decent one right across the street from here. If they're still open, that is.'

'Great,' Maria said. 'Let's go see.'

'So, you happen to be in town?' Maddie asked as they stepped inside the elevator and rode down to the first floor.

'No, I drove down specifically to speak with you,' she revealed. 'Three hours straight in the car, which is why I need a coffee.'

In Eva's, they took a seat at a two-person wooden table, close to the back of the cafe and made polite conversation until the waiter had taken their order. Detective González was dressed in tight stonewashed jeans with a thick sweater. Her long black hair was tied back behind her head.

As soon as the waiter was out of earshot, Detective González sat forward, lacing her fingers together on the tabletop. 'Look. I'll come straight to the point: the guy has struck again. I need you to understand how much I really need your help on this.'

Maddie saw through to the desperation in the woman's eyes.

'I don't want to have to go down the clichéd *I'm-not-leaving-here-until-you-say-yes* route, but that's kind of the essence of it. We're pursuing every lead we can but, in truth, we know as much about this guy now as we did back when he first started...which is next to nothing, by the way.'

'Do you have a good DNA sample?' she asked.

Detective González nodded. 'Yes. We consider this individual to be a very dangerous man, Madison; with each next crime, he's upping the ante. With his growing confidence, he's also becoming more careful and more extreme in what he's doing to these women. We really need to catch him before he strikes again.'

The waiter arrived with the coffees, giving Maddie a moment to think before answering. 'We've never tackled a live case before.'

'Listen. I wouldn't set aside a whole day from this investigation to come and persuade you, if I thought we were even close to catching this guy using standard procedural methods. We're literally waiting for him to do it again in the messed-up hope that he makes a mistake, so we'll have something more to go on.' She leaned forward across the table and lowered her voice. 'Truth is, we didn't reveal everything to the media. They know he takes his victims from their homes, murders them before dumping their bodies in churchyards around Twin Falls,' she glanced around her before continuing. 'What we didn't disclose—and I'm telling you this in the strictest confidence—is that, after he abducts them, he takes the women off someplace, maybe a woodland or forest, where he releases them—'

'He *releases* them?' Maddie questioned.

Detective González nodded. 'It's like some kind of sick game to him. He releases them into the woods and then hunts them down. Once they're dead, he hauls them back and leaves them in random churchyards around Twin Falls.'

'Jesus,' Maddie muttered.

'Exactly,' Detective González agreed, drinking some of her coffee. 'The attacks are becoming more frequent, more audacious and more barbaric. I don't want to wait for another girl to die. We're clinging to some flimsy hope that he'll leave us enough of a clue for us to catch him; I want to get him right now.'

'You do know that what we do isn't instant or overnight? He could strike again before we even got anywhere with the case,' Maddie replied. 'I've got cases—equally heinous, tragic, awful cases—sitting on shelves, still unsolved, that I agreed to take on two years ago.'

'I know that, yes,' she said. 'I've done my homework on you. But I can't *not* try. What's your reticence, exactly, may I ask?'

'My team,' Maddie answered.

'Not up to it?'

'The opposite: they're not—*I'm* not—law-enforcement-trained and I don't trust that—with the stakes that high—they would ever stop to eat or use the bathroom or go to bed; this is a harrowing case for which they have no mental-health support outside of me and each other.'

For the first time, Detective González smiled. 'I'm confident that between us we can do this. I can help with any law-enforcement issues or questions you or they may have and, as their boss, I'm sure you can direct their work-life balance. And, I can arrange to have a therapist we use come down and speak with them as often as they need it.'

Maddie stared at the single pink flower sitting in a small white vase on the table between them, weighing the decision. One thing, which the detective had said, struck a chord with her; that the investigation had reached a point where they were essentially waiting for him to strike again. She exhaled, drank some coffee and said, 'I'm not promising anything at all, but I *will* take a look. When I get home, I'll send you a link to the forms that you need to complete and information about getting the DNA tested at FamilyTreeDNA. We'll just have to wait and take things from there.'

The detective smiled and leaned sideways, as she pulled out her cellphone. She tapped the screen, then placed the phone in front of Maddie. 'There you go: the kit number and password.'

Maddie looked from the cell to the detective. 'You've already had the kit processed?'

'Like I said to you before, I wasn't going to leave here until I got a 'yes'.'

'No, you said you *weren't* going to say that because it was a cliché,' Maddie countered, making a note on her own cellphone of the kit number and password.

The detective finished her coffee and offered Maddie her hand to shake. 'Thank you for seeing me, Madison. I really appreciated it.'

'It's Maddie,' she said, shaking her hand.

'I'm going to tell you something. For the first time since we started this investigation, I actually feel a real cause to hope that we're going to catch him.'

'We'll see,' Maddie said.

The drive back home on the I-15 wasn't so bad; the snowplows were doing a pretty good job of keeping the roads clear. Maddie had left Salt Lake City with the feeling that she wouldn't be going back in for quite some time. Thanks to the coronavirus, her home in South Jordan was now going to be her entire world: the kids would be there; her mom would be there; her work would be there. But Michael would not be there. And, for the first time, her gut told her that he would never be there ever again. He was gone and wouldn't be coming back. Besides which, the only person, who might have known anything about what had happened to him, was dead.

Emmanuel Gribbin.

Acknowledgements

A book of this complexity, and with such a range of specific specialist areas, did not happen without considerable assistance from various people around the world, to whom I am extremely grateful; I literally could not have written this book without their kind assistance.

My first thanks must go to those who gave considerable time to my endless questions about police procedure: Detective John Free, Detective Thomas Fedele and Chief Scott Mahoney. I'm really thankful for all your help.

To Barbara Rae-Venter, I would like to extend my sincere gratitude for answering my questions regarding the procedures of investigative genetic genealogy. Barbara was included in the *Time 100* list of most influential people of 2018 for her work in helping to solve cold cases, including the Golden State Killer, and her work in identifying unknown human remains. The conversation with someone at the top of this field, regarding investigative genetic genealogy, was an invaluable source for my initial research. I have, however, applied the veneer of creative license to that which she shared with me and any procedural mistakes, exaggerations and inconsistencies come from me and my fictionalizing.

My thanks also go to Judy Russell for answering my questions so willingly regarding US law and to Dave Dowell for taking the time to regularly send me information relevant to the field of genetic genealogy. Thank you to the DNA-guru, Blaine Bettinger, whose presentation, *DNA, Genealogy, and Law Enforcement,* delivered at RootsTech 2020, answered a great number of questions regarding the transactions between law enforcement and genetic genealogy companies.

Laura Wilkinson Hedgecock, Mags Gaulden and Kirk Wennerstrom were a great help in suggesting ways to be introduced into this world and some of its main figures, some of whom are mentioned above, and for that and their efforts made on my behalf, I am very grateful.

As always, my thanks must go to Patrick Dengate, who has completed another outstanding book cover, despite my dithering and changing my ideas many times. You are a patient man. It must be in your genes.

Thank you to my early readers: Mags Gaulden, Connie Parrott, Dr.

Karen Cummings, Helen Smith, Cheryl Hudson Passey, Elizabeth O'Neal, Laura Wilkinson Hedgecock and Lorna Cowan. You have all done a sterling job of identifying errors, omissions, errant Britishisms and potentially saving me from an expensive lawsuit for inadvertent, unlicensed use of song lyrics (thanks, Laura!).

And, finally, to my husband, Robert John Bristow, for supporting and encouraging the writing of this book, as well as accompanying me on location hunts around Salt Lake City; wandering around the Kearns Building, hiring scooters, skiing Park City, getting pizza in RedRock and eating lunch in Eva's Boulangerie (all in the name of research, you understand), as well as offering his usual honest and constructive criticism in improving the story.

Further Information

Website & Newsletter: www.nathandylangoodwin.com
Twitter: @NathanDGoodwin
Facebook: www.facebook.com/NathanDylanGoodwin
Pinterest: www.pinterest.com/NathanDylanGoodwin
Blog: theforensicgenealogist.blogspot.co.uk
LinkedIn: www.linkedin.com/in/NathanDylanGoodwin

Have you tried *The Forensic Genealogist* series, featuring Morton Farrier? Start the series with the short story, *The Asylum*, available to download for FREE from www.nathandylangoodwin.com

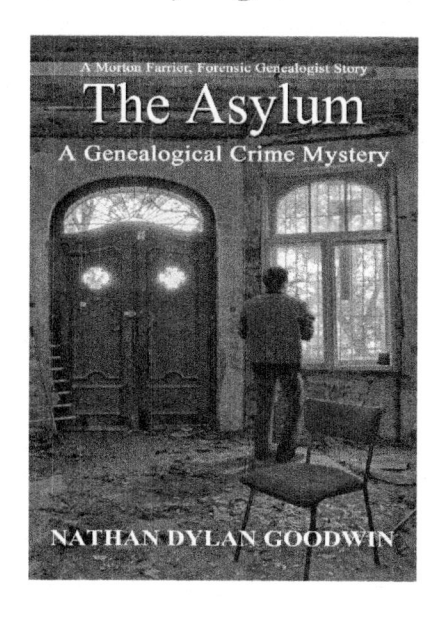

The job presented to forensic genealogist, Morton Farrier, ought to have been simple and easy. But the surprise discovery of an additional marriage to his client's father leads Morton on an enquiry, revolving around a mysterious death in the county asylum. Requiring his various investigative genealogical skills, Morton must work to unravel this complex eighty-year-old secret and finally reveal the truth to his client.

This is the first story in the Morton Farrier genealogical crime mystery series.